ENIGMA

ROBERT HARRIS

ARROW

First published by Arrow Books in 1996
This edition published by Arrow Books in 2001

3 5 7 9 10 8 6 4

First published in the United Kingdom in 1995 by Hutchinson

Arrow Books
The Random House Group Limited
20 Vauxhall Bridge Road, London, SW1V 2SA

Random House Australia (Pty) Limited
20 Alfred Street, Milsons Point, Sydney
New South Wales 2061, Australia

Random House New Zealand Limited
18 Poland Road, Glenfield, Auckland 10, New Zealand

Random House (Pty) Limited
Endulini, 5a Jubilee Road, Parktown 2193, South Africa

The Random House Group Limited Reg. No. 954009

www.randomhouse.co.uk

A CIP catalogue record for this book
is available from the British Library

Papers used by Random House
are natural, recyclable products made from wood grown in
sustainable forests. The manufacturing processes conform to
the environmental regulations of the country of origin

Typeset by MATS, Southend-on-Sea, Essex
Printed and bound in Germany by
Elsnerdruck, Berlin

ISBN 0 09 941688 3

For Gill,
and for Holly and Charlie
QXQF VFLR TXLG VLWD PRUA

Author's Note

This novel is set against the background of an actual historical event. The German naval signals quoted in the text are all authentic. The characters, however, are entirely fictional.

'It looks as if Bletchley Park is the single greatest achievement of Britain during 1939-45, perhaps during this century as a whole.'

George Steiner

'A mathematical proof should resemble a simple and clear-cut constellation, not a scattered cluster in the Milky Way. A chess problem also has unexpectedness, and a certain economy; it is essential that the moves should be surprising, and that every piece on the board should play its part.'

G.H. Hardy, *A Mathematician's Apology*

ONE

WHISPERS

WHISPERS: the sounds made by an enemy wireless transmitter immediately before it begins to broadcast a coded message.

A Lexicon of Cryptography
('Most Secret', Bletchley Park, 1943)

CAMBRIDGE IN THE fourth winter of the war: a ghost town.

A ceaseless Siberian wind with nothing to blunt its edge for a thousand miles whipped off the North Sea and swept low across the Fens. It rattled the signs to the air-raid shelters in Trinity New Court and battered on the boarded-up windows of King's College Chapel. It prowled through the quadrangles and staircases, confining the few dons and students still in residence to their rooms. By mid-afternoon the narrow cobbled streets were deserted. By nightfall, with not a light to be seen, the university was returned to a darkness it hadn't known since the Middle Ages. A procession of monks shuffling over Magdalene Bridge on their way to Vespers would scarcely have seemed out of place.

In the wartime blackout the centuries had dissolved.

It was to this bleak spot in the flatlands of eastern England that there came, in the middle of February 1943, a young mathematician named Thomas Jericho. The authorities of his college, King's, were given less than a day's notice of his arrival – scarcely enough time to reopen his rooms, put sheets on his bed, and have more than three years' worth of dust swept from his shelves and carpets. And they would not have gone to even that much trouble, it being wartime and servants so scarce – had not the Provost himself been telephoned at the Master's Lodge by an obscure but very senior official of His Majesty's Foreign Office, with a request that 'Mr Jericho be looked after until he is well enough to return to his duties'.

'Of course,' replied the Provost, who couldn't for the life of him put a face to the name of Jericho. 'Of course. A pleasure to welcome him back.'

As he spoke, he opened the college register and flicked through it until he came to: Jericho, T. R. G.; matriculated, 1935; Senior Wrangler, Mathematics Tripos, 1938; Junior Research Fellow at two hundred pounds a year; not seen in the university since the outbreak of war.

Jericho? Jericho? To the Provost he was at best a dim memory, a fuzzy adolescent blob on a college photograph. Once, perhaps, he would have remembered the name, but the war had shattered the sonorous rhythm of intake and graduation and all was chaos – the Pitt Club was a British Restaurant, potatoes and onions were growing in the gardens of St John's . . .

'He has recently been engaged upon work of the gravest national importance,' continued the caller. 'We would appreciate it if he were not disturbed.'

'Understood,' said the Provost. 'Understood. I shall see to it he is left alone.'

'We are obliged to you.'

The official rang off. *Work of the gravest national importance*, by God . . . The old man knew what that meant. He hung up and looked thoughtfully at the receiver for a few moments, then went in search of the domestic bursar.

A Cambridge college is a village, with a village's appetite for gossip – all the keener when that village is nine-tenths empty – and the return of Jericho provoked hours of analysis among the college staff.

There was, for a start, the manner of his arrival – a few hours after the call to the Provost, late on a snowy night, swaddled in a travelling rug, in the back of a cavernous official Rover driven by a young chauffeuse in the dark blue uniform of the Women's Royal Navy. Kite, the porter, who offered to carry the visitor's bags to his rooms, reported that Jericho clung to his pair of battered leather suitcases and refused to let go of either, even though he looked so pale and worn out that Kite doubted he would make it up the spiral staircase unaided.

Dorothy Saxmundham, the bedder, saw him next, when she went in the following day to tidy up. He was propped on his pillows staring out at the sleet pattering across the river, and he never turned his head, never even looked at her, didn't seem to know she was there, poor lamb. Then she went to move one of his cases and he was up in a flash – 'Please don't touch that, thank you so much, Mrs Sax, thank you' – and she was out on the landing in a quarter of a minute.

He had only one visitor: the college doctor, who saw him twice, stayed for about fifteen minutes on each occasion, and left without saying a word.

He took all his meals in his room for the first week

– not that he ate very much, according to Oliver Bickerdyke, who worked in the kitchens: he took up a tray three times a day, only to take it away again an hour later, barely touched. Bickerdyke's great coup, which led to at least an hour of speculation around the coke stove in the Porter's Lodge, was to come upon the young man working at his desk, wearing a coat over his pyjamas, a scarf and a pair of mittens. Normally, Jericho 'sported his oak' – that is to say, he kept the heavy outer door to his study firmly shut – and called politely for his tray to be left outside. But on this particular morning, six days after his dramatic arrival, he had left it slightly ajar. Bickerdyke deliberately brushed the wood lightly with his knuckles, so quietly as to be inaudible to any living creature, save possibly a grazing gazelle, and then he was across the threshold and within a yard of his quarry before Jericho turned round. Bickerdyke just had time to register piles of papers ('covered in figures and circuits and Greek and suchlike') before the work was hastily covered up and he was sent on his way. Thereafter the door remained locked.

Listening to Bickerdyke's tale the next afternoon, and not wishing to be outdone, Dorothy Saxmundham added a detail of her own. Mr Jericho had a small gas fire in his sitting room and a grate in his bedroom. In the grate, which she had cleaned that morning, he had obviously burned a quantity of paper.

There was silence while this intelligence was digested.

'Could be *The Times*,' said Kite eventually. 'I puts a

copy of *The Times* under his door every morning.'

No, declared Mrs Sax. It was not *The Times*. They were still in a pile by the bed. 'He doesn't seem to read them, not as I've noticed. He just does the crosswords.'

Bickerdyke suggested he was burning letters. 'Maybe love letters,' he added, with a leer.

'Love letters? Him? Get away.' Kite took off his antique bowler hat, inspected its frayed brim, then replaced it carefully on his bald head. 'Besides, he ain't had any letters, not a single one, not since he's been here.'

And so they were forced to the conclusion that what Jericho was burning in his grate was his work – work so secret, nobody could be allowed to see even a fragment of the waste. In the absence of hard fact, fantasy was piled upon fantasy. He was a government scientist, they decided. No, he worked in Intelligence. No, no – he was a genius. He had had a nervous breakdown. His presence in Cambridge was an official secret. He had friends in high places. He had met Mr Churchill. He had met the King . . .

In all of which speculation, they would have been gratified to learn, they were absolutely and precisely correct.

Three days later, early on the morning of Friday 26 February, the mystery was given a fresh twist.

Kite was sorting the first delivery of mail, stuffing a small sackful of letters into the few pigeon holes whose owners were still in college, when he came across not one but three envelopes addressed to T. R. G. Jericho

Esq, originally sent care of the White Hart Inn, Shenley Church End, Buckinghamshire, and subsequently forwarded to King's. For a moment, Kite was taken aback. Did the strange young man, for whom they had constructed such an exotic identity, in reality manage a *pub?* He pushed his spectacles up on to his forehead, held the envelope at arm's length, and squinted at the postmarks.

Bletchley.

There was an old Ordnance Survey map hanging at the back of the lodge, showing the dense triangle of southern England enclosed by Cambridge, Oxford and London. Bletchley sat astride a big railway junction exactly midway between the two university towns. Shenley Church End was a tiny hamlet about four miles north-west of it.

Kite studied the more interesting of the three envelopes. He raised it to his bulbous, blue-veined nose. He sniffed it. He had been sorting mail for more than forty years and he knew a woman's handwriting when he saw it: clearer and neater, more looped and less angular than a man's. A kettle was boiling on the gas ring at the back of the stove. He glanced around. It was not yet eight, and barely light outside. Within seconds he had stepped into the alcove and was holding the flap of the envelope to the steam. It was made of thin, shoddy wartime paper, sealed with cheap glue. The flap quickly moistened, curled, opened, and Kite extracted a card.

He had just about read through to the end when he heard the lodge door open. A blast of wind shook the windows. He stuffed the card back into the envelope, dipped his little finger into the glue pot kept ready by the stove, stuck down the flap, then casually poked his head round the corner to see who had come in. He almost had a stroke.

'Good heavens – morning – Mr Jericho – sir . . .'

'Are there any letters for me, Mr Kite?' Jericho's voice was firm enough, but he seemed to sway slightly and held on to the counter like a sailor who had just stepped ashore after a long voyage. He was a pale young man, quite short, with dark hair and dark eyes – twin darknesses that served to emphasise the pallor of his skin.

'Not as I've noticed, sir. I'll look again.'

Kite retreated with dignity to the alcove and tried to iron out the damp envelope with his sleeve. It was only slightly crumpled. He slipped it into the middle of a handful of letters, came out to the front, and performed – even if he said so himself – a virtuoso pantomime of searching through them.

'No, no, nothing, no. Ah, yes, here's something. Gracious. And two more.' Kite proffered them across the counter. 'Your birthday, sir?'

'Yesterday.' Jericho stuffed the envelopes into the inside pocket of his overcoat without glancing at them.

'Many happy returns, sir.' Kite watched the letters disappear and gave a silent sigh of relief. He folded his arms and leaned forward on the counter. 'Might I hazard a guess at your age, sir? Came up in 'thirty-five, as I recall. Would that make you, perhaps, twenty-six?'

'I say, is that my newspaper, Mr Kite? Perhaps I might take it. Save you the trouble.'

Kite grunted, pushed himself back up on his feet and fetched it. He made one last attempt at conversation as he handed it over, remarking on the satisfactory progress of the war in Russia since Stalingrad and Hitler being finished if you asked him – but, of course, that he, Jericho, would surely be more up to date about such matters than he, Kite . . . ? The younger man merely smiled.

'I doubt if my knowledge about anything is as up to date as yours, Mr Kite, not even about myself. Knowing your methods.'

For a moment, Kite was not sure he had heard correctly. He stared sharply at Jericho, who met his gaze and held it with his dark brown eyes, which seemed suddenly to have acquired a glint of life. Then, still smiling, Jericho nodded 'Good morning', tucked his paper under his arm and was gone. Kite watched him through the lodge's mullioned window – a slender figure in a college scarf of purple and white, unsteady on his feet, head bowed into the wind. 'My methods,' he repeated to himself. *'My methods?'*

That afternoon, when the trio gathered for tea as usual around the coke stove, he was able to advance a whole new explanation for Jericho's presence in their midst. Naturally, he could not disclose how he came by his information, only that it was especially reliable (he hinted at a man-to-man chat). Forgetting his earlier scorn about love letters, Kite now asserted with

confidence that the young fellow was obviously
suffering from a broken heart.

2

Jericho did not open his letters immediately. Instead he
squared his shoulders and tilted forwards into the
wind. After a week in his room, the richness of
the oxygen pummelling his face made him feel light-
headed. He turned right at the Junior Combination
Room and followed the flagstone path that led through
the college and over the little hump-back bridge to the
water meadow beyond. To his left was the college hall,
to his right, across a great expanse of lawn, the massive
cliff-face of the chapel. A tiny column of choirboys was
bobbing through its grey lee, gowns flapping in the
gale.

He stopped, and a gust of wind rocked him on his
heels, forcing him half a step backwards. A stone
passageway led off from one side of the path, its arch
grown over with untended ivy. He glanced, by force of
habit, at the set of windows on the second floor. They
were dark and shuttered. Here, too, the ivy had been
allowed to grow unchecked, so that several of the small,
diamond-shaped panes were lost behind thick foliage.

He hesitated, then stepped off the path, under the
keystone, into the shadows.

The staircase was just as he remembered it, except
that now this wing of the college was closed and the

wind had blown dead leaves into the well of the steps. An old newspaper curled itself around his legs like a hungry cat. He tried the light switch. It clicked uselessly. There was no bulb. But he could still make out the name, one of three painted on a wooden board in elegant white capitals, now cracked and faded.

TURING, A.M.

How nervously he had climbed these stairs for the first time – when? in the summer of 1938? a world ago – to find a man barely five years older than himself, as shy as a freshman, with a hank of dark hair falling across his eyes: the great Alan Turing, the author of *On Computable Numbers,* the progenitor of the Universal Computing Machine . . .

Turing had asked him what he proposed to take as his subject for his first year's research.

'Riemann's theory of prime numbers.'

'But I am researching Riemann myself.'

'I know,' Jericho had blurted out, 'that's why I chose it.'

And Turing had laughed at this outrageous display of hero worship, and had agreed to supervise Jericho's research, even though he hated teaching.

Now Jericho stood on the landing and tried Turing's door. Locked, of course. The dust smeared his hand. He tried to remember how the room had looked. Squalor had been the overwhelming impression. Books, notes, letters, dirty clothes, empty bottles and tins of food had been strewn across the floor. There had been a teddy bear called Porgy on the mantelpiece above the gas fire, and a battered violin

12

leaning in the corner, which Turing had picked up in a junk shop.

Turing had been too shy a man to get to know well. In any case, from the Christmas of 1938 he was hardly ever to be seen. He would cancel supervisions at the last minute saying he had to be in London. Or Jericho would climb these stairs and knock and there would be no reply, even though Jericho could sense he was behind the door. When, at last, around Easter 1939, not long after the Nazis had marched into Prague, the two men had finally met, Jericho had nerved himself to say: 'Look, sir, if you don't want to supervise me . . .'

'It's not that.'

'Or if you're making progress on the Riemann Hypothesis and you don't want to share it . . .'

Turing had smiled. 'Tom, I can assure you I am making no progress on Riemann whatsoever.'

'Then what . . . ?'

'It's not Riemann.' And then he had added, very quietly: 'There are other things now happening in the world, you know, apart from mathematics . . .'

Two days later Jericho had found a note in his pigeonhole.

'Please join me for a glass of sherry in my rooms this evening. F.J. Atwood.'

Jericho turned from Turing's room. He felt faint. He gripped the worn handrail, taking each step carefully, like an old man.

Atwood. Nobody refused an invitation from Atwood, professor of ancient history, dean of the college before Jericho was even born, a man with a spider's web of connections in Whitehall. It was tantamount to a summons from God.

'Speak any languages?' had been Atwood's opening question as he poured the drinks. He was in his fifties, a bachelor, married to the college. His books were arranged prominently on the shelf behind him. *The Greek and Macedonian Art of War. Caesar as Man of Letters. Thucydides and His History.*

'Only German.' Jericho had learned it in adolescence to read the great nineteenth-century mathematicians – Gauss, Kummer, Hilbert.

Atwood had nodded and handed over a tiny measure of very dry sherry in a crystal glass. He followed Jericho's gaze to the books. 'Do you know Herodotus, by any chance? Do you know the story of Histiaeus?'

It was a rhetorical question; Atwood's questions mostly were.

'Histiaeus wished to send a message from the Persian court to his son-in-law, the tyrant Aristagoras, at Miletus, urging him to rise in revolt. However, he feared any such communication would he intercepted. His solution was to shave the head of his most trusted slave, tattoo the message onto his naked scalp, wait for his hair to grow, then send him to Aristagoras with a request that he be given a haircut. Unreliable but, in his case, effective. Your health.'

Jericho learned later that Atwood told the same stories to all his recruits. Histiaeus and his bald slave gave way to Polybius and his cipher square, then came Caesar's letter to Cicero using an alphabet in which *a* was enciphered as *d*, *b* as *e*, *c* as *f*, and so forth. Finally, still circling the subject, but closer now, had come the lesson in etymology.

'The Latin *crypta*, from the Greek root κρυπτη meaning "hidden, concealed". Hence *crypt*, burial place of the dead, and *crypto*, secret. Crypto-communist, crypto-fascist . . . By the way, you're not either, are you?'

'I'm not a burial place of the dead, no.'

'*Cryptogram* . . .' Atwood had raised his sherry to the light and squinted at the pale liquid. '*Cryptanalysis* . . . Turing tells me he thinks you might be rather good . . .'

Jericho was running a fever by the time he reached his rooms. He locked the door and flopped face down on his unmade bed, still wearing his coat and scarf. Presently he heard footsteps and someone knocked.

'Breakfast, sir.'

'Just leave it outside. Thank you.'

'Are you all right, sir?'

'I'm fine.'

He heard the clatter of the tray being set down, and steps retreating. The room seemed to be lurching and swelling out of all proportion, a corner of the ceiling was suddenly huge and close enough to touch. He closed his eyes and the visions came up at him through the darkness –

– Turing, smiling his shy half smile: 'Tom, I can assure you, I am making no progress on Riemann whatsoever . . .'

– Logie, pumping his hand in the Bombe Hut, shouting above the noise of the machinery, 'The Prime

Minister has just been on the telephone with his congratulations . . .'

– Claire, touching his cheek, whispering, 'Poor you, I've really got under your skin, haven't I, poor you . . .'

– 'Stand back' – a man's voice, Logie's voice – 'Stand back, give him air . . .'

And then there was nothing.

When he woke, the first thing he did was look at his watch. He'd been unconscious for about an hour. He sat up and patted his overcoat pockets. Somewhere he had a notebook in which he recorded the duration of each attack, and the symptoms. It was a distressingly long list. He found instead the three envelopes.

He laid them out on the bed and considered them for a while. Then he opened two of them. One was a card from his mother, the other from his aunt, both wishing a happy birthday. Neither woman had any idea what he was doing and both, he knew, were guiltily disappointed he wasn't in uniform and being shot at, like the sons of most of their friends.

'But what do I tell people?' his mother had asked him in despair during one of his brief visits home, after he had refused yet again to tell her what he did.

'Tell them I'm in government communications,' he had replied, using the formula they had been instructed to deploy in the face of persistent enquiries.

'But perhaps they'd like to know a little more than that.'

'Then they're acting suspiciously and you should call the police.'

His mother had contemplated the social catastrophe of her bridge four being interviewed by the local inspector, and had fallen silent.

And the third letter? Like Kite before him, he turned it over and sniffed it. Was it his imagination or was there a trace of scent? Ashes of Roses by Bourjois, a minuscule bottle of which had practically bankrupted him just a month earlier. He used his slide rule as a paperknife and slit the envelope open. Inside was a cheap card, carelessly chosen – it showed a bowl of fruit, of all things – and a standard message for the circumstances, or so he guessed, never having been in this situation before. 'Dearest T . . . always see you as a friend . . . perhaps in the future . . . sorry to hear about . . . in haste . . . much love . . .' He closed his eyes.

Later, after he had filled in the crossword, after Mrs Sax had finished the cleaning, after Bickerdyke had deposited another tray of food and taken it away again untouched, Jericho got down on his hands and knees and tugged a suitcase from beneath his bed and unlocked it. Folded into the middle of his 1930 Doubleday first edition of *The Complete Sherlock Holmes* were six sheets of foolscap covered in his tiny writing. He took them over to the rickety desk beside the window and smoothed them out.

'The cipher machine converts the input(plain language, P) into the cipher (Z) by means of a function f. Thus $Z = f(P, K)$ where K denotes the key . . .'

He sharpened his pencil, blew away the shavings and bent over the sheets.

'Suppose K has N possible values. For each of the N assumptions we must see if $f^{-1}(Z,K)$ produces plain language, where f^{-1} is the deciphering function which produces P if K is correct . . .'

The wind ruffled the surface of the Cam. A flotilla of ducks rode the waves, without moving, like ships at anchor. He put down his pencil and read her card again, trying to measure the emotion, the meaning behind the flat phrases. Could one, he wondered, construct a similar formula for letters – for love letters or for letters signalling the end of love?

'The input (sentiment, S) is converted into a message (M) by the woman, by means of the function w. Thus $M=w(S,V)$ where V denotes the vocabulary. Suppose V has N possible values . . .'

The mathematical symbols blurred before his eyes. He took the card into the bedroom, to the grate, knelt and struck a match. The paper flared briefly and twisted in his hand, then swiftly turned to ash.

Gradually his days acquired a shape.

He would rise early and work for two or three hours. Not at cryptanalysis – he burned all that on the day he burned her card – but at pure mathematics. Then he would take a nap. He would fill in *The Times* crossword before lunch, timing himself on his father's old pocket watch – it never took him more than five minutes to complete it, and once he finished it in three minutes forty. He managed to solve a series of complex chess problems – 'the hymn tunes of mathematics', as G.H. Hardy called them – without using pieces or a board. All this reassured him his brain had not been permanently impaired.

After the crossword and the chess he would skim through the war news while trying to eat something at his desk. He tried to avoid the Battle of the Atlantic (DEAD MEN AT THE OARS: U-BOAT VICTIMS FROZEN IN LIFEBOATS) and concentrated instead on the Russian Front: Pavlograd, Demiansk, Rzhev . . . the Soviets seemed to recapture a new town every few hours and he was amused to find *The Times* reporting Red Army Day as respectfully as if it were the King's Birthday.

In the afternoon he would walk, a little further on each occasion – at first confining himself to the college grounds, then strolling through the empty town, and finally venturing into the frozen countryside – before returning as the light faded to sit by the gas fire and read his Sherlock Holmes. He began to go into Hall for dinner, although he declined politely the Provost's offer of a place at High Table. The food was as bad as at Bletchley, but the surroundings were better, the candlelight flickering on the heavy-framed portraits and gleaming on the long tables of polished oak. He learned to ignore the frankly curious stares of the college staff. Attempts at conversation he cut off with a nod. He didn't mind being solitary. Solitude had been his life. An only child, a stepchild, a 'gifted' child – always there had been something to set him apart. At one time he couldn't speak about his work because hardly anyone would understand him. Now he couldn't speak of it because it was classified. It was all the same.

By the end of his second week he had actually started to sleep through the night, a feat he hadn't managed for more than two years.

Shark, Enigma, kiss, bombe, break, pinch, drop, crib – all the weird vocabulary of his secret life he slowly succeeded in erasing from his conscious mind. To his astonishment, even Claire's image became diffuse. There were still vivid flashes of memory, especially at night – the lemony smell of newly washed hair, the wide grey eyes as pale as water, the soft voice half amused, half bored – but increasingly the parts failed to cohere. The whole was vanishing.

He wrote to his mother and persuaded her not to visit him.

'Nurse Time,' the doctor had said, snapping shut his bag of tricks, 'that's who'll cure you. Mr Jericho. Nurse Time.'

Rather to Jericho's surprise it seemed that the old boy was right. He was going to be well again. 'Nervous exhaustion' or whatever they called it was not the same as madness after all.

And then, without warning, on Friday 12 March, they came for him.

The night before it happened he had overheard an elderly don complaining about a new air base the Americans were building to the east of the city.

'I said to them, you do realise you're standing on a fossil site of the Pleistocene era? That I myself have removed from here the horncores of *Bos primigenius*? D'you know, the fellow merely *laughed* . . .'

Good for the Yanks, thought Jericho, and he decided there and then it would make a suitable destination for his afternoon walk. Because it would take him at least three miles further than he had attempted so far, he left earlier than usual, straight after lunch.

He strode briskly along the Backs, past the Wren Library and the icing sugar towers of St John's, past the sports field in which two dozen little boys in purple shirts were playing football, and then turned left, trudging beside the Madingley Road. After ten minutes he was in open country.

Kite had gloomily predicted snow, but although it was still cold it was sunny and the sky was a glory – a pure blue dome above the flat landscape of East Anglia, filled for miles with the silver specks of aircraft and the white scratches of contrails. Before the war he had cycled through this quiet countryside almost every week and had barely seen a car. Now an endless succession of big American trucks lumbered past him, forcing him on to the verge – brasher, faster, more modern than British Army lorries, covered over at the back with camouflaged tarpaulins. The white faces of the US airmen peered out of the shadows. Sometimes the men shouted and waved and he waved back, feeling absurdly English and self-conscious.

Eventually he came within sight of the new base and stood beside the road watching three Flying Fortresses take off in the distance, one after the other – vast aircraft, almost too heavy, or so it seemed to Jericho, to escape the ground. They lumbered along the fresh concrete runway, roaring with frustration, clawing at the air for liberation until suddenly a crack of daylight appeared beneath them, and the crack widened, and they were aloft.

He stood there for almost half an hour, feeling the air pulse with the vibrations of their engines, smelling the faint scent of aviation spirit carried on the cold air. He had never seen such a demonstration of power. The fossils of the Pleistocene era, he reflected with grim delight, must now be so much dust. What was that line of Cicero that Atwood was so fond of quoting? *'Nervos belli, pecuniam infinitam.'* The sinews of war, unlimited money.

He looked at his watch and realised he had better turn back if he was going to reach the college before dark.

He had gone about a mile when he heard an engine behind him. A jeep overtook him, swerved and stopped. The driver, wrapped in a heavy overcoat, stood up and beckoned to him.

'Hey, fella! Wanna lift?'

'That would be kind. Thank you.'

'Jump in.'

The American didn't want to talk, which suited Jericho. He gripped the edges of his seat and stared ahead as they bounced and rattled at speed down the darkening lanes and into the town. The driver dropped him at the back of the college, waved, gunned the engine, and was gone. Jericho watched him disappear, then turned and walked through the gate.

Before the war, this three-hundred-yard walk, at this

time of day, at this time of year, had been Jericho's favourite: the footpath running across a carpet of mauve and yellow crocuses, the worn stones lit by ornate Victorian lamps, the spires of the chapel to the left, the lights of the college to the right. But the crocuses were late, the lanterns had not been switched on since 1939, and a static water tank disfigured the famous aspect of the chapel. Only one light gleamed faintly in the college and as he walked towards it he gradually realised it was *his* window.

He stopped, frowning. Had he left his desk light on? He was sure he hadn't. As he watched, he saw a shadow, a movement, a figure in the pale yellow square. Two seconds later the light went on in his bedroom.

It wasn't possible, was it?

He started to run. He covered the distance to his staircase in thirty seconds and took the steps like an athlete. His boots clattered on the worn stone. 'Claire?' he shouted. 'Claire?' On the landing his door stood open.

'Steady on, old thing,' said a male voice from within, 'you'll do yourself a mischief.'

3

Guy Logie was a tall, cadaverous man, ten years older than Jericho. He lay on his back on the sofa facing the door, his neck on one armrest, his bony ankles dangling over the other, long hands folded neatly on his stomach. A pipe was clamped between his teeth and he was blowing smoke rings at the ceiling. Distended haloes drifted upwards, twisted, broke and melted into haze. He took his pipe from his mouth and gave an elaborate yawn which seemed to take him by surprise.

'Oh, God. Sorry.' He opened his eyes and swung himself into a sitting position. 'Hello, Tom.'

'Oh please. Please, don't get up,' said Jericho. 'Please, I insist, make yourself at home. Perhaps I could get you some tea?'

'Tea. What a grand idea.' Before the war Logie had been head of mathematics at a vast and ancient public school. He had a Blue in rugger and another in hockey and irony bounced off him like pebbles off an advancing rhinoceros. He crossed the room and grasped Jericho by the shoulders. 'Come here. Let me look at you, old thing,' he said, turning him this way and that towards the light. 'Oh dear oh dear, you do look bloody terrible.'

Jericho shrugged himself free. 'I *was* fine.'

'Sorry. We did knock. Your porter chap let us in.'

'Us?'

There was a noise from the bedroom.

'We came in the car with the flag on it. Greatly impressed your Mr Kite.' Logie followed Jericho's gaze to the bedroom door. 'Oh, that? That's Leveret! Don't mind him.' He took out his pipe and called: 'Mr Leveret! Come and meet Mr Jericho. The *famous* Mr Jericho.'

A small man with a thin face appeared at the entrance to the bedroom.

'Good afternoon, sir.' Leveret wore a raincoat and trilby. His voice had a slight northern accent.

'What the hell are you doing in there?'

'He's just checking you're alone,' said Logie sweetly.

'Of course I'm bloody well alone!'

'And is the whole staircase empty, sir?' enquired Leveret. 'Nobody in the rooms above or below?'

Jericho threw up his hands in exasperation. 'Guy, for God's sake!'

'I think it's all clear,' said Leveret to Logie. 'I've already closed the blackout curtain in there.' He turned to Jericho. 'Mind if I do the same here, sir?' He didn't wait for permission. He crossed to the small leaded window, opened it, took off his hat and thrust his head out, peering up and down, left and right. A freezing mist was off the river and a blast of chill air filled the room. Satisfied, Leveret ducked back inside, closed the window and drew the curtains.

There was a quarter of a minute's silence. Logie broke it by rubbing his hands and saying: 'Any chance of a fire, Tom? I'd forgotten what this place was like in winter. Worse than school. And tea? You mentioned tea? Would you like some tea, Mr Leveret?'

'I would indeed, sir.'

'And what about some toast? I noticed you had some bread, Tom, in the kitchen over there. Toast in front of a college fire? Wouldn't that take us back?'

Jericho looked at him for a moment. He opened his mouth to protest then changed his mind. He took a box of matches from the mantelpiece, struck a light and held it to the gas fire. As usual the pressure was low and the match went out. He lit another and this time it caught. A worm of flame glowed blue and began to spread. He went across the landing to the little kitchen, filled the kettle and lit the gas ring. In the bread bin there was indeed a loaf – Mrs Saxmundham must have put it there earlier in the week – and he sawed off three grey slices. In the cupboard he found a pre-war pot of jam, surprisingly presentable after he had scraped the white fur of mould from its surface, and a smear of margarine on a chipped plate. He arranged his delicacies on a tray and stared at the kettle.

Perhaps he *was* having a dream? But when he looked back into his sitting room, there was Logie stretched out again on the sofa, and Leveret perched uneasily on the edge of one of the chairs, his hat in his hands, like an unreliable witness waiting to go into court with an under-rehearsed story.

Of course they had brought bad news. What else could it be but bad news? The acting head of Hut 8 wouldn't travel fifty miles across country in the deputy director's precious bloody car just to pay a social call. They were going to sack him. *'Sorry, old thing, but we can't carry passengers . . .'* Jericho felt suddenly very tired. He massaged his forehead with the heel of his hand. The familiar headache was beginning to return, spreading up from his sinuses to the back of his eyes.

He had thought it was her. That was the joke. For about half a minute, running towards the lighted window, he had been happy. It was pitiful.

The kettle was beginning to boil. He prised open the tea caddy to find age had reduced the tea leaves to dust.

Nevertheless he spooned them into the pot and tipped in the hot water.

Logie pronounced it nectar.

Afterwards they sat in silence in the semi-darkness. The only illumination was provided by the faint gleam of the desk lamp behind them and the blue glow of the fire at their feet. The gas jet hissed. From beyond the blackout curtains came a faint flurry of splashes and the mournful quacking of a duck. Logie sat on the floor, his long legs outstretched, fiddling with his pipe. Jericho slouched in one of the two easy chairs, prodding the carpet absent-mindedly with the toasting fork. Leveret had been told to stand guard outside: 'Would you mind closing both doors, old thing? The inner door and the outer door, if you'd be so kind?'

The warm aroma of toast hung over the room. Their plates had been pushed to one side.

'This really is most companionable,' murmured Logie. He struck a match and the objects on the mantelpiece threw brief shadows on the damp wall. 'Although one appreciates that one is, in a sense, *fortunate* to be in a place like Bletchley, given where else one might be, one does start to get rather *down* with the sheer *drabness* of it all. Don't you find?'

'I suppose so.' Oh, do get on with it, thought Jericho, stabbing at a couple of crumbs. Just sack me and leave.

Logie made a contented sucking noise through his pipe, then said quietly: 'You know, we've all been terribly worried about you, Tom. I do hope you haven't felt abandoned.'

At this unexpected display of concern, Jericho was surprised and humiliated to find tears pricking at his eyes. He kept looking down at the carpet. 'I'm afraid I made the most frightful ass of myself, Guy. The worst of it is, I can't remember much of what happened. There's almost a week that's pretty well a blank.'

Logie gave a dismissive wave of his pipe. 'You're not the first to bust his health in that place, old thing. Did you see in *The Times* poor Dilly Knox died last week? They gave him a gong at the end. Nothing too fancy – CMG, I think. Insisted on receiving it at home, personally, propped up in his chair. Dead two days later. Cancer. Ghastly. And then there was Jeffreys. Remember him?'

'He was sent back to Cambridge to recover as well.'

'That's the man. Whatever happened to Jeffreys?'

'He died.'

'Ah. Shame.' Logie performed a bit more pipe smoker's business, tamping down the tobacco and striking another match.

Just don't let them put me in admin, prayed Jericho. Or Welfare. There was a man in Welfare, Claire had told him, in charge of billeting, who made the girls sit on his knee if they wanted digs with a bathroom.

'It was Shark, wasn't it,' said Logie, giving him a shrewd look through a cloud of smoke, 'that did for you?'

'Yes. Perhaps. You could say that.'

Shark nearly did for all of us, thought Jericho.

'But you broke it,' pursued Logie. 'You broke Shark.'

'I wouldn't put it quite like that. *We* broke it.'

'No. *You* broke it.' Logie twirled the spent match in his long finger. 'You broke it. And then it broke you.'

Jericho had a sudden memory-flash of himself on a bicycle, under a starlit sky. A cold night and the cracking of ice.

'Look,' he said, suddenly irritated 'd'you think we could get to the point here, Guy? I mean, tea in front of the college fire talking about old times? It's all very pleasant, but come on –'

'This *is* the point, old thing.' Logie drew his knees up under his chin and wrapped his hands around his shins. 'Shark, Limpet, Dolphin, Oyster, Porpoise, Winkle. The six little fishes in our aquarium, the six German naval Enigmas. And the greatest of these is Shark.' He stared into the fire and for the first time Jericho was able to have a good look at his face, ghostly in the blue light, like a skull. The eye sockets were hollows of darkness. He looked like a man who hadn't slept for a week. He yawned again. 'You know, I was trying to remember, in the car coming over, who decided to call it Shark in the first place.'

'I can't recall,' said Jericho. 'I've an idea it was Alan. Or maybe it was me. Anyway, what the devil does it matter? It just emerged. Nobody argued. Shark was the perfect name for it. We could tell at once it was going to be a monster.'

'And it was.' Logie puffed on his pipe. He was starting to disappear in a bank of fumes. The cheap wartime tobacco smelled like burning hay. 'And it is.'

Something in the way he delivered that last word –

some slight hesitation – made Jericho look up sharply.

The Germans called it Triton, after the son of Poseidon, the demigod of the ocean who blew through a twisted seashell to raise the furies of the deep. 'German humour,' Puck had groaned when they discovered the code name, 'German fucking humour . . .' But at Bletchley they stuck to Shark. It was a tradition, and they were British and they liked their traditions. They named all the enemy's ciphers after sea creatures. The main German naval cipher they called Dolphin. Porpoise was the Enigma key for Mediterranean surface vessels and shipping in the Black Sea. Oyster was an 'officer only' variation on Dolphin. Winkle was the 'officer only' variant of Porpoise.

And Shark? Shark was the operational cipher of the U-boats.

Shark was unique. Every other cipher was produced on a standard three-rotor Enigma machine. But Shark came out of an Enigma with a specially adapted fourth rotor which made it twenty-six times more difficult to break. Only U-boats were allowed to carry it.

It came into service on 1 February 1942 and it blacked out Bletchley almost completely.

Jericho remembered the months that followed as a prolonged nightmare. Before the advent of Shark, the cryptanalysts in Hut 8 had been able to break most U-boat transmissions within a day of interception, allowing ample time to re-route convoys around the wolf packs of German submarines. But in the ten months after the introduction of Shark they read the traffic on just three occasions, and even then it took them seventeen days each time, so that the intelligence, when it did arrive, was virtually useless, was ancient history.

To encourage them in their labours a graph was posted in the code-breakers' hut, showing the monthly tonnages of shipping sunk by the U-boats in the North Atlantic. In January, before the blackout, the Germans destroyed forty-eight Allied ships. In February they sank seventy-three. In March, ninety-five. In May, one hundred and twenty . . .

'The weight of our failure,' said Skynner, the head of the Naval Section, in one of his portentous weekly addresses, 'is measured in the bodies of drowned men.'

In September, ninety-five ships were sunk. In November, ninety-three . . .

And then came Fasson and Grazier.

Somewhere in the distance the college clock began to toll. Jericho found himself counting the chimes.

'Are you all right, old thing? You've gone terribly silent.'

'Sorry. I was just thinking. Do you remember Fasson and Grazier?'

'Fasson and who? Sorry, I don't think I ever met them.'

'No. Nor did I. None of us did.'

Fasson and Grazier. He never knew their Christian names. A first lieutenant and an able-bodied seaman. Their destroyer had helped trap a U-boat, the *U-459*, in the eastern Mediterranean. They had depth-charged her and forced her to the surface. It was about ten o'clock at night. A rough sea, a wind blowing up. After the surviving Germans had abandoned the submarine, the two British sailors had stripped off and swum out to her, lit by searchlights. The U-boat was already low in the waves, holed in the conning tower by cannon fire, shipping water fast. They'd brought off a bundle of secret papers from the radio room, handing them to a boarding party in a boat alongside, and had just gone back for the Enigma machine itself when the U-boat suddenly went bows up and sank. They went down with her – half a mile down, the Navy man had said when he told them the story in Hut 8. *'Let's just hope they were dead before they hit the bottom.'*

And then he'd produced the code books. This was on 24 November 1942. More than nine and a half months into the blackout.

At first glance they scarcely looked worth the cost of two men's lives: two little pamphlets, the Short Signal Book and the Short Weather Cipher, printed in soluble ink on pink blotting paper, designed to be dropped into water by the wireless operator at the first sign of trouble. But to Bletchley they were beyond price, worth more than all the sunken treasure ever raised in history. Jericho knew them by heart even now. He closed his eyes and the symbols were still there, burned into the back of his retina.

T = Lufttemperatur in ganzen Celsius-Graden. –28C = a. –27C = b. –26C = c . . .

U-boats made daily weather reports: air temperature, barometric pressure, wind-speed, cloud-cover . . .

The Short Weather Cipher book reduced that data to a half-dozen letters. Those half-dozen letters were enciphered on the Enigma. The message was then broadcast from the submarine in Morse code and picked up by the German Navy's coastal weather stations. The weather stations used the U-boats' data to compile meteorological reports of their own. These reports were then re-broadcast, an hour or two later, in a standard three-rotor Enigma weather cipher – *a cipher Bletchley could break* – for the use of every German vessel.

It was the back door into Shark.

First, you read the weather report. Then you put the weather report back into the short weather cipher. And what you were left with, by a process of logical deduction, was the text that had been fed into the four-rotor Enigma a few hours earlier. It was a perfect crib. A cryptanalyst's dream.

But still they couldn't break it.

Every day the code-breakers, Jericho among them, fed their possible solutions into the bombes – immense electro-mechanical computers, each the size of a walk-in wardrobe, which made a noise like a knitting machine – and waited to be told which guess was correct. And every day they received no answer. The task was simply too great. Even a message enciphered on a three-rotor enigma might take twenty-four hours to decode, as the bombes clattered their way through the billions of permutations. A four-rotor Enigma, multiplying the numbers by a factor of twenty-six, would theoretically take the best part of a month.

For three weeks Jericho worked round the clock, and when he did grab an hour or two's sleep it was only to dream fitfully of drowning men. *'Let's just hope they were dead before they hit the bottom . . .'* His brain was beyond tiredness. It ached physically, like an over-worked muscle. He began to suffer blackouts. These only lasted a matter of seconds but they were frightening enough. One moment he might be working in the Hut, bent over his slide-rule, and the next everything around him had blurred and jumped on, as if a film had slipped its sprockets in a projector. He managed to beg some Benzedrine off the camp doctor but that only made his mood swings worse, his frenzied highs followed by increasingly protracted lows.

Curiously enough, the solution, when it came, had nothing to do with mathematics, and afterwards he was to reproach himself furiously for becoming too immersed in detail. If he had not been so tired, he might have stepped back and seen it earlier.

It was a Saturday night, the second Saturday in December. At about nine o'clock Logie had sent him home. Jericho had tried to argue, but Logie had said: 'No, you're going to kill yourself if you go on at this rate, and that won't be any use to anyone, old love, especially you.' So Jericho had cycled wearily back to his digs above the pub in Shenley Church End and had crawled beneath the bedclothes. He heard last orders called downstairs, listened as the final few regulars departed and the bar was closed up. In the dead hours after midnight he lay looking at the ceiling wondering if he would ever sleep again, his mind churning like a piece of machinery he couldn't switch off.

It had been obvious from the moment Shark had first surfaced that the only acceptable, long-term solution was to redesign the bombes to take account of the fourth rotor. But that was proving a nightmarishly slow process. If only they could somehow complete the mission Fasson and Grazier had begun so heroically and steal a Shark Enigma. That would make the redesign easier. But Shark Enigmas were the crown jewels of the German Navy. Only the U-boats had them. Only the U-boats and, of course, U-boat communication headquarters in Sainte-Assise, southeast of Paris.

A commando raid on Sainte-Assise, perhaps? A parachute drop? He played with the image for a moment and then dismissed it. Impossible. And, in any case, useless. Even if, by some miracle, they got away with a machine, the Germans would know about it, and switch to a different system of communications. Bletchley's future rested on the Germans continuing to believe that Enigma was impregnable. Nothing could ever be done which might jeopardise that confidence.

Wait a minute.

Jericho sat upright.

Wait a bloody minute.

If only the U-boats and their controllers in Saint-Assise were allowed to have four-rotor Enigmas – and Bletchley knew for a fact that that was the case – how the hell were the coastal weather stations deciphering the U-boat's transmissions?

It was a question no one had bothered to stop and ask, yet it was fundamental.

To read a message enciphered on a four-rotor machine you had to have a four-rotor machine.

Or did you?

If it is true, as someone once said, that genius is 'a zigzag of lightning across the brain', then, in that instant, Jericho knew what genius was. He saw the solution lit up like a landscape before him.

He seized his dressing gown and pulled it over his pyjamas. He grabbed his overcoat, his scarf, his socks and his boots and in less than a minute he was on his bike, wobbling down the moonlit country lane towards the Park. The stars were bright, the ground was iron-hard with frost. He felt absurdly euphoric, laughing like a madman, steering directly into the frozen puddles along the edge of the road, the ice crusts rupturing under his tyres like drum skins. Down the hill he free-wheeled into Bletchley. The countryside fell away and the town spread out beneath him in the moonlight, familiarly drab and ugly but on this night beautiful, as beautiful as Prague or Paris, perched on either bank of a gleaming river of railway tracks. In the still air he could hear a train half a mile away being shunted in the sidings – the sudden, frantic chugging of a locomotive followed by a series of clanks, then a long exhalation of steam. A dog barked and set off another. He passed the church and the war memorial, braked to avoid skidding on the ice, and turned left into Wilton Avenue.

He was panting with exertion by the time he reached the Hut, fifteen minutes later, so much so he could barely blurt out his discovery and catch his breath and stop himself from laughing at the same time: '– They're – using – it – as – a – three-rotor – machine – they're – leaving – the – fourth – rotor – in – neutral – when – they – do – the – weather – stuff – the – silly – bloody – buggers –'

His arrival caused a commotion. The night shift all stopped working and gathered in a concerned half-circle round him – he remembered Logie, Kingcome, Puck and Proudfoot – and it was clear from their expressions they thought he really had gone mad. They sat him down and gave him a mug of tea and told him to take it again, slowly, from the beginning.

He went through it once more, step by step, suddenly anxious there might be a flaw in his logic. Four-rotor Enigmas were restricted to U-boats and Sainte-Assise: correct? Correct. Therefore, coastal stations could only decipher three-rotor Enigma messages: correct? Pause. Correct. Therefore, when the U-boats sent their weather reports, the wireless operators must logically disengage the fourth rotor, probably by setting it at zero.

After that, everything happened quickly. Puck ran along the corridor to the Big Room and laid out the best of the weather cribs on one of the trestle tables. By 4 A.M. they had a menu for the bombes. By breakfast one of the bombe bays was reporting a drop and Puck ran through the canteen like a schoolboy shouting: 'It's out! It's out!'

It was the stuff of legend.

At midday Logie telephoned the Admiralty and told

the Submarine Tracking Room to stand by. Two hours
later, they broke the Shark traffic for the previous
Monday and the Teleprincesses, the gorgeous girls in
the Teleprinter Room, began sending the translated
decrypts down the line to London. They were indeed
the crown jewels. Messages to raise the hairs on the
back of your neck.

```
FROM: U-BOAT TO CAPTAIN SCHRÖDER
FORCED TO SUBMERGE BY DESTROYERS. NO CONTACT.
LAST POSITION OF ENEMY AT 0815 NAVAL GRID SQUARE
1849.
COURSE 45 DEGREES, SPEED 9 KNOTS.


FROM: GILADORNE
HAVE ATTACKED. CORRECT POSITION OF CONVOY IS
AK1984. 050 DEGREES. AM RELOADING AND KEEPING
CONTACT.


FROM: HAUSE
AT 0115 IN SQUARE 3969 ATTACKED, FLARES AND
GUNFIRE, DIVED, DEPTH CHARGES. NO DAMAGE. AM IN
NAVAL GRID SQUARE AJ3996. ALL TIN FISH, 70 CBM.


FROM: FLAG OFFICER, U-BOATS
TO: 'DRAUFGÄNGER' WOLF PACK
TOMORROW AT 1700 BE IN NEW PATROL LINE FROM
NAVAL GRID SQUARE AK2564 TO 2994. OPERATIONS
AGAINST EASTBOUND CONVOY WHICH AT 1200/7/12 WAS
IN NAVAL GRID SQUARE AK4189. COURSE 050 TO 070
DEGREES. SPEED APPROX 8 KNOTS.
```

By midnight they had broken, translated and teleprintered to London ninety-two Shark signals giving the Admiralty the approximate whereabouts and tactics of half the Germans' U-boat fleet.

Jericho was in the Bombe Hut when Logie found him. He had been chasing about for the best part of nine hours and now he was supervising a changeover on one of the machines, still wearing his pyjamas under his overcoat, to the great amusement of the Wrens who tended the bombe. Logie clasped Jericho's hand in both of his and shook it vigorously.

'The Prime Minister!' he shouted in Jericho's ear, above the clattering of the bombes.

'What?'

'The Prime Minister has just been on the telephone with his congratulations!'

Logie's voice seemed a long way away. Jericho bent forward to hear better what Churchill had said and then the concrete floor melted beneath his feet and he was pitching forward into darkness.

'Is,' said Jericho.

'What, old thing?'

'Just now, you said Shark *was* a monster and then you said it *is* a monster.' He pointed the fork at Logie. 'I know why you've come. You've lost it, haven't you?'

Logie grunted and stared into the fire and Jericho felt as though someone had laid a stone on his heart. He sat back in his chair, shaking his head, then gave a snort of laughter.

'Thank you, Tom,' said Logie, quietly. 'I'm glad you find it funny.'

'And all the time I thought you'd come here to give me the push. That's funny. That's pretty funny, isn't it, *old thing?*'

'What day is it today?' asked Logie.

'Friday.'

'Right, right.' Logie extinguished his pipe with his thumb and stuffed it into his pocket. He sighed. 'Let me see. That means it must have happened on Monday. No, Tuesday. Sorry. We haven't had a lot of sleep lately.'

He passed a hand through his thinning hair and Jericho noticed for the first time that he'd turned quite grey. So it's not just me, he thought, it's all of us, we're all falling to pieces. No fresh air. No sleep. Not enough fresh food. Six-day weeks and twelve-hour days . . .

'We were still just about ahead of the game when you left,' said Logie. 'You know the drill. Of course you do. You wrote the bloody book. We'd wait for Hut 10 to break the main naval weather cipher, then, by lunchtime, with a bit of luck we'd have enough cribs to tackle the day's short weather codes. That would give us three of the four rotor settings and then we'd get stuck into Shark. The time-lag varied. Sometimes we'd break it in one day, sometimes three or four. Anyway, the stuff was gold-dust and we were Whitehall's blue-eyed boys.'

'Until Tuesday.'

'Until Tuesday.' Logie glanced at the door and

dropped his voice. 'It's an absolute tragedy, Tom. We'd cut losses in the North Atlantic by 75 per cent. That's about three hundred thousand tons of shipping a month. The intelligence was amazing. We knew where the U-boats were almost as precisely as the Germans did. Of course, looking back, it was too good to last. The Nazis aren't fools. I always said: "Success in this game breeds failure, and the bigger the success, the bigger the failure's likely to be." You'll remember me saying it. The other side gets suspicious, you see. I said –'

'What happened on Tuesday, Guy?'

'Right-ho. Sorry. Tuesday. It was about eight in the evening. We got a call from one of the intercept stations. Flowerdown, I think, but Scarborough heard it too. I was in the canteen. Puck came and fetched me out. They'd started picking up something in the early afternoon. A single word, broadcast on the hour, every hour. It was coming out of Sainte-Assise on both main U-boat radio nets.'

'This word was enciphered in Shark, I take it?'

'No, that's just it. That's what they were so excited about. It wasn't in cipher. It wasn't even in Morse. It was a human voice. A man. Repeating this one word: *Akelei.*'

'*Akelei,*' murmured Jericho. '*Akelei* . . . That's a flower, isn't it?'

'Ha!' Logie clapped his hands. 'You are a bloody marvel, Tom. See how much we miss you? We had to go and ask one of the German swots on Z-watch what it meant. *Akelei:* a five-petalled flower of the buttercup family, from the Latin *Aquilegia*. We vulgarians call it columbine.'

'*Akelei*,' repeated Jericho. 'This is a prearranged signal of some sort, presumably?'

'It is.'

'And it means?'

'It means trouble, is what it means, old love. We found out just how much trouble at midnight yesterday.' Logie leaned forwards. The humour had left his voice. His face was lined and grave. '*Akelei* means: "Change the Short Weather Code Book." They've gone over to a new one and we haven't a bloody clue what to do about it. They've closed off our way into Shark, Tom. They've blacked us out again.'

It didn't take Jericho long to pack. He'd bought nothing since he arrived in Cambridge except a daily newspaper, so he took out exactly what he'd carried in three weeks earlier: a pair of suitcases filled with clothes, a few books, a fountain pen, a slide rule and pencils, a portable chess set and a pair of walking boots. He laid his cases on the bed and moved slowly about the room collecting his possessions while Logie watched him from the doorway.

Running round and round in his head, unbidden from some hidden depth in his subconscious, was a nursery rhyme: 'For want of a nail, the horse was lost; for want of a horse, the rider was lost; for want of a rider, the battle was lost; for want of a battle, the kingdom was lost; and all for the want of a horseshoe nail . . .'

He folded a shirt and laid it on top of his books.

For want of a Short Weather Code Book they might lose the Battle of the Atlantic. So many men, so much material, threatened by so small a thing as a change in weather codes. It was absurd.

'You can always tell a boarding-school boy,' said Logie, 'they travel light. All those endless train journeys, I suppose.'

'I prefer it.'

He stuffed a pair of socks down the side of the case. He was going back. They wanted him back. He couldn't decide whether he was elated or terrified.

'You don't have much stuff in Bletchley, either, do you?'

Jericho swung round to look at him. 'How do you know that?'

'Ah.' Logie winced with embarrassment. 'I'm afraid we had to pack up your room, and, ah, give it to someone else. Pressure of space and all that.'

'You didn't think I'd be coming back?'

'Well, let's say we didn't know we'd need you back so soon. Anyway, there's fresh digs for you in town, so at least it'll be more convenient. No more long cycle rides late at night.'

'I rather like long cycle rides late at night. They clear the mind.' Jericho closed the lids on the suitcases and snapped the locks.

'I say, you are up to this, old love? Nobody wants to force you into anything.'

'I'm a damn sight fitter than you are, by the look of you.'

'Only I'd hate you to feel pressured . . .'

'Oh do shut up, Guy.'

'Right-ho. I suppose we haven't left you with much choice, have we? Can I help you with those?'

'If I'm well enough to go back to Bletchley, I'm well enough to manage a couple of suitcases.'

He carried them to the door and turned off the light. In the sitting room he extinguished the gas fire and took a last look around. The overstuffed sofa. The scratched chairs. The bare mantelpiece. This was his life, he thought, a succession of cheaply furnished rooms provided by English institutions: school, college, government. He wondered what the next room would be like. Logie opened the doors and Jericho turned off the desk light.

The staircase was in darkness. The bulb had long since died. Logie got them down the stone steps by striking a series of matches. At the bottom, they could just make out the shape of Leveret, standing guard, his silhouette framed against the black mass of the chapel. He turned round. His hand went to his pocket.

'All right, Mr Leveret,' said Logie. 'It's only me. Mr Jericho's coming with us.'

Leveret had a blackout torch, a cheap thing swathed in tissue paper. By its pale beam, and by the faint residue of light still left in the sky, they made their way through the college. As they walked alongside the Hall they could hear the clatter of cutlery and the sound of the diners' voices, and Jericho felt a pang of regret. They passed the Porter's Lodge and stepped through the man-sized gate cut in the big oak door. A crack of light appeared in one of the lodge's windows as someone inside pulled back the curtain a fraction. With Leveret in front of him and Logie behind, Jericho had a curious sensation of being under arrest.

The deputy director's Rover was pulled up on the cobbled pavement. Leveret carefully unlocked it and ushered them into the back seat. The interior was cold and smelled of old leather and cigarette ash. As Leveret was stowing the suitcases in the boot Logie said suddenly: 'Who's Claire, by the way?'

'Claire?' Jericho heard his voice in the darkness, guilty and defensive.

'When you came up the staircase I thought I heard you shouting "Claire". Claire?' Logie gave a low whistle. 'I say, she's not the arctic blonde in Hut 3, is she? I bet she is. You lucky bugger . . .'

Leveret started the engine. It stuttered and backfired. He let out the brake and the big car rocked over the cobbles on to King's Parade. The long street was deserted in both directions. A wisp of mist shone in the shaded headlamps. Logie was still chuckling to himself as they swung left.

'I bet she jolly well is. You lucky, lucky bugger . . .'

Kite stayed at his post by the window, watching the red tail-lights until they vanished past the corner of Gonville and Caius. He let the curtain drop.

Well, well . . .

This would give them something to talk about the next morning. Listen to this, Dottie. Mr Jericho was taken away at dead of night – oh, all right then, eight o'clock – by two men, one a tall fellow and the other very obviously a plain clothes copper. Escorted from the premises and not a word to anyone. The tall chap and the copper had arrived about five o'clock while the young master was still out walking and the big one – the detective, presumably – had asked Kite all sorts of questions: 'Has he seen anyone since he's been here? Has he written to anyone? Has anyone written to him? What's he been doing?' Then they'd taken his keys and searched Jericho's room before Jericho got back.

It was murky. Very murky.

A spy, a genius, a broken heart – and now what? A criminal of some sort? Quite possibly. A malingerer? A runaway? A deserter! Yes, that was it: a deserter!

Kite went back to his seat by the stove and opened his evening paper.

NAZI SUB TORPEDOES PASSENGER LINER, he read. WOMEN AND CHILDREN LOST.

Kite shook his head at the wickedness of the world. It was disgusting, a young man of that age, not wearing uniform, hiding away in the middle of England while mothers and kiddies were being killed.

TWO

CRYPTOGRAM

CRYPTOGRAM: message written in cipher or in some other secret form which requires a key _qy_ for its meaning to be discovered.

A Lexicon of Cryptography
('Most Secret', Bletchley Park, 1943)

1

THE NIGHT WAS impenetrable, the cold irresistible. Huddled in his overcoat inside the icy Rover, Tom Jericho could barely see the flickering of his breath or the mist it formed on the window beside him. He reached across and rubbed a porthole in the condensation, smearing his fingers with cold, wet grime. Occasionally their headlamps flashed on white-washed cottages and darkened inns, and once they passed a convoy of lorries heading in the opposite direction. But mostly they seemed to travel in a void. There were no street lights or signposts to guide them, no lit windows; not even a match glimmered in the blackness. They might have been the last three people alive.

Logie had started to snore within fifteen minutes of leaving King's, his head dropping further forwards onto his chest each time the Rover hit a bump, a motion which caused him to mumble and nod, as if in profound agreement with himself. Once, when they turned a corner sharply, his long body toppled sideways and Jericho had to fend him off gently with his forearm.

In the front seat Leveret hadn't uttered a word, except to say, when Jericho asked him to turn it on, that the heater was broken. He was driving with exaggerated care, his face hunched inches from the windscreen, his right foot alternating cautiously between the brake pedal and the accelerator. At times they seemed to be travelling scarcely faster than walking-pace, so that although in daylight the journey to Bletchley might take little more than an hour and a half, Jericho calculated that tonight they would be lucky to reach their destination before midnight.

'I should get some sleep if I were you, old thing,' Logie had said, making a pillow of his overcoat. 'Long night ahead.'

But Jericho couldn't sleep. He stuffed his hands deep into his pockets and stared uselessly into the night.

Bletchley, he thought with disgust. Even the sensation of the name in the mouth was unpleasant, stranded somewhere between blanching and retching. Of all the towns in England, why did they have to choose *Bletchley?* Four years ago he'd never even heard of the place. And he might have lived the rest of his life in happy ignorance had it not been for that glass of sherry in Atwood's rooms in the spring of 1939.

How odd it was, how absurd to trace one's destiny and to find that it revolved around a couple of fluid ounces of pale manzanilla.

It was immediately after that first approach that Atwood had arranged for him to meet some 'friends' in London. Thereafter, every Friday morning for four months, Jericho would catch an early train and make his way to a dusty office block near St James's tube station. Here, in a shabby room furnished by a blackboard and a clerk's desk, he was initiated into the secrets of cryptography. And it was just as Turing had predicted: he loved it.

He loved the history, all of it, from the ancient runic systems and the Irish codes of the Book of Ballymote with their exotic names ('Serpent through the heather', 'Vexation of a poet's heart'), through the codes of Pope Sylvester II and Hildegard von Bingen, through the invention of Alberti's cipher disk – the first poly-alphabetic cipher – and Cardinal Richelieu's grilles, all the way down to the machine-generated mysteries of the German Enigma, which were gloomily held to be unbreakable.

And he loved the secret vocabulary of cryptanalysis, with its homophones and polyphones, its digraphs and bigraphs and nulls. He studied frequency analysis. He was taught the intricacies of superencipherment, of placode and enicode. At the beginning of August 1939 he was formally offered a post at the Government Code and Cipher School at a salary of three hundred pounds a year and was told to go back to Cambridge and await developments. On 1 September he woke to hear on the wireless that the Germans had invaded Poland. On 3 September, the day Britain declared war, a telegram arrived at the Porter's Lodge ordering him to report the following morning to a place called Bletchley Park.

He left King's as instructed, as soon as it was light, wedged into the passenger seat of Atwood's antiquated sports car. Bletchley turned out to be a small Victorian railway town about fifty miles west of Cambridge. Atwood, who liked to cut a dash, insisted on driving with the roof off, and as they rattled down the narrow streets Jericho had an impression of smoke and soot, of little, ugly terraced houses and the tall, black chimneys of brick kilns. They passed under a railway bridge, along a lane, and were waved through a pair of high gates by armed sentries. To their right, a lawn sloped down to a lake fringed by large trees. To their left was a mansion – a long, low, late-Victorian monstrosity of red brick and sand-coloured stone that reminded Jericho of the veterans' hospital his father had died in. He looked around, half expecting to see wimpled nurses wheeling broken men in Bath chairs.

'Isn't it perfectly hideous?' squeaked Atwood with delight. 'Built by a Jew. A stockbroker. *A friend of Lloyd George.*' His voice rose with each statement, suggesting an ascending scale of social horror. He parked abruptly at a crazy angle, with a spurt of gravel, narrowly missing a sapper unrolling a large drum of electrical cable.

Inside, in a panelled drawing room overlooking the lake, sixteen men stood around drinking coffee. Jericho was surprised at how many he recognised. They glanced at one another, embarrassed and amused. *So,* their faces said, *they got you too.* Atwood moved serenely among them, shaking hands and making sharp remarks they all felt obliged to smile at.

'It's not fighting the Germans I object to. It's going to war on behalf of these beastly Poles.' He turned to a handsome, intense-looking young man with a broad, high forehead and thick hair. 'And what's your name?'

'Pukowski,' said the young man, in perfect English. 'I'm a beastly Pole.'

Turing caught Jericho's eye and winked.

In the afternoon the cryptanalysts were split into teams. Turing was assigned to work with Pukowski, redesigning the 'bombe', the giant decryptor which the great Marian Rejewski of the Polish Cipher Bureau had built in 1938 to attack Enigma. Jericho was sent to the stable block behind the mansion to analyse encrypted German radio traffic.

How odd they were, those first nine months of the war, how unreal, how – it seemed absurd to say it now – *peaceful*. They cycled in each day from their digs in various country pubs and guesthouses around the town. They lunched and dined together in the mansion. In the evenings they played chess and strolled through the grounds before cycling home to bed. There was even a Victorian maze of yew hedges to get lost in. Every ten days or so, someone new would join the party – a classicist, a mathematician, a museum curator, a dealer in rare books – each recruited because he was a friend of someone already resident in Bletchley.

A dry and smoky autumn of golds and browns, the rooks whirling in the sky like cinders, gave way to a winter off a Christmas card. The lake froze. The elms drooped under the weight of snow. A robin pecked at breadcrumbs outside the stable window.

Jericho's work was pleasantly academic. Three or four times a day, a motorcycle dispatch-rider would clatter into the courtyard at the back of the big house bearing a pouch of intercepted German cryptograms. Jericho sorted them by frequency and call sign and marked them up on charts in coloured crayons – red for the Luftwaffe, green for the German Army – until gradually, from the unintelligible babble, shapes emerged. Stations in a radio net allowed to talk freely to one another made, when plotted on the stable wall, a crisscross pattern within a circle. Nets in which the only line of communication was two-way, between a headquarters and its out-stations, resembled stars. Circle-nets and star-nets. *Kreis und Stern.*

This idyll lasted eight months, until the German offensive in May 1940. Up to then, there had been scarcely enough material for the cryptanalysts to make a serious attack on Enigma. But as the Wehrmacht swept through Holland, Belgium, France, the babble of wireless traffic became a roar. From three or four motorcycle pouches of material, the volume increased to thirty or forty; to a hundred; to two hundred.

It was late one morning about a week after this had started that Jericho felt a touch on his elbow and turned to find Turing, smiling.

'There's someone I want you to meet, Tom.'

'I'm rather busy at present, Alan, to be honest.'

'Her name's Agnes. I really think you ought to see her.'

Jericho almost argued. A year later he would have argued, but at that time he was still too much in awe of Turing not to do as he was told. He tugged his jacket off the back of his chair and walked out, shrugging it on, into the May sunshine.

By this time the Park had already started to be transformed. Most of the trees at the side of the lake had been chopped down to make way for a series of large wooden huts. The maze had been uprooted and replaced by a low brick building, outside which a small crowd of cryptanalysts had gathered. There was a sound coming from within it, of a sort Jericho had never heard before, a humming and a clattering, something between a loom and a printing press. He followed Turing through the door. Inside, the noise was deafening, reverberating off the whitewashed walls and the corrugated iron ceiling. A brigadier, an air commodore, two men in overalls and a frightened-looking Wren with her fingers in her ears were standing round the edge of the room staring at a large machine full of revolving drums. A blue flash of electricity arced across the top. There was a fizz and a crackle, a smell of hot oil and overheated metal.

'It's the redesigned Polish bombe,' said Turing. 'I thought I'd call her Agnes.' He rested his long, pale fingers tenderly on the metal frame. There was a bang and he snatched them away again. 'I do hope she works all right . . .'

Oh yes, thought Jericho, rubbing another window into the condensation, oh yes, she worked all right.

The moon slid from beneath a cloud, briefly lighting the Great North Road. He closed his eyes.

She worked all right, and after that the world was different.

Despite his earlier wakefulness Jericho must have fallen asleep, for when he next opened his eyes Logie was sitting up and the Rover was passing through a small town. It was still dark and at first he couldn't get his bearings. But then they passed a row of shops, and when the headlights flickered briefly on the billboard of the County Cinema (NOW SHOWING: 'THE NAVY COMES THROUGH', 'SOMEWHERE I'LL FIND YOU'), he muttered to himself, and heard the weariness already creeping back into his voice: 'Bletchley.'

'Too bloody right,' said Logie.

Down Victoria Road, past the council offices, past a school . . . The road curved and suddenly, in the distance, above the pavements, a myriad of fireflies were swarming towards them. Jericho passed his hands across his face and found that his fingers were numb. He felt mildly sick.

'What time is it?'

'Midnight,' said Logie. 'Shift change.'

The specks of light were blackout torches.

Jericho guessed the Park's workforce must now be about five or six thousand, toiling round the clock in eight-hour shifts – midnight till eight, eight till four, four till midnight. That meant maybe four thousand people were now on the move, half coming off shift, half going on, and by the time the Rover had turned into the road leading to the main gate it was barely possible to advance a yard without hitting someone. Leveret was alternately leaning out of the window, shouting and hammering on the horn. Crowds of people had spilled out into the road, most on foot, some on bicycles. A convoy of buses was struggling to get past. Jericho thought: the odds are two to one that Claire's among them. He had a sudden desire to shrink down in his seat, to cover his head, to get away.

Logie was looking at him curiously. 'Are you *sure* you're up to this, old thing?'

'I'm fine. It's just – it's hard to think it started with sixteen of us.'

'Wonderful, isn't it? And it'll be twice the size next year.' The pride in Logie's voice abruptly gave way to alarm. 'For God's sake, Leveret, look out man, you nearly ran that lady over!'

In the headlights a blonde head spun angrily and Jericho felt a rush of nausea. But it wasn't her. It was a woman he didn't recognise, a woman in an army uniform, a slash of scarlet lipstick like a wound across her face. She looked as if she was tarted up and on her way to meet a man. She shook her fist and mouthed 'Bugger off' at them.

'Well,' said Logie, primly, 'I *thought* she was a lady.'

When they reached the guard post they had to dig out their identity cards. Leveret collected them and passed them on through the window to an RAF corporal. The sentry hitched his rifle and studied the cards by torchlight, then ducked down and directed the beam in turn on to each of their faces. The brilliance struck Jericho like a blow. Behind them he could hear a second sentry rummaging through the boot.

He flinched from the light and turned to Logie. 'When did all this start?' He could remember a time when they weren't even asked for passes.

'Not sure now you mention it.' Logie shrugged. 'They seem to have tightened up in the last week or two.'

Their cards were returned. The barrier rose. The sentry waved them through. Beside the road was a freshly painted sign. They had been given a new name some time around Christmas and Jericho could just about read the white lettering in the darkness: 'Government Communication Headquarters'.

The metal barrier came down after them with a crash.

2

Even in the blackout you could sense the size of the place. The mansion was still the same, and so were the huts, but these were now just a fraction of the overall site. Stretching away beyond them was a great factory of intelligence: low, brick-built offices and bombproof bunkers of concrete and steel, A-Blocks and B-Blocks and C-Blocks, tunnels and shelters and guard posts and garages . . . There was a big military camp just beyond the wire. The barrels of anti-aircraft batteries poked through camouflaged netting in the nearby woods. And more buildings were under construction. There had never been a day when Jericho hadn't heard the racket of mechanical diggers and cement mixers, the ringing of pickaxes and the splintering of falling trees. Once, just before he left, he had paced out the distance from the new assembly hall to the far perimeter fence and had reckoned it at half a mile. What was it all for? He had no idea. Sometimes he thought they must be monitoring every radio transmission on the planet.

Leveret drove the Rover slowly past the darkened mansion, past the tennis court and the generators, and drew up a short distance from the huts.

Jericho clambered stiffly from the back seat. His legs had gone to sleep and the sensation of the blood returning made his knees buckle. He leaned against the side of the car. His right shoulder was rigid with cold. A duck splashed somewhere on the lake and its cry made him think of Cambridge – of his warm bed and his crosswords – and he had to shake his head to clear the memory.

Logie was explaining to him that he had a choice: Leveret could take him over to his new digs and he could have a decent night's kip, or he could come in straight away and take a look at things immediately.

'Why don't we start now?' said Jericho. His re-entry into the hut would be an ordeal. He'd prefer to get it over with.

'That's the spirit, old love. Leveret will look after your cases, won't you, Leveret? And take them to Mr Jericho's room?'

'Yes, sir.' Leveret looked at Jericho for a moment, then stuck out his hand. 'Good luck, sir.'

Jericho took it. The solemnity surprised him. Anyone would think he was about to make a parachute jump into hostile territory. He tried to think of something to say. 'Thank you very much for driving us.'

Logie was fiddling with Leveret's blackout torch. 'What the hell's wrong with this thing?' He knocked it against his palm. 'Bloody thing. Oh, sod it. Come on.'

He strode away on his long legs and after a moment's hesitation Jericho wrapped his scarf tight around his neck and followed. In the darkness they had to feel their way along the blastproof wall surrounding Hut 8. Logie banged into what sounded like a bicycle and Jericho heard him swear. He dropped the torch. The impact made it come on. A trickle of light revealed the entrance to the hut. There was a smell of lime and damp here – lime and damp and creosote: the odours of Jericho's war. Logie rattled the handle, the door opened and they stepped into the dim glow.

Because he had changed so much in the month he had been away, somehow – illogically – he had expected that the hut would have changed as well. Instead, the instant he crossed the threshold, the familiarity of it almost overwhelmed him. It was like a recurrent dream in which the horror lay in knowing precisely what would happen next – the certainty that it always had been, and always would be, exactly like this.

A narrow, ill-lit corridor, perhaps twenty yards long, stretched in front of him, with a dozen doors leading off it. The wooden partitions were flimsy and the noise of a hundred people working at full stretch leaked from room to room – the clump and thud of boots and shoes on the bare boards, the hum of conversation, the occasional shout, the scrape of chair legs, the ringing of telephones, the *clack clack clack* of the Type-X machines in the Decoding Room.

The only tiny difference was that the walk-in

cupboard on the right, immediately next to the entrance, now had a nameplate on it: 'Lt. Kramer US Navy Liaison Officer'.

Familiar faces loomed towards him. Kingcome and Proudfoot were whispering together outside the Catalogue Room and drew back to let him pass. He nodded to them. They nodded in return but didn't speak. Atwood hurried out of the Crib Room, saw Jericho, gawped, then put his head down. He muttered, 'Hello, Tom,' then almost ran towards Research.

Clearly, nobody had ever expected to see him again. He was an embarrassment. A dead man. A ghost.

Logie was oblivious, both to the general astonishment and to Jericho's discomfort. 'Hello, everybody.' He waved to Atwood. 'Hello, Frank. Look who's back! The prodigal returns! Give them a smile, Tom, old thing, it's not a ruddy funeral. Not yet, anyway.' He stopped outside his office and fiddled with his key for half a minute, then discovered the door was unlocked. 'Come in, come in.'

The room was scarcely bigger than a broom store. It had been Turing's cubbyhole until just before the break into Shark, when Turing had been sent to America. Now Logie had it – his tiny perquisite of rank – and he looked absurdly huge as he bent over his desk, like an adult poking around in a child's den. There was a fireproof safe in one corner, leaking intercepts, and a rubbish bin labelled CONFIDENTIAL WASTE. There was a telephone with a red handset. Paper was everywhere – on the floor, on the table, on the top of the radiator where it had baked crisp and yellow, in wire baskets and in box files, in tall stacks and in piles that had subsided into fans.

'Bugger, bugger, bugger.' Logie had a message slip in his hands and was frowning at it. He took his pipe out of his pocket and chewed on the stem. He seemed to have forgotten Jericho's presence until Jericho coughed to remind him.

'What? Oh. Sorry, old love.' He traced the words of the message with his pipe. 'The Admiralty's a bit exercised, apparently. Conference in A-Block at eight o'clock with Navy brass up from Whitehall. Want to know the score. Skynner's in a spin and demands to see me forthwith. Bugger, bugger.'

'Does Skynner know I'm back?' Skynner was the head of Bletchley's Naval Section. He'd never cared for Jericho, probably because Jericho had never concealed his opinion of him: that he was a bombast and a bully whose chief war aim was to greet the peace as Sir Leonard Skynner, OBE, with a seat on the Security Executive and a lease on an Oxford mastership. Jericho had a vague memory of actually telling Skynner some of this, or all of it, or possibly more, shortly before he was sent back to Cambridge to recover his senses.

'Of course he knows you're back, old thing. I had to clear it with him first.'

'And he doesn't mind?'

'Mind? No. The man's desperate. He'd do anything to get back into Shark.' Logie added quickly: 'Sorry, I don't mean . . . that's not to say that bringing you back is an act of desperation. Only, well, you know . . .' He sat down heavily and looked again at the message. He rattled his pipe against his worn yellow teeth. 'Bugger, bugger, bugger . . .'

Looking at him then it occurred to Jericho that he knew almost nothing about Logie. They had worked together for two years, would regard themselves as friends, yet they'd never had a proper conversation. He didn't know if Logie was married, or if he had a girl.

'I'd better go and see him, I suppose. Excuse me, old love.'

Logie squeezed past his desk and shouted down the corridor: 'Puck!' Jericho could hear the cry being taken up somewhere in the recesses of the hut by another voice. 'Puck!' And then another: 'Puck! Puck!'

Logie ducked his head back into the office. 'One analyst per shift co-ordinates the Shark attack. Puck this shift, Baxter next, then Pettifer.' His head disappeared again. 'Ah-ha, here he comes. Come on, old thing. Look alive. I've a surprise for you. See who's in here.'

'So there you are, my dear Guy,' came a familiar voice from the corridor. 'Nobody knew where to find you.'

Adam Pukowski slid his lithe frame past Logie, saw Jericho and stopped dead. He was genuinely shocked. Jericho could almost see his mind struggling to regain control of his features, forcing his famous smile back on to his face. At last he managed it. He even threw his arms round Jericho and hugged him. 'Tom, it's . . . I had begun to think you were never returning. It's marvellous.'

'It's good to see you again, Puck.' Jericho patted him politely on the back.

Puck was their mascot, their touch of glamour, their link with the adventure of war. He had arrived in the first week to brief them on the Polish bombe, then flown back to Poland. When Poland fell he had fled to France, and when France collapsed he had escaped across the Pyrenees. Romantic stories clustered around him: that he had hidden from the Germans in a goatherd's cottage, that he had smuggled himself aboard a Portuguese steamer and ordered the captain to sail to England at pistol-point. When he had popped up again in Bletchley in the winter of 1940 it was Pinker, the Shakespearian, who had shortened his name to Puck ('that merry wanderer of the night'). His mother was British, which explained his almost perfect English, distinctive only because he pronounced it so carefully.

'You have come to give us assistance?'

'So it seems.' He shyly disengaged himself from Puck's embrace. 'For what it's worth.'

'Splendid, splendid.' Logie regarded them fondly for a moment, then began rummaging among the litter on his desk. 'Now where is that thing? It was here this morning . . .'

Puck nodded at Logie's back and whispered: 'Do you see, Tom? As organised as ever.'

'Now, now, Puck, I heard that. Let me see. Is this it? No. Yes. Yes!'

He turned and handed Jericho a typewritten document, officially stamped and headed 'By Order of

64

the War Office'. It was a billeting notice, served on a Mrs Ethel Armstrong, entitling Jericho to lodgings in the Commercial Guesthouse, Albion Street, Bletchley.

'I'm afraid I don't know what it's like, old thing. Best I could do.'

'I'm sure it's fine.' Jericho folded the chit and stuffed it into his pocket. Actually, he was quite sure it *wasn't* fine – the last decent rooms in Bletchley had disappeared three years ago, and people now had to travel in from as far away as Bedford, twenty miles distant – but what was the point in complaining? On past experience he wouldn't be using the room much anyway, except to sleep in.

'Now don't you go exhausting yourself, my boy,' said Logie. 'We don't expect you to work a full shift. Nothing like that. You just come and go as you please. What we want from you is what you gave us last time. Insight. Inspiration. Spotting that something we've all missed. Isn't that so, Puck?'

'Absolutely.' His handsome face was more haggard than Jericho had ever seen it, more tired even than Logie's. 'God knows, Tom, we are certainly up against it.'

'I take it then we're no further forw rd?' said Logie. 'No good news I can give our lord and master?'

Puck shook his head.

'Not even a glimmer?'

'Not even that.'

'No. Well, why should there be? Damn bloody *admirals*.' Logie screwed up the message slip, aimed it at his rubbish bin and missed. 'I'd show you round myself, Tom, but the Skynner waits for no man, as you'll recall. All right with you, Puck? Give him the grand tour?'

'Of course, Guy. As you wish.'

Logie ushered them out into the passage and tried to lock the door, then gave up on it. As he turned he opened his mouth and Jericho nerved himself for one of Logie's excruciating housemaster's pep talks – something about innocent lives depending on them, and the need for them to do their best, and the race being not to the swift nor the battle to the strong (he had actually said this once) – but instead his mouth just widened into a yawn.

'Oh, dear. Sorry, old thing. Sorry.'

He shuffled off down the corridor, patting his pockets to make sure he had his pipe and tobacco pouch. They heard him mutter again, something about 'bloody admirals', and he was gone.

Hut 8 was thirty-five yards long by ten wide and Jericho could have toured it in his sleep, probably *had* toured it in his sleep, for all he knew. The outside walls were thin and the damp from the lake seemed to rise through the floorboards so that at night the rooms were chilly, cast in a sepia glow by bare, low-wattage bulbs. The furniture was mostly trestle tables and folding wooden chairs. It reminded Jericho of a church hall on a winter's night. All that was missing was a badly tuned piano and somebody thumping out 'Land of Hope and Glory'.

It was laid out like an assembly line, the main stage

in a process that originated somewhere far out in the darkness, maybe two thousand miles away, when the grey hull of a U-boat rose close to the surface and squirted off a radio message to its controllers. The signals were intercepted at various listening-posts and teleprinted to Bletchley and within ten minutes of transmission, even as the U-boats were preparing to dive, they were emerging via a tunnel into Hut 8's Registration Room. Jericho helped himself to the contents of a wire basket labelled 'Shark' and carried them to the nearest light. The hours immediately after midnight were usually the busiest time. Sure enough, six messages had been intercepted in the last eighteen minutes. Three consisted of just eight letters: he guessed they were weather reports. Even the longest of the other cryptograms was no more than a couple of dozen four-letter groups:

```
JRLO GOPL DNRZ LOBT –
```

Puck made a weary face at him, as if to say: What can you do?

Jericho said: 'What's the volume?'

'It varies. One hundred and fifty, perhaps two hundred messages a day. And rising.'

The Registration Room didn't just handle Shark. There was Porpoise and Dolphin and all the other different Enigma keys to log and then pass across the corridor to the Crib Room. Here, the cribsters sifted them for clues – radio station call signs they recognised (Kiel was JDU, for example, Wilhelmshaven KYU), messages whose contents they could guess at, or cryptograms that had already been enciphered in one key and then retransmitted in another (they marked these 'XX' and called them 'kisses'). Atwood was the champion cribster and the Wrens said cattily behind his back that these were the only kisses he had ever had.

It was in the big room next door – which they called, with their solemn humour, the Big Room – that the cryptanalysts used the cribs to construct possible solutions that could be tested on the bombes. Jericho took in the rickety tables, the hard chairs, the weak lighting, the fug of tobacco, the college-library atmosphere, the night chill (most of the cryptanalysts were wearing coats and mittens) and he wondered why – *why?* – he had been so ready to come back. Kingcome and Proudfoot were there, and Upjohn and Pinker and de Brooke, and maybe half a dozen newcomers whose faces he didn't recognise, including one young man sitting bold as you please in the seat which had once been reserved for Jericho. The tables were stacked with cryptograms, like ballot papers at an election count.

Puck was muttering something about back-breaks but Jericho, fascinated by the sight of someone else in his place, lost track and had to interrupt him. 'I'm sorry, Puck. What was that?'

'I was saying that from twenty minutes ago we are up to date. Shark is now fully read to the point of the code change. So that there is nothing left to us. Except history.' He gave a weak smile and patted Jericho's shoulder. 'Come. I'll show you.'

When a cryptanalyst believed he'd glimpsed a possible break into a message, his guess was sent out of the hut to be tested on a bombe. And if he'd been skilful enough, or lucky enough, then in an hour, or a day, the bombe would churn through a million permutations and reveal how the Enigma machine had been set up. That information was relayed back from the bombe bays to the Decoding Room.

Because of its noise, the Decoding Room was tucked away at the far end of the hut. Personally, Jericho liked the clatter. It was the sound of success. His worst memories were of the nights when the building was silent. A dozen British Type-X enciphering machines had been modified to mimic the actions of the German Enigma. They were big, cumbersome devices – typewriters with rotors, a plugboard and a cylinder – at which sat young and well-groomed debutantes.

Baxter, who was the hut's resident Marxist, had a theory that Bletchley's workforce (which was mainly female) was arranged in what he called 'a paradigm of the English class system'. The wireless interceptors, shivering in their coastal radio stations, were generally working-class and laboured in ignorance of the Enigma secret. The bombe operators, who worked in the grounds of some nearby country houses and in a big new installation just outside London, were petit-bourgeois and had a vague idea. And the Decoding Room girls, in the heart of the Park, were mostly upper-middle-class, even aristocratic, and they saw it all – the secrets literally passed through their fingers. They typed out the letters of the original cryptogram, and from the cylinder on the right of the Type-X a strip of sticky-backed paper, the sort you saw gummed down on telegram forms, slowly emerged, bearing the decrypted plaintext.

'Those three are doing Dolphin,' said Puck, pointing across the room, 'and the two by the door are just starting on Porpoise. And this charming young lady here, I believe' – he bowed to her – 'has Shark. May we?'

She was young, about eighteen, with curly red hair and wide hazel eyes. She looked up and smiled at him, a dazzling *Tatler* smile, and he leaned across her and began uncoiling the strip of tape from the cylinder. Jericho noticed as he did so that he left one hand resting casually on her shoulder, just as simply as that, and he thought how much he envied Puck the ease of that gesture. It would have taken him a week to pluck up the nerve. Puck beckoned him down to read the decrypt.

VONSCHULZEQU88521DAMPFER1TANKERWAHRSCHEINLICHAM6
3TANKERFACKEL ...

Jericho ran his finger along it, separating the words and translating it in his mind: U-boat commander von Schulze was in grid square 8852 and had sunk one steamship (for certain) and one tanker (probably) and had set one other tanker on fire . . .

'What date is this?'

'You can see it there,' said Puck. '*Sechs drei.* The sixth of March. We've broken everything from this week up to the code change on Wednesday night, so now we go back and pick up the intercepts we missed earlier in the month. This is – what? – six days old. Herr Kapitän von Schulze may be five hundred miles away by now. It is of academic interest only, I fear.'

'Poor devils,' said Jericho, passing his finger along the tape for a second time. *IDAMPFERITANKER*... What freezing and drowning and burning were concentrated in that one line! What were the ships called, he wondered, and had the families of the crews been told?

'We have approximately a further eighty messages from the sixth still to run through the Type-Xs. I shall put two more operators on to it. A couple of hours and we should be finished.'

'And then what?'

'Then, my dear Tom? Then I suppose we shall make a start on back-breaks from February. But that barely qualifies even as history. February? February in the Atlantic? Archaeology!'

'Any progress on the four-wheel bombe?'

Puck shook his head. 'First, it is impossible. It is out of the question. Then there is a design, but the design is theoretical nonsense. Then there is a design that should work, but doesn't. Then there is a shortage of materials. Then there is a shortage of engineers. . .' He made a weary gesture with his hand, as if he were pushing it all out of the way.

'Has anything else changed?'

'Nothing that affects us. According to the direction finders, U-boat HQ has moved from Paris to Berlin. They have some wonderful new transmitter at

Magdeburg they say will reach a U-boat forty-five feet under water at a range of two thousand miles.'

Jericho murmured: 'How very ingenious of them.'

The red-headed girl had finished deciphering the message. She tore off the tape, stuck it on the back of the cryptogram and handed it to another girl, who rushed out of the room. Now it would be turned into recognisable English and teleprintered to the Admiralty.

Puck touched Jericho's arm. 'You must be tired. Why don't you go now and rest?'

But Jericho didn't feel like sleeping. 'I'd like to see all the Shark traffic we haven't been able to break. Everything since midnight on Wednesday.'

Puck gave a puzzled smile. 'Why? There's nothing you can do with it.'

'Maybe so. But I'd like to see it.'

'Why?'

'I don't know.' Jericho shrugged. 'Just to handle it. To get a feel of it. I've been out of the game for a month.'

'You think we may have missed something, perhaps?'

'Not at all. But Logie has asked me.'

'Ah yes. The celebrated Jericho "inspiration" and "intuition".' Puck couldn't conceal his irritation. 'And so from science and logic we descend to superstition and "feelings".'

'For heaven's sake, Puck!' Jericho was starting to become annoyed himself. 'Just humour me, if that's how you prefer to look at it.'

Puck glared at him for a moment, and then, as quickly as they had arisen, the clouds seemed to pass. 'Of course.' He held up his hands in a gesture of surrender. 'You must see it all. Forgive me. I'm tired. We're all tired.'

Five minutes later, when Jericho walked into the Big Room carrying the folder of Shark cryptograms, he found his old seat had been vacated. Someone had also laid out in his place a new pile of jotting paper and three freshly sharpened pencils. He looked around, but nobody seemed to be paying him any attention.

He laid the intercepts out on the table. He loosened his scarf. He felt the radiator – as ever, it was lukewarm. He blew some warmth on to his hands and sat down.

He was back.

3

Whenever anyone asked Jericho why he was a mathematician – some friend of his mother, perhaps, or an inquisitive colleague with no interest in science – he would shake his head and smile and claim he had no idea. If they persisted, he might, with some diffidence, direct them to the definition offered by G. H. Hardy in his famous *Apology*: 'a mathematician, like a painter or a poet, is a *maker* of patterns'. If that didn't satisfy them, he would try to explain by quoting the most basic illustration he could think of: pi – 3.14 – the ratio of a circle's circumference to its diameter. Calculate pi to a thousand decimal places, he would say, or a million or more, and you will discover no pattern to its unending sequence of digits. It appears random, chaotic, ugly. Yet Leibnitz and Gregory can take the same number and tease from it a pattern of crystalline elegance:

$$\frac{pi}{4} = 1 - \frac{1}{3} + \frac{1}{5} - \frac{1}{7} + \frac{1}{9} - -$$

and so on to infinity. Such a pattern had no practical usefulness, it was merely beautiful – as sublime, to Jericho, as a line in a fugue by Bach – and if his questioner still couldn't see what he was driving at, then, sadly, he would give up on them as a waste of time.

On the same principle, Jericho thought the Enigma machine was beautiful – a masterpiece of human ingenuity that created both chaos and a tiny ribbon of meaning. In the early days at Bletchley he used to fantasise that some day, when the war was over, he would track down its German inventor, Herr Arthur Scherbius, and buy him a glass of beer. But then he'd heard that Scherbius had died in 1929, killed – of all ludicrously illogical things – by a runaway horse, and hadn't lived to see the success of his patent.

If he had, he would have been a rich man. By the end of 1942 Bletchley estimated that the German had manufactured at least a hundred thousand Enigmas. Every Army headquarters had one, every Luftwaffe base, every warship, every submarine, every port, every big railway station, every SS brigade and Gestapo HQ.

Never before had a nation entrusted so much of its secret communications to a single device.

In the mansion at Bletchley the cryptanalysts had a roomful of captured Enigmas and Jericho had played with them for hours. They were small (little more than a foot square by six inches deep), portable (they weighed just twenty-six pounds) and simple to operate. You set up your machine, typed in your message, and the ciphertext was spelled out, letter by letter, on a panel of small electric bulbs. Whoever received the enciphered message merely had to set up his machine in exactly the same way, type in the cryptogram, and there, spelled out on the bulbs, would be the original plaintext.

The genius lay in the vast number of different permutations the Enigma could generate. Electric current on a standard Enigma flowed from keyboard to lamps via a set of three wired rotors (at least one of which turned a notch every time a key was struck) and a plugboard with twenty-six jacks. The circuits changed constantly; their potential number was astronomical, but calculable. There were five different rotors to choose from (two were kept spare) which meant they could be arranged in any one of sixty possible orders. Each rotor was slotted on to a spindle and had twenty-six possible starting positions. Twenty-six to the power of three was 17,576. Multiply that by the sixty potential rotor-orders and you got 1,054,560. Multiply *that* by the possible number of plugboard connections – about 150 million million – and you were looking at a machine that had around 150 million million *million* different starting positions. It didn't matter how many Enigma machines you captured or how long you played with them. They were useless unless you knew the rotor order, the rotor starting positions and the plugboard connections. And the Germans changed these daily, sometimes twice a day.

The machine had only one tiny – but, as it turned out, crucial – flaw. It could never encipher a letter as itself: an *A* would never emerge from it as an *A*, or *a B* as a *B*, or a *C* as *a C* . . . *Nothing is ever itself:* that was the great guiding principle in the breaking of Enigma, the infinitesimal weakness that the bombes exploited.

Suppose one had a cryptogram that began:

IGWH BSTU XNTX EYLK PEAZ ZNSK UFJR CADV _

And suppose one knew that this message originated from the Kriegsmarine's weather station in the Bay of Biscay, a particular friend of the Hut 8 cribsters, which always began its reports in the same way:

WEUBYYNULLSEQSNULLNULL

('Weather survey 0600', WEUB being an abbreviation for WETTERÜBERSICHT and SEQS for SECHS; YY and NULL being inserted to baffle eavesdroppers).

The cryptanalyst would lay out the ciphertext and slide the crib beneath it and on the principle that *nothing is ever itself* he would keep sliding it until he found a position in which there were no matching letters between the top and bottom lines. The result in this case would be:

Enigma

```
BSTUXNTXEYLKPEAZZNSKUF
WEUBYYNULLSEQSNULLNULL
```

And at this point it became theoretically possible to calculate the original Enigma settings that alone could have produced this precise sequence of letter pairings. It was still an immense calculation, one which would have taken a team of human beings several weeks. The Germans assumed, rightly, that whatever intelligence might be gained would be too old to be of use. But Bletchley – and this was what the Germans had never reckoned on – *Bletchley didn't use human beings.* It used bombes. For the first time in history, a cipher mass-manufactured by machine was being broken by machine.

Who needed spies now? What need now of secret inks and dead-letter drops and midnight assignations in curtained *wagons-lits?* Now you needed mathematicians and engineers with oilcans and fifteen hundred filing clerks to process five thousand secret messages a day. They had taken espionage into the machine age.

But none of this was of much help to Jericho in breaking Shark.

Shark defied every tool he could bring to bear on it. For a start, there were almost no cribs. In the case of a surface Enigma key, if Hut 8 ran out of cribs, they had tricks to get round it – 'gardening', for example. 'Gardening' was arranging for the RAF to lay mines in a particular naval grid square outside a German harbour. An hour later, you could guarantee, the harbour master, with Teutonic efficiency, would send a message using that day's Enigma settings, warning ships to beware of mines in naval grid square such-and-such. The signal would be intercepted, flashed to Hut 8, and give them their missing crib.

But you couldn't do that with Shark and Jericho could make only the vaguest guesses at the contents of the cryptograms. There were eight long messages originating from Berlin. They would be orders, he supposed, probably directing the U-boats into 'wolf packs' and stationing them in front of the oncoming convoys. The shorter signals – there were a hundred and twenty-two, which Jericho sorted into a separate pile – had been sent by the submarines themselves. These could contain anything: reports of ships sunk and of engine trouble; details of survivors floating in the water and of crewmen washed overboard; requests for spare parts and fresh orders. Shortest of all were the U-boats' weather messages or, very occasionally, contact reports: 'Convoy in naval grid square BE9533 course 70 degrees speed 9 knots . . .' But these were encoded, like the weather bulletins, with one letter of the alphabet substituting for each piece of information. And then they were enciphered in Shark.

He tapped his pencil against the desk. Puck was quite right. There was not enough material to work with.

And even if there had been, there was still the wretched fourth rotor on the Shark Enigma, the innovation that made U-boat messages twenty-six times more difficult to break than those of surface ships. One hundred and fifty million million million multiplied by twenty-six. A phenomenal number. The engineers had been struggling for a year to develop a four-rotor bombe — but still, apparently, without success. It seemed to be just that one step beyond their technical ability.

No cribs, no bombes. Hopeless.

Hours passed during which Jericho tried every trick he could think of to prompt some fresh inspiration. He arranged the cryptograms chronologically. Then he arranged them by length. Then he sorted them by frequency. He doodled on the pile of paper. He prowled around the hut, oblivious now to who was looking at him and who wasn't. This was what it had been like for ten interminable months last year. No wonder he had gone mad. The chorus-lines of meaningless letters danced before his eyes. But they were not meaningless. They were loaded with the most vital meaning imaginable, if only he could find it. But where was the pattern? Where was the pattern? Where was the *pattern*?

It was the practice on the night shift at about four o'clock in the morning for everyone to take a meal-break. The cryptanalysts went off when they liked, depending on the stage they'd reached in their work. The Decoding Room girls and the clerks in the Registration and Catalogue rooms had to leave according to a rota so that the hut was never caught short-staffed.

Jericho didn't notice the drift of people towards the door. He had both elbows on the table and was leaning over the cryptograms, his knuckles pressed to his temples. His mind was eidetic – that is to say, it could hold and retrieve images with photographic accuracy, be they mid-game positions in chess, crossword puzzles or enciphered German naval signals – and he was working with his eyes closed.

' "Below the thunders of the upper deep," ' intoned a muffled voice behind him, ' "Far, far beneath in the abysmal sea,/His ancient, dreamless, uninvaded sleep . . ." '

' " . . . The Kraken sleepeth." ' Jericho finished the quotation and turned to find Atwood pulling on a purple balaclava. 'Coleridge?'

'Coleridge?' Atwood's face abruptly emerged wearing an expression of outrage. '*Coleridge?* It's Tennyson, you barbarian. We wondered whether you'd care to join us for refreshment.'

Jericho was about to refuse, but decided that would be rude. In any case, he was hungry. He'd eaten nothing except toast and jam for twelve hours.

'That's kind. Thank you.'

He followed Atwood, Pinker and a couple of the others along the length of the hut and out into the night. At some stage while he'd been lost in the cryptograms it must have rained and the air was still moist. Along the road to the right he could hear people moving in the shadows. The beams of torches glistened on the wet tarmac. Atwood conducted them past the mansion and the arboretum and through the main gate. Discussing work outside the hut was forbidden and Atwood, purely to annoy Pinker, was declaiming on the suicide of Virginia Woolf, which he held to be the greatest day for English letters since the invention of the printing press.

'I c-c-can't believe you mmm-mmm-mmm . . .' When Pinker snagged himself on a word, his whole body seemed to shake with the effort of trying to get himself free. Above his bow-tie, his face bloomed scarlet in the torchlight. They stopped and waited patiently for him. 'Mmm-mmm . . .'

'Mean that?' suggested Atwood.

'Mean that, Frank,' gasped Pinker with relief. 'Thank you.'

Someone came to Atwood's support, and then Pinker's shrill voice started to argue again. They moved off. Jericho lagged behind.

The canteen, which lay just behind the perimeter fence, was as big as an aircraft hangar, brightly lit and thunderously noisy, with perhaps five or six hundred people sitting down to eat or queuing for food.

One of the new cryptanalysts shouted to Jericho: 'I bet you've missed this!' Jericho smiled and was about to say something in return but the young man went off to collect a tray. The din was dreadful, and so was the smell – a blended steam of institutional food, of cabbage and boiled fish and custard, laced with cigarette smoke and damp clothes. Jericho felt simultaneously intimidated by it and detached from it, like a prisoner returning from solitary confinement, or a patient from an isolation ward released on to the street after a long illness.

He queued and didn't pay much attention to the food being slopped on his plate. It was only after he had handed over his two shillings and sat down that he took a good look at it – boiled potatoes in a curdled yellow grease and a slab of something ribbed and grey. He stabbed at the lump with his fork, then lifted a fragment cautiously to his mouth. It tasted like fishy liver, like congealed cod liver oil. He winced.

'This is perfectly vile.'

Atwood said, through a full mouth: 'It's whale meat.'

'Good heavens.' Jericho put his fork down hurriedly.

'Don't waste it, dear boy. Don't you know there's a war on? Pass it over.'

Jericho pushed the plate across the table and tried to swill the taste away with the milk-water coffee.

The pudding was some kind of fruit tart, and that was better, or, rather, it tasted of nothing more noxious than cardboard, but halfway through it, Jericho's wavering appetite finally died. Atwood was now giving them his opinion of Gielgud's interpretation of Hamlet, spraying the table in the process with particles of whale, and at that point Jericho decided he'd had enough. He took the leftovers that Atwood didn't want and scraped them into a milk churn labelled 'PIG SWILL'.

When he was halfway to the door he was suddenly overcome with remorse at his rudeness. Was this the behaviour of a good colleague, what Skynner would call 'a team player'? But then, when he turned and looked back, he saw that nobody had missed him. Atwood was still talking, waving his fork in mid-air, Pinker was shaking his head, the others were listening.

Jericho turned once more for the door and the salvation of the fresh air.

Thirty seconds later he was out on the pavement, picking his way carefully in the darkness towards the guard post, thinking about Shark.

He could hear the *click click* of a woman's heels hurrying about twenty paces in front of him. There was no one else around. It was between sittings: everyone was either working or eating. The rapid footsteps stopped at the barrier and a moment later the sentry shone his torch directly in the woman's face. She glanced away with a murmur of annoyance, and Jericho saw her then, for an instant, spot-lit in the blackout, looking straight in his direction.

It was Claire.

For a fraction of a second, he thought she must have seen him. But he was in the shadows and reeling backwards in panic, four or five steps backwards, and she was dazzled by the light. With what seemed like infinite slowness she brought her hand up to shield her eyes. Her blonde hair gleamed white.

He couldn't hear what was said but very quickly the torch was quenched and everything was dark again. And then he heard her moving off down the path on the other side of the barrier, *click click click,* obviously in a rush about something, fading into the night.

He had to catch her up. He stumbled quickly to the guard post, searching for his wallet, searching for his pass, nearly tripping off the kerbstone, but he couldn't find the damned thing. The torch came on, blinding him – *'evening sir'*, *'evening corporal'* – and his fingers were useless, he couldn't make them work, and the pass wasn't in his wallet, wasn't in his overcoat pockets, wasn't in his jacket pockets, breast pocket – he couldn't hear her footsteps now, just the sentry's boot tapping impatiently – and, yes, it *was* in his breast pocket, *'here you are'*, *'thank you sir'*, *'thank you corporal'*, *'night sir'*, *'night corporal'*, night, night, night . . .

She was gone.

The sentry's light had robbed him of what little vision he had. When he closed his eyes there was only the imprint of the torch and when he opened them the darkness was absolute. He found the edge of the road with his foot and followed its curve. It took him once again past the mansion and brought him out close to the huts. Far away, on the opposite bank of the lake, someone – perhaps another sentry — started to whistle 'We'll Gather Lilacs in the Spring Again', then stopped.

It was so quiet, he could hear the wind moving in the trees.

While he was hesitating, wondering what to do, a dot of light appeared along the footpath to his right, and then another. For some reason Jericho drew back into the shadows of Hut 8 as the torches bobbed towards him. He heard voices he didn't recognise – a man's and a woman's – whispered but emphatic. When they were almost level with him, the man threw his cigarette into the water. A cascade of red points ended in a hiss. The woman said: 'It's just a week, darling,' and went to embrace him. The fireflies danced and separated and moved on.

He stepped out onto the path again. His night vision was coming back. He looked at his watch. It was 4.30. Another ninety minutes and it would start to get light.

On impulse he walked down the side of Hut 8, keeping close to the blastproof wall. This brought him to the edge of Hut 6, where the ciphers of the German Army and Luftwaffe were broken. Straight ahead was a narrow alleyway of rough grass separating Hut 6 from the end wall of the Naval Section. And at the end of that, crouched low in the darkness, just about visible, was the side of another hut – Hut 3 – to which the decrypted ciphers from Hut 6 were sent for translation and dispatch.

Hut 3 was where Claire worked.

He glanced around. There was no one in sight.

He left the path and started to stumble down the passage. The ground was slippery and uneven and several times something grabbed at his ankle – ivy, maybe, or a tendril of discarded cable – and almost sent him sprawling. It took him about a minute to reach Hut 3.

Here, too, was a concrete wall, designed, optimistically, to shield the flimsy wooden structure from an exploding bomb. It was neck-high, but although he was short he was just about able to peer over the top.

A row of windows was set into the side of the building. Over these, from the outside, blackout shutters were fastened every day at dusk. All that was visible was the ghosts of squares, where the light seeped around the edges of the frames. The floor of Hut 3, like Hut 8's, was made of wood, suspended above a concrete base, and he could hear the muffled clumps and thuds of people moving about.

She must be on duty. She must be working the midnight shift. She might be three feet from where he stood.

He was on tiptoe.

He had never been inside Hut 3. For reasons of security, workers in one section of the Park were not encouraged to stray into another, not unless they had good reason. From time to time his work had taken him over the threshold of Hut 6, but Hut 3 was a mystery to him. He had no idea of what she did. She'd tried to tell him once, but he'd said gently that it was best he didn't know. From odd remarks he gathered it was something to do with filing and was 'deadly dull, darling'.

He stretched out as far as he could, until his fingertips were brushing the asbestos cladding of the hut.

What are you doing, darling Claire? Are you busy with your boring filing, or are you flirting with one of the night-duty officers, or gossiping with the other girls, or puzzling over that crossword you can never do?

Suddenly, about fifteen yards to his left, a door opened. From the oblong of dim light a uniformed man emerged, yawning. Jericho slid silently to the ground until he was kneeling in the wet earth and pressed his chest against the wall. The door closed and the man began to walk towards him. He stopped about ten feet away, breathing hard. He seemed to be listening. Jericho closed his eyes and shortly afterwards he heard a pattering and then a drilling noise and when he opened them he saw the faint silhouette of the man pissing against the wall, very hard. It went on for a wondrously long time and Jericho was close enough to get a whiff of pungent, beery urine. A fine spray was being borne downwind on the breeze. He had to put his hand to his nose and mouth to stop himself gagging. Eventually, the man gave a deep sigh – a groan, almost – of satisfaction, and fumbled with the buttons of his fly. He moved away. The door opened and closed again and Jericho was alone.

There was a certain humour in the situation, and later even he was to see it. But at the time he was on the edge of panic. What, in the name of reason, did he think he was doing? If he were to be caught, kneeling in the darkness, with his ear pressed to a hut in which he had no business, he would have – to put it mildly – a hard time explaining himself. For a moment he considered simply marching inside and demanding to see her. But his imagination recoiled at the prospect. He might be thrown out. Or she might appear in fury and create a scene. Or she might appear and be the soul of sweetness, in which case what did he say? *'Oh, hello, darling. I just happened to be passing. You look in good form. By the way, I've been meaning to ask you, why did you wreck my life?'*

He used the wall to help him scramble to his feet. The quickest way back to the road was straight head, but that would take him past the door of the hut. He decided that the safest course would be to go back the way he had come.

He was more cautious after his scare. Each time he took a step he planted his foot carefully and on every fifth pace he paused to make sure that no one else was moving around in the blackout. Two minutes later he was back outside the entrance to Hut 8.

He felt as if he had been on a cross-country run. He was out of breath. There was a small hole in his left shoe and his sock was wet. Bits of damp grass were sticking to the bottoms of his trouser legs. His knees were sodden. And where he had rubbed against the concrete wall the front of his overcoat was streaked luminously white. He took out his handkerchief and tried to clean himself up.

He had just about finished when he heard the others coming back from the canteen. Atwood's voice carried in the night: 'A dark horse, that one. Very dark. I recruited him, you know,' to which someone else chimed in: 'Yes, but he was once very good, wasn't he?'

Jericho didn't stop to hear the rest. He pushed open the door and almost ran down the passage, so that by the time the cryptanalysts appeared in the Big Room he was already seated at his desk, bent over the intercepts, knuckles to his temples, eyes closed.

He stayed like that for three hours.

At about six o'clock, Puck stopped by to drop on the table another forty encrypted signals, the latest batch of Shark traffic, and to enquire – not without a degree of sarcasm – if Jericho had 'solved it yet?' At seven, there was a rattle of step ladders against the outside wall and the blackout shutters were unfastened. A pale grey light filtered into the hut.

What was she doing, hurrying into the Park at that time of night? That was what he did not understand. Of course, the mere fact of seeing her again after a month spent trying to forget her was disturbing. But it was the circumstances, in retrospect, that troubled him more. She had not been in the canteen, he was sure of that. He had scrutinised every table, every face – had been so distracted he had barely even looked at what he was being given to eat. But if she had not been in the canteen, where had she been? Had she been with someone? Who? Who? And the way she was walking so hurriedly. Was there not something furtive, even panicky, about it?

His memory replayed the scene frame by frame: the footsteps, the flash of light, the turn of her head, her cry, the halo of her hair, the way she had vanished . . . That was something else. Could she really have walked the entire distance to the hut in the time it took him to fumble for his pass?

Just before eight o'clock he gathered the crypto-grams together and slipped them into the folder. All around him, the cryptanalysts were preparing to go off shift – stretching and yawning and rubbing at tired eyes, pulling together their work, briefing their replacements. Nobody noticed Jericho walk quickly down the corridor to Logie's office. He knocked once. There was no reply. He tried the door. As he remembered: unlocked.

He closed it behind him and picked up the

telephone. If he delayed for a second his nerve would fail him. He dialled '0' and on the seventh ring, just as he was about to give up, a sleepy operator answered.

His mouth was almost too dry to get the words out. 'Duty Officer, Hut 3, please.'

Almost immediately a man's voice said, irritably: 'Colonel Coker.'

Jericho nearly dropped the receiver.

'Do you have a Miss Romilly there?' He didn't need to disguise his voice: it was so strained and quavering it was unrecognisable. 'A Miss Claire Romilly?'

'You've come through to *completely* the wrong office. Who is this?'

'Welfare.'

'Oh bloody *hell!*' There was a deafening bang, as if the colonel had thrown the telephone across the room, but the connection held. Jericho could hear the clatter of a teleprinter and a man's voice, very cultured, somewhere in the background: 'Yes, yes, I've got that. Right-oh. Cheerio.' The man ended one conversation and started another. 'Army Index here . . .' Jericho glanced at the clock above the window. Now it was past eight. Come on, come on . . . Suddenly there was more loud banging, much closer, and a woman said softly in Jericho's ear: 'Yes?'

He tried to sound casual but it came out as a croak. 'Claire?'

'No, I'm afraid it's Claire's day off. She won't be back on duty until eight tomorrow morning. Can I help?'

Jericho gently replaced the receiver in its cradle, just

as the door was thrown open behind him.

'Oh, *there* you are, old thing . . .'

4

Daylight diminished the huts.

The blackout had touched them with a certain mystery but the morning showed them up for what they were: squat and ugly, with brown walls and tarred roofs and a premature air of dereliction. Above the mansion, the sky was glossy white with streaks of grey, a dome of polished marble. A duck in drab winter plumage waddled across the path from the lake looking for food, and Logie almost kicked it as he strode past, sending it protesting back to the water.

He had not been in the least perturbed to find Jericho in his office and Jericho's carefully prepared excuse – that he was returning the Shark intercepts – had been waved away.

'Just dump 'em in the Crib Room and come with me.'

Drawn across the northern edge of the lake, next to the huts, was A-Block, a long, two-storey affair with brick walls and a flat top. Logie led the way up a flight of concrete steps and turned right. At the far end of the corridor a door opened and Jericho heard a familiar voice booming: '. . . all our resources, human and material, into this problem . . .' and then the door closed again and Baxter peered down the passage towards them.

'So there you are. I was just coming to find you. Hello, Guy. Hello, Tom. How are you? Hardly recognised you. Upright.' Baxter had a cigarette in his mouth and didn't bother to remove it, so it bobbed as he spoke and sprayed ash down the front of his pullover. Before the war he had been a lecturer at the London School of Economics.

'What have we got?' said Logie, nodding towards the closed door.

'Our American "lee-ay-son officer", plus another American – some big shot from the Navy. A man in a suit – a lounge lizard from Intelligence by the look of him. Three from our Navy, of course, one of them an admiral. All up from London specially.'

'An admiral?' Logie's hand went automatically to his tie and Jericho noticed he had changed into a pre-war double-breasted suit. He licked his fingers and tried to plaster down his hair. 'I don't like the sound of an admiral. And how's Skynner?'

'At the moment? I'd say heavily out-gunned.' Baxter was staring at Jericho. The corners of his mouth twitched down briefly, the nearest Jericho had seen him come to a smile. 'Well, well, I suppose you don't look too bad, Tom.'

'Now, Alec, don't you go upsetting him.'

'I'm fine, Alec, thank you. How's the revolution?'

'Coming along, comrade. Coming along.'

Logie patted Jericho on the arm. 'Don't say anything when we get inside, Tom. You're only here for show, old love.'

Only here for show, thought Jericho, what the hell

does that mean? But before he could ask, Logie had opened the door and all he could hear was Skynner – 'we must expect these setbacks from time to time' – and they were on.

There were eight men in the room. Leonard Skynner, the head of the Naval Section, sat at one end of the table, with Atwood to his right and an empty chair to his left, which Baxter promptly reclaimed. Gathered around the other end were five officers in dark blue naval uniform, two of them American and three British. One of the British officers, a lieutenant, had an eye-patch. They looked grim.

The eighth man had his back to Jericho. He turned as they came in and Jericho briefly registered a lean face with fair hair.

Skynner stopped speaking. He stood and held out a meaty hand. 'Come in Guy, come in Tom.' He was a big square-faced man with thick black hair and wide bushy eyebrows that almost met above the bridge of his nose and reminded Jericho of the Morse code symbol for M. He beckoned to the newcomers eagerly, obviously thankful to see Allied reinforcements. 'This is Guy Logie,' he said to the admiral, 'our chief cryptanalyst, and Tom Jericho, of whom you may have heard. Tom was instrumental in getting us into Shark just before Christmas.'

The admiral's leathery old face was immobile. He was smoking a cigarette – they were all smoking cigarettes except for Skynner – and he regarded Jericho, as did the Americans, blankly, through a fog of tobacco, without the slightest interest. Skynner rattled off the introductions, his arm sweeping round the table like the hand of a clock. 'This is Admiral Trowbridge. Lieutenant Cave. Lieutenant Villiers. Commander Hammerbeck –' the older of the two Americans nodded '– Lieutenant Kramer, US Navy Liaison. Mr Wigram is observing for the cabinet Office.' Skynner gave a little bow to everybody and sat down again. He was sweating.

Jericho and Logie each collected a folding chair from a stack beside the table and took up positions next to Baxter.

Almost the whole of the wall behind the admiral was taken up by a map of the North Atlantic. Clusters of coloured discs showed the positions of Allied convoys and their escorts: yellow for the merchantmen, green for the warships. Black triangles marked the suspected whereabouts of German U-boats. Beneath the chart was a red telephone, a direct link to the Submarine Tracking Room in the basement of the Admiralty. The only other decoration on the whitewashed walls was a pair of framed photographs. One was of the King, signed, looking nervous, presented after a recent visit. The other was of Grand Admiral Karl Dönitz, commander in chief of the German Navy: Skynner liked to think of himself as locked in a personal battle with the wily Hun.

Now, though, he seemed to have lost the thread of what he was saying. He sorted through his notes and in the time it took Logie and Jericho to take their places, one of the Royal Navy men – Cave, the one with the eye-patch – received a nod from the admiral and started speaking.

'Perhaps, if you've finished outlining your problems, it might be helpful for us now to set out the operational situation.' His chair scraped on the bare floor as he rose to his feet. His tone was insultingly polite. 'The position at twenty-one hundred . . .'

Jericho passed his hand over his unshaven chin. He couldn't make up his mind whether to keep his overcoat on or take it off. On, he decided – the room was cold, despite the number of people in it. He undid the buttons and loosened his scarf. As he did so, he noticed the admiral watching him. They couldn't believe it, these senior officers, whenever they came up to visit – the lack of discipline, the scarves and cardigans, the first-name terms. There was a story about Churchill, who'd visited the Park in 1941 and given a speech to the cryptanalysts on the lawn. Afterwards, as he was being driven away, he'd said to the director: 'When I told you to leave no stone unturned recruiting for this place, I didn't expect you to take me literally.' Jericho smiled at the memory. The admiral glowered and flicked cigarette ash on the floor.

The one-eyed naval officer had picked up a pointer and was standing in front of the Atlantic chart, holding a sheaf of notes.

'It must be said, unfortunately, that the news you've given us couldn't have come at a worse moment. No fewer than three convoys have left the United States in the past week and are presently at sea. Convoy SC-122.' He rapped it once with the pointer, hard, as if he had a grudge against it, and read out his notes. 'Departed New York last Friday. Carrying fuel oil, iron ore, steel, wheat, bauxite, sugar, refrigerated meat, zinc, tobacco and tanks. Fifty merchant ships.'

Cave spoke in a clipped, metallic voice, without looking at his audience. His one good eye was fixed on the map.

'Convoy HX-229.' He tapped it. 'Departed New York Monday. Forty merchant vessels. Carrying meat, explosives, lubricating oil, refrigerated dairy produce, manganese, lead, timber, phosphate, diesel oil, aviation spirit, sugar and powdered milk.' He turned to them for the first time. The whole of the left side of his face was a mass of purple scar tissue. 'That, I might say, is two weeks' supply of powdered milk for the entire British Isles.'

There was some nervous laughter. 'Better not lose that,' joked Skynner. The laughter stopped at once. He looked so forlorn in the silence Jericho almost felt sorry for him.

Again, the pointer crashed down.

'And Convoy HX-229A. Left New York Tuesday. Twenty-seven ships. Similar cargoes to the others. Fuel oil, aviation spirit, timber, steel, naval diesel, meat, sugar, wheat, explosives. Three convoys. A total of one hundred and seventeen merchant ships, with a gross registered tonnage of just under one million tons, plus cargo of another million.'

One of the Americans – it was the senior one, Hammerbeck – raised his hand. 'How many men involved?'

'Nine thousand merchant seamen. One thousand passengers.'

'Who are the passengers?'

'Mainly servicemen. Some ladies from the American Red Cross. Quite a lot of children. A party of Catholic missionaries, curiously enough.'

'Jesus Christ.'

Cave permitted himself a crimped smile. 'Quite.'

'And whereabouts are the U-boats?'

'Perhaps I might let my colleague answer that.'

Cave sat down and the other British officer, Villiers, took the floor. He flourished the pointer.

'Submarine Tracking Room had three U-boat packs operational as of zero-zero-hundred Thursday – heah, heah, and heah.' His accent barely qualified as recognisable English, it was the sort that pronounced 'cloth' as 'clawth' and 'really' as 'rarely', and when he spoke his lips hardly moved, as if it were somehow ungentlemanly – a betrayal of the amateur ethos – to put too much effort into talking. 'Gruppe Raubgraf heah, two hundred miles off the coast of Greenland. Gruppe Neuland, heah, almost precisely mid-ocean. And Gruppe Westmark heah, due south of Iceland.'

'Zero-zero *Thursday*? You mean more than thirty hours ago?' Hammerbeck's hair was the colour and thickness of steel wool, close-cropped to his scalp. It glinted in the fluorescent light as he leaned forwards. 'Where the hell are they now?'

'I'm afraid I've no ideah. I thought that was why we were heah. They've blipped awf the screen.'

Admiral Trowbridge lit another cigarette from the

tip of his old one. He had transferred his attention from Jericho and now he was staring at Hammerbeck through small, rheumy eyes.

Again, the American raised his hand. 'How many subs are we talking about in these three wolf packs?'

'I'm sorry to say, ah, they're quite large, ah, we estimate forty-six.'

Skynner squirmed in his chair. Atwood made a great show of rummaging through his papers.

'Let me get this straight,' said Hammerbeck. (He was certainly persistent – Jericho was beginning to admire him.) 'You're telling us one million tons of shipping – '

'Merchant shipping,' interrupted Cave.

'– merchant shipping, pardon me, one million tons of *merchant* shipping, with ten thousand people on board, including various ladies of the American Red Cross and assorted Catholic Bible-bashers, is steaming towards forty-six U-boats, and you have no idea where those U-boats are?'

'I'm rather afraid I am, yes.'

'Well, I'll be fucked,' said Hammerbeck, sitting back in his chair. 'And how long before they get there?'

'That's hard to say.' It was Cave again. He had an odd habit of turning his face away when he talked, and Jericho realised he was trying not to show his shattered cheekbone. 'The SC is the slower convoy. She's making about seven knots. The HXs are both faster, one ten knots, one eleven. I'd say we've got three days, at the maximum. After that, they'll be within operational range of the enemy.'

Hammerbeck had begun whispering to the other American. He was shaking his head and making short chopping motions with his hand. The admiral leaned over and muttered something to Cave, who said quietly: 'I'm afraid so, sir.'

Jericho looked up at the Atlantic, at the yellow discs of the convoys and the black triangles of the U-boats, sewn like shark's teeth across the sea lanes. The distance between the ships and the wolf packs was roughly eight hundred miles. The merchantmen were making maybe two hundred and forty miles every twenty-four hours. Three days was about right. My God, he thought, no wonder Logie was so desperate to get me back.

'Gentlemen, please, if I may?' said Skynner loudly, bringing the meeting back to order. Jericho saw he'd plastered on his 'come let us smile in the face of disaster' expression – invariably a sign of incipient panic. 'I think we should guard against too much pessimism. The Atlantic does cover thirty-two million square miles, you know.' He risked another laugh. 'That's an awful lot of ocean.'

'Yes,' said Hammerbeck, 'and forty-six is one hell of a lot of U-boats.'

'I agree. It's probably the largest concentration of hearses we've faced,' said Cave. 'I'm afraid we must assume the enemy will make contact. Unless, of course, we can find out where they are.'

He gave Skynner a significant look, but Skynner ignored it and pressed on. 'And let's not forget – these convoys are not unprotected?' He glanced around the table for support. 'They do have an escort?'

'Indeed.' Cave again. 'They have an escort of – ' he consulted his notes '– seven destroyers, nine corvettes and three frigates. Plus various other vessels.'

'Under an experienced commander . . .'

The British officers glanced at one another, and then at the admiral.

'Actually, it's his first command.'

'Jesus Christ!' Hammerbeck rocked forwards in his chair and brought his fists down on the table.

'If I might step in heah. Obviously, we didn't know last Friday when the escorts were forming up that our intelligence was going to be shut awf.'

'How long will this blackout last?' This was the first time the admiral had spoken and everyone turned to look at him. He gave a sharp, explosive cough, which sounded as if small pieces of machinery were flying around loose in his chest, then sucked in another lungful of smoke and gestured with his cigarette. 'Will it be over in four days, d'you think?'

The question was addressed directly to Skynner and they all turned to look at him. He was an administrator, not a cryptanalyst – he'd been vice-chancellor of some northern university before the war – and Jericho knew he hadn't a clue. He didn't know whether the blackout would last four days, four months or four years.

Skynner said carefully: 'It's possible.'

'Yes, well, all things are possible.' Trowbridge gave an unpleasant rasping laugh that turned into another cough. 'Is it likely? Is it likely you can break this, whatever you call it – this Shark – before our convoys come within range of the U-boats?'

'We'll give it every priority.'

'I know damn well you'll give it every priority, Leonard. You keep saying you'll give it every priority. That's not the question.'

'Well, sir, as you press me, sir, yes.' Skynner stuck his big jaw out heroically. In his mind's eye he was steering his ship manfully into the face of the typhoon. 'Yes, I think we may be able to do it.'

You're mad, thought Jericho.

'And you all believe that?' The admiral stared hard in their direction. He had eyes like a bloodhound's, red-lidded and watery.

Logie was the first to break the silence. He looked at Skynner and winced and scratched the back of his head with the stem of his pipe. 'I suppose we do have the advantage of knowing more about Shark than we did before.'

Atwood jumped in: 'If Guy thinks we can do it, I certainly respect his opinion. I'd go along with whatever he estimates.' Baxter nodded judiciously. Jericho inspected his watch.

'And you?' said the admiral. 'What do you think?'

In Cambridge, they would just about be finishing breakfast. Kite would be steaming open the mail. Mrs Sax would be rattling round with her brushes and pails. In Hall on Saturday they served vegetable pie with potatoes for lunch . . .

He was aware that the room had gone quiet and he looked up to find all eyes were on him. The fair-haired man in the suit was staring at him with particular curiosity. He felt his face begin to colour.

And then he felt a spasm of irritation.

Afterwards Jericho was to think about this moment many times. What made him act as he did? Was it tiredness? Was he simply disoriented, plucked out of Cambridge and set down in the middle of this nightmare? Was he still ill? Illness would certainly help explain what happened later. Or was he so distracted by the thought of Claire that he wasn't thinking straight? All he remembered for certain was an overwhelming feeling of annoyance. *'You're only here for show, old love.'* You're only here to make up the numbers, so Skynner can put on a good act for the Yanks. You're only here to do as you're told, so keep your views to yourself, and don't ask questions. He was suddenly sick of it all, sick of everything – sick of the blackout, sick of the cold, sick of the chummy first-name terms and the lime smell and the damp and the whale meat – *whale meat* – at four o'clock in the morning . . .

'Actually, I'm not sure I am as optimistic as my colleagues.'

Skynner interrupted him at once. You could almost hear the klaxons going off in his mind, see the airmen sprinting across the deck and the big guns swivelling skywards as HMS *Skynner* came under threat. 'Tom's been ill, sir, I'm afraid. He's been away from us for the best part of a month . . .'

'Why not?' The admiral's tone was dangerously friendly. 'Why aren't you optimistic?'

'. . . so I'm not sure he's altogether fully *au fait* with the situation. Wouldn't you admit that, Tom?'

'Well, I'm certainly *au fait* with Enigma, ah,

Leonard.' Jericho could hardly believe his own words. He plunged on. 'Enigma is a very sophisticated cipher system. And Shark is its ultimate refinement. I've spent the past eight hours reviewing the Shark material and, ah, forgive me if I'm speaking out of turn, but it seems to me we are in a very serious situation.'

'But you *were* breaking it successfully?'

'Yes, but we'd been given a key. The weather code was the key that unlocked the door. The Germans have now changed the weather code. That means we've lost our key. Unless there's been some development I'm not aware of, I don't understand how we're going to . . .' Jericho searched for a metaphor. '. . . pick the lock.'

The other American naval officer, the one who hadn't spoken so far – Jericho had momentarily forgotten his name – said: 'And you still haven't gotten those four-wheel bombes you promised us, Frank.'

'That's a separate issue,' muttered Skynner. He gave Jericho a murderous look.

'Is it?' Kramer – that was it. He was called Kramer. 'Surely if we had a few four-wheel bombes right now we wouldn't need the weather cribs?'

'Just stop there for a moment,' said the admiral, who had been following this conversation with increasing impatience. 'I'm a sailor, and an old sailor at that. I don't understand all this – *talk* – about keys and cribs and bombs with wheels. We're trying to keep the sea-lanes open from America and if we can't do that we're going to lose this war.'

'Hear, hear,' said Hammerbeck. 'Well said, Jack.'

'Now will somebody please give me a straight answer

to a straight question? Will this blackout definitely be over in four days' time or won't it? Yes or no?'

Skynner's shoulders sagged. 'No,' he said wearily. 'If you put it like that, sir, I can't say *definitely* it will be over, no.'

'Thank you. So, if it isn't over in four days, when will it be over? You. You're the pessimist. What do you think?'

Once again Jericho was conscious of everyone watching him.

He spoke carefully. Poor Logie was peering inside his tobacco pouch as if he wished he could climb in and never come out 'It's very hard to say. All we have to measure it by is the last blackout.'

'And how long did that go on?'

'Ten months.'

It was as if he had detonated a bomb. Everybody made a noise. The Navy men shouted. The admiral started coughing. Baxter and Atwood said 'No!' simultaneously. Logie groaned. Skynner, shaking his head, said: 'That really is defeatist of you, Tom.' Even Wigram, the fair-headed man, gave a snort and stared at the rafters, smiling at some private joke.

'I'm not saying it will definitely take us ten months,' Jericho resumed when he could make himself heard. 'But that's the measure of what we're up against and I think that four days is unrealistic. I'm sorry. I do.'

There was a pause, and then Wigram said, softly: '*Why*, I wonder . . .'

'Mr Wigram?'

'Sorry, Leonard.' Wigram bestowed his smile

around the table, and Jericho's immediate thought was how *expensive* he looked – blue suit, silk tie, Jermyn Street shirt, pomaded hair swept back and scented with some masculine cologne – he might have stepped out of the lobby of the Ritz. *A lounge lizard*, Baxter had called him, which was Bletchley code for *spy*.

'Sorry,' Wigram said again. 'Thinking aloud. I was just wondering *why* Dönitz should have decided to change this *particular* bit of code and *why* he should have chosen to do so *now*.' He stared at Jericho. 'From what you were saying, it sounds as though he couldn't have chosen any one thing more damaging to us.'

Jericho didn't have to reply; Logie did it for him. 'Routine. Almost certainly. They change their code books from time to time. Just our bad luck they did it now.'

'Routine,' repeated Wigram. 'Right.' He smiled once more. 'Tell me, Leonard, how many people know about this weather code and how important it is to us?'

'Really, Douglas,' laughed Skynner, 'whatever are you suggesting?'

'How many?'

'Guy?'

'A dozen, perhaps.'

'Couldn't make me a little list, could you?'

Logie looked to Skynner for approval. 'I, ah, well, I, ah . . .'

'Thanks.'

Wigram resumed his examination of the ceiling.

The silence that followed was broken by a long sigh from the admiral. 'I think I gather the sense of the meeting.' He stubbed out his cigarette and reached down beside his chair for his briefcase. He began stuffing his papers into it and his lieutenants followed suit. 'I can't pretend it's the happiest of messages to take back to the First Sea Lord.'

Hammerbeck said: 'I guess I'd better signal Washington.'

The admiral stood and immediately they all pushed back their chairs and got to their feet.

'Lieutenant Cave will act as Admiralty liaison.' He turned to Cave: 'I'd like a daily report. On second thoughts, perhaps better make that twice a day.'

'Yes, sir.'

'Lieutenant Kramer: you'll carry on here and keep Commander Hammerbeck informed?'

'I sure will, sir. Yes, sir.'

'So.' He pulled on his gloves. 'I suggest we reconvene this meeting as and when there are developments to report. Which hopefully will be within four days.'

At the door, the old man turned. 'It's not just one million tons of shipping and ten thousand men, you know. It's one million tons of shipping and ten thousand men *every two weeks*. And it's not just the convoys. It's our obligation to send supplies to Russia. It's our chances of invading Europe and driving the Nazis out. It's everything. It's the whole war.' He gave another of his wheezing laughs. 'Not that I want to put any pressure on you, Leonard.' He nodded. 'Good morning, gentlemen.'

As they mumbled their 'good morning sirs', Jericho

heard Wigram say quietly to Skynner: 'I'll talk to you later, Leonard.'

They listened to the visitors clatter down the concrete stairs, and then to the crunch of their feet on the path outside, and suddenly the room was quiet. A mist of blue tobacco hung over the table like smoke rising after a battle.

Skynner's lips were compressed. He was humming to himself. He gathered his papers into a pile and squared off the edges with exaggerated care. For what seemed a long time, nobody spoke.

'Well,' said Skynner eventually, 'that was a triumph. Thank you, Tom. Thank you very much indeed. I'd forgotten what a tower of strength you could be. We've missed you.'

'It's my fault, Leonard,' said Logie. 'Bad briefing. Should have put him in the picture better. Sorry. Bit of a rush first thing.'

'Why don't you just get back to the Hut, Guy? In fact, why don't you all go back, and then Tom and I can have a little chat.'

'Bloody fool,' said Baxter to Jericho.

Atwood took his arm. 'Come on, Alec.'

'Well, he is. Bloody fool.'

They left.

The moment the door closed Skynner said: 'I never wanted you back.'

'Logie didn't mention that.' Jericho folded his arms to stop his hands shaking. 'He said I was needed here.'

'I never wanted you back, not because I think you're a fool – Alec's wrong about that. You're not a fool. But you're a wreck. You're ruined. You've cracked once before under pressure and you'll do it again, as your little performance just now showed. You've outlived your usefulness to us.'

Skynner was leaning his large bottom casually against the edge of the table. He was speaking in a friendly tone and if you had seen him from a distance you would have thought he was exchanging pleasantries with an old acquaintance.

'Then why am I here? I never asked to come back.'

'Logie thinks highly of you. He's the acting head of the Hut and I listen to him. And, I'll be honest, after Turing, you probably have – or, rather, *had* – the best reputation of any cryptanalyst on the Park. You're a little bit of history, Tom. A little bit of a legend. Bringing you back, letting you attend this morning, was a way of showing our masters how seriously we take this, ah, temporary crisis. It was a risk. But obviously I was wrong. You've lost it.'

Jericho was not a violent man. He had never hit another person, not even as a boy, and he knew it was a mercy he had avoided military service: given a rifle he would have been a menace to no one except his own side. But there was a heavy brass ashtray on the table – the sawn-off end of a six-inch shell-case, brimful of cigarette stubs – and Jericho was seriously tempted to ram it into Skynner's smug face. Skynner seemed to sense this. At any rate, he pulled his bottom off the table and began to pace the floor. This must be one of the benefits of being a madman, thought Jericho, people can never take you entirely for granted.

'It was so much simpler in the old days, wasn't it?' said Skynner. 'A country house. A handful of eccentrics. Nobody expecting very much. You potter along. And then suddenly you're sitting on the greatest secret of the war.'

'And then people like you arrive.'

'That's right, people like myself are needed, to make sure this remarkable weapon is used properly.'

'Oh is that what you do, Leonard? You make sure the weapon is used properly. I've often wondered.'

Skynner stopped smiling. He was a big man, nearly a foot taller than Jericho. He came up very close, and Jericho could smell the stale cigarette smoke and the sweat on his clothes.

'You've no conception of this place any more. No idea of the problems. The Americans, for instance. In front of whom you've just humiliated me. Us. We're negotiating a deal with the Americans that – ' He stopped himself. 'Never mind. Let's just say that when you – when you *indulge* yourself as you just did, you can't even conceive of the seriousness of what's at stake.'

Skynner had a briefcase with a royal crest stamped on it and 'G VI R' in faded gold lettering. He slipped his papers into it and locked it with a key attached to his belt by a long chain.

'I'm going to arrange for you to be taken off cryptanalytical work and put somewhere you can't do any damage. In fact, I'm going to have you transferred out of Bletchley altogether.' He pocketed the key and patted it. 'You can't return to civilian life, of course, not until the war's over, not knowing what you know.

Still, I hear the Admiralty's on the lookout for an extra brain to work in statistics. Dull stuff, but cushy enough for a man of your . . . delicacy. Who knows? Perhaps you'll meet a nice girl. Someone more – how shall we say? – more *suitable* for you than the person I gather you *were* seeing.'

Jericho did try to hit him then, but not with the ashtray, only with his fist, which in retrospect was a mistake. Skynner stepped to one side with surprising grace and the blow missed and then his right hand shot out and grabbed Jericho's forearm. Skynner dug his fingers very hard into the soft muscle.

'You are an ill man, Tom. And I am stronger than you, in every way.' He increased the pressure for a second or two, then abruptly let go of the arm. 'Now get out of my sight.'

5

God, but he was tired. Exhaustion stalked him like a living thing, clutching at his legs, squatting on his sagging shoulders. Jericho leaned against the outside wall of A-Block, rested his cheek against the smooth, damp concrete, and waited for his pulse to return to normal.

What had he done?

He needed to lie down. He needed to find some hole to crawl into and get some rest. Like a drunk searching for his keys, he felt first in one pocket and then another and finally pulled out the billeting chit and squinted at it. Albion Street? Where was that? He had a vague memory. He would know it when he saw it.

He pushed himself away from the wall and began to make his way, carefully, away from the lake towards the road that led to the main gate. A small, black car was parked about ten yards ahead and as he came closer the driver's door opened and a figure in a blue uniform appeared.

'Mr Jericho!'

Jericho stared with surprise. It was one of the Americans. 'Lieutenant Kramer?'

'Hi. Going home? Can I give you a ride?'

'Thank you. No. Really, it's only a short walk.'

'Aw, come on.' Kramer patted the roof of the car. 'I just got her. It'd be my pleasure. Come on.'

Jericho was about to decline again, but then he felt his legs begin to crumple.

'Whoa there, feller.' Kramer sprang forward and took his arm. 'You're all in. Long night, I guess?'

Jericho allowed himself to be guided to the passenger door and pushed into the front seat. The interior of the little car was cold and smelled as if it hadn't been used in a long while. Jericho guessed it must have been someone's pride and joy until petrol rationing forced it off the road. The chassis rocked as Kramer clambered in the other side and slammed the door.

'Not many people around here run their own cars.' Jericho's voice sounded oddly in his ears, as if from a distance. 'You have trouble getting fuel?'

'No, sir.' Kramer pressed the starter button and the engine rattled into life. 'You know us. We can get as much as we want.'

The car was carefully inspected at the main gate. The barrier rose and they headed out, past the canteen and the assembly hall, towards the end of Wilton Avenue.

'Which way?'

'Left, I think.'

Kramer flicked out one of the little amber indicators and they turned into the lane that led down to the town. His face was handsome – boyish and square-cut, with a faded tan that suggested service overseas. He was about twenty-five and looked formidably fit.

'I guess I'd like to thank you for that.'

'Thank me?'

'At the conference. You told the truth when the others all talked bull-shit. "Four days" – Jesus!'

'They were just being loyal.'

'Loyal? Come on, Tom. D'you mind if I call you Tom? I'm Jimmy, by the way. They'd been fixed.'

'I don't think this is a conversation we should be having . . .' The dizziness had passed and in the clarity that always followed it occurred to Jericho that the American must have been waiting for him to emerge from the meeting. 'This will do fine, thank you.'

'Really? But we've hardly gone any distance.'

'Please, just pull over.'

Kramer swerved into the kerb beside a row of small cottages, braked and turned off the engine.

'Listen, will you, Tom, just a minute? The Germans brought in Shark three months after Pearl Harbor –'

'Look –'

'Relax. Nobody's listening.' This was true. The lane was deserted. 'Three months after Pearl Harbor, and suddenly we're losing ships like we're going out of business. But nobody tells us why. After all, we're the new boys around here – we just route the convoys the way London tells us. Finally, it's getting so bad, we ask you guys what's happened to all this great intelligence you used to have.' He jabbed his finger at Jericho. 'Only *then* are we told about Shark.'

'I can't listen to this,' said Jericho. He tried to open the door but Kramer leaned across and seized the handle.

'I'm not trying to poison your mind against your own people. I'm just trying to tell you what's going on here. After we were told about Shark last year, we started to do some checking. Fast. And eventually, after one hell of a fight, we began to get some figures. D'you know how many bombes you guys had by the end of last summer? This is after two years of manufacture?'

Jericho was staring straight ahead. 'I wouldn't be privy to information like that.'

'Fifty! And d'you know how many our people in Washington said they could build within *four months*? Three hundred and sixty!'

'Well, build them, then,' said Jericho, irritably, 'if you're so bloody marvellous.'

'Oh no,' said Kramer. 'You don't understand. That's not allowed. Enigma is a British baby. Official. Any change in status has to be negotiated.'

'Is it being negotiated?'

'In Washington. Right now. That's where your Mr

Turing is. In the meantime, we just have to take whatever you give us.'

'But that's absurd. Why not just build the bombes anyway?'

'Come on, Tom. Think about it for a minute. You have all the intercept stations over here. You have all the raw material. We're three thousand miles away. Damn hard to pick up Magdeburg from Florida. And what's the point in having three hundred and sixty bombes if there's nothing to put in them?'

Jericho shut his eye sand saw Skynner's flushed face, heard his rumbling voice: '*You've no conception of this place any more . . . We're negotiating a deal with the Americans . . . You can't even conceive of the seriousness . . .*' Now, at least, he understood the reason for Skynner's anger. His little empire, so painfully put together, brick by bureaucratic brick, was mortally threatened by Shark. But the threat came not from Berlin. It came from Washington.

'Don't get me wrong,' Kramer was saying, 'I've been here a month and I think what you've all achieved is astounding. Brilliant. And nobody on our side is talking about a takeover. But it can't go on like this. Not enough bombes. Not enough typewriters. Those huts. Christ! "Was it dangerous in the war, Daddy?" "Sure was, I damned near froze to death." Did you know the whole operation almost stopped one time because you ran out of coloured pencils? I mean, what are we saying here? That men have to die because you don't have enough *pencils?*'

Jericho felt too tired to argue. Besides, he knew

enough to know it was true: all true. He remembered a night, eighteen months ago, when he'd been asked to keep an eye open for strangers at the Shoulder of Mutton, standing near the door in the blackout, sipping halves of shandy, while Turing, Welchman and a couple of the other big chiefs met in a room upstairs and wrote a joint letter to Churchill. Exactly the same story: not enough clerks, not enough typists, the factory at Letchworth that made the bombes – it used to make cash registers, of all things – short of parts, short of manpower . . . There'd been one hell of a row when Churchill got the letter – a tantrum in Downing Street, careers broken, machinery shaken up – and things had improved, for a while. But Bletchley was a greedy child. Its appetite grew with the feeding. *'Nervos belli, pecuniam infinitam.'* Or, as Baxter had put it, more prosaically, it all comes down to money in the end. The Poles had had to give Enigma to the British. Now the Brits would have to share it with the Yanks.

'I can't have anything to do with this. I've got to get some sleep. Thanks for the lift.'

He reached for the handle and this time Kramer made no attempt to stop him. He was halfway out of the door when Kramer said: 'I heard you lost your old man in the last war.'

Jericho froze. 'Who told you that?'

'I forget. Does it matter?'

'No. It's not a secret.' Jericho massaged his forehead. He had a filthy headache coming on. 'It happened before I was born. He was wounded by a shell at Ypres. He lived on for a bit but he wasn't much use after that.

He never came out of hospital. He died when I was six.'

'What did he do? Before he got hit?'

'He was a mathematician.'

There was a moment's silence.

'I'll see you around,' said Jericho. He got out of the car.

'My brother died,' said Kramer suddenly. 'One of the first. He was in the Merchant Marine. Liberty ships.'

Of course, thought Jericho.

'This was during the Shark blackout, I suppose?'

'You got it.' Kramer looked bleak, then forced a smile. 'Let's keep in touch, Tom. Anything I can do for you – just ask.'

He reached over and pulled the door shut with a bang. Jericho stood alone on the roadside and watched as Kramer executed a rapid U-turn. The car backfired, then headed at speed up the hill towards the Park, leaving a little puff of dirty smoke hanging in the morning air.

THREE

PINCH

PINCH: (1) <u>vb</u>., to steal enemy
cryptographic material; (2) <u>n</u>.,
any object stolen from the enemy
that enhances the chances of
breaking his codes or ciphers.

<u>A Lexicon of Cryptography</u>
('Most Secret', Bletchley Park, 1943)

1

BLETCHLEY WAS A railway town. The great main line
from London to Scotland split it down the middle, and
then the smaller branch line from Oxford to
Cambridge sliced it into quarters, so that wherever you
stood there was no escaping the trains: the noise of
them, the smell of their soot, the sight of their brown
smoke rising above the clustered roofs. Even the
terraced houses were mostly railway-built, cut from the
same red brick as the station and the engine sheds,
constructed in the same dour, industrial style.

The Commercial Guesthouse, Albion Street, was
about five minutes' walk from Bletchley Park and
backed on to the main line. Its owner, Mrs Ethel
Armstrong, was, like her establishment, a little over
fifty years old, solidly built, with a forbidding, late-
Victorian aspect. Her husband had died of a heart
attack a month after the outbreak of war, whereupon
she had converted their four-storey property into a
small hotel. Like the other townspeople – and there
were about seven thousand of them – she had no idea
of what went on in the grounds of the mansion up the
road, and even less interest. It was profitable, that was
all that mattered to her. She charged thirty-eight
shillings a week and expected her five residents, in
return for meals, to hand over all their food-rationing

coupons. As a result, by the spring of 1943, she had a thousand pounds in War Savings Bonds and enough edible goods hoarded in her cellar to open a medium-sized grocery store.

It was on the Wednesday that one of her rooms had become vacant, and on the Friday that she had been served a billeting notice requiring her to provide accommodation to a Mr Thomas Jericho. His possessions from his previous address had been delivered to her door that same morning: two boxes of personal effects and an ancient iron bicycle. The bicycle she wheeled into the back yard. The boxes she carried upstairs.

One carton was full of books. A couple of Agatha Christies. *A Synopsis of Elementary Results in Pure and Applied Mathematics,* two volumes, by a fellow named George Shoobridge Garr. *Principia Mathematica,* whatever that was. A pamphlet with a suspiciously Germanic ring to it – *On Computable Numbers, with an Application to the Entscheidungsproblem* – inscribed 'To Tom, with fond respect, Alan'. More books full of mathematics, one so repeatedly read it was almost falling to pieces and stuffed full of markers – bus and tram tickets, a beer mat, even a blade of grass. It fell open at a heavily underlined passage:

there is one purpose at any rate which the real mathematics may serve in war. When the world is mad, a mathematician may find in mathematics an incomparable anodyne. For mathematics is, of all the arts and sciences, the most remote.

Well, the last line's true enough, she thought. She closed the book, turned it around and squinted at the spine: *A Mathematician's Apology* by G. H. Hardy, Cambridge University Press.

The other box also yielded little of interest. A Victorian etching of King's College Chapel. A cheap Waralarm clock, set to go off at eleven, in a black fibre case. A wireless. An academic mortarboard and a dusty gown. A bottle of ink. A telescope. A copy of *The Times* dated 23 December 1942, folded to the crossword, which had been filled in by two different hands, one very small and precise, the other rounder, probably feminine. Written above it was 2712815. And, finally, at the bottom of the carton, a map, which, when she unfolded it, proved not to be of England, or even (as she had suspected and secretly hoped) of Germany, but of the night sky.

She was so put off by this dreary collection that when, at half past midnight that night, there was a knock on the door and another two suitcases were delivered by a small man with a northern accent, she didn't even bother to open them but dumped them straight in the empty room.

Their owner arrived at nine o'clock on Saturday morning. She was sure of the time, she explained later to her next-door neighbour, Mrs Scratchwood, because the religious service was just ending on the wireless and the news was about to start. And he was exactly as she'd suspected he would be. He wasn't very tall. He was thin. Bookish. Ill-looking, and nursing his arm, as if he'd just injured it. He hadn't shaved, was as white as

– well, she was going to say 'as a sheet', but she hadn't seen sheets that white since before the war, certainly not in her house. His clothes were of good quality, but in a mess: she noticed there was a button missing on his overcoat. He was pleasant enough, though. Nicely spoken. Very good manners. A quiet voice. She'd never had any children herself, never had a son, but if she had, he would have been about the same age. Well, let's just say he needed feeding up, anyone could see that.

She was strict about the rent. She always demanded a month in advance – the request was made down in the hall, before she took them up to see the room – and there was usually an argument, at the end of which she grumpily agreed to settle for two weeks. But he paid up without a murmur. She asked for seven pounds six shillings and he gave her eight pounds, and when she pretended she hadn't any change, he said: 'Fine, give it me later.' When she mentioned his ration book he looked at her for a moment, very puzzled, and then he said (and she would remember it for the rest of her life): 'Do you mean this?'

'*Do you mean this*?' She repeated it in wonderment. As if he'd never seen one before! He gave her the little brown booklet – the precious weekly passport to four ounces of butter, eight ounces of bacon, twelve ounces of sugar – and told her she could do what she liked with it. 'I've never had any use for it.'

By this time she was so flustered she hardly knew what she was doing. She tucked the money and the ration book into her apron before he could change his mind and led him upstairs.

Now Ethel Armstrong was the first to admit that the fifth bedroom of the Commercial Guest House was not up to much. It was at the end of the passage, up a little twist of stairs, and the only furniture in it was a single bed and a wardrobe. It was so small the door wouldn't open properly because the bed got in the way. It had a tiny window flecked with soot which looked out over the wide expanse of railway tracks. In two and a half years it must have had thirty different occupants. None had stayed more than a couple of months and some had refused to sleep in it at all. But this one just sat on the edge of the bed, squeezed in between his boxes and his cases, and said wearily, 'Very pleasant, Mrs Armstrong.'

She quickly explained the rules of the house. Breakfast was at seven in the morning, dinner at six thirty in the evening, 'cold collations' would be left in the kitchen for those working irregular shifts. There was one bathroom at the far end of the passage, shared between the five guests. They were permitted one bath a week each, the depth of water not to exceed five inches (a line was marked on the enamel) and he would have to arrange his turn with the others. He would be given four lumps of coal per evening to heat his room. The fire in the parlour downstairs was extinguished at 9 p.m., sharp. Anyone caught cooking, drinking alcohol or entertaining visitors in their room, especially of the opposite sex – he'd smiled faintly at that – would be evicted, balance of rent to be paid as a forfeit.

She'd asked if he had any questions, to which he

made no reply, which was a mercy, because at that moment a nonstop express shrieked past at sixty miles an hour no more than a hundred feet from the bedroom window, shaking the little room so violently that Mrs Armstrong had a brief and horrifying vision of the floor giving way and them both plummeting downwards, down through her own bedroom, down through the scullery, crashing down to land amid the waxy legs of ham and tinned peaches so carefully stacked and hidden in her Aladdin's cave of a cellar.

'Well, then,' she said, when the noise (if not yet the house) had finally subsided, 'I'll leave you to get some peace and quiet.'

Tom Jericho sat on the edge of the bed for a couple of minutes after listening to her footsteps descending the stairs. Then he took off his jacket and shirt and examined his throbbing forearm. He had a pair of bruises just below the elbow as neat and black as damsons, and he remembered now whom Skynner had always reminded him of: a prefect at school called Fane, the son of a bishop, who liked to cane the new boys in his study at teatime, and make them all say 'thank you, Fane' afterwards.

It was cold in the room and he started to shiver, his skin puckering into rashes of gooseflesh. He felt desperately tired. He opened one of his suitcases and took out a pair of pyjamas and changed into them quickly. He hung up his jacket and thought about unpacking the rest of his clothes, but decided against it. He might be out of Bletchley by the next morning.

That was a point – he passed his hand across his face – he'd just given away eight pounds, more than a week's salary, for a room he might not need. The wardrobe vibrated as he opened it and the wire coat hangers sounded a melancholy chime. Inside it stank of mothballs. He quickly shoved the cardboard boxes into it and pushed the cases under the bed. Then he drew the curtains, lay down on the lumpy mattress, and pulled the blankets up under his chin.

For three years Jericho had led a nocturnal life, rising with the darkness, going to bed with the light, but he'd never got used to it. Lying there listening to the distant sounds of a Saturday morning made him feel like an invalid. Downstairs someone was running a bath. The water tank was in the attic directly above his head, and the noise of it emptying and refilling was deafening. He closed his eyes and all he could see was the chart of the North Atlantic. He opened them and the bed shook slightly as a train went by and that reminded him of Claire. The 15.06 out of London Euston – '*calling at Willesden, Watford, Apsley, Berkhamsted, Tring, Cheddington and Leighton Buzzard, arriving Bletchley four-nineteen*' – he could recite the station announcement even now, and see her now as well. It had been his first glimpse of her.

This must have been – what? – a week after the break into Shark? A couple of days before Christmas, anyway. He and Logie, Puck and Atwood had been ordered to present themselves at the office block in Broadway, near St James's tube station, from which Bletchley Park was run. 'C' himself had made a little speech about the value of their work. In recognition of their 'vital breakthrough', and on the orders of the Prime Minister, they had each received an iron handshake and an envelope containing a cheque for a hundred pounds, drawn on an ancient and obscure City bank. Afterwards, slightly embarrassed, they'd said goodbye to one another on the pavement and gone their various ways – Logie to lunch at the Admiralty, Puck to meet a girl, Atwood to a concert at the National Portrait Gallery – and Jericho back to Euston to catch the train to Bletchley, '*calling at Willesden, Watford, Apsley . . .*'

There would be no more cheques now, he thought. Perhaps Churchill would ask for his money back.

A million tons of shipping. Ten thousand people. Forty-six U-boats. And that was just the beginning of it.

'*It's everything. It's the whole war.*'

He turned his face to the wall.

Another train went by, and then another. Someone else began to run a bath. In the back yard, directly beneath his window, Mrs Armstrong hung the parlour carpet over the washing line and began to beat it, hard and rhythmically, as if it were a tenant behind with his rent or some prying inspector from the Ministry of Food.

Darkness closed around him.

The dream is a memory, the memory a dream.

A teeming station platform – iron girders and pigeons fluttering against a filthy glass cupola. Tinny carols playing over the public address system. Steel light and splashes of khaki.

A line of soldiers bent sideways by the weight of kitbags runs towards the guard's van. A sailor kisses a pregnant woman in a red hat and pats her bottom. School children going home for Christmas, salesmen in threadbare overcoats, a pair of thin and anxious mothers in tatty furs, a tall, blonde woman in a well-cut, ankle-length grey coat, trimmed with black velvet at the collar and cuffs. A prewar coat, *he thinks,* nothing so fine is made nowadays . . .

She walks past the window and he realises with a jolt that she's noticed he is staring at her. He glances at his watch, snaps the lid shut with his thumb and when he looks up again she's actually stepping into his compartment. Every seat is taken. She hesitates. He stands to offer her his place. She smiles her thanks and gestures to show there's just sufficient room for her to squeeze between him and the window. He nods and sits again with difficulty.

Doors slam along the length of the train, a whistle blows, they shudder forwards. The platform is a blur of waving people.

He's wedged so tightly he can barely move. Such intimacy would never have been tolerated before the war, but nowadays, on these endless uncomfortable journeys, men and women are always being thrown together, often literally so. Her thigh is pressed to his, so hard he can feel the firmness of muscle and bone beneath the padding of her flesh. Her shoulder is to his. Their legs touch. Her stocking rustles against his calf. He can feel the warmth of her, and smell her scent.

He looks past her and pretends to stare out of the

window at the ugly houses sliding by. She's much younger than he thought at first. Her face in profile is not conventionally pretty, but striking – angular, strong – he supposes 'handsome' is the word for it. She has very blonde hair, tied back. When he tries to move, his elbow brushes the side of her breast and he thinks he might die of embarrassment. He apologies profusely but she doesn't seem to notice. She has a copy of The Times, *folded up very small so that she can hold it in one hand.*

The compartment is packed. Servicemen lie on the floor and jam the corridor outside. An RAF corporal has fallen asleep in the luggage rack and cradles his kit bag like a lover. Someone begins to snore. The air smells strongly of cheap cigarettes and unwashed bodies. But gradually, for Jericho, all this begins to disappear. There are just the two of them, rocking with the train. Where they touch his skin is burning. His calf muscles ache with the strain of neither moving too close nor drawing apart.

He wonders how far she's going. Each time they stop at one of the little stations he fears she might get off. But no: she continues to stare down at her square of newsprint. The dreary hinterland of northern London gives way to a dreary countryside, monochrome in the darkening December afternoon – frosted fields barren of livestock, bare trees and the straggling dark lines of hedgerows, empty lanes, little villages with smoking chimneys that stand out like smudges of soot in the white landscape.

An hour passes. They're clear of Leighton Buzzard and within five minutes of Bletchley when she suddenly says: 'German town partly in French disagreement with Hamelin.'

He isn't sure he's heard her properly, or even if the remark is addressed to him.

'I'm sorry?'

'German town partly in French disagreement with Hamelin.' She repeats it, as if he's stupid. 'Seven down. Eight letters.'

'Ah yes,' he says. 'Ratisbon.'

'How do you get that? I don't think I've even heard of it.' She turns her face to him. He has an impression of large features – a sharp nose, a wide mouth – but it is the eyes that hold him. Grey eyes – a cold grey, with no hint of blue. They're not dove-grey, he decides later, or pearl-grey. They're the grey of snow clouds waiting to break.

'It's a cathedral city. On the Danube, I believe. Partly in French – well, bon, obviously. Disagreement with Hamelin. That's easy. Hamelin – Pied Piper – rats. Rat is bon. Rat is good. Not the view in Hamelin.'

He starts to laugh then stops himself. Just hark at yourself, he thinks, you're babbling like an idiot.

'Fill up ten. Nine letters.'

'That's an anagram,' he says immediately. 'Plentiful.'

'Morning snack as far as it goes. Five letters.'

'Ambit.'

She shakes her heard, filling in the answers. 'How do you get it so quickly?'

'It's not hard. You learn to know the way they think. Morning – that's a.m., obviously. Snack as far as it goes – bit with the e missing. As far as it goes – well, within one's ambit. One's limit. May I?'

He reaches over and takes the paper and pencil. Half his brain studies the puzzle, the other half studies her –

*how she takes a cigarette from her handbag and lights it,
how she watches him, her head resting slightly to one side.
Aster, tasso, loveage, landau . . . It's the first and only
time in their relationship he's ever fully in control, and by
the time he's completed the thirty clues and given her back
the paper they're pulling through the outskirts of a small
town, crawling past narrow gardens and tall chimneys.
Behind her head he sees the familiar lines of washing, the
air raid shelters, the vegetable plots, the little red-brick
houses coated black by the passing trains. The compartment darkens as they pass beneath the iron canopy of
the station. 'Bletchley,' calls the guard. 'Bletchley station!'*

He says, 'I'm afraid this is my stop.'

*'Yes.' She looks thoughtfully at the finished crossword,
then turns and smiles at him. 'Yes. D'you know, I rather
guessed it might be.'*

'Mr Jericho!' someone calls. 'Mr Jericho!'

'Mr Jericho!'

He opened his eyes. For a moment he was
disoriented. The wardrobe loomed over him like a thief
in the dim light.

'Yes.' He sat up in the strange bed. 'I'm sorry. Mrs
Armstrong?'

'It's a quarter past six, Mr Jericho.' She was shouting
to him from halfway up the stairs. 'Will you be wanting
supper?'

A quarter past six? The room was almost dark. He
pulled his watch out from beneath his pillow and
flicked it open. To his astonishment he found he had
slept through the entire day.

'That would be very kind, Mrs Armstrong. Thank you.'

The dream had been disturbingly vivid – more substantial, certainly, than this shadowy room – and as he threw off the blankets and swung his bare feet on to the cold floor, he felt himself to be in a no-man's-land between two worlds. He had a peculiar conviction that Claire had been thinking of him, that his subconscious had somehow acted like a radio receiver and had picked up a message from her. It was an absurd thought for a mathematician, a rationalist, to entertain, but he couldn't rid himself of it. He found his sponge-bag and slipped his overcoat over his pyjamas.

On the first floor a figure in a blue flannel dressing gown and white paper curlers hurried out of the bathroom. He nodded politely but the woman gave a squeak of embarrassment and scuttled down the passage. Standing at the basin, he laid out his toiletries: a sliver of carbolic soap, a safety razor with a six-month-old blade, a wooden toothbrush worn down to a fuzz of bristles, an almost empty tin of pink tooth powder. The taps clanked. There was no hot water. He scraped at his chin for ten minutes until it was red and pricked with blood. This was where the devil of the war resided, he thought, as he dabbed at his skin with the hard towel: in the details, in the thousand petty humiliations of never having enough toilet paper or soap or matches or baths or clean clothes. Civilians had been pauperised. They smelled, that was the truth of it. Body odour lay over the British Isles like a great sour fog.

There were two other guests downstairs in the

dining room, a Miss Jobey and a Mr Bonnyman, and the three of them made discreet conversation while they waited for their food. Miss Jobey was dressed in black with a cameo brooch at her throat. Bonnyman wore mildew-coloured tweeds with a set of pens in his breast pocket and Jericho guessed he might be an engineer on the bombes. The door to the kitchen swung open as Mrs Armstrong brought in their plates.

'Here we go,' whispered Bonnyman. 'Brace yourself old boy.'

'Now, don't you go getting her worked up again, Arthur,' said Miss Jobey. She gave his arm a playful pinch, at which Bonnyman's hand slid beneath the table and squeezed her knee. Jericho poured them all a glass of water and pretended not to notice.

'It's potato pie,' announced Mrs Armstrong, defiantly. 'With gravy. And potatoes.'

They contemplated their steaming plates.

'How very, ah, substantial,' said Jericho, eventually.

The meal passed in silence. Pudding was some kind of stewed apple with powdered custard. Once that had been cleared away Bonnyman lit his pipe and announced that, as it was a Saturday night, he and Miss Jobey would be going to the Eight Bells Inn on the Buckingham Road.

'Naturally, you're very welcome to join us,' he said, in a tone which implied that Jericho, naturally, wouldn't be welcome at all. 'Do you have any plans?'

'It's kind of you, but as a matter of fact I do have plans. Or, rather, *a* plan.'

After the others had gone, he helped Mrs Armstrong

clear away the dishes, then went out into the back yard to check his bicycle. It was almost dark and there was a sharpness in the air that promised frost. The lights still worked. He cleaned the dirt off the regulation white patch on the mudguard and pumped some air into the tyres.

By eight o'clock he was back up in his room. At half past ten, Mrs Armstrong was on the point of laying aside her knitting to go up to bed when she heard him coming downstairs. She opened the door a crack, just in time to see Jericho hurrying along the passage and out into the night.

2

The moon defied the blackout, shining a blue torch over the frozen fields, quite bright enough for a man to cycle by. Jericho lifted himself out of the saddle and trod hard on the pedals, rocking from side to side as he toiled up the hill out of Bletchley, pursuing his own shadow, cast sharp on the road before him. From far in the distance came the drone of a returning bomber.

The road began to level out and he sat back on the saddle. For all his efforts with the pump, the tyres remained half-flat, the wheels and chain were stiff for want of oil. It was hard going, but Jericho didn't mind. He was taking action, that was the point. It was the same as code-breaking. However hopeless the situation, the rule was always to do *something*. No cryptogram, Alan Turing used to say, was ever solved by simply staring at it.

He cycled on for about two miles, following the lane as it continued to rise gently towards Shenley Brook End. This was hardly a village, more a tiny hamlet of perhaps a dozen houses, mostly farmworkers' cottages. He couldn't see the buildings, which sheltered in a slight hollow, but when he rounded a bend and caught the scent of woodsmoke he knew he must be close.

Just before the hamlet, on the left, there was a gap in the hawthorn hedge where a rutted track led to a little cottage that stood alone. He turned into it and skittered to a halt, his feet slipping on the frozen mud. A white owl, improbably huge, rose from a nearby branch and flapped soundlessly across the field. Jericho squinted at the cottage. Was it his imagination or was there a hint of light in the downstairs window? He dismounted and began to wheel his bike towards it.

He felt wonderfully calm. Above the thatched roof the constellations spread out like the lights of a city – Ursa Minor and Polaris, Pegasus and Cepheus, the flattened M of Cassiopeia with the Milky Way flowing through it. No glow from earth obscured their brilliance. *You can at least say this for the blackout,* he thought, *it has given us back the stars.*

The door was stout and iron-studded. It was like knocking on stone. After half a minute he tried again.

'Claire?' he called. 'Claire?'

There was a pause, and then: 'Who is it?'

'It's Tom.'

He took a breath and braced himself, as if for a blow.

The handle turned and the door opened slightly, just enough to reveal a dark-haired woman, thirtyish, about Jericho's height. She was wearing round spectacles and a thick overcoat and was holding a prayer book.

'Yes?'

For a moment he was speechless. 'I'm sorry,' he said, 'I was looking for Claire.'

'She's not in.'

'Not in?' he repeated, hopelessly. He remembered now that Claire shared the cottage with a woman called Hester Wallace (*'she works in Hut 6, she's a sweetie'*) but for some reason he had forgotten all about her. She did not look very sweet to Jericho. She had a thin face, split like a knife by a long, sharp nose. Her hair was wrenched back off a frowning forehead. 'I'm Tom Jericho.' She made no response. 'Perhaps Claire's mentioned me?'

'I'll tell her you called.'

'Will she be back soon?'

'I've no idea, I'm sorry.'

She began to close the door. Jericho pressed his foot against it. 'I say, I know this is awfully rude of me, but I couldn't possibly come in and wait, could I?'

The woman glanced at his foot, and then at his face. 'I'm afraid that's impossible. Good evening, Mr Jericho.' She pushed the door closed with surprising force.

Jericho took a step backwards on to the track. This was not a contingency envisaged in his plan. He looked at his watch. It was just after eleven. He picked up his bicycle and wheeled it back towards the lane, but at the

135

last moment, instead of going out on to the road, he turned left and followed the line of the hedge. He laid the bicycle flat and drew into the shadows to wait.

After about ten minutes, the cottage door opened and closed and he heard the rattle of a bicycle being wheeled over stone. It was as he thought: Miss Wallace had been dressed to go out because she was working the midnight shift. A pinprick of yellow light appeared, wobbled briefly from side to side, and then began to bob towards him. Hester Wallace passed within twenty feet in the moonlight, knees pumping, elbows stuck out, as angular as an old umbrella. She stopped at the entrance to the lane and slipped on a luminous armlet. Jericho edged further into the hawthorn. Half a minute later she was gone. He waited a full quarter of an hour in case she'd forgotten something, then headed back to the cottage.

There was only one key – ornate and iron and big enough to fit a cathedral. It was kept, he recalled, under a piece of slate beneath a flowerpot. Damp had warped the door and he had to push hard to open it, scraping an arc on the flagstone floor. He replaced the key and closed the door behind him before turning on the light.

He had only been inside once before, but there wasn't much to remember. Two rooms on the ground floor: a sitting room with low beams and a kitchen straight ahead. To his left, a narrow staircase led up to a little landing. Claire's bedroom was at the front, looking towards the lane. Hester's was at the rear. The lavatory was a chemical toilet just outside the back door, reached via the kitchen. There was no bathroom.

A galvanised metal tub was kept in the shed next to the kitchen. Baths were taken in front of the stove. The whole place was cold and cramped and smelled of mildew. He wondered how Claire stuck it.

'Oh, but darling, it's so much better than having some ghastly landlady telling one what to do . . .'

Jericho took a couple of steps across the worn rug and stopped. For the first time he began to feel uneasy. Everywhere he looked he saw evidence of a life being lived quite contentedly without him – the ill-assorted blue-and-white china in the dresser, the vase full of daffodils, the stack of pre-war *Vogues*, even the arrangement of the furniture (the two armchairs and the sofa drawn up cosily around the hearth). Every tiny domestic detail seemed significant and premeditated.

He had no business here.

He very nearly left at that moment. All that stopped him was the faintly pathetic realisation that he had nowhere else particularly to go. The Park? Albion Street? King's? His life seemed to have become a maze of dead ends.

Better to make a stand here, he decided, than run away again. She was bound to be back quite soon.

God, but it was cold! His bones were ice. He walked up and down the cramped room, ducking to avoid the heavy beams. In the hearth was white ash and a few blackened fragments of wood. He sat first in one armchair, then tried the other. Now he was facing the door. To his right was the sofa. Its covers were of frayed pink silk, its cushions hollowed and leaking feathers. The springs had gone and when you sat in it you sank almost to the floor and had to struggle to get out. He remembered that sofa and he stared at it for a long time, as a soldier might stare at a battlefield where a war had been irretrievably lost.

They leave the train together and walk up the footpath to the Park. To their left is a playing field, ploughed into allotments for the Dig for Victory campaign. To their right, through the perimeter fence, is the familiar huddle of low buildings. People walk briskly to ward off the cold. The December afternoon is raw and misty, the day is leaking into dusk.

She tells him she's been up to London to celebrate her birthday. How old does he think she is?

He hasn't a clue. Eighteen perhaps?

Twenty, she says triumphantly, ancient. And what was he doing in town?

He can't tell her, of course. Just business, he says. Just business.

Sorry, she says, she shouldn't have asked. She still can't get the hang of all this 'need to know'. She has been at the Park three months and hates it. Her father works at the Foreign Office and wangled her the job to keep her out of mischief. How long has he been here?

Three years, says Jericho, she shouldn't worry, it'll get better.

Ah, she says, that's easy for him to say, but surely he does something interesting?

Not really, he says, but then he thinks that makes him sound boring, so he adds: 'Well, quite interesting, I suppose.'

In truth he's finding it hard to keep up his end of the conversation. It's distracting enough merely to walk alongside her. They lapse into silence.

There's a noticeboard close to the main gate advertising a performance of Bach's Musikalisches Opfer *by the Bletchley Park Music Society. 'Oh, now look at that,' she says. 'I adore Bach', to which Jericho replies with genuine enthusiasm, that Bach is his favourite composer. Grateful at last to have found something to talk about, he launches into a long dissertation about the* Musikalisches Opfer*'s six-part fugue, which Bach is supposed to have improvised on the spot for King Frederick the Great, a feat equivalent to playing and winning sixty games of blindfold chess simultaneously. Perhaps she knows that Bach's dedication to the King –* Regis Iussu Cantio et Reliqua Canonica Arte Resoluta *– rather interestingly yields the acrostic* RICERCAR, *meaning 'to seek'?*

No, oddly enough, she doesn't know that.

This increasingly desperate monologue carries them as far as the huts where they both stop and, after another awkward pause, introduce themselves. She offers him her hand – her grip is warm and firm, but her nails are a shock: painfully bitten back, almost to the quick. Her surname is Romilly. Claire Romilly. It has a pleasant ring. Claire Romilly. He wishes her a merry Christmas and turns away but she calls him back. She hopes he won't think it too fresh of her, but would he like to go with her to the concert?

He isn't sure, he doesn't know . . .

She writes down the date and time just above The Times *crossword – 27 December at 8.15 – and thrusts it into his hands. She'll buy the tickets. She'll see him there.*

Please don't say no.

And before he can think of an excuse, she's gone.

He's due to be on shift on the evening of the 27th but he doesn't know where to find her to tell her he can't go. And anyway, he realises, he rather does want to go. So he calls in a favour he's owed by Arthur de Brooke and waits outside the assembly hall, and waits, and waits. Eventually, after everyone else has gone in, and just when he's about to give up, she comes running out of the darkness, smiling her apologies.

The concert is better than he'd hoped. The quintet all work at the Park and once played professionally. The harpsichordist is particularly fine. The women in the audience are wearing evening frocks, the men are wearing suits. Suddenly, and for the first time he can recall, the war seems a long way away. As the last notes of the third canon ('per Motum contrarium') are dying in the air he risks a glance at Claire only to discover that she is looking at him. She touches his arm and when the fourth canon ('per Augmentationem, contrario Motu') begins, he is lost.

Afterwards he has to go straight back to the hut: he's promised he'd be back before midnight. 'Poor Mr Jericho,' she says, 'just like Cinderella . . .' But at her suggestion they meet again for the following week's concert – Chopin – and when that's over they walk down the hill to the station to have cocoa in the platform buffet.

'So,' she says, as he returns from the counter bearing two cups of brown froth, 'how much am I allowed to know about you?'

'Me? Oh, I'm very boring.'

'I don't think you're boring at all. In fact, I've heard a rumour you're rather brilliant.' She lights a cigarette and he notices again her distinctive way of inhaling, seeming almost to swallow the smoke, then tilting her head back and breathing it out through her nostrils. Is this some new fashion, he wonders? *'I suppose you're married?'* she says.

He almost chokes on his cocoa. *'Good God, no. I mean, I would hardly be —'*

'Fiancée? Girlfriend?'

'Now you're teasing me.' He pulls out a handkerchief and dabs at his chin.

'Brothers? Sisters?'

'No, no.'

'Parents? Even you must have parents.'

'Only one still alive.'

'I'm the same,' she says. *'My mother's dead.'*

'How awful for you. I'm sorry. My mother, I must say, is very much alive.'

And so it goes on, this hitherto untasted pleasure of talking about oneself. Her grey eyes never leaving his face. The trains steam past in the darkness, trailing a wash of soot and hot air. Customers come and go. *'Who cares if we're without a light?'* sings a crooner on the wireless in the corner, *'they can't blackout the moon . . .'* He finds himself telling her things he's never really spoken of before — about his father's death and his mother's remarriage, about his stepfather (a businessman, whom he dislikes), about his discovery of astronomy and then of mathematics . . .

'And your work now?' she says. *'Does that make you happy?'*

'*Happy?*' He warms his hands on his cup and considers the question. '*No. I couldn't say happy. It's too demanding – frightening, even, in a way.*'

'*Frightening?*' The wide eyes widen further with interest. '*Frightening how?*'

'*What might happen . . .*' (*You're showing off, he warns himself, stop it.*) '*What might happen if you get it wrong, I suppose.*'

She lights another cigarette. '*You're in Hut 8, aren't you? Hut 8's the naval section?*'

This brings him up with a jolt. He looks around quickly. Another couple are holding hands at the next table, whispering. Four airmen are playing cards. A waitress in a greasy apron is polishing the counter. Nobody seems to have heard.

'*Talking of which,*' he says, brightly, '*I think I ought to get back.*'

On the corner of Church Green Road and Wilton Avenue she kisses him, briefly, on the cheek.

The following week it is Schumann, followed by steak-and-kidney pudding and jam roly-poly at the British Restaurant in Bletchley Road ('*two courses for eleven-pence*') and this time it's her turn to talk. Her mother died when she was six, she says, and her father trailed her from embassy to embassy. Family has been a procession of nannies and governesses. At least she's learned some languages. She'd wanted to join the Wrens, but the old man wouldn't let her.

Jericho asks what London was like in the Blitz.

'*Oh, a lot of fun, actually. Loads of places to go. The Milroy, the Four Hundred. A kind of desperate gaiety.*'

We've all had to learn to live for the moment, don't you think?'

When they say goodbye she kisses him again, her lips to one cheek, her cool hand to the other.

In retrospect, it is around this time, in the middle of January, that he should have started keeping a record of his symptoms, for it is now that he begins to lose his equilibrium. He wakes with a feeling of mild euphoria. He bounces into the hut, whistling. He goes for long walks around the lake between shifts, taking bread to feed the ducks – just for the exercise, he tells himself, but really he is scanning the crowds for her, and twice he sees her, and once she sees him and waves.

For their fourth date (the fifth, if you count their meeting on the train) she insists they do something different, so they go to the County Cinema on the High Street to see the new Noël Coward picture, In Which We Serve.

'And you really mean to tell me you've never once been here?'

They're queuing for tickets. The film's only been showing for a day and the line extends round the corner into Aylesbury Street.

'I haven't, actually, to be honest, no.'

'God, Tom, you are a funny old darling. I think I'd die stuck in Bletchley without the flicks to go to.'

They sit near the back and she laces her arm through his. The light from the projector high up behind them makes a kaleidoscope of blues and greys in the dust and cigarette smoke. The couple next to them are kissing. A woman giggles. A fanfare of trumpets announces a *newsreel and there, on the screen, long columns of German prisoners, an impossible number, are shown trekking through snow, while the announcer talks excitedly about Red Army breakthroughs on the eastern front. Stalin appears, presenting medals, to loud applause. Someone shouts:* 'Three cheers for Uncle Joe!' *The lights come up, then dim again, and Claire squeezes his arm. The main film begins –* 'This is the story of a ship' *– with Coward as an improbably suave Royal Navy captain. There's a lot of clipped excitement.* 'Vessel on fire bearing green three-oh . . . Torpedo track, starboard, sir . . . Carry on firing . . .' *At the climax of the sea battle, Jericho looks around at the flickering of the celluloid explosions on the rapt faces, and it strikes him that he is a part of all this – a distant, vital part – and that nobody knows, nobody will ever know . . . After the final credits the loudspeakers play* 'God Save the King' *and they all stand, many of the audience so moved by the film they begin to sing.*

They've left their bicycles near the end of an alley running beside the cinema. A few paces further on a shape rubs itself against the wall. As they come closer they can see it is a soldier with his greatcoat wrapped around a girl. Her back is to the bricks. Her white face stares at them from the shadows like an animal in its hide. The movement stops for the time it takes Claire and Jericho to collect their bicycles, then it starts again.

'What very peculiar behaviour.'

He says it without thinking. To his surprise, Claire bursts out laughing.

'What's the matter?'

144

'Nothing,' she says.

They stand on the pavement holding their bicycles, waiting for an Army lorry with dimmed headlights to pass, its gearbox grinding as it heads north along Watling Street. Her laughter stops.

'Do come and see my cottage, Tom.' She says it almost plaintively. 'It's not that late. I'd love to show it you.'

He can't think of an excuse, doesn't want to think of one.

She leads the way through the town and out past the Park. They don't speak for fifteen minutes and he begins to wonder how far she's taking him. At last, when they're rattling down the path that leads to the cottage, she calls over her shoulder, 'Isn't it a perfect sweetheart?'

'It's, ah, off the beaten track.'

'Now don't be horrible,' she says, pretending to be hurt.

She tells him how she found it standing derelict, how she charmed the farmer who owns it into letting her rent it. Inside, the furniture is shabby-grand, rescued from an aunt's house in Kensington that was shut up for the Blitz and never reopened.

The staircase creaks so alarmingly, Jericho wonders if their combined weight might pull it away from the wall. The place is a ruin, freezing cold. 'And this is where I sleep,' she says, and he follows her into a room of pinks and creams, crammed full of pre-war silks and furs and feathers, like a large dressing-up box. A loose floorboard goes off like a gunshot beneath his feet. There's too much detail for the eye to register, so many hat boxes, shoe boxes, bits of jewellery, cosmetic bottles . . . She slips off her coat and lets it fall to the floor and flings herself flat out on the *bed, then props herself up on her elbows and kicks off her shoes. She seems amused by something.*

'And what's this?' Jericho, in a turmoil, has retreated to the landing and is staring at the only other door.

'Oh, that's Hester's room,' she calls.

'Hester?'

'Some bureaucratic beast found out where I was and said if I had a second bedroom I had to share. So in came Hester. She works in Hut 6. She's a sweetie, really. Got a bit of a crush on me. Take a look. She won't mind.'

He knocks, there's no reply, he opens the door. Another tiny room, but this one spartan, like a cell: a brass bedstead, a jug and bowl on a washstand, some books piled on a chair. Ableman's German Primer. *He opens it.* 'Der Rhein ist etwas länger als die Elbe,' *he reads. The Rhine is somewhat longer than the Elbe. He hears the gunshot of the floorboard behind him and Claire lifts the book from his hands.*

'Don't snoop, darling. It's rude. Come on, let's make a fire and have a drink.'

Downstairs, he kneels by the hearth and rolls a copy of The Times *into a ball. He piles on kindling and a couple of small logs, and lights the paper. The chimney draws voraciously, sucking up the smoke with a roar.*

'Look at you, you haven't even taken off your coat.'

He stands, brushing the dust away, and turns to face her. Grey skirt, navy cashmere sweater, a single loop of milk-white pearls at her creamy throat – the ubiquitous, unchanging uniform of the upper-class Englishwoman. She somehow contrives to look both very young and very mature at the same time.

'Come here. Let me do it.'

She sets down the drinks and begins to unbutton his overcoat.

'Don't tell me, Tom,' she whispers, 'don't tell me you didn't know what they were doing behind that cinema?'

Even barefoot she is as tall as he is.

'Of course I knew . . .'

'In London nowadays the girls all call it a "wall job". What do you think? They say you can't get pregnant this way . . .'

Instinctively, he draws his coat around her. She wraps her arms about his back.

3

Damn it, damn it, damn it.

He pitched himself forwards and out of the chair, sending the images scattering and smashing on the cold stone floor. He prowled around the tiny sitting room a couple of times, then went into the kitchen. Everything was clean and swept and put away. That would be Hester's handiwork, he guessed, not Claire's. The stove had burned down very low and was lukewarm to the touch, but he resisted the temptation to shovel in some coal. It was quarter to one. Where was she? He wandered back into the sitting room, hesitated at the foot of the stairs, and began to climb. The plaster on the walls was damp and flaking beneath his fingers. He decided to try Hester's room first. It was exactly as it had been six weeks earlier. A pair of sensible shoes beside the bed. A cupboard full of dark clothes. The same German primer. *'An seinen Ufern sind Berge, Felsen und malerische Schlosser aus den ältesten Zeiten.'* On its shores are mountains, rocks and picturesque castles from the oldest times. He closed it and went back out on the landing.

And so, at last, to Claire's room.

He was quite clear now about what he was going to do, even though conscience told him it was wrong and logic told him it was stupid. And, in principle, he agreed. Like any good boy he had learned his Aesop, knew that 'listeners never hear good of themselves' – but since when, he thought, as he began opening drawers, since when has that pious wisdom stopped anybody? A letter, a diary, a message – anything that might tell him *why* – he had to see it, he had to, even though the chances of its yielding any comfort were nil. Where was she? Was she with another man? Was she doing what all the girls in London, darling, call a wall job?

He was suddenly in a rage and he went through her room like a housebreaker, pulling out drawers and upending them, sweeping jewellery and trinkets off the shelves, pulling her clothes down on to the floor, throwing off her sheets and blankets and wrenching up her mattress, raising clouds of dust and scent and ostrich feathers.

After ten minutes he crawled into the corner and laid his head on a pile of silks and furs.

'You're a wreck,' Skynner had said. *'You're ruined.*

You've lost it. Find someone more suitable than the person you were seeing.'

Skynner knew about her, and Logie had seemed to know as well. What was it he'd called her? The 'arctic blonde'? Perhaps they all knew? Puck, Atwood, Baxter, everybody?

He had to get out, get away from the smell of her perfume and the sight of her clothes.

And it was that action that changed everything, for it was only when he stood on the landing, leaning with his back to the wall and his eyes closed, that he realised there *was* something he'd missed.

He walked back slowly and deliberately into her room. Silence. He stepped across the threshold and repeated the action. Silence again. He got down on his knees. One of auntie's Kensington rugs covered the floorboards, something oriental, stained, and tastefully threadbare. It was only about two yards square. He rolled it up and laid it on the bed. The wooden planks which had lain beneath it were bowed with age, worn smooth, fixed down by rust-coloured nails, untouched for two centuries – except in one place, where a shorter length of the old planking, perhaps, eighteen inches long, was secured by four very modern, very shiny screws. He slapped the floor in triumph.

'Is there any other point to which you would wish to draw my attention, Mr Jericho?'

'To the curious incident of the creaking floorboard.'

'But the floorboard didn't creak.'

'That was the curious incident.'

In the mess of her bedroom he could see no suitable

tool. He went down into the kitchen and found a knife. It had a mother-of-pearl handle with an 'R' engraved on it. Perfect. He almost skipped across the sitting room. The tip of the knife slotted into the head of the screw and the thread turned easily, it came away like a dream. So did the other three. The floorboard lifted up to reveal the horsehair and plaster of the downstairs ceiling. The cavity was about six inches deep. He took off his overcoat and his jacket and rolled up his sleeve. He lay on his side and thrust his hand into the space. To begin with he brought out nothing except handfuls of debris, mostly lumps of old plaster and small pieces of brick, but he kept on working his way around until at last he gave a cry of delight as his hand touched paper.

He put everything back in its place, more or less. He hung the clothes back up from the beams, piled her underclothes and her scarves back into the drawers and replaced the drawers in the mahogany chest. He heaped the trinkets of jewellery into their leather case and draped others artfully along the shelves, together with her bottles and pots and packets, most of which were empty.

He did all this mechanically, an automaton.

He remade the bed, lifting off the rug and smoothing down the eiderdown, throwing the lace cover over it where it settled like a net. Then he sat on the edge of the mattress and surveyed the room. Not bad. Of course, once she began looking for things, then she would know someone had been through it, but at a casual glance it looked the same as before – apart, that is, from the hole in the floor. He didn't know yet what to do about that. It depended on whether or not he replaced the intercepts. He pulled them out from under the bed and examined them again.

There were four, on standard-size sheets, eight inches by ten. He held one up to the light. It was cheap wartime paper, the sort Bletchley used by the ton. He could practically see a petrified forest in its coarse yellow weave – the shadows of foliage and leaf-stalks, the faint outlines of bark and fern.

In the top left-hand corner of each signal was the frequency on which it had been transmitted – 12260 kilocycles per second – and in the top right its TOI, Time of Interception. The four had been sent in rapid succession on 4 March, just nine days earlier, at roughly twenty-five-minute intervals, beginning at 9.30 p.m. and ending just before midnight. Each consisted of a call sign – ADU – and then about two hundred five-letter groups. That in itself was an important clue. It meant, whatever else they were, they weren't naval: the Kriesgmarine's signals were transmitted in groups of four letters. So they were presumably German Army or Luftwaffe.

She must have stolen them from Hut 3.

The enormity of the implications hit Jericho for a second time, winding him like a punch in the stomach. He arranged the intercepts in sequence on her pillow and tried very hard, like a defending King's Counsel, to come up with some innocent explanation. A piece of silly mischief? It was possible. She had certainly never paid much attention to security – shouting about Hut 8 in the station buffet, demanding to know what he did, trying to tell him what *she* did. A dare? Again, possible. She was capable of anything. But that hole in the floorboards, the cool deliberation of it, drew his gaze and mocked his advocacy.

A sound, a footstep downstairs, dragged him out of his reverie and made him jump to his feet.

He said, 'Hello?' in a loud voice that suggested more courage than he felt. He cleared his throat. 'Hello?' he repeated. And then he heard another nose, definitely a footstep, and definitely *outside* now, and a charge of adrenaline snapped in. He moved quickly to the bedroom door and turned the light off, so that the only illumination in the cottage came from the sitting room. Now, if anyone came up the stairs, he would be able to see their silhouette, while remaining hidden. But nothing happened. Perhaps they were trying to come round the back? He felt horribly vulnerable. He moved cautiously down the stairs, flinching at every creak. A blast of cold air struck him.

The front door was wide open.

He threw himself down the last half-dozen steps and ran outside, just in time to see the red rear light of a bicycle shoot out of the track and vanish down the lane.

He set off in pursuit but gave up after twenty paces. He didn't stand a chance of catching the cyclist.

There was a heavy frost. In every direction the ground shone a dull and luminous blue. The branches of the bare trees were raised against the sky like blood vessels. In the glittering ice, two sets of tyre-tracks were imprinted: incoming and outgoing. He followed them back to the door, where they ended in a series of sharp footprints.

Sharp, large, *male* footprints.

Jericho looked at them for half a minute, shivering in his shirtsleeves. An owl shrieked in the nearby copse and it seemed to him that its call had the rhythm of Morse: dee-dee-dee-*dah*, dee-dee-dee-*dah*.

He hurried back into the cottage.

Upstairs, he rolled the intercepts very tightly into a cylinder. He used his teeth to tear a small hole in the lining of his overcoat and pushed the signals into it. Then he quickly screwed down the floorboards and replaced the rug. He put on his jacket and coat, turned off the lights, locked the door, replaced the key.

His bicycle added a third set of impressions in the frost.

At the entrance to the lane he stopped and looked back at the darkened cottage. He had a strong sensation – foolish, he told himself – that he was being watched. He glanced around. A gust of wind stirred in the trees; in the blackthorn hedge beside him, icicles clinked and chimed.

Jericho shivered again, remounted the bike and pointed it down the hill, towards the south, towards Orion and Procyon, and to Hydra, which hung suspended in the night sky above Bletchley Park like a knife.

FOUR

KISS

KISS: the coincidence of two
different cryptograms, each
transmitted in a different cipher,
yet each containing the same
original plaintext, the solution
of one thereby leading to the
solution of the other.

A Lexicon of Cryptography

('Most Secret', Bletchley Park, 1943)

1

HE DOESN'T KNOW what wakes him — some faint sound, some movement in the air that hooks him in the depths of his dreams and hauls him to the surface.

At first his darkened room seems entirely normal — the familiar jet-black spar of the low oak beam, the smooth grey plains of wall and ceiling — but then he realises that a faint light is rising from the foot of his bed.

'Claire?' he says, propping himself up. 'Darling?'

'It's all right, darling. Go on back to sleep.'

'What on earth are you doing?'

'I'm just going through your things.'

'You're . . . what?'

His hand fumbles across the bedside table and switches on the lamp. His Waralarm shows him it is half past three.

'That's better,' she says, and she turns off the blackout torch. 'Useless thing, anyway.'

And she is doing exactly what she says. She is naked except for his shirt, she is kneeling, and she is going through his wallet. She removes a couple of one-pound notes, turns the wallet inside out and shakes it.

'No photographs?' she says.

'You haven't given me one yet.'

'Tom Jericho,' she smiles, replacing the money, 'I do declare, you're becoming almost smooth.'

She checks the pockets of his jacket, his trousers, then

157

shuffles on her knees across to his chest of drawers. He laces his hands behind his head and leans back against the iron bedstead and watches her. It is only the second time they have slept together – a week after the first – and at her insistence they have done it not in her cottage but in his room, creeping through the darkened bar of the White Hart Inn and up the creaking stair. Jericho's bedroom is well away from the rest of the household so there is no danger of them being overheard. His books are lined up on the top of the chest of drawers and she picks up each in turn, holds it upside down and flicks through the pages.

Does he see anything odd in all this? No, he does not. It merely seems amusing, flattering, even – one further intimacy, a continuation of all the rest, a part of the waking dream his life has become, governed by dream rules. Besides, he has no secrets from her – or, at least, he thinks he hasn't. She finds Turing's paper and studies it closely.

'And what are computable numbers with an application to the Entscheidungsproblem, *when they're at home?'*

Her pronunciation of the German, he registers with surprise, is immaculate.

'It's a theoretical machine, capable of an infinite number of numerical operations. It supports the assumptions of Hilbert and challenges those of Godel. Come back to bed, darling.'

'But it's only a theory?'

He sighs and pats the mattress next to him. They're sleeping in a single bed. 'Turing believes there's no inherent reason why a machine shouldn't be capable of doing everything a human brain can do. Calculate. Communicate. Write a sonnet.'

158

'Fall in love?'

'If love is logical.'

'Is it?'

'Come to bed.'

'This Turing, does he work at the Park?'

He makes no reply. She leafs through the paper, squinting with disgust at the mathematics, then replaces it with the books and opens one of the drawers. As she leans forwards the shirt rides higher. The lower part of her back gleams white in the shadows. He stares, mesmerised, at the soft triangle of flesh at the base of her vertebrae as she rummages among his clothes.

'Ah,' she says, 'now here is something.' She withdraws a slip of paper. 'A cheque for a hundred pounds, drawn on the Foreign Office Contingency Fund, made out to you —'

'Give me that.'

'Why?'

'Put it back.'

He is across the room and standing beside her within a couple of seconds, but she is quicker than he is. She is on her feet, on tiptoe, holding the cheque aloft, and she — absurdly — is just that half-inch taller than him. The money flutters like a pennant beyond his reach.

'I knew there would be something. Come on, darling, what's it for?'

He should have banked the damn thing weeks ago. He'd quite forgotten it. 'Claire, please . . .'

'You must have done something frightfully clever in that naval hut of yours. A new code? Is that it? You broke some new important code, my clever, clever darling?'

She may be taller than he is, she may even be stronger,

but he has the advantage of desperation. He seizes the firm muscle of her bicep and pulls her arm down and twists her round. They struggle for a moment and then he throws her back on the narrow bed. He prises the cheque out of her bitten-down fingers and retreats with it across the room.

'Not funny, Claire. Some things just aren't that funny.'

He stands there on the rough matting – naked, slender, panting with exertion. He folds the cheque and slips it into his wallet, puts the wallet into his jacket, and turns to hang the jacket in the wardrobe. As he does so, he is aware of a peculiar noise coming from behind him – a frightening, animal noise, something between a rasping breath and a sob. She has curled herself up tight on the bed, her knees drawn up to her stomach, her forearms pressed to her face.

My God, what has he done?

He starts to gabble his apologies. He hadn't meant to frighten her, let alone to hurt her. He goes across to the bed and sits beside her. Tentatively, he touches her shoulder. She doesn't seem to notice. He tries to pull her towards him, to roll her over on her back, but she has become as rigid as a corpse. The sobs are shaking the bed. It is like a fit, a seizure. She is somewhere beyond grief, somewhere far away, beyond him.

'It's all right,' he says. 'It's all right.'

He can't tug the bedclothes out from under her, so he fetches his overcoat and lays that across her, and then he lies beside her, shivering in the January night, stroking her hair.

They stay like that for half an hour until, at last, when she is calm again, she gets up off the bed and begins to dress. He cannot bring himself to look at her and he knows better than to speak. He can just hear her moving around the room, collecting her scattered clothes. Then the door closes quietly. The stairs creak. A minute later he hears the click of her bicycle being wheeled away from beneath his window.

And now his own nightmare begins.

First, there is guilt, that most corrosive of emotions, more torturing even than jealousy (although jealousy is added to the brew a few days later, when he happens to see her walking through Bletchley with a man he doesn't recognise: the man could be anyone, of course – cousin, friend, colleague – but naturally his imagination can't accept that). Why did he respond so dramatically to so small a provocation? The cheque could, after all, have been a reward for anything. He didn't have to tell her the truth. Now that she's gone, a hundred plausible explanations for the money come to mind. What had he done to provoke such terror in her? What awful memory had he reawakened?

He groans and draws the blankets over his head.

The next morning he takes the cheque to the bank and exchanges it for twenty large, crisp, white five-pound notes. Then he searches out the dreary little jewellery shop on Bletchley Road and asks for a ring, any ring as long as it is worth a hundred pounds, at which the jeweller – a ferret of a man with pebble-thick glasses, who clearly can't believe his luck – produces a diamond worth less than half that amount, and Jericho buys it.

He will make it up to her. He will apologise. It will all be right.

But luck is not with Jericho. He has become the victim

of his own success. A Shark decrypt discloses that a U-boat tanker – the U-459, under Korvettenkapitän von Williamowitz-Mollendorf, with 700 tons of fuel on board – is to rendezvous with, and refuel, the Italian submarine Kalvi, *300 miles east of St Paul's Rock, in the middle of the Atlantic. And some fool at the Admiralty, forgetting that no action, however tempting, must ever be taken that will endanger the Enigma secret, orders a squadron of destroyers to intercept. The attack is made. It fails. The U-459 escapes. And Dönitz, that crafty fox in his Paris lair, is immediately suspicious. In the third week of January, Hut 8 decrypts a series of signals ordering the U-boat fleet to tighten its cipher security. Shark traffic dwindles. There is barely enough material to make a menu for the bombes. At Bletchley, all leave is cancelled. Eight-hour shifts drag on to twelve hours, to sixteen hours . . . The daily battle to break the codes is almost as great a nightmare as it was in the depths of the Shark blackout, and Skynner's lash is felt on everybody's back.*

Jericho's world has gone from perpetual sunshine to bleak midwinter in the space of a week. His messages to Claire, of entreaty and remorse, vanish, unanswered, into a void. He can't get out of the Hut to see her. He can't work. He can't sleep. And there's no one he can talk to. To Logie, lost and vague behind his smokescreen of tobacco? To Baxter, who would regard a dalliance with a woman like Claire Romilly as a betrayal of the world proletariat? To Atwood – Atwood! – whose sexual adventures have hitherto been confined to taking the prettier male undergraduates on golfing weekends to Brancaster, where they quickly discover that all the locks have been removed

*from the bathroom doors? Puck would have been a
possibility, but Jericho could guess at his advice – 'Take
out someone else, my dear Thomas, and fuck her' – and
how could he admit the truth: that he didn't want to 'fuck'
anyone else, that he had never 'fucked' anyone else?*

On the final day of January, collecting a copy of The
Times *from Brinklow's the newsagent in Victoria Road,
he spots her, at a distance, with the other man, and he
shrinks into a doorway to avoid being seen. Apart from
that, he never meets her: the Park has become too big, there
are too many changes of shift. Eventually, he's reduced to
lying in wait in the lane opposite her cottage, like a
Peeping Tom. But she seems to have stopped coming home.*

And then he almost walks right into her.

*It is 8 February, a Monday, at four o'clock. He's
walking wearily back to the hut from the canteen; she is
part of a flood of workers streaming towards the gate at the
end of the afternoon shift. He has rehearsed for his moment
so many times, but in the end all he manages is a whine of
complaint: 'Why don't you answer my letters?'*

'Hello, Tom.'

*She tries to walk on, but he won't let her get away this
time. He has a pile of Shark intercepts waiting for him on
his desk but he doesn't care. He catches at her arm.*

'I need to talk to you.'

*Their bodies block the pavement. The flow of people has
to pass around them, like a river round a rock.*

'Mind out,' *says someone.*

'Tom,' *she hisses,* 'for God's sake, you're making a
scene.'

'Good. Let's get out of here.'

He is pulling at her arm. His pressure is insistent and reluctantly she surrenders to it. The momentum of the crowd sweeps them through the gate and along the road. His only thought is to put some distance between them and the Park. He doesn't know how long they walk for – fifteen minutes, perhaps, or twenty – until, at last, the pavements are deserted and they are passing through the hinterland of the town. It is a raw, clear afternoon. On either side of them, semidetached suburban villas hide behind dirty privet hedges, their wartime gardens filled with chicken runs and the half-buried, corrugated-iron hoops of bomb shelters. She shakes her arm free.

'There's no point in this.'

'You're seeing someone else?' He hardly dares to ask the question.

'I'm always seeing someone else.'

He stops but she walks on. He lets her go for fifty yards then hurries to catch her up. By now the houses have petered out and they're in a kind of no-man's land between town and country, on Bletchley's western edge, where people dump their rubbish. A flock of seagulls cries and rises, like a swirl of waste paper caught by the wind. The road has dwindled to a track which leads under the railway to a row of abandoned Victorian brick kilns. Three red-brick chimneys, as in a crematorium, rise fifty feet against the sky. A sign says: DANGER, FLOODED CLAY PIT – VERY DEEP WATER.

Claire draws her coat around her shoulders and shivers – 'What a filthy place!' – but she still walks on ahead.

For ten minutes, the derelict brick works provide a welcome distraction. Indeed, they wander through the ruined kilns and workshops in a silence that is almost companionable. Amorous couples have scratched their formulae on the crumbling walls: AE + GS, Tony = Kath, Sal 4 Me. Lumps of masonry and brick litter the ground. Some of the buildings are open to the sky, the walls are scorched — there's clearly been a fire — and Jericho wonders if the Germans could have mistaken it for a factory, and bombed it. He turns to say as much to Claire, but she has disappeared.

He finds her outside, her back to him, staring across the flooded clay pit. It is huge, a quarter of a mile across. The surface of the water is coal-black and perfectly still, the stillness hinting at unimaginable depths.

She says: 'I ought to get back.'

'What do you want to know?' he says. 'I'll tell you everything you want to know.'

And he will, if she wants it. He doesn't care about security or the war. He'll tell her about Shark and Dolphin and Porpoise. He'll tell her about the Bay of Biscay weather crib. He'll tell her all their little tricks and secrets, and draw her a diagram of how the *bombe* works, if that's what she wants. But all she says is: 'I do hope you're not going to be a bore about this, Tom.'

A bore. Is that what he is? He is being a bore?

'Wait,' he calls after her, 'you might as well have this.'

He gives her the little box with the ring in it. She opens it and tilts the stone to catch the light, then snaps the lid shut and hands it back.

'Not my style.'

'Poor you,' he remembers her saying a minute or two later,

'*I've really got under your skin, haven't I? Poor you . . .*'

And by the end of the week he's in the deputy director's Rover, being borne back through the snow to King's.

2

The smells and sounds of an English Sunday breakfast curled up the staircase of the Commercial Guesthouse and floated across the landing like a call to arms: the hiss of hot fat frying in the kitchen, the dirge-like strains of a church service being relayed by the BBC, the muffled crack of Mrs Armstrong's worn slippers flapping like castanets on the linoleum floor.

They were a ritual in Albion Street, these Sunday breakfasts, served up with appropriate solemnity on plain white utility crockery: one piece of bread, as thick as a hymn book, dunked in fat and fried, with two spoonfuls of powdered egg, scrambled and slopped on top, the whole mass sliding freely on a rainbow film of grease.

It was not, Jericho had to acknowledge, a great meal, nor even a particularly edible one. The bread was rust-coloured, flecked with black, and obscurely flavoured by the kippers that had been cooked in the same fat the previous Friday. The egg was pale yellow and tasted of stale biscuits. Yet such was his appetite after the excitements of the night that, despite his anxiety, he ate every scrap of it, washed it down with two cups of greyish tea, mopped up the last of the grease with a fragment of bread, and even, on his way out, complimented Mrs Armstrong on the quality of her cooking — an unprecedented gesture which caused her to poke her head around the kitchen door and search his features for a trace of irony. She found none. He also attempted a cheerful 'Good morning' to Mr Bonnyman, who was just groping his way down the banisters ('Feeling a bit rough, to be honest, old boy — something wrong with the beer in that place') and by seven forty-five he was back in his room.

If Mrs Armstrong could have seen the changes he had wrought up there, she would have been astonished. Far from preparing to evacuate it after his first night, like so many of the bedroom's previous tenants, Jericho had unpacked. His suitcases were empty. His one good suit hung in the wardrobe. His books were lined along the mantelpiece. Balanced on the top of them was his print of King's College Chapel.

He sat on the edge of the bed and stared at the picture. It was not a skilful piece of work. In fact, it was rather ugly. The twin Gothic spires were hastily drawn, the sky was an improbable blue, the blob-like figures clustered around its base could have been the work of a child. But even bad art can sometimes have its uses. Behind its scratched glass, and behind the cheap Victorian mezzotint itself, laid flat and carefully secured, were the four undecrypted intercepts he had removed from Claire's bedroom.

He should have returned them to the Park, of course. He should have cycled straight from the cottage to the huts, should have sought out Logie or some other figure of authority, and handed them in.

Even now, he couldn't disentangle all his motives for not doing so, couldn't sort out the selfless (his wish to protect her) from the selfish (his desire to have her in his power, just once). He only knew he could not bring himself to betray her, and that he was able to rationalise this by telling himself that there was no harm in waiting till the morning, no harm in giving her a chance to explain.

And so he had cycled on, past the main gate, had tiptoed up to his room and had hidden the cryptograms behind the print, increasingly aware that he had strayed across whatever border it is that separates folly from treason, and that with every passing hour it would be harder for him to find his way back.

For the hundredth time, sitting on his bed, he ran though all the possibilities. That she was crazy. That she was being blackmailed. That her room was being used as a hiding place without her knowledge. That she was a spy.

A spy? The notion seemed fantastic to him – melodramatic, bizarre, *illogical*. For one thing, why would a spy with any sense steal cryptograms? A spy would be after decodes, surely: the answers not the riddles; the hard proof that Enigma was being broken?

He checked the door, then gently took down the picture and dismantled the frame, working the thumbtacks loose with his fingers and lifting away the hardboard backing. Now he thought about it, there *was* something distinctly odd about these cryptograms, looking at them again he realised what it was. They should have had the thin paper strips of decode produced by the Type-X machines gummed to their backs. But not only were there no strips, there weren't even any marks to show where the strips had been torn off. So, by the look of them, these signals had never even been broken. Their secrets were intact. They were virgin.

None of it made any sense.

He stroked one of the signals between finger and thumb. The yellowish paper had a slight but perceptible odour. What was it? He held it close to his nose and inhaled. The scent of a library or an archive, perhaps? Quite a rich smell – warm, almost smoky – as evocative as perfume.

He realised suddenly that despite his fear he was actually beginning to treasure the cryptograms, as another man might treasure a favourite snapshot of a girl. Only these were better than any photographs, weren't they, for photographs were merely *likenesses*, whereas these were clues to *who she was*, and therefore wasn't he, by possessing them, in a sense, possessing her . . .?

He would give her just one chance. No more.

He looked at his watch. Twenty minutes had passed since breakfast. It was time to go. He slipped the cryptograms behind the picture, reassembled the frame and replaced it on the mantelpiece, then opened the door a fraction. Mrs Armstrong's regular guests had all come in from the night-shift. He could hear their murmured voices in the dining room. He put on his overcoat and stepped out on to the landing. Such were his efforts to seem natural, Mrs Armstrong would later swear she heard him humming to himself as he descended the stairs.

'I see you smiling in the cigarette glow
Though the picture fades too soon
But I see all I want to know
They can't black out the moon . . .'

From Albion Street to Bletchley Park was a walk of less than half a mile – left out of the door and along the street of terraced houses, left under the blackened railway bridge and sharp right across the allotments.

He strode quickly over the frozen ground, his breath steaming before him in the cold sunshine. Officially it was almost spring but someone had forgotten to pass the news on to winter. Patches of ice, not yet melted from the night before, cracked beneath the soles of his shoes. Rooks called from the tops of skeletal elms.

It was well past eight o'clock by the time he turned off the footpath into Wilton Avenue and approached the main gate. The shift change was over; the suburban road was almost deserted. The sentry – a giant young corporal, raw-faced from the cold – came stamping out of the guard post and barely glanced at his pass before waving him into the grounds.

Past the mansion he went, keeping his head down to avoid having to speak to anyone, past the lake (which was fringed with ice) and into Hut 8, where the silence emanating from the Decoding Room told him all he needed to know. The Type-X machines had worked their way through the backlog of Shark intercepts and now there was nothing for them to do until Dolphin and Porpoise came on stream, probably around mid-morning. He caught a glimpse of Logie's tall figure at the end of the corridor and darted into the Registration Room. There, to his surprise, was Puck, sitting in a corner, being watched by a pair of love-struck Wrens. His face was grey and lined, his head resting against the wall. Jericho thought he might be asleep but then he opened a piercing blue eye.

'Logie's looking for you.'

'Really?' Jericho took off his coat and scarf and hung them on the back of the door. 'He knows where to find me.'

'There's a rumour going around that you hit Skynner. For God's sake tell me it's true.'

One of the Wrens giggled.

Jericho had forgotten all about Skynner. He passed his hand through his hair. 'Do me a favour, Puck, will you?' he said. 'Pretend you haven't seen me?'

Puck regarded him closely for a moment, then shut his eyes. 'What a man of mystery you are,' he murmured, sleepily.

Back in the corridor Jericho walked straight into Logie.

'Ah, there you are, old love. I'm afraid we need to have a talk.'

'Fine, Guy. Fine.' Jericho patted Logie on the shoulder and squeezed past him. 'Just give me ten minutes.'

'No, not in ten minutes,' Logie shouted after him, 'now!'

Jericho pretended he hadn't heard. He trotted out into the fresh air, walked briskly round the corner, past Hut 6, towards the entrance to Hut 3. Only when he was within twenty paces of it did his footsteps slow, then stop.

The truth was, he knew very little about Hut 3, except that it was the place where the decoded messages of the German Army and Luftwaffe were processed. It was about twice the size of the other huts and was arranged in the shape of an L. It had gone up at the same time as the rest of the temporary buildings, in the winter of 1939 – a timber skeleton rising out of the freezing Buckinghamshire clay, clothed in a sheath of asbestos and flimsy wooden boarding – and to heat it, he remembered, they had cannibalised a big cast-iron stove from one of the Victorian greenhouses. Claire used to complain she was always cold. Cold, and that her job was 'boring'. But where exactly she worked within its warren of rooms, let alone what this 'boring' job entailed, was a mystery to him.

A door slammed somewhere behind him and he glanced over his shoulder to see Logie emerging from around the corner of the naval hut. Damn, damn. He dropped to one knee and pretended to fumble with his shoelace but Logie hadn't seen him. He was marching purposefully towards the mansion. That seemed to settle Jericho's resolve. Once Logie was out of sight, he counted himself down then launched himself across the path and through the entrance into the hut.

He did his best to look as if he had a right to be there. He pulled out a pen and set off down the central corridor, thrusting past airmen and Army officers, glancing officiously from side to side into the busy rooms. It was much more overcrowded even than Hut

8. The racket of typewriters and telephones was amplified by the membrane of wooden walls to create a bedlam of activity.

He had barely gone halfway down the passage when a colonel with a large moustache stepped smartly out of a doorway and blocked his path. Jericho nodded and tried to edge past him, but the colonel moved deftly to one side.

'Hold on, stranger. Who are you?'

On impulse Jericho stuck out his hand. 'Tom Jericho,' he said. 'Who are you?'

'Never mind who the hell I am.' The colonel had jug ears and thick black hair with a wide, straight parting that stood out like a firebreak. He ignored the proffered hand. 'What's your section?'

'Naval. Hut 8.'

'Hut 8? State your business here.'

'I'm looking for Dr Weitzman.'

An inspired lie. He knew Weitzman from the Chess Society: a German Jew, naturalised British, who always played Queen's Gambit Declined.

'Are you, by God?' said the colonel. 'Haven't you Navy people ever heard of the telephone?' He stroked his moustache and looked Jericho up and down. 'Well, you'd better come with me.'

Jericho followed the colonel's broad back along the passage and into a large room. Two groups of about a dozen men sat at tables arranged in a pair of semicircles, working their way through wire baskets stacked high with decrypts. Walter Weitzman was perched on a stool in a glass booth behind them.

'I say, Weitzman, d'you know this chap?'

Weitzman's large head was bent over a pile of German weapons manuals. He looked up, vague and distracted, but when he recognised Jericho his melancholy face brightened into a smile. 'Hello, Tom. Yes, of course I know him.'

'"*Kriegsnachrichten Für Seefahrer,*"' said Jericho, a fraction too quickly. 'You said you might have something by now.'

For a moment, Weitzman didn't react and Jericho thought he was done for, but then the old man said slowly, 'Yes. I believe I have that information for you.' He lowered himself carefully from his stool. 'You have a problem, colonel?'

The colonel thrust his chin forward. 'Yes, actually, Weitzman, I do, now you mention it. "Inter-hut communication, unless otherwise authorised, must be conducted by telephone or written memorandum." Standard procedure.' He glared at Weitzman and Weitzman stared back, with exquisite politeness. The belligerence seemed to leak out of the colonel. 'Right,' he muttered. 'Yes. Remember that in future.'

'Arsehole,' hissed Weitzman, as the colonel moved away. 'Well, well. You'd better come over here.'

He led Jericho to a rack of card-index files, selected a drawer, pulled it out and began riffling through it. Every time the translators came across a term they couldn't understand, they consulted Weitzman and his famous index-system. He'd been a philologist at Heidelberg until the Nazis forced him to emigrate. The Foreign Office, in a rare moment of inspiration, had dispatched him to Bletchley in 1940. Very few phrases defeated him.

'"*Kriegsnachrichten Für Seefahrer,*" "*War notices for Marines.*" First intercepted and catalogued, November ninth last year. As you knew perfectly well already.' He held the card within an inch of his nose and studied it through his thick spectacles. 'Tell me, is the good colonel still looking at us?'

'I don't know. I think so.' The colonel had bent down to read something one of the translators had written, but his gaze kept returning to Jericho and Weitzman. 'Is he always like that?'

'Our Colonel Coker? Yes, but worse today, for some reason.' Weitzman spoke softly, without looking at Jericho. He tugged open another drawer and pulled out a card, apparently absorbed. 'I suggest we stay here until he leaves the room. Now here's a U-boat term we picked up in January: "*Fluchttiefe.*"'

'"Evasion depth,"' replied Jericho. He could play this game for hours. *Vorhalt-Rechner* was a deflection-angle computer. A cold-soldered joint was a *kalte Lötstelle*. Cracks in a U-boat's bulkheads were *Stirnwandrisse* . . .

'"Evasion depth,"' Weitzman nodded. 'Quite right.'

Jericho risked another look at the colonel. 'He's going out of the door . . . now. It's all right. He's gone.'

Weitzman gazed at the card for a moment, then slipped it back among the rest and closed the drawer. 'So. Why are you asking me questions to which you already know the answers?' His hair was white, his small brown eyes overshadowed by a jutting forehead.

Wrinkles at their edges suggested a face that had once creased readily into laughter. But Weitzman didn't laugh much any more. He was rumoured to have left most of his family behind in Germany.

'I'm looking for a woman called Claire Romilly. Do you know her?'

'Of course. The beautiful Claire. Everyone knows her.'

'Where does she work?'

'She works here.'

'I know here. Here where?'

'"Inter-hut communication, unless otherwise authorised, must be conducted by telephone or written memorandum. Standard procedure."' Weitzman clicked his heels. 'Heil Hitler!'

'Bugger standard procedure.'

One of the translators turned round, irritably. 'I say, you two, put a sock in it, will you?'

'Sorry.' Weitzman took Jericho by the arm and led him away. 'Do you know, Tom,' he whispered, 'in three years, this is the first time I have heard you swear?'

'Walter. Please. It's important.'

'And it can't wait until the end of the shift?' He gave Jericho a careful look. 'Obviously not. Well, well again. Which way did Coker go?'

'Back towards the entrance.'

'Good. Follow me.'

Weitzman led Jericho almost to the other end of the hut, past the translators, through two long narrow rooms where scores of women were labouring over a pair of giant card indexes, around a corner and through a room lined with teleprinters. The din here was terrific. Weitzman put his hands to his ears, looked over his shoulder and grinned. The noise pursued them down a short length of passage, at the end of which was a closed door. Next to it was a sign, in a schoolgirl's best handwriting: GERMAN BOOK ROOM.

Weitzman knocked on the door, opened it and went inside. Jericho followed. His eye registered a large room. Shelves stacked with ledgers and files. Half a dozen trestle tables pushed together to form one big working area. Women, mostly with their backs to him. Six, perhaps, or seven? Two typing, very fast, the others moving back and forth arranging sheaves of papers into piles.

Before he could take in any more, a plump, harassed-looking woman in a tweed jacket and skirt advanced to meet them. Weitzman was beaming now, exuding charm, for all the world as if he were still in the tearoom of Heidelberg's Europäischer Hof. He took her hand and bowed to kiss it.

'*Guten Morgen, mein liebes Fräulein Monk. Wie geht's?*'

'*Gut, danke, Herr Doktor. Und dir?*'

'*Danke, sehr gut.*'

It was clearly a familiar routine between them. Her shiny complexion flushed pink with pleasure. 'And what can I do for you?'

'My colleague and I, my dear Miss Monk – ' Weitzman patted her hand, then released it and gestured towards Jericho '– are looking for the delightful Miss Romilly.'

At the mention of Claire's name, Miss Monk's flirtatious smile evaporated. 'In that case you must join the queue, Dr Weitzman. Join the queue.'

'I am sorry. The queue?'

'We are all trying to find Claire Romilly. Perhaps you, or your colleague, have an idea where we might start?'

To say that the world stands still is a solipsism, and Jericho knew it even as it seemed to happen – knew that it isn't ever the world that slows down, but rather the individual, confronted by an unexpected danger, who receives a charge of adrenaline and speeds up. Nevertheless, for him, for an instant, everything did freeze. Weitzman's expression became a mask of bafflement, the woman's of indignation. As his brain tried to compute the implications, he could hear his own voice, far away, begin to babble: 'But I thought . . . I was told – assured – yesterday – she was supposed to be on duty at eight this morning . . .'

'Quite right,' Miss Monk was saying. 'It really is most thoughtless of her. And terribly inconvenient.'

Weitzman gave Jericho a peculiar look, as if to say, What have you got me into? 'Perhaps she's ill?' he suggested.

'Then surely a note would have been considerate? A message? Before I let the entire night-shift go? We can barely cope when there are eight of us. When we're down to seven . . .'

She started to prattle on to Weitzman about '3A' and '3M' and all the staffing memos she'd written and how no one appreciated her difficulties. As if to prove her point, at that moment the door opened and a woman came in with a stack of files so high she had to

wedge her chin on top of them to keep control. She let
them fall on the table and there was a collective groan
from Miss Monk's girls. A couple of signals fluttered
over the edge of the table and on to the floor and
Jericho, primed for action, swooped to retrieve them.
He got a brief glimpse of one –

ZZZ

BATTLE HEADQUARTERS GERMAN AFRIKA KORPS LOCATED
MORNING THIRTEENTH £ THIRTEENTH ONE FIVE
KILOMETRES WEST OF BEN GARDANE £ BEN GARDANE

– before it was snatched out of his hands by Miss
Monk. She seemed for the first time to become aware
of his presence. She cradled the secrets to her plump
breast and glared at him.

'I'm sorry, you are – who are you exactly?' she asked.
She edged to one side to block his view of the table.
'You are – what? – a friend of Claire, I take it?'

'It's all right, Daphne,' said Weitzman, 'he's a friend
of mine.'

Miss Monk flushed again. 'I beg your pardon,
Walter,' she said. 'Of course, I didn't mean to imply –'

Jericho cut in: 'I wonder, could I ask you, has she
done this before? Failed to turn up, I mean, without
telling you?'

'Oh no. Never. I will not tolerate slacking in my
section. Dr Weitzman will vouch for that.'

'Indeed,' said Weitzman, gravely. 'No slacking here.'

Miss Monk was of a type that Jericho had come to
know well over the past three years: mildly hysterical at

moments of crisis; jealous of her precious rank and her extra fifty pounds a year; convinced that the war would be lost if her tiny fiefdom were denied a gross of lead pencils or an extra typist. She would hate Claire, he thought: hate her for her prettiness and her confidence and her refusal to take anything seriously.

'She hasn't been behaving at all oddly?'

'We have important work to do. We've no time here for oddness.'

'When did you last see her?'

'That would be Friday.' Miss Monk obviously prided herself on her memory for detail. 'She came on duty at four, went off at midnight. Yesterday was her rest day.'

'So I don't suppose it's likely she came back into the hut, say, early on Saturday morning?'

'No. I was here. Anyway, why should she do that? Normally, she couldn't wait to get away.'

I bet she couldn't. He glanced again at the girls behind Miss Monk. What on earth were they all doing? Each had a mound of paperclips in front of her, a pot of glue, a pile of brown folders and a tangle of rubber bands. They seemed – could this be right? – to be compiling new files out of old ones. He tried to imagine Claire here, in this drab room, among these sensible drones. It was like picturing some gorgeous parakeet in a cage full of sparrows. He wasn't sure what to do. He took out his watch and flicked open the lid. Eight thirty-five. She had already been missing more than half an hour.

'What will you do now?'

'Obviously – because of the level of classification –

there's a certain procedure we have to follow. I've already notified Welfare. They'll send someone round to her room to turf her out of bed.'

'And if she isn't there?'

'Then they'll contact her family to see if they know where she is.'

'And if they don't?'

'Well, then it's serious. But it never gets that far.' Miss Monk drew her jacket tight across her pigeon chest and folded her arms. 'I'm sure there's a *man* at the bottom of this somewhere.' She shuddered. 'There usually is.'

Weitzman was continuing to give Jericho imploring glances. He touched him on the arm. 'We ought to go now, Tom.'

'Do you have an address for her family? Or a telephone number?'

'Yes, I think so, but I'm not sure I should . . .' She turned towards Weitzman, who hesitated fractionally, shot another look at Jericho, then forced a smile and a nod.

'I can vouch for him.'

'Well,' said Miss Monk, doubtfully, 'if you think it's permissible . . .' She went over to a filing cabinet beside her desk and unlocked it.

'Coker will kill me for this,' whispered Weitzman, while her back was turned.

'He'll never find out. I promise you.'

'The curious thing is,' said Miss Monk, almost to herself, 'that she'd really become much more *attentive* of late. Anyway, this is her card.'

Next-of-kin: Edward Romilly.
Relation: Father.
Address: 27 Stanhope Gardens, London SW.
Telephone: Kensington 2257.

Jericho glanced at it for a second and handed it back.

'I don't think there's any need to trouble him, do you?' asked Miss Monk. 'Certainly not yet. No doubt Claire will arrive at any moment with some silly story about oversleeping –'

'I'm sure,' said Jericho.

'– in which case,' she added shrewdly, 'who shall I say was looking for her?'

'Auf Wiedersehen, Fraulein Monk.' Weitzman had had enough. He was already half out of the room, pulling Jericho after him with surprising force. Jericho had a last vision of Miss Monk, standing bewildered and suspicious, before the door closed on her schoolroom German.

'Auf Wiedersehen, Herr Doktor, und Herr . . .'

Weitzman didn't lead Jericho back the way they had come. Instead he bundled him out of the rear exit. Now, in the cold daylight, Jericho could see why he had found it so difficult stumbling around out here the other night. They were on the edge of a building site. Trenches had been carved four feet deep into the grass. Pyramids of sand and gravel were covered in a white mould of frost. It was a miracle he hadn't broken his neck.

Weitzman shook a cigarette out of a crumpled pack

of Passing Clouds and lit it. He leaned against the wall of the hut and exhaled a sigh of steam and smoke. 'Useless for me to ask, I suppose, what in God's name is going on?'

'You don't want to know, Walter. Believe me.'

'Troubles of the heart?'

'Something like that.'

Weitzman mumbled a couple of words in Yiddish that might have been a curse and continued to smoke.

About thirty yards away, a group of workmen were huddled around a brazier, finishing a tea break. They dispersed reluctantly, trailing pickaxes and spades across the hard ground, and Jericho had a sudden memory of himself as a boy, holding hands with his mother, walking along a seaside promenade, his spade clattering on the concrete road behind him. Somewhere beyond the trees, a generator kicked into life sending a scattering of rooks cawing into the sky.

'Walter, what's the German Book Room?'

'I'd better get back,' said Weitzman. He licked the ends of his thumb and forefinger and nipped off the glowing tip of his cigarette, slipping the unsmoked portion into his breast pocket. Tobacco was far too precious to waste even a few shreds.

'Please, Walter . . .'

'Ach!' Weitzman made a sudden gesture of disgust with his arm, as if sweeping Jericho aside, and began making his way, unsteadily but wonderfully quickly for a man of his age, down the side of the hut towards the path. Jericho had to scramble to keep pace with him.

'You ask too much, you know – '

'I know I do.'

'I mean, my God, Coker already suspects I am a Nazi spy. Can you believe that? I may be a Jew, but for him one German is no different from another. Which, of course, is precisely *our* argument. I suppose I should be flattered.'

'I wouldn't – it's just – there's nobody else . . .'

A pair of sentries with rifles rounded the corner and strolled towards them. Weitzman clamped his jaw shut and abruptly turned right off the path towards the tennis court. Jericho followed him. Weitzman opened the gate and they stepped on to the asphalt. The court had been put in – at Churchill's personal instigation, so it was said – two years earlier. It hadn't been used since the autumn. The white lines were barely visible beneath the frost. Drifts of leaves had collected against the chain-link fence. Weitzman closed the gate after them and walked towards the net post.

'It's all changed since we started, Tom. Nine-tenths of the people in the hut I don't even know any more.' He kicked moodily at the leaves and Jericho noticed for the first time how small his feet were; dancer's feet. 'I've grown old in this place. I can remember a time when we thought we were geniuses if we read fifty messages a week. Do you know what the rate is now?'

Jericho shook his head.

'Three thousand a *day*.'

'Good God.' *That's a hundred and twenty-five an hour,* thought Jericho, *that's one every thirty seconds . . .*

'Is she in trouble, then, your girl?'

'I think so. I mean, yes – yes, she is.'

184

'I'm sorry to hear it. I like her. She laughs at my jokes. Women who laugh at my jokes must be cherished. Especially if they are young. And pretty.'

'Walter . . .'

Weitzman turned towards Hut 3. He had chosen his ground well, with the instinct of a man who has been forced at some time, as a matter of personal survival, to learn how to find privacy. Nobody could come up behind them without entering the tennis court. Nobody could approach from the front without being seen. And if anyone was watching from a distance – well, what was there to see but two old colleagues, having a private chat?

'It's organised like a factory line.' He curled his fingers into the wire netting. His hands were white with cold. They clenched the steel like claws. 'The decrypts arrive by conveyor belt from Hut 6. They go first to the Watch for translation – you know that, that's my post. Two Watches per shift, one for urgent material, the other for back-breaks. Translated Luftwaffe signals are passed to 3A, Army to 3M. A for air, M for military. God in heaven, it's cold. Are you cold? I'm shaking.' He pulled out a filthy handkerchief and blew his nose. 'The duty officers decide what's important and give it a Z-priority. A single Z is low-grade – Hauptmann Fischer is to be transferred to the German Air Fleet in Italy. A weather report would be three Zs. Five Zs is pure gold – where Rommel will be tomorrow afternoon, an imminent air attack. The intelligence is summarised, then three copies are dispatched – one to SIS in Broadway, one to the appropriate service ministry in Whitehall, one to the relevant commander in the field.'

'And the German Book Room?'

'Every proper name is indexed: every officer, every piece of equipment, every base. For example, Hauptmann Fischer's transfer may at first seem quite worthless as intelligence. But then you consult the Air Index and you see his last posting was to a radar station in France. Now he is going to Bari. So: the Germans are installing radar in Bari. Let them build it. And then, when it is almost finished, bomb it.'

'And that's the German Book?'

'No, no.' Weitzman shook his head crossly, as if Jericho were some dim student at the bottom of his class at Heidelberg. 'The German Book is the very end of the process. All this paper – the intercept, the decode, the translation, the Z-signal, the list of cross-references, all these thousands of pages – it all comes together at the end to be filed. The German Book is a verbatim transcription of all decoded messages in their original language.'

'Is that an important job?'

'In intellectual terms? No. Purely clerical.'

'But in terms of access? To classified material?'

'Ah. Different.' Weitzman shrugged. 'It would depend on the person involved, of course, whether they could be bothered to read what they were handling. Most don't.'

'But in theory?'

'In theory? On an average day? A girl like Claire would probably see more operational detail about the German armed forces than Adolf Hitler.' He glanced at

Jericho's incredulous face and smiled. 'Absurd, isn't it? What is she? Nineteen? Twenty?'

'Twenty,' muttered Jericho. 'She always told me her job was boring.'

'Twenty! I swear it's the greatest joke in the history of warfare. Look at us: the hare-brained debutante, the weakling intellectual and the half-blind Jew. If only the master race could see what we're doing to them – sometimes the thought of it is all that keeps me going.' He held his watch up very close to his face. 'I must get back. Coker will have issued a warrant for my arrest. I fear I have talked too much.'

'Not at all.'

'Oh, I have, I have.'

He turned towards the gate. Jericho made a move to follow but Weitzman held up a hand to stop him. 'Why don't you wait here, Tom? Just for a moment. Let me get clear.'

He slipped out of the court. As he passed by on the other side of the fence, something seemed to occur to him. He slowed and beckoned Jericho closer to the wire netting.

'Listen,' he said softly, 'if you think I can help you again, if you need any more information – please, don't ask me. I don't want to know.'

Before Jericho could answer he had crossed the path and disappeared around the back of Hut 3.

Within the grounds of Bletchley Park, just beyond the mansion, in the shadow of a fir tree, stood an ordinary red telephone box. Inside it, a young man in motorcycle leathers was finishing a call. Jericho, leaning against the tree, could hear his singsong accent, muffled but audible.

'Right you are . . . OK, doll . . . See you.'

The dispatch rider put the receiver down with a clatter and pushed open the door.

'All yours, pal.'

The motorcyclist didn't move away at first. Jericho stood in the kiosk, pretending to fish in his pockets for change, and watched him through the glass. The man adjusted his leggings, put on his helmet, fiddled with the chin strap . . .

Jericho waited until he had moved away before dialling zero.

A woman's voice said: 'Operator speaking.'

'Good morning. I'd like to make a call, please, to Kensington double-two five seven.'

She repeated the number. 'That'll be fourpence, caller.'

A sixty-mile land line connected all Bletchley Park numbers to the Whitehall exchange. As far as the operator could tell, Jericho was merely calling one London borough from another. He pressed four pennies into the slot and after a series of clicks he heard a ringing tone.

It took fifteen seconds for a man to answer.

'Ye-es?'

It was exactly the voice Jericho had always imagined for Claire's father. Languid and assured, it stretched that single short syllable into two long ones. Immediately there was a series of pips and Jericho pushed the A-button. His money tinkled into the coin-box.

Already, he felt at a disadvantage – an indigent without access to a telephone of his own.

'Mr Romilly?'

'Ye-es?'

'I'm so sorry to trouble you, sir, especially on a Sunday morning, but I work with Claire . . .'

There was a faint noise, and then a pause, during which he could hear Romilly breathing. A crackle of static cut across the line. 'Are you still there, sir?'

The voice, when it came again, was quiet, and it sounded hollow, as if emanating from a vast and empty room. 'How did you get this number?'

'Claire gave it me.' It was the first lie that came into Jericho's head. 'I wondered if she was with you.'

Another long pause. 'No. No, she isn't. Why should she be?'

'She's not turned up for her shift this morning. Yesterday was her day off. I wondered if she might have gone down to London.'

'Who is this speaking?'

'My name is Tom Jericho.' Silence. 'She may have spoken of me.'

'I don't believe so.' Romilly's voice was barely audible. He cleared his throat. 'I'm awfully sorry, Mr Jericho. I'm afraid I can't help you. My daughter's movements are as much a mystery to me as they seem to be to you. Goodbye.'

There was a fumbling noise and the connection was broken off.

'Hello?' said Jericho. He thought he could still hear somebody breathing on the line. 'Hello?' He held on to the heavy bakelite receiver for a couple of seconds, straining to hear, then carefully replaced it.

He leaned against the side of the telephone box and massaged his temples. Beyond the glass, the world went silently about its business. A couple of civilians with bowler hats and rolled umbrellas, fresh from the London train, were being escorted up the drive to the mansion. A trio of ducks in winter camouflage came in to land on the lake, feet splayed, ploughing furrows in the grey water.

'My daughter's movements are as much a mystery to me as they seem to be to you.'

That was not right, was it? That was not the reaction one would expect of a father on being told his only child was missing?

Jericho groped in his pocket for a handful of change. He spread the coins out on his palm and stared at them, stupidly, like a foreigner just arrived in an unfamiliar country.

He dialled zero again.

'Operator speaking.'

'Kensington double-two five seven.'

Once again, Jericho inserted four pennies into the metal slot. Once again there was a series of short clicks, then a pause. He tightened his finger on the button. But this time there was no ringing tone, only the *blip-blip-blip* of an engaged signal, pulsing in his ear like a heartbeat.

Over the next ten minutes Jericho made three more attempts to get through. Each met the same response.

Either Romilly had taken his telephone off the hook, or he was involved in a long conversation with someone.

Jericho would have tried the number a fourth time, but a woman from the canteen with a coat over her apron had turned up and started rapping a coin on the glass, demanding her turn. Finally, Jericho let her in. He stood on the roadside and tried to decide what to do.

He glanced back at the huts. Their squat, grey shapes, once so boring and familiar, now seemed vaguely threatening.

Damn it. What did he have to lose?

He buttoned his jacket against the cold and turned towards the gate.

3

St Mary's Parish Church, eight solid centuries of hard white stone and Christian piety, lay at the end of an avenue of elderly yew trees, less than a hundred yards beyond Bletchley Park. As Jericho walked through the gate he saw bicycles, fifteen or twenty of them, stacked neatly around the porch, and a moment later heard the piping of the organ and the mournful lilt of a Church of England congregation in mid-hymn. The graveyard was perfectly still. He felt like a late guest approaching a house where a party was already in full swing.

'We blossom and flourish as leaves on a tree,
And wither, and perish, but naught changeth thee . . .'

Jericho stamped his feet and beat his arms. He considered slipping inside and standing at the back of the nave until the service ended, but experience had taught him there was no such thing as a quiet entry into a church. The door would bang, heads would turn, some officious sidesman would come hurrying down the aisle with a prayer sheet and a hymn book. Such attention was the last thing he wanted.

He left the path and pretended to study the tombstones. Frosted cobwebs of improbable size and delicacy shone like ectoplasm between the memorials: marble monuments for the well-to-do, slate for the farmworkers, weathered wooden crosses for the poor and infants. Ebenezer Slade, aged four years and six months, asleep in the arms of Jesus. Mary Watson, wife of Albert, taken after a long illness, rest in peace . . . On a few of the graves, bunches of dead flowers, petrified by ice, testified to some continuing flicker of interest among the living. On others, yellow lichen had obscured the inscriptions. He bent and scratched away at it, hearkening to the voices of the righteous beyond the stained glass window.

'O ye Dews and Frosts, bless ye the Lord: praise him and magnify him for ever.

O ye Frost and Cold, bless ye the Lord: praise him and magnify him for ever . . .'

Odd images chased through his mind.

He thought of his father's funeral, on just such a

day as this: a freezing, ugly Victorian church in the industrial Midlands, medals on the coffin, his mother weeping, his aunts in black, everyone studying him with sad curiosity, and he all the time a million miles away, factoring the hymn numbers in his head ('Forward out of error,/Leave behind the night' – number 392 in *Ancient and Modern* – came out very prettily, he remembered, as $2 \times 7 \times 2 \times 7 \times 2 \ldots$)

And for some reason he thought of Alan Turing, restless with excitement in the hut one winter night, describing how the death of his closest friend had made him seek a link between mathematics and the spirit, insisting that at Bletchley they were creating a new world: that the bombes might soon be modified, the clumsy electro-mechanical switches replaced by relays of pentode valves and GT1C-thyatrons to create computers, machines that might one day mimic the actions of the human brain and unlock the secrets of the soul . . .

Jericho wandered among the dead. Here was a small stone cross garlanded with stone flowers, there a stern-looking angel with a face like Miss Monk. All the time he kept listening to the service. He wondered whether anyone from Hut 8 was among the congregation and, if so, who. With all else failing, might Skynner be offering up a prayer to God? He tried to imagine what fresh reserves of sycophancy Skynner would draw on to communicate with a being even higher than the First Lord of the Admiralty, and found he couldn't do it.

'The blessing of God Almighty, the Father, the Son, and

the Holy Ghost, be amongst you and remain with you always. Amen.'

The service was over. Jericho wove quickly through the headstones, away from the church, and stationed himself behind a pair of large bushes. From here he had a clear view of the porch.

Before the war the faithful would have emerged to an uplifting peal of grandsire triples. But church bells now were to be rung only in the event of invasion, so that when the door opened and the elderly priest stationed himself to say farewell to his parishioners, the silence gave the ceremony a subdued, even melancholy air. One by one the worshippers stepped into the daylight. Jericho didn't recognise any of them. He began to think he might have come to the wrong conclusion. But then, sure enough, a small, lean young woman in a black coat appeared, still holding the prayer book from the night before.

She shook hands briefly, even curtly, with the vicar, said nothing, looped her carpetbag over the handles of her bicycle and wheeled it towards the gate. She walked quickly, with short, rapid steps, her sharp chin held high. Jericho waited until she had gone some way past him, then stepped out from his hiding place and shouted after her: 'Miss Wallace!'

She stopped and glanced back in his direction. Her weak eyesight made her frown. Her head moved vaguely from side to side. It wasn't until he was within two yards of her that her face cleared.

'Why, Mr . . .'

'Jericho.'

'Of course. Mr Jericho. The stranger in the night.' The cold had reddened the sharp point of her nose and painted two neat discs of colour, the size of half-crowns, on her white cheeks. She had long, thick, black hair which she wore piled up, shot through and secured by an armoury of pins. 'What did you make of the sermon?'

'Uplifting?' he said, tentatively. It seemed easier than telling the truth.

'Did you really? I thought it the most frightful rot I've heard all year. "Suffer not a woman to teach, nor to usurp authority over the man, but to be in silence . . ."' She shook her head furiously. 'Is it a heresy, do you suppose, to call St Paul an *ass*?'

She resumed her brisk progress towards the lane. Jericho fell in beside her. He had picked up a few details about Hester Wallace from Claire – that before the war she'd been a teacher at a girls' private school in Dorset, that she played the organ and was a clergyman's daughter, that she received the quarterly newsletter of the Jane Austen Society – just enough clues to suggest the sort of woman who might indeed go straight from an eight-hour night-shift to Sunday matins.

'Do you attend most Sundays?'

'Always,' she said. 'Although increasingly one wonders why. And you?'

He hesitated. 'Occasionally.'

It was a mistake and she was on to it at once.

'Whereabouts d'you sit? I don't recall ever seeing you.'

'I try to keep at the back.'

'So do I. Exactly at the back.' She gave him a second look, her wire-framed round spectacles flashing in the winter sun. 'Really, Mr Jericho, a sermon you obviously didn't hear, a pew you never occupy: one might almost suspect you of laying claim to a piety you don't rightly possess.'

'Ah . . .'

'I'll bid you good day.'

They had reached the gate. She swung herself on to the saddle of her bicycle with surprising grace. This was not how Jericho had planned it. He had to reach out and hold on to the handlebars to stop her pedalling away.

'I wasn't in church. I'm sorry. I wanted to talk to you.'

'Kindly remove your hand from my machine, Mr Jericho.' A couple of elderly parishioners turned to stare at them. 'At once, if you please.' She twisted the handlebars back and forth but Jericho held on.

'I am so sorry. It really won't take a moment.'

She glared at him. For an instant he thought she might be about to reach down for one of her stout and sensible shoes and hammer his fingers loose. But there was curiosity as well as anger in her eyes, and curiosity won. She sighed and dismounted.

'Thank you. There's a bus shelter over there.' He nodded to the opposite side of Church Green Road. 'Just spare me five minutes. Please.'

'Absurd. Quite absurd.'

The wheels of her bicycle clicked like knitting

needles as they crossed the road to the shelter. She refused to sit. She stood with her arms folded, looking down the hill towards the town.

He tried to think of some way of broaching the subject. 'Claire tells me you work in Hut 6. That must be interesting.'

'Claire has no business telling you where I work. Or anyone else for that matter. And, no, it is not interesting. Everything interesting seems to be done by men. Women do the rest.'

She could be pretty, he thought, if she put her mind to it. Her skin was as smooth and white as Parian. Her nose and chin, though sharp, were delicate. But she wore no make-up, and her expression was permanently cross, her lips drawn into a thin, sarcastic line. Behind her spectacles, her small, bright eyes glinted with intelligence.

'Claire and I, we were . . .' He fluttered his hands and searched for the word. He was so hopeless at all this. '"Seeing one another" I suppose is the phrase. Until about a month ago. Then she refused to have anything more to do with me.' His resolution was wilted by her hostility. He felt a fool, addressing her narrow back. But he pressed on. 'To be frank, Miss Wallace, I'm worried about her.'

'How odd.'

He shrugged. 'We were an unlikely couple, I agree.'

'No.' She turned to him. 'I meant how *odd* that people always feel obliged to disguise their concern for themselves as concern for other people.'

The corners of her mouth twitched down in her

version of a smile and Jericho realised he was beginning to dislike Miss Hester Wallace, not least because she had a point.

'I don't deny an element of self-interest,' he conceded, 'but the fact is, I am worried about her. I think she's disappeared.'

She sniffed. 'Nonsense.'

'She hasn't turned up for her shift this morning.'

'An hour late for work hardly constitutes a disappearance. She probably overslept.'

'I don't think she went home last night. She certainly wasn't back by two.'

'Then perhaps she overslept *somewhere else*,' said Miss Wallace, maliciously. The spectacles flashed gain. 'Incidentally, might I ask *how* you know she didn't come home?'

He had learned it was better not to lie. 'Because I let myself in and waited for her.'

'So. A housebreaker as well. I can see why Claire wants nothing more to do with you.'

To hell with this, thought Jericho.

'There are other things you should know. A man came to the cottage last night while I was there. He ran away when he heard my voice. And I just called Claire's father. He claims he doesn't know where she is, but I think he's lying.'

That seemed to impress her. She chewed on the inside of her lip and looked away, down the hill. A train, an express by the sound of it, was passing through Bletchley. A curtain of brown smoke, half a mile long, rose in percussive bursts above the town.

'None of this is my concern,' she said at last.

'She didn't mention she was going away?'

'She never does. Why should she?'

'And she hasn't seemed odd to you lately? Under any sort of strain?'

'Mr Jericho, we could probably fill this bus shelter – no, we could probably fill an entire double-decker bus – with young men who are worried about their relationships with Claire Romilly. Now I'm really very tired. Much too tired and inexpert in these matters to be of any help to you. Excuse me.'

For the second time she mounted her bicycle, and this time Jericho didn't try to stop her. 'Do the letters ADU mean anything to you?'

She shook her head irritably and pushed herself away from the kerb.

'It's a call sign,' he shouted after her. 'Probably German Army or Luftwaffe.'

She applied the brakes with such force she slid off the saddle, her flat heels skittering in the gutter. She looked up and down the empty road. 'Have you gone utterly mad?'

'You'll find me in Hut 8.'

'Wait a moment. What has this to do with Claire?'

'Or, failing that, the Commercial Guesthouse in Albion Street.' He nodded politely. 'ADU, Miss Wallace. Angels Dance Upwards. I'll leave you in peace.'

'Mr Jericho . . .'

But he didn't want to answer any of her questions. He crossed the road and hurried down the hill. As he turned left into Wilton Avenue towards the main gate he glanced back. She was still where he had left her, her thin legs planted either side of the pedals, staring after him in astonishment.

4

Logie was waiting for him when he got back to Hut 8. He was prowling around the confined space of the Registration Room, his bony hands clasped behind his back, the bowl of his pipe jerking around as he chomped furiously on its stem.

'This your coat?' was his only greeting. 'Better bring it with you.'

'Hello, Guy. Where are we going?' Jericho unhooked his coat from the back of the door and one of the Wrens gave him a rueful smile.

'*We're* going to have a chat, old cock. Then *you're* going home.'

Once inside his office, Logie threw himself into his chair and swung his immense feet up on to his desk. 'Close the door then, man. Let's at least *try* and keep this between ourselves.'

Jericho did as he was told. There was nowhere for him to sit so he leaned his back against it. He felt surprisingly calm. 'I don't know what Skynner's been telling you,' he began, 'but I didn't actually land a punch.'

'Oh, well, that's fine, then.' Logie raised his hands in

mock relief. 'I mean to say, as long as there's no *blood*, none of your actual *broken bones* – '

'Come on, Guy. I never touched him. He can't sack me for that.'

'He can do whatever he sodding well likes.' The chair creaked as Logie reached across the desk and picked up a brown folder. He flicked it open. 'Let us see what we have here. "Gross insubordination," it says. "Attempted physical assault," it says. "Latest in a long series of incidents which suggest the individual concerned is no longer fit for active duties."' He tossed the file back on his desk. 'Not sure I disagree, as a matter of fact. Been waiting for you to show your face around here ever since yesterday afternoon. Where've you been? Admiralty? Taking a swing at the First Sea Lord?'

'You said not to work a full shift. "Just come and go as you please." Your very words.'

'Don't get smart with me, old love.'

Jericho was silent for a moment. He thought of the print of King's College Chapel with the intercepts hidden behind it. Of the German Book Room and Weitzman's frightened face. Of Edward Romilly's shaken voice. *My daughter's movements are as much a mystery to me as they seem to be to you.*' He was aware that Logie was studying him carefully.

'When does he want me to go?'

'Well, now, you bloody idiot. "Send him back to King's and this time letter the bugger walk" – I seem to recall those were my specific instructions.' He sighed and shook his head. 'You shouldn't have made him look a fool, Tom. Not in front of his clients.'

'But he *is* a fool.' Outrage and self-pity were welling in him. He tried to keep his voice steady. 'He hasn't the foggiest idea of what he's talking about. Come on, Guy. Do you honestly believe, for one minute, that we can break back into Shark within the next three days?'

'No. But there are ways of saying it and there are ways of saying it, if you follow me, especially when our dearly beloved American brethren are in the same room.'

Someone knocked and Logie shouted: 'Not now, old thing, thanks all the same!'

He waited until whoever it was had gone and then said, quietly: 'I don't think you quite appreciate how much things have changed round here.'

'That's what Skynner said.'

'Well, he's right. For once. You saw it for yourself at the conference yesterday. It's not 1940 any more, Tom. It's not plucky little Britain stands alone. We've moved on. We have to take account of what other people think. Just look at the map, man. Read the newspapers. These convoys embark from *New York*. A quarter of the ships are American. The cargo's *all* American. American troops. American crews.' Logie suddenly covered his face with his hands. 'My God, I can't believe you tried to hit Skynner. You really are pretty potty, aren't you? I'm not at all sure you're safe to walk the streets.' He lifted his feet off the desk and picked up the telephone. 'Look, I don't care what he says, I'll see if I can get the car to take you back.'

'No!' Jericho was surprised at the vehemence in his

voice. In his mind he could see, perfectly replicated, the Atlantic plot – the brown landmass of North America, the Rorschach inkblots of the British Isles, the blue of the ocean, the innocent yellow discs, the shark's teeth, set and loaded like a mantrap. And Claire? Impossible to find her even now, when he had access to the Park. Shipped back to Cambridge, stripped of his security clearance, he might as well be on another planet. 'No,' he said, more calmly. 'You can't do that.'

'It's not my decision.'

'Give me a couple of days.'

'What?'

'Tell Skynner you want to give me a couple of days. Give me a couple of days to see if I can find a way back into Shark.'

Logie stared at Jericho for five seconds, then started to laugh. 'You get madder and madder as the week wears on, old son. Yesterday you're telling us Shark can't be broken in three days. Now you're saying you might be able to do it in two.'

'Please, Guy. I'm begging you.' And he was. He had his hands on Logie's desk and was leaning over it. He was pleading for his life. 'Skynner doesn't just want me out of the hut, you know. He wants me out of the Park altogether. He wants me locked up in some garret in the Admiralty doing long division.'

'There are worse places to spend the war.'

'Not for me there aren't. I'd hang myself. I belong here.'

'I have already stuck my neck out so far for you, my lad.' Logie jabbed his pipe into Jericho's chest.

'"Jericho?" they said. "You can't be serious. We're in a crisis and you want *Jericho*?"' He jabbed his pipe again. 'So I said: "Yes, I know he's half bloody cracked and keeps on fainting like a maiden bloody aunt, but he's got something, got that extra two per cent. Just trust me."' Jab, jab. 'So I beg a bloody car – no joke round here, as you've gathered – and instead of getting my kip I come and drink stale tea in King's and plead with you, bloody *plead*, and the first thing you do is make us all look idiots and then you slug the head of section – all right, all right, *try* to slug him. Now, I ask you: who's going to listen to me now?'

'Skynner.'

'Come off it.'

'Skynner will have to listen, he will if you insist you need me. I know – ' Jericho was inspired. 'You could threaten to tell that admiral, Trowbridge, that I've been removed – at a vital moment in the Battle of the Atlantic – just because I spoke the truth.'

'Oh, I could, could I? Thank you. Thanks very much. Then we'll both be doing long division in the Admiralty.'

'"There are worse places to spend the war."'

'Don't be cheap.'

There was another knock, much louder this time. 'For God's sake,' yelled Logie, 'piss off!' But the handle started to turn anyway. Jericho moved out of the way, the door opened and Puck appeared.

'Sorry, Guy. Good morning, Thomas.' He gave them each a grim nod. 'There's been a development, Guy.'

'Good news?'

'Frankly, no, to be entirely honest. It is probably not good news. You had better come.'

'Hell, *hell!*' muttered Logie. He gave Jericho a murderous look, grabbed his pipe and followed Puck out into the corridor.

Jericho hesitated for a second, then set off after them, down the passage and into the Registration Room. He had never seen it so full. Lieutenant Cave was there, along, it seemed, with almost every cryptanalyst in the hut – Baxter, Atwood, Pinker, Kingcome, Proudfoot, de Brooke – as well as Kramer, like a matinee idol in his American naval uniform. He gave Jericho a friendly nod.

Logie glanced around the room with surprise. 'Hail, hail, the gang's all here.' Nobody laughed. 'What's up, Puck? Holding a rally? Going on strike?'

Puck inclined his head towards the three young Wrens who made up the Registration Room's day shift.

'Ah yes,' said Logie, 'of course,' and he flashed his smoker's teeth at them in an ochre smile. 'Bit of business to attend to, girls. Hush hush. I wonder if you wouldn't mind leaving the gentlemen alone for a few minutes.'

'I happened to show this to Lieutenant Cave,' said Puck, when the Wrens had gone. 'Traffic analysis.' He held aloft the familiar yellow log sheet, as if he were about to perform a conjuring trick. 'Two long signals intercepted in the last twelve hours coming out of the

Nazis' new transmitter near Magdeburg. One just before midnight: one hundred and eight four-letter groups. One just after: two hundred and eleven groups. Rebroadcast twice, over both the Diana and Hubertus radio nets. Four-six-oh-one kilocycles. Twelve-nine-fifty.'

'Oh, do get on with it,' said Atwood, under his breath.

Puck affected not to hear. 'In the same period, the total number of Shark signals intercepted from the North Atlantic U-boats up to oh-nine-hundred this morning: five.'

'Five?' repeated Logie. 'Are you sure, old love?' He took the log sheet and ran his finger down the neatly inked columns of entries.

'What's the phrase?' said Puck. '"As quiet as the grave"?'

'Our listening posts,' said Baxter, reading the log sheet over Logie's shoulder. 'There must be something wrong with them. They must have fallen asleep.'

'I rang the intercept control room ten minutes ago. After I'd spoken to the lieutenant. They say there's no mistake.'

An excited murmur of conversation broke out.

'And what say you, O wise one?'

It took Jericho a couple of seconds to realise that Atwood was talking to him. He shrugged. 'It's very few. Ominously few.'

Puck said: 'Lieutenant Cave believes there's a pattern.'

'We've been interrogating captured U-boat crew

about tactics.' Lieutenant Cave leaned forwards and
Jericho saw Pinker flinch at the sight of his scarred face.
'When Dönitz sniffs a convoy, he draws his hearses up
line abreast across the route he expects it to take.
Twelve boats, say, maybe twenty miles apart. Possibly
two lines, possibly three – nowadays he's got the
hearses to put on a pretty big show. Our estimate,
before the blackout, was forty-six operational in that
sector of the North Atlantic alone.' He broke off,
apologetically. 'Sorry,' he said, 'do stop me if I'm
telling my grandmothers how to suck eggs.'

'Our work's rather more – ah – theoretical,' said
Logie. He looked around and several of the cryptanalysts nodded in agreement.

'All right. There are basically two types of line.
There's your picket line, which basically means the U-
boats stay stationary on the surface waiting for the
convoy to steam into them. And there's your patrol
line, which involves the hearses sweeping forwards in
formation to intercept it. Once the lines are established, there's one golden rule. Absolute radio silence
until the convoy's sighted. My hunch is that that's
what's happening now. The two long signals coming
out of Magdeburg – those are most likely Berlin
ordering the U-boats into line. And if the boats are now
observing radio silence . . .' Cave shrugged: he was sorry
to have to state the obvious. 'That means they must be
on battle stations.'

Nobody said anything. The intellectual abstractions
of cryptanalysis had taken solid form: two thousand
German U-boat men, ten thousand Allied seamen and

passengers, converging to do battle in the North Atlantic winter, a thousand miles from land. Pinker looked as if he might be sick. Suddenly the oddity of their situation struck Jericho. Pinker was probably personally responsible for sending – what? – a thousand German sailors to the bottom of the ocean, yet Cave's face was the closest he had come to the brutality of the Atlantic war.

Someone asked what would happen next.

'If one of the U-boats finds the convoy? It'll shadow it. Send a contact signal every two hours – position, speed, direction. That'll be picked up by the other hearses and they'll start to converge on the same location. Same procedure, to try to draw in as many hunters as possible. Usually, they try to get right inside the convoy, in among our ships. They'll wait until nightfall. They prefer to attack in the dark. Fires from the ships that have been hit illuminate other targets. There's more panic. Also, night-time makes it harder for our destroyers to catch them.'

'Of course, the weather's appalling,' added Cave, his sharp voice cutting in to the silence, 'even for the time of year. Snow. Freezing fog. Green water breaking over the bows. That's actually in our favour.'

Kramer said: 'How long do we have?'

'Less time than we originally thought, that's for certain. The U-boat is faster than any convoy, but it's still a slow beast. On the surface it moves at the speed of a man on a bicycle, underwater it's only as fast as a man on foot. But if Dönitz knows about the convoys? Perhaps a day and a half. The bad weather will give them visibility problems. Even so – yes – I'd guess a day and a half at the outside.'

Cave excused himself to go and telephone the bad news to the Admiralty. The cryptanalysts were left alone. At the far end of the hut a faint clacking noise began as the Type-X machines started their day's work.

'That'll be D-D-Dolphin,' said Pinker. 'Will you excuse me, G-G-Guy?'

Logie raised a hand in benediction and Pinker hurried out of the room.

'If only we had a four-wheel bombe,' moaned Proudfoot.

'Well, we ain't got one, old love, so don't let's waste time on that.'

Kramer had been leaning against one of the trestle tables. Now he pushed himself on to his feet. There wasn't room for him to pace, so he performed a kind of restless shuffle, smacking his fist into the palm of his left hand.

'Goddamn it, I feel so *helpless*. A day and a half. A measly, goddamn *day and a half*. Jesus! There must be *something*. I mean, you guys did break this thing once, didn't you, during the last blackout?'

Several people spoke at once.

'Oh, yes.'

'D'you remember that?'

'That was Tom.'

Jericho wasn't listening. Something was stirring in his mind, some tiny shift in the depths of his subconscious, beyond the reach of any power of analysis. What was it? A memory? A connection? The more he tried to concentrate on it, the more elusive it became.

'Tom?'

He jerked his head up in surprise.

'Lieutenant Kramer was asking you, Tom' said Logie, with weary patience, 'about how we broke Shark during the blackout.'

'What?' He was irritated at having his thoughts interrupted. His hands fluttered. 'Oh, Dönitz was promoted to admiral. We took a guess that U-boat headquarters would be pleased as Punch. So pleased, they'd transmit Hitler's proclamation verbatim to all boats.'

'And did they?'

'Yes. It was a good crib. We put six bombes onto it. Even then it still took us nearly three weeks to read one day's traffic.'

'With a good crib?' said Kramer. 'Six bombes. *Three weeks?*'

'That's the effect of a four-wheel Enigma.'

Kingcome said: 'It's a pity Dönitz doesn't get a promotion every day.'

This immediately brought Atwood to life. 'The way things are going, he probably will.'

Laughter momentarily lightened the gloom. Atwood looked pleased with himself.

'Very good, Frank,' said Kingcome. 'A daily promotion. Very good.'

Only Kramer refused to laugh. He folded his arms and stared down at his gleaming shoes.

They began to talk about some theory of de Brooke's which had been running on a pair of bombes for the past nine hours, but the methodology was hopelessly skewed, as Puck pointed out.

'Well, at least I've had an idea,' said de Brooke, 'which is more than you have.'

'That is because, my dear Arthur, if I have a terrible idea, I keep it to myself.'

Logie clapped his hands. 'Boys, boys. Let's keep the criticism constructive, shall we?'

The conversation dragged on but Jericho had stopped listening a long time ago. He was chasing the phantom in his mind again, searching back through his mental record of the past ten minutes to find the word, the phrase, that could have stirred it into life. Diana, Hubertus, Magdeburg, picket line, radio silence, contact signal . . .

Contact signal.

'Guy, where d'you keep the keys to the Black Museum?'

'What, old thing? Oh, in my desk. Top right-hand drawer. Hey, where're you going? Just a minute, I haven't finished talking to you yet . . .'

It was a relief to get out of the claustrophobic atmosphere of the hut and into the cold, fresh air. He trotted up the slope towards the mansion.

He seldom went into the big house these days but whenever he did it reminded him of a stately home in a twenties murder mystery. (*'You will recall, inspector, that the colonel was in the library when the fatal shots were fired . . .*') The exterior was a nightmare, as if a giant handcart full of the discarded bits of other buildings had been tipped out in a heap. Swiss gables, Gothic battlements, Greek pillars, suburban bay windows, municipal red brick, stone lions, the entrance porch of a cathedral – the styles sulked and raged against one another, capped by a bell-shaped roof of beaten green copper. The interior was pure Gothic horror, all stone arches and stained glass windows. The polished floors rang hollow beneath Jericho's feet and the walls were decorated with dark wooden panelling of the sort that springs open in the final chapter to reveal a secret labyrinth. He was hazy about what went on here now. Commander Travis had the big office at the front looking out over the lake while upstairs in the bedrooms all sorts of mysterious things were done: he'd heard rumours they were breaking the ciphers of the German Secret Service.

He walked quickly across the hall. An Army captain loitering outside Travis's office was pretending to read that morning's *Observer*, listening to a middle-aged man in tweeds trying to chat up a young RAF woman. Nobody paid any attention to Jericho. At the foot of the elaborately carved oak staircase, a corridor led off to the right and wound around the back of the house. Midway along it was a door which opened to reveal steps down to a secondary passage. It was here, in a locked room in the cellar, that the cryptanalysts from huts 6 and 8 stored their stolen treasures.

Jericho felt along the wall for the light switch.

The larger of the two keys unlocked the door to the

museum. Stacked on metal shelves along one wall were a dozen or more captured Enigma machines. The smaller key fitted one of a pair of big iron safes. Jericho knelt and opened it and began to rummage through the contents. Here they all were, their precious pinches: each one a victory in the long war against the Enigma. There was a cigar box with a label dated February 1941, containing the haul from the armed German trawler *Krebs:* two spare rotors, the Kriegsmarine grid map of the North Atlantic and the naval Enigma settings for February 1941. Behind these was a bulging envelope marked *München* – a weather ship whose capture three months after the *Krebs* had enabled them to break the meterological code – and another labelled 'U-110'. He pulled out armfuls of papers and charts.

Finally, from the bottom shelf at the back, he withdrew a small package wrapped in brown oilcloth. This was the haul for which Fasson and Grazier had died, still in its original covering, as it had been passed out of the sinking U-boat. He never saw it without thanking God that they'd found something waterproof to wrap it in. The smallest exposure to water would have dissolved the ink. To have plucked it from a drowning submarine, at night, in a high sea . . . It was enough to make even a mathematician believe in miracles. Jericho removed the oilcloth tenderly, as a scholar might unwrap the papyri of an ancient civilisation, or a priest uncover holy relics. Two little pamphlets, printed in Gothic lettering on pink blotting paper. The second edition of the U-boats' Short Weather Cipher, now useless, thanks to the code book change. And – exactly as he had remembered – the Short Signal Book. He flicked through it. Columns of letters and numbers.

A typed notice was stuck on the back of the safe door: 'It is strictly forbidden to remove any item without my express permission. (Signed) L.F.N. Skynner, Head of Naval Section.'

Jericho took particular pleasure in slipping the Short Signal Book into his inside pocket and running with it back to the hut.

Jericho tossed the keys to Logie who fumbled and then just caught them.

'Contact signal.'

'What?'

'Contact signal,' repeated Jericho.

'Praise the Lord!' said Atwood, throwing up his hands like a revivalist preacher. 'The Oracle has spoken.'

'All right, Frank. Just a minute. What about it, old love?'

Jericho could see it all much faster than he could convey it. Indeed, it was quite hard to formulate it in words at all. He spoke slowly, as if translating from a foreign language, reordering it in his mind, turning it into a narrative.

'Do you remember, in November, when we got the Short Weather Cipher Book off the U-459? When we also got the Short Signal Book? Only we decided not to concentrate on the Short Signal Book at the time, because it never yielded anything long enough to make a worthwhile crib? I mean, a convoy contact signal on

214

its own, it isn't worth a damn, is it? It's just five letters once in a blue moon.' Jericho withdrew the little pink pamphlet carefully from his pocket. 'One letter for the speed of the convoy, a couple for its course, a couple more for the grid reference . . .'

Baxter stared at the code book as if hypnotised. 'You've removed that from the safe *without permission*?'

'But if Lieutenant Cave is correct, and whichever U-boat finds the convoy is going to send a contact signal every *two hours*, and if it's going to shadow it till nightfall, then it's possible – theoretically possible – it might send as many as four, or even five signals, depending on what time of day it makes its first sighting.' Jericho sought out the only uniform in the room. 'How long does daylight last in the North Atlantic in March?'

'About twelve hours,' said Kramer.

'Twelve hours, you see? And if a number of other U-boats attach themselves to the same convoy, on the same day, in response to the original signal, and *they* all start sending contact signals every two hours . . .'

Logie, at least, could see what he was driving at. He withdrew his pipe slowly from his mouth. 'Bloody hell!'

'Then again, *theoretically*, we could have, say, twenty letters of crib off the first boat, fifteen off the second – I don't know, if it's an attack by eight boats, let's say, we could easily get to a hundred letters. It's just as good as the weather crib.' Jericho felt as a proud as a father, offering the world a glimpse of his newborn child. 'It's beautiful, don't you see?' He gazed at each of the cryptanalysts in turn: Kingcome and Logie were beginning to look excited, de Brooke and Proudfoot seemed thoughtful, Baxter, Atwood and Puck appeared downright hostile. 'It was never possible till this moment, because until now the Germans have never been able to throw so many U-boats against such a mass of shipping. It's the whole story of Enigma in a nutshell. The very scale of the Germans' achievement breeds such a mass of material for us, it'll sow the seeds of their eventual defeat.'

He paused.

'Aren't there rather a lot of *ifs* there?' said Baxter drily. '*If* the U-boat finds the convoy early enough in the day, *if* it reports every two hours, *if* the others all do the same, *if* we manage to intercept every transmission . . .'

'And *if,*' said Atwood, 'the Short Signal Book we pinched in November wasn't changed last week at the same time as the Weather Cipher Book . . .'

That was a possibility Jericho hadn't considered. He felt his enthusiasm crumble slightly.

Now Puck joined in the attack. 'I agree. The concept is quite brilliant, Thomas. I applaud your – inspiration, I suppose. But your strategy depends on failure, does it not? We will only break Shark, on your admission, if the U-boats find the convoy, which is exactly what we want to avoid. And suppose we do come up with that day's Shark settings – so what? Marvellous. We can read all the U-boats' signals to Berlin, boasting to Dönitz about how many Allied ships they've sunk. And twenty-four hours later, we're blacked out again.'

Several of the cryptanalysts groaned in agreement.

'No, no,' Jericho shook his head emphatically. 'Your logic is flawed, Puck. What we hope, obviously, is that the U-boats don't find the convoys. Yes – that's the whole point of the exercise. But if they do, we can at least turn it to our advantage. And it won't just be one day, not if we're lucky. If we break the Shark settings for twenty-four hours, then we'll pick up the encoded weather messages for that entire period. And, remember, we'll have our own ships in the area, able to give us the precise weather data the U-boats are encoding. We'll have the plaintext, we'll have the Shark cipher settings, so we'll be able to make a start on reconstructing the new Weather Code Book. We could get our foot back in the door again. Don't you see?'

He ran his hands through his hair and tugged at it in exasperation. Why were they all being so dim?

Kramer had been scribbling furiously in a notebook. 'He's on to something, you know.' He tossed his pencil into the air and caught it. 'Come on. It's worth a try. At least it puts us back in the fight.'

Baxter grunted. 'I still don't see it.'

'Nor do I,' said Puck.

'I suppose you don't see it, Baxter,' said Atwood, 'because it doesn't represent a triumph for the world proletariat?'

Baxter's hands curled into fists. 'One of these days, Atwood, someone's going to knock your bloody smug block off.'

'Ah. The first impulse of the totalitarian mind: violence.'

'Enough!' Logie banged his pipe like a gavel on one

of the trestle tables. None of them had ever heard him shout before and the room went quiet. 'We've had quite enough of that already.' He stared hard at Jericho. 'Now, it's quite right we should be cautious. Puck, your point's taken. But we've also got to face facts. We've been blacked out four days and Tom's is the only decent idea we've got. So bloody good work, Tom.'

Jericho stared at an ink stain on the floor. *Oh God*, he thought, *here comes the housemaster's pep talk*.

'Now, there's a lot resting on us here, and I want every man to remember he's part of a team.'

'No man is an island, Guy,' said Atwood, deadpan, his chubby hands clasped piously on his wide stomach.

'Thank you, Frank. Quite right. No they're not. And if ever any of us – any of us – is tempted to forget it, just think of those convoys, and all the other convoys this war depends on. Got it? Good. Right. Enough said. Back to work.'

Baxter opened his mouth to protest, but then seemed to think better of it. He and Puck exchanged grim glances on their way out. Jericho watched them go and wondered why they were so determinedly pessimistic. Puck couldn't abide Baxter's politics and normally the two men kept their distance. But now they seemed to have made common cause. What was it? A kind of academic jealousy? Resentment that he had come in after all their hard work and made them look like fools?

Logie was shaking his head. 'I don't know, old love, what are we to do with you?' He tried to look stern, but he couldn't hide his pleasure. He put his hand on

Jericho's shoulder.

'Give me my job back.'

'I'll have to talk to Skynner.' He held the door open and ushered Jericho out into the passage. The three Wrens watched them. 'My God,' said Logie, with a shudder. 'Can you imagine what he's going to say? He's going to love it, isn't he, having to tell his friends the admirals that the best chance of getting back into Shark is if the convoys are attacked? Oh, bugger, I suppose I'd better go and call him.' He went halfway into his office, then came out again. 'And you're quite sure you never actually hit him?'

'Quite sure, Guy.'

'Not a scratch?'

'Not a scratch.'

'Pity, said Logie, half to himself. 'In a way. Pity.'

5

Hester Wallace couldn't sleep. The blackout curtains were drawn against the day. Her tiny room was a study in monochrome. A nosegay of lavender sent a soothing fragrance filtering through her pillow. But even though she lay dutifully on her back in her cotton nightgown, her legs pressed together, her hands folded on her breast, like a maiden on a marble tomb, oblivion still eluded her.

'ADU, Miss Wallace. Angels Dance Upwards . . .'

The mnemonic was infuriatingly effective. She

couldn't get it out of her brain, even though the arrangement of letters meant nothing to her.

'It's a call sign. Probably German Army or Luft-waffe . . .'

No surprise in that. It was almost bound to be. After all, there were so many of them: thousands upon thousands. The only reliable rule was that Army and Luftwaffe call-signs never began with a D, because D always indicated a German commercial station.

ADU . . . ADU . . .

She couldn't place it.

She turned on her side, brought her knees up to her stomach and tried to fill her mind with soothing thoughts. But no sooner had she rid herself of the intense, pale face of Tom Jericho than her memory showed her the wizened priest of St Mary's, Bletchley, that croaking mouthpiece of St Paul's misogynies. 'It is a shame for women to speak in the church . . .' (1 Corinthians 14.xxxv). 'Silly women laden with sins, led away with divers lusts . . .' (2 Timothy 3.vi). From such texts he had woven a polemical sermon against the wartime employment of the female sex – women driving lorries, women in trousers, women drinking and smoking in public houses unaccompanied by their husbands, women neglecting their children and their homes. 'As a jewel of gold in a swine's mouth, so is a fair woman which is without discretion.' (Proverbs 11.xxii).

If only it were true! she thought. If only women *had* usurped authority over men! The Brylcreemed figure of Miles Mermagen, her head of section, rose greasily before her inner eye. 'My dear Hester, a transfer at the present moment is really quite out of the question.' He had been a manager at Barclays Bank before the war and liked to come up behind the girls as they worked and massage their shoulders. At the Hut 6 Christmas Party he had manoeuvred her under the mistletoe and clumsily taken off her glasses. ('Thank you, Miles,' she'd said, trying miserably to make a joke of it, 'without my spectacles you too look almost tolerably attractive . . .') His lips on hers were unpleasantly moist, like the underside of a mollusc, and tasted of sweet sherry.

Claire, of course, had known immediately what to do.

'Oh, darling, poor you, and I suppose he's got a wife?'

'He says they were married too young.'

'Well, she's your answer. Tell him you think it's only fair you go and have a talk with her first. Tell him you want to be her friend.'

'But what if he says yes?'

'Oh, God! Then I suppose you'll just have to kick him in the balls.'

Hester smiled at the memory. She shifted her position in the bed again and the cotton sheet rode up and corrugated beneath her. It was quite hopeless. She reached out and switched on the little bedside lamp, fumbling around its base for her glasses.

Ich lerne deutsch, ich lernte deutsch, ich habe deutsch gelernt . . .

German, she thought: German would be her

salvation. A working knowledge of written German would lift her out of the grind of the Intercept Control Room, away from the clammy embrace of Miles Mermagen, and propel her into the rarefied air of the Machine Room, where the *real* work was done – where she should have been put in the first place.

She propped herself up in bed and tried to focus on *Abelman's German Primer*. Ten minutes of this was usually quite enough to send her off to sleep.

'Intransitive verbs showing a change of place or condition take the auxiliary *sein* instead of *haben* in the compound tenses . . .'

She looked up. Was that a noise downstairs?

'In subordinate word order the auxiliary must stand last, directly after the past participle or the infinitive . . .'

And there it was again.

She slipped her warm feet into her cold outdoor shoes, wrapped a woollen shawl about her shoulders, and went out onto the landing.

A knocking sound was coming from the kitchen.

She began to descend the stairs.

There had been two men waiting for her when she arrived back from church. One had been standing on the doorstep, the other had emerged casually from the back of the cottage. The first man was young and blond with a languid, aristocratic manner and a kind of decadent Anglo-Saxon handsomeness. His companion was older, smaller, slim and dark, with a northern accent. They both had Bletchley Park passes and said they'd come from Welfare and were looking for Miss Romilly. She hadn't turned up for work: any idea where she might be?

Hester had said she hadn't. The older man had gone upstairs and had spent a long time searching around. The blond, meanwhile – she never caught his name – had sprawled on the sofa and asked a lot of questions. There was something offensively patronising about him, for all his good manners. This is what Miles Mermagen would be like, she found herself thinking, if he'd had five thousand pounds' worth of private education. What was Claire like? Who were her friends? Who were the men in her life? Had anyone been asking after her? She mentioned Jericho's visit of the previous night and he made a note of it with a gold propelling pencil. She almost blurted out the story of Jericho's peculiar approach in the churchyard ('*ADU, Miss Wallace* . . .') but by this time she had taken so strongly against the blond man's manner she bit back the words.

Knock, knock, knock from the kitchen . . .

Hester took the poker that stood beside the sitting-room fireplace and slowly opened the kitchen door.

It was like stepping into a refrigerator. The window was banging in the wind. It must have been open for hours.

At first she felt relieved, but that lasted only until she tried to close it. Then she discovered that the metal catch, weakened by rust, had been snapped clean off. Part of the wooden window frame around it was splintered.

She stood in the cold and considered the implications and quickly concluded there was only one plausible explanation. The dark-haired man who had appeared from behind the cottage on her return from church had obviously been in the process of breaking in.

They had told her there was nothing to worry about. But if there was nothing to worry about, why had they been prepared to force entry into the house?

She shivered and drew the shawl around her.

'Oh Claire,' she said aloud, 'oh, Claire, you silly, stupid, *stupid* girl, what *have* you done?'

She used a piece of blackout tape to try and secure the window. Then, still holding the poker, she went back upstairs and into Claire's room. A silver fox was hanging over the end of the bed, its glass-bead eyes staring, its needle teeth bared. Out of habit, she folded it neatly and placed it on the shelf where it normally lived. The room was such an expression of Claire, such an extravagance of colour and fabric and scent, that it seemed to resonate with her presence, even now, when she was away, to hum with it, like the last vibrations of a tuning fork . . . Claire, holding some ridiculous dress to herself and laughing and asking her what she thought, and Hester pretending to frown with an older sister's disapproval. Claire, as moody as an adolescent, on her stomach on the bed, leafing through a pre-war *Tatler*. Claire combing Hester's hair (which, when she let it down, fell almost to her waist), running her brush through it with slow and languorous strokes that made Hester's limbs turn weak. Claire insisting on painting Hester in her make-up, dressing her up like a doll and standing back in mock surprise: *'Why, darling, you're beautiful!* Claire, in nothing but a pair of white silk knickers and a string of pearls, prancing about the room in search of something, long-legged as an athlete, turning and seeing that Hester was secretly watching her in the mirror, catching the look in her eyes, and standing there for a moment, hip thrust forward, arms outstretched, with a smile that was something between an invitation and a taunt, before sweeping back into motion . . .

And on that cold, bright Sabbath afternoon, Hester Wallace, the clergyman's daughter, leaned against the wall and closed her eyes and pressed her hand between her legs with shame.

An instant later the noise from the kitchen started again and she thought her heart might burst with panic. She fled across the landing and into her room, pursued by the dry whine of the vicar of St Mary's – or was it really the voice of her father? – reciting from the Book of Proverbs:

'For the lips of a strange woman drop as an honeycomb, and her mouth is smoother than oil: But her end is bitter as wormwood, sharp as a two-edged sword. Her feet go down to death; her steps take hold on hell . . .'

6

For the first time in more than a month, Tom Jericho found that he was busy.

He had to supervise the copying of the Short Signal Code Book, six typewritten transcripts of which were duly produced and stamped MOST SECRET. Every line had to be checked, for a single error could spell the difference between a successful break and days of failure. The intercept controllers had to be briefed. Teleprintered orders had to be sent to all the duty officers of every Hut 8 listening post – from Thurso, clinging to the cliffs on the northernmost tip of Scotland, right down to St Erth, near Land's End. Their brief was simple: concentrate everything you have on the known Atlantic U-boat frequencies, cancel all leave, bring in the lame and the sick and the blind if you have to, and pay even greater attention than usual to very short bursts of Morse preceded by E-bar – *dot dot dash dot dot* – the Germans' priority code which cleared the wavelength for convoy contact reports. Not one such signal was to be missed, understand? *Not one.*

From the Registry, Jericho withdrew three months' worth of Shark decrypts to bring himself back up to speed, and, that afternoon, sitting in his old place by the window in the Big Room, proved by slide-rule calculation what he already knew by instinct: that seventeen convoy contact reports, if harvested in the same twenty-four-hour stretch, would yield eighty-five letters of cipher encode which might – *might*, if the cryptanalysts had the requisite percentage of luck – give them a break into Shark, provided they could get at least ten bombes working in relay for a minimum of thirty-six hours . . .

And all the time he thought of Claire.

There was very little, practically, he could do about her. Twice during the day he managed to get out to the telephone box to try to call her father: once as they all went off to lunch, when he was able to drop back, unnoticed by the rest, just before they reached the main gate; and the second time in the late afternoon when he pretended he needed to stretch his legs. On each occasion, the connection was made, but the phone merely rang, unanswered. He had a vague but growing feeling of dread, made worse by his powerlessness. He couldn't return to Hut 3. He didn't have the time to check out her cottage. He would have liked to go back to his room to rescue the intercepts – hidden behind a *picture* on top of the *mantelpiece*? was he *insane*? – but the round trip would have taken him the best part of twenty minutes and he couldn't get away.

In the event, it was to be well past seven before he got away. Logie was passing through the Big Room when he stopped off at Jericho's table and told him, for God's sake, to get back to his digs and get some rest. 'There's nothing more for you to do here, old love. Except wait. I expect it'll be around this time tomorrow that we'll start to sweat.'

Jericho reached thankfully for his coat. 'Did you talk to Skynner?'

'About the plan, yes. Not about you. He didn't ask and I certainly wasn't going to bring it up.'

'Don't tell me he's forgotten?'

Logie shrugged. 'There's some other flap on that seems to have taken his mind off things.'

'What other flap?'

But Logie had moved away. 'I'll see you in the morning. You just make sure you get some kip.'

Jericho returned the stack of Shark intercepts to the Registry and went outside. The March sun, which had barely risen above the trees all day, had sunk behind the mansion, leaving a fading streak of primrose and pale orange at the rim of an indigo sky. The moon was already out and Jericho could hear the sound of bombers, far away, a lot of them, forming up for the night's attack on Germany. As he walked, he gazed around him in wonder. The lunar disc on the still lake, the fire on the horizon – it was an extraordinary conjunction of lights and symbols, almost like a portent. He was so engrossed he had almost passed the telephone box before he realised that it was empty.

One last try? He glanced at the moon. Why not?

The Kensington number still wasn't answering so he decided, on a whim, to try the Foreign Office. The operator put him through to a duty clerk and he asked for Edward Romilly.

'Which department?'

'I don't know, I'm afraid.'

The line went silent. The chances of Edward Romilly being at his desk on a Sunday night were slim. He rested his shoulder against the glass panel of the booth. A car went past slowly, then pulled up about ten yards down the road. Its brake lights glowed red in the dusk. There was a click and Jericho returned his attention to the call.

'Putting you through.'

A ringing tone, and then a cultured female voice said: 'German Desk.'

German Desk? He was momentarily disconcerted. 'Ah, Edward Romilly, please.'

'And who shall I say is calling?'

My God, he *was* there. He hesitated again.

'A friend of his daughter.'

'Wait, please.'

His fingers were clamped so tight around the receiver that they were aching. He made an effort to relax. There was no good reason why Romilly *shouldn't* work on the German Desk. Hadn't Claire told him once that her father had been a junior official at the Berlin Embassy, just as the Nazis were coming to power? She would have been about ten or eleven. That must have been where she learned her German.

'I'm afraid, sir, Mr Romilly's already left for the evening. Who shall I say called?'

'Thank you. It doesn't matter. Good night.'

He hung up quickly. He didn't like the sound of that. And he didn't like the look of this car, either. He came out of the telephone box and began to walk towards it – a low, black machine with wide running boards, edged white for the blackout. Its engine was still running. As he came closer it suddenly catapulted forwards and shot round the curving road towards the main gate. He trotted after it but by the time he reached the entrance it had gone.

As Jericho went down the hill, the vague outline of the town evaporated into the darkness. No generation for at least a century could have witnessed such a spectacle. Even in his great-grandfather's day there would have been some illumination – the gleam of a gaslight or a carriage lantern, the bluish glow of a night watchman's paraffin lamp – but not any more. As the light faded, so did Bletchley. It seemed to sink into a black lake. He could have been anywhere.

He was aware, now, of a certain paranoia, and the night magnified his fears. He passed an urban pub close to the railway bridge, an elaborate Victorian mausoleum with FINE WHISKYS, PORTS AND STOUTS inlaid in gold on the black masonry like an epitaph. He could hear a badly tuned piano playing 'The Londonderry Air' and for a moment he was tempted to go in, buy a drink, find someone to talk to. But then he imagined the conversation –

'So, what's your line then, pal?'

'Just government work.'

'Civil service?'

'Communications. Nothing much. Look, I say, can I get you another drink?'

'Local are you?'

'Not exactly . . .'

– and he thought: no, better to keep clear of strangers; best, really, not to drink at all. As he was turning into Albion Street he heard the scrape of a footstep behind him and spun round. The pub door had opened, there was a moment of colour and music, then it closed and the road was dark again.

The guesthouse was about half way down Albion Street, on the right and he had almost reached it when he noticed, on the left, a car. He slowed his pace. He couldn't be sure it was the same one that had behaved so oddly at the Park, although it looked quite similar. But then, when he was almost level with it, one of the occupants struck a match. As the driver leaned over to cup his hand to the light, Jericho saw on his sleeve the three white stripes of a police sergeant.

He let himself into the guesthouse and prayed he could make the stairs before Mrs Armstrong rose like a night fighter to intercept him in the hall. But he was too late. She must have been waiting for the sound of his key in the latch. She appeared from the kitchen through a cloud of steam that smelled of cabbage and offal. In the dining room, somebody made a retching noise and there was a shout of laughter.

Jericho said weakly, 'I don't think I'm very hungry, Mrs Armstrong, thanks all the same.'

She dried her hands on her apron and nodded towards a closed door. 'You've got a visitor.'

He had just planted his foot defiantly on the first stair. 'Is it the police?'

'Why, Mr Jericho, whatever would the police be doing here? It's a very nice-looking young gentleman. I've put him,' she added, with heavy significance, 'in the parlour.'

The parlour! Open nightly to any resident from eight till ten on weekdays, and from teatime onwards, Saturday and Sunday: as formal as a ducal drawing room, with its matching three-piece suite and antimacassars (made by the proprietress herself), its mahogany standard lamp with tasselled shade, its row of grinning Toby jugs, precisely lined above its freezing hearth. Who had come to see him, wondered Jericho, who warranted admission to the *parlour*?

At first he didn't recognise him. Golden hair, a pale and freckled face, pale blue eyes, a practised smile. Advancing across the room to meet him, right hand outstretched, left hand holding an Anthony Eden hat, fifty guineas' worth of Savile Row coat draped over manly shoulders. A blur of breeding, charm and menace.

'Wigram. Douglas Wigram. Foreign Office. We met yesterday but weren't introduced properly.'

He took Jericho's hand lightly and oddly, a finger crooked back into his palm, and it took Jericho a moment to realise he had just been the recipient of a masonic handshake.

'Digs all right? Super room, this. Super. Mind if we go somewhere else? Whereabouts are you based? Upstairs?'

Mrs Armstrong was still in the hall, fluffing up her hair in front of the oval mirror.

'Mr Jericho suggests we might have our little chat upstairs in his room, if that's OK with you, Mrs A?' He didn't wait for a reply. 'Let's go then, shall we?'

He held out his arm, still smiling, and Jericho found himself being ushered up the stairs. He felt as though he had been tricked or robbed but he couldn't work out how. On the landing he rallied sufficiently to turn and say, 'It's very small, you know, there's barely room to sit.'

'That's perfectly all right, my dear chap. As long as it's private. Onwards and upwards.'

Jericho switched on the dim light and stood back to

let Wigram go in first. There was a faint whiff of eau de cologne and cigars as he brushed past. Jericho's eyes went straight to the picture of the chapel, which, he was relieved to note, looked undisturbed. He closed the door.

'See what you mean about the room,' said Wigram, cupping his hands to the glass to peer out of the window. 'The hell we have to go through, what? And a railway view thrown in. Bliss.' He closed the curtains and turned back to Jericho. He was cleaning his fingers on a handkerchief with almost feminine delicacy. 'We're rather worried.' His smile widened. 'We're rather worried about a girl called Claire Romilly.' He folded the blue silk square and thrust it back into his breast pocket. 'Mind if I sit down?'

He shrugged off his overcoat and laid it on the bed, then hitched up his pinstriped trousers a fraction at the knees to avoid damaging the crease. He sat on the edge of the mattress and bounced up and down experimentally. His hair was blond; so were his eyebrows, his eyelashes, the hairs on the back of his neat white hands . . . Jericho felt his skin prickle with fear and disgust.

Wigram patted the eiderdown beside him. 'Let's talk.' He didn't seem the least put out when Jericho stayed where he was. He merely folded his hands contentedly in his lap.

'All right,' he said, 'we'll make a start, then, shall we? Claire Romilly. Twenty. Clerical grade staff. Officially missing for –' he looked at his watch '– twelve hours. Failed to show for her morning shift. Actually, when you start to check, not seen since midnight, Friday – dear oh dear, that's nearly two days ago now – when she left the Park after work. Alone. The girl she lives with swears she hasn't seen her since Thursday. Her father says he hasn't seen her since before Christmas. Nobody else – girls she works with, family, so forth – nobody seems to have the foggiest. Vanished.' Wigram snapped his fingers. 'Just like that.' For the first time he'd stopped smiling. 'Rather a good friend of yours, I gather?'

'I haven't seen her since the beginning of February. Is this why there are police outside?'

'But good enough? Good enough that you've *tried* to see her? Out to her cottage last night, according to our little Miss Wallace. Scurry, scurry. Questions, questions. Then, this morning, into Hut 3 – questions, questions, again. Phone call to her father – oh, yes,' he said, noticing Jericho's surprise, 'he rang us straight away to say you'd called. You've never met Ed Romilly? Lovely bloke. Never achieved his full potential, so they say. Rather lost the plot after his wife died. Tell me, Mr Jericho, why the interest?'

'I'd been away for a month. I hadn't seen her.'

'But surely you've got plenty more important things to worry about, especially just now, than renewing one acquaintance?'

His last words were almost lost in the roar of a passing express train. The room vibrated for fifteen seconds, which was the exact duration of his smile. When the noise was over, he said: 'Were you surprised to be brought back from Cambridge?'

'Yes. I suppose I was. Look, Mr Wigram, who are you, exactly?'

'Surprised when you were told *why* you were needed back?'

'Not surprised. No.' He searched for the word. 'Shocked.'

'Shocked. Ever talk to the girl about your work?'

'Of course not.'

'Of course not. Strike you as odd, though – possibly more than a coincidence, possibly even sinister – that one day the Germans black us out in the North Atlantic and two days later the girlfriend of a leading Hut 8 cryptanalyst goes missing? Actually on the same day he comes back?'

Jericho's gaze flickered involuntarily to the print of the chapel. 'I told you. I never talked to Claire about my work. I hadn't seen her for a month. And she wasn't my girlfriend.'

'No? What was she then?'

What was she then? A good question. 'I just wanted to see her,' he said lamely. 'I couldn't find her. I was concerned.'

'Got a photo of her? Something recent?'

'No. Actually, I don't have any pictures of her.'

'Really? Now here's another funny thing. Pretty girl like that. But can we find a picture? We'll just have to use the ID copy from her Welfare file.'

'Use it for what?'

'Can you fire a gun, Mr Jericho?'

'I couldn't hit a duck at a funfair.'

'Now that's what I would have thought, though one shouldn't always judge a chap by his looks. Only the Bletchley Park Home Guard had a little burglary at their armoury on Friday night. Two items missing. A Smith and Wesson .38 revolver, manufactured in Springfield, Massachusetts, issued by the War Office last year. And a box containing thirty-six rounds of ammunition.'

Jericho said nothing. Wigram looked at him for a while, as if he were making up his mind about something. 'No reason why *you* shouldn't know, I suppose. Trustworthy fellow like you. Come and sit down.' He patted the eiderdown again. 'I can't keep shouting the biggest frigging secret in the British Empire across your frigging bedroom. Come on. I won't bite, I promise.'

Reluctantly, Jericho sat down. Wigram leaned forwards. As he did so, his jacket parted slightly, and Jericho glimpsed a flash of leather and gunmetal against the white shirt.

'You want to know who I am?' he said softly. 'I'll tell you who I am. I'm the man our masters have decreed should find out just what's what down here in your little *anus mundi*.' He was speaking so quietly, Jericho was obliged to move his head in close to hear. 'Bells are going off, you see. Horrible, horrible bells. Five days ago, Hut 6 decoded a German Army signal from the Middle East. General Rommel's becoming a bit of a bad sport. Seems to think the only reason he's losing is that somehow, by some miracle, we always appear to know where exactly he's going to attack. Suddenly, the Afrika Korps want an enquiry into cipher security. Oh dear. *Ding dong*. Twelve hours later, Admiral Dönitz, for reasons as yet unknown, suddenly decides to tighten Enigma procedure by changing the U-boat weather code. *Ding dong* again. Today, it's the Luftwaffe. Four German merchant ships loaded with goodies for the aforementioned Rommel were recently "surprised" by the RAF and sunk halfway to Tunisia. This morning, we read that the German C-in-C, Mediterranean, Field Marshal Kesselring himself, no less, is demanding to know whether the enemy could have read his codes.' Wigram patted Jericho's knee. 'Peals of alarms, Mr Jericho. A Westminster-Abbey-on-Coronation-Day peal of alarms. And in the middle of them all, your lady friend disappears, at the same time as a shiny new shooter and a box of bullets.'

'Exactly who or what are we dealing with here?' said Wigram. He had taken out a small black leather notebook and a gold propelling pencil. 'Claire Alexandra Romilly. Born: London, twenty-first of the twelfth, 'twenty-two. Father: Edward Arthur Macauley Romilly, diplomat. Mother: the Honourable Alexandra Romilly, *née* Harvey, deceased in motor accident, Scotland, August 'twenty-nine. The child is educated privately abroad. Father's postings: Bucharest, 'twenty-eight to 'thirty-one; Berlin, 'thirty-one to 'thirty-four; Washington, 'thirty-four to 'thirty-eight. A year in Athens, then back to London. The girl by now is at some fancy finishing school in Geneva. She returns to London on the outbreak of war, aged seventeen. Principal occupation for the next three years, as far as one can gather: having a good time.' Wigram licked his finger and turned the page. 'Some voluntary civil defence work. Nothing too arduous. July 'forty-one:

translator at the Ministry of Economic Warfare. August 'forty-two: applies for clerical position, Foreign Office. Good languages. Recommended for position at Bletchley Park. See attached letter from father, blah, blah. Interviewed 10th of September. Accepted, cleared, starts work the following week.' Wigram flicked the pages back and forth. 'That's the lot. Not exactly a rigorous process of selection, is it? But then she does come from a *frightfully* good family. And Papa *does* work down at head office. And there *is* a war on. Care to add anything to the record?'

'I don't think I can.'

'How'd you meet her?'

For the next ten minutes Jericho answered Wigram's questions. He did this carefully and – mostly – truthfully. Where he lied it was only by omission. They had gone to a concert for their first date. After that they had gone out in the evenings a few times. They had seen a picture. Which one? *In Which We Serve.*

'Like it?'

'Yes.'

'I'll tell Noël.'

She had never talked about politics. She had never discussed her work. She had never mentioned other friends.

'Did you sleep with her?'

'Mind your own bloody business.'

'I'll put that down as yes.'

More questions. No, he had noticed nothing odd about her behaviour. No, she had not seemed tense or nervous, secretive, silent, aggressive, inquisitive, moody, depressed or elated – no, none of these – and at the end, they hadn't quarrelled. Really? No. So they had . . . what, then?

'I don't know. Drifted apart.'

'She was seeing someone else?'

'Perhaps. I don't know.'

'Perhaps. You don't know.' Wigram shook his head in wonder. 'Tell me about last night.'

'I cycled over to her cottage.'

'What time?'

'About ten, ten-thirty. She wasn't there. I talked with Miss Wallace for a bit. Then I came home.'

'Mrs Armstrong says she didn't hear you come in until around two o'clock this morning.'

So much for tiptoeing past her door, thought Jericho.

'I must have cycled around for a while.'

'I'll say you did. In the frost. In the blackout. You must have cycled around for about three hours.'

Wigram gazed down at his notes, tapping the side of his nose. 'Not right, Mr Jericho. Can't quite put my finger on it, but definitely *not right*. Still.' He snapped the notebook shut and gave a reassuring smile. 'Time to go into all that later, what?' He put his hand on Jericho's knee and pushed himself to his feet. 'First, we must catch our rabbit. You've no idea where she might be, I suppose? No favourite haunts? No little den to run to?' He gazed down at Jericho, who was staring at the floor. 'No? No. Thought not.'

By the time Jericho felt he could trust himself to look up again, Wigram had draped his beautiful over-coat back around his shoulders and was preoccupied

ROBERT HARRIS

picking tiny pieces of lint from its collar.

'It could all be a coincidence,' said Jericho. 'You do realise that? I mean, Dönitz always seems to have been suspicious about Enigma. That's why he gave the U-boats Shark in the first place.'

'Oh absolutely,' said Wigram cheerfully. 'But let's look at it another way. Let's imagine the Germans *have* got a whisper of what we're up to here. What would they do? They couldn't exactly chuck out a hundred thousand Enigma machines overnight, could they? And then what about all those experts of theirs, who've always said Enigma is unbreakable? They're not going to change their minds without a fight. No. They'd do what they look as though they might be doing. They'd start checking every suspicious incident. And in the meantime, they'd try and find hard proof. A person, perhaps. Better still, a person with documentary evidence. God, there are enough of them about. Thousands right here, who either know all the story, or a bit of it, or enough to put two and two together. And what kind of people are they?' He withdrew a sheet of paper from his inside pocket and unfolded it. 'This is the list I asked for yesterday. Eleven people in the Naval Section knew about the importance of the Weather Code Book. Some rum names here, if you stop to think about them. Skynner we can exclude, I suppose. And Logie – he seems sound enough. But Baxter? Now Baxter's a communist, isn't he?'

'I think you'll find that communists don't have much time for Nazis. As a rule.'

'What about Pukowski?'

240

'Puck lost his father and his brother when Poland was invaded. He loathes the Germans.'

'The American, then. Kramer. *Kramer*? He's a second-generation German immigrant, did you know that?'

'Kramer also lost a brother to the Germans. Really, Mr Wigram, this is ridiculous . . .'

'Atwood. Pinker. Kingcome. Proudfoot. de Brooke. *You* . . . Who *are* you all, exactly?' Wigram looked around the tiny room with distaste: the frayed blackout curtains, the tatty wardrobe, the lumpy bed. For the first time he seemed to notice the print of the chapel above the mantelpiece. 'I mean, just because a bloke's been to King's College, Cambridge . . .'

He picked up the picture and held it at an angle under the light. Jericho watched him, transfixed.

'E. M. Forster,' said Wigram thoughtfully. 'Now he's still at King's, isn't he?'

'I believe so.'

'Know him?'

'Only to nod to.'

'What was that essay of his? How did it go? The one about choosing between your friend and your country?'

'"I hate the idea of causes, and if I had to choose between betraying my country and betraying my friend, I hope I should have the guts to betray my country." But he did write that before the war.'

Wigram blew some dust off the frame and set the print carefully back on the top of Jericho's books.

'So I should hope,' he said, standing back to admire it. He turned and smiled at Jericho. 'So I should frigging well hope.'

After Wigram had gone, it was some minutes before Jericho felt able to move.

He lay full length on the bed, still wearing his scarf and overcoat, and listened to the sounds of the house. Some mournful string quartet which the BBC judged suitable entertainment for a Sunday night was scraping away downstairs. There were footsteps on the landing. A whispered conversation ensued which ended with a woman – Miss Jobey, was it? – having a fit of the giggles. A door slammed. The cistern above his head emptied and refilled. Then silence again.

When he did move, after about a quarter of an hour, his actions had a frantic, fumbling haste. He carried the chair over from the bedside to the door and tilted it against the flimsy panelling. He took the print and laid it face down on the threadbare carpet, pulled out the tacks, lifted off the back, rolled the intercepts into a tube, and took them over to the grate. On top of the little bucket of coal beside the hearth was a matchbox containing two matches. The first was damp and wouldn't strike but the second did, just, and Jericho twisted it round to make sure the yellow flame caught and grew, then he applied it to the bottom of the intercepts. He held on to them as they writhed and blackened until the very last moment, until the pain obliged him to drop them in the grate, where they disintegrated into tiny flakes of ash.

FIVE

CRIB

CRIB: a piece of evidence (usually
a captured code book or a length
of plaintext) which provides clues
for the breaking of a cryptogram;
'without question, the crib . . .
is the single most essential tool
of any cryptanalyst' (Knox
et al., op. cit., page 27).

A Lexicon of Cryptography
('Most Secret', Bletchley Park, 1943)

1

THE WARTIME LIPSTICK was hard and waxy – it was like trying to colour your lips with a Christmas candle. When, after several minutes of hard rubbing, Hester Wallace replaced her glasses, she peered into the mirror with distaste. Make-up had never featured much in her life, not even before the war, when there had been plenty in the shops. But now, when there was nothing to be had, the lengths one was expected to go to were quite absurd. She knew of girls in the hut who made lipstick out of beetroot and sealed it in place with Vaseline, who used shoe polish and burnt cork for mascara and margarine wrappers as a skin softener, who dusted bicarbonate of soda into their armpits to disguise their sweat . . . She formed her lips into a cupid's bow, which she immediately drew back into a grimace. Really, it was quite, quite absurd.

The shortage of cosmetics seemed to have caught up at last even with Claire. Although there was a profusion of pots and bottles all over her little dressing table – Max Factor, Coty, Elizabeth Arden: each name redolent of pre-war glamour – most of them turned out on closer inspection to be empty. Nothing was left except a trace of scent. Hester sniffed at each in turn and her mind was filled with images of luxury – of satin cocktail dresses by Worth of London and gowns with daring *décolletage*, of fireworks at Versailles and the Duchess of Westminster's summer ball, and a dozen other wonderful nonsenses that Claire had prattled on about. Eventually she found a half-full pot of mascara and a glass-stoppered jar with an inch of rather lumpy face powder and set to work with those.

She had no qualms about helping herself. Hadn't Claire always told her she should? Making-up was fun, that was Claire's philosophy, it made one feel good about oneself, it turned one into someone else, and, besides, '*if this is what it takes, then, darling heart, this is simply what one does*'. Very well. Hester dabbed grimly at her pallid cheeks. If *this* was what it bloody well *took* to help persuade Miles Mermagen to approve a transfer, this was what he'd bloody well *get*.

She regarded her reflection without enthusiasm, then carefully replaced everything in its proper place and went downstairs. The sitting room was freshly swept. Daffodils above the hearth. A fire laid. The kitchen, too, was spotless. She had made a carrot flan earlier in the evening, enough for two, with ingredients she had grown herself in the little vegetable patch outside the kitchen door, and now she laid a place for Claire, and left a note telling her where to find the flan and instructions on how to heat it. She hesitated, then added at the end: 'Welcome back – from wherever you've been! – much love, H.' She hoped it didn't sound too fussy and inquisitive; she hoped she wasn't turning into her mother.

'ADU, *Miss Wallace* . . .'

Of course Claire would come back. It was all a stupid panic, too absurd for words.

She sat in one of the armchairs and waited for her until a quarter to midnight, when she dared leave it no longer.

As her bicycle bounced along the track towards the lane she startled a white owl which rose silently like a ghost in the moonlight.

In a way it was all Miss Smallbone's fault. If Angela Smallbone hadn't pointed out in the common room after prep that the *Daily Telegraph* was holding a crossword competition, then Hester Wallace's life would have gone on undisturbed. It was not a particularly thrilling life – a placid, provincial life in a remote and eccentric girls' preparatory school near the Dorset town of Beaminster, less than ten miles from where Hester had grown up. And it was not a life much touched by war, either, save for the pale faces of the evacuee children on some of the nearby farms, the barbed wire along the beach near Lyme Regis, and the chronic shortage of teaching staff – a shortage which meant that when the Michaelmas term began in the autumn of 1942, Hester was having to take divinity (her usual subject) *and* English *and* some Latin and Greek.

Hester had a gift for crosswords and when Angela read out that night that the prize-money was twenty pounds . . . well, she thought, why not? The first hurdle, an abnormally difficult puzzle printed in the next day's paper, she passed with ease. She sent off her solution and a letter arrived almost by return of post inviting her to the final, to be held in the *Telegraph's* staff canteen, a fortnight hence, a Saturday. Angela agreed to take over hockey practice, Hester caught the train from Crewkerne up to London, joined fifty other finalists – and won. She completed the crossword in three minutes and twenty-two seconds and Lord Camrose himself presented her with the cheque. She gave five pounds to her father for his church restoration fund, she spent seven pounds on a new winter coat (second-hand, actually, but good as new), and the rest she put in her Post Office savings account.

It was on the Thursday that the second letter had arrived, this one very different. Registered post, long buff envelope. On His Majesty's Service.

Afterwards, she could never quite decide. Had the *Telegraph* held the competition at the instigation of the War Office, as a way of trawling the country for men and women with an aptitude for word puzzles? Or had some bright spark at the War Office merely seen the results of the competition and asked the *Telegraph* for a list of the finalists? Whatever the truth, five of the most suitable were summoned to be interviewed in a grim Victorian office block on the wrong side of the Thames, and three of them were ordered to report to Bletchley.

The school hadn't wanted her to go. Her mother had cried. Her father had detested the idea, just as he detested all change, and for days beforehand he was filled with foreboding ('He shall return no more to his house, neither shall his place know him any more' Job 7.x). But the law was the law. She had to go. Besides, she thought, she was twenty-eight. Was she doomed to live out the rest of her life in the same place, tucked away in this drowsy quilt of tiny fields and honey-stoned villages? Here was her chance of escape. She had picked up enough clues at the interview to guess that the work would be codes, and her fantasies were all of quiet, book-lined libraries and the pure, clear air of the intellect.

Arriving at Bletchley station in her second-hand coat on a soaking Monday morning, she was taken straight by shooting brake to the mansion and given a copy of the Official Secrets Act to sign. The Army Captain who inducted them laid his pistol on the desk and said that if any of them, ever, breathed a word of what they were about to be told, he'd use it on them. Personally. Then they were assigned. The two male finalists became cryptanalysts, while she, the woman who had beaten them, was dispatched to a bedlam called Control.

'You take this form here, see, and in this first column you enter the code name of the intercept station. Chicksands, right, that's CKS, Beaumanor is BMR, Harpendon is HPN – don't worry, dear, you'll soon get used to it. Now here, see, you put the time of interception, here frequency, here call sign, here number of letter groups . . .'

Her fantasies were dust. She was a glorified clerk, Control a glorified funnel between the intercept stations and the cryptanalysts, a funnel down which poured the ceaseless output of some forty thousand different radio call signs, using more than sixty separately identified Enigma keys.

'German Air Force, right, they're usually either

insects or flowers. So you've got Cockroach, say, that's the Enigma key for western fighters, based in France. Dragonfly is Luftwaffe in Tunis. Locust is Luftwaffe, Sicily. You've got a dozen of those. Your flowers are the Luftgau – Foxglove: eastern front, Daffodil: western front, Narcissus: Norway. Birds are for the German Army. Chaffinch and Phoenix, they're Panzerarmee Afrika. Kestrel and Vulture – Russian front. Sixteen little birdies. Then there's Garlic, Onion, Celery – all the vegetables are weather Enigmas. They go straight to Hut 10. Got it?'

'What are Skunk and Porcupine?'

'Skunk is Fliegerkorps VIII, eastern front. Porcupine is ground-air cooperation, southern Russia.'

'Why aren't they insects as well?'

'God knows.'

The charts they had to fill in were called either 'blists' or 'hankies', the filing cabinet for miscellaneous trivia was known as Titicaca ('an Andes lake fed by many rivers,' said Mermagen portentously, 'but with no outflow'). The men gave one another silly names – 'the Unicorn-Zebra', 'the Mock Turtle' – while the girls mooned after the handsomer cryptanalysts in the Machine Room. Sitting in the freezing hut that winter, compiling her endless lists, Hester had a sense of Nazi Germany only as an endless, darkened plain, with thousands of tiny, isolated lights, flickering at one another in the blackness. Oddly enough, she thought, it was all, in its way, as remote from the war as the meadows and thatched barns of Dorset.

*

She parked her bicycle in the shed beside the canteen and was borne along by the stream of workers to be deposited near the entrance to Hut 6. Control was already in a fine state of uproar, Mermagen bustling self-importantly between the desks, knocking his head against the low-hanging lampshades, sending pools of yellow light spilling crazily in all directions. Fourth Panzer Army was reporting the successful recapture of Kharkov from the Russians and the ninnies in Hut 3 were demanding that *every* frequency in the southern sector, eastern front, be double-backed *immediately*.

'Hester, Hester, just in time. Will you talk to Chicksands, there's a good girl, and see what they can do? And while you're on, the Machine Room reckon they've got a corrupt text on the last batch of Kestrel – the operator needs to check her notes and re-send. Then the eleven o'clock from Beaumanor all need blisting. Grab someone to help you. Oh, and the Index could do with a sorting out.'

All this before she had even taken off her coat.

It was two o'clock before there was enough of a lull for her to get away and talk to Mermagen in private. He was in his broom-cupboard office, his feet up on the desk, studying a handful of papers through half-closed eyes, in a terrific man-of-destiny pose she guessed he'd copied from some actor in the pictures.

'I wondered if I might have a word, Miles.'

Miles. She found this insistence on first-name terms a tiresome affectation, but informality was a rigid rule, an essential part of the Bletchley ethos: *we*, the civilian amateurs shall defeat *them*, the disciplined Hun.

Mermagen continued to study his papers.

She tapped her foot. 'Miles?'

He flicked over a page. 'You have my completely divided attention.'

'My request for a transfer –'

He groaned and turned over another page. 'Not that again.'

'I've been learning German –'

'How brave.'

'You did say that *not* having German made a transfer impossible.'

'Yes, but I didn't say that *having* it made a transfer *likely*. Oh, bloody hell! Well, come in, then.'

With a sigh he put aside his papers and beckoned her over the threshold. Someone must have told him once that Brylcreem made him look racy. His oily black hair, swept back off his forehead and behind his ears, glistened like a swimmer's cap. He was trying to grow a Clark Gable moustache but it was slightly too long on the left-hand side.

'Transfers of personnel from section to section are, as I've told you before, extremely rare. We do have security to consider.'

Security to consider: this must have been how he turned down loans before the war. Suddenly he was staring at her intently and she realised he had noticed the make-up. He couldn't have looked more startled if she'd painted herself with woad. His voice seemed to drop an octave.

'Look here, Hester, the last thing I want is to be difficult. What you need is a change of scene for a day or two.' He touched his moustache lightly and gave a faint smile of recognition, as if he were surprised to find it still in place. 'Why don't you go up and take a look round one of the intercept stations, get a feel for where you fit into the chain? I know,' he added, 'I could do with a refresher myself. We could go up together.'

'Together? Yes . . . Why not? And find a little pub somewhere we could stop off for lunch?'

'Excellent. Make a real break of it.'

'Possibly a pub with rooms, so we could stay overnight if it got late?'

He laughed nervously. 'I still couldn't guarantee a transfer, you know.'

'But it would help?'

'Your words.'

'Miles?'

'Mmmm?'

'I'd rather die.'

'Frigid little bitch.'

She filled the basin with cold water and splashed her face furiously. The icy water numbed her hands and stung her face. It trickled down inside the neck of her shirt and up the sleeves. She welcomed the shock and the discomfort. She deserved it as a punishment for her folly and delusion.

She pressed her flat stomach against the edge of the basin and stared myopically at the chalk-white face in the mirror.

Useless to complain, of course. It was her word against his. She would never be believed. And even if she was – so what? My dear, it was *simply* the way of the world. Miles could ram her up against Lake bloody Titicaca if he liked, and put his hand up her skirt, and they'd still never let her go: nobody, once they'd seen as much as she had, was ever allowed to leave.

She felt a pricking of self-pity in the corners of her eyes and immediately lowered her head back over the basin and drenched her face, scrubbing at her cheeks and mouth with a sliver of carbolic soap until the powder stained the water pink.

She wished she could talk to Claire.

'*ADU, Miss Wallace . . .*'

Behind her in the cubicle the toilet flushed. Hurriedly, she pulled the plug out of the basin and dried her face and hands.

Name of intercept station, time of interception, frequency, call sign, letter groups . . . Name of intercept station, time of interception, frequency, call sign, letter groups . . .

Hester's hand moved mechanically across the paper.

At four o'clock the first half of the night-shift began drifting off to the canteen.

'Coming, Hetty?'

'Too much to do, unfortunately. I'll catch you up.'

'Poor you!'

'Poor you and *bloody* Miles,' said Beryl McCann, who had been to bed with Mermagen, once, and wished to God she hadn't.

Hester bent her head lower over her desk and continued to write in her careful schoolmistress copperplate. She watched the other women putting on their coats and filing out, their shoes clumping on the wooden floor. Ah, but Claire had been so *funny* about them. It was one of the things Hester loved in her the most, the way she mimicked everyone: Anthea Leigh-Delamere, the huntswoman, who liked to come on shift in jodhpurs; Binnie with the waxy skin who wanted to be a Catholic nun; the girl from Solihull who held the telephone a foot away from her mouth because her mother had told her the receiver was full of germs . . . As far as Hester knew, Claire had never even *met* Miles Mermagen, yet she could impersonate him to perfection. The ghastliness of Bletchley had been their shared and private joke, their conspiracy against the bores.

The opening of the outside door let in a sudden blast of freezing air. Blists and hankies rustled and fluttered in the chill.

Bores. Boring. Claire's favourite words. The Park was boring. The war was boring. The town was *terrifically* boring. And the men were the biggest bores of all. The men – my God, what scent was it she gave off? – there were always two or three of them at least, hanging round her like tomcats on heat. And how she mocked them, on those precious evenings when she and Hester were alone together, sitting companionably by the fireside like an old married couple. She mocked their clumsy fumblings, their corny dialogue, their absurd self-importance. The only man she didn't mock, now Hester came to think of it, was the curious Mr Jericho, whom she had never even mentioned.

'*ADU, Miss Wallace . . .*'.

Now that she had made up her mind to do it – and hadn't she always *known*, secretly, that she was going to do it? – she was astonished at how calm she felt. It would only be the briefest of glances, she told herself, and where was the harm in that? She even had the perfect excuse to slip across to the Index, for hadn't the beastly Miles, in everybody's hearing, commanded her to ensure the volumes were all arranged in proper order?

She finished the blist and slotted it into the rack. She forced herself to wait a decent interval, pretending to check the others' work, and then moved as casually as she could towards the Index Room.

2

Jericho drew back the curtains to unveil another cold, clear morning. It was only his third day in the Commercial Guesthouse but already the view had acquired a weary familiarity. First came the long and narrow garden (concrete yard with washing line, vegetable patch, bomb shelter) which petered out after seventy yards into a wilderness of weeds and a tumbledown, rotted fence. Then there was a drop he couldn't see, like a ha-ha, and then a broad expanse of railway lines, a dozen or more, which led the eye, at last, to the centrepiece: a huge Victorian engine shed with LONDON MIDLAND & SCOTTISH RAILWAY in white letters just visible beneath the grime.

What a day in prospect: the sort of day one waded through with no aim higher than to reach the other end intact. He looked at his Waralarm. It was a quarter past seven. It would be dark in the North Atlantic for at least another four hours. By his reckoning there would be nothing for him to do until – at the earliest – midnight, British time, when the first elements of the convoy would begin to enter the U-boat danger zone. Nothing to do except sit around the hut and wait and brood.

There had been three occasions during the night when Jericho had made up his mind to seek out Wigram and make a full confession, on the last of which he had actually got as far as putting on his coat. But in the end the judgement was too fine a one to call. On the one hand, yes, it was his duty to tell Wigram all he knew. On the other, no, what he knew would make little practical difference to the task of finding her, so why betray her? The equations cancelled one another out. By dawn he had surrendered, gratefully, to the old inertia, the product of always seeing both sides of every question.

And it could all still be some ghastly mistake – couldn't it, just? Some prank gone badly wrong? Eleven hours had passed since his conversation with Wigram. They might have found her by now. More likely, she would have turned up, either at the cottage or the hut – wide-eyed and wondering, darlings, what on earth the fuss was all about.

He was on the point of turning away from the

window when his eye was caught by a movement at the far end of the engine shed. Was it a large animal of some sort, or a big man crawling on all fours? He squinted through the sooty glass but the thing was too far away for him to make it out exactly, so he fetched his telescope from the bottom of the wardrobe. The window sash was stuck but a few heavy blows from the heel of his hand were enough to raise it six inches. He knelt and rested the telescope on the sill. At first he couldn't find anything to focus on amid the dizzying crisscross of tracks but then, suddenly, it was filling his eye – an Alsatian dog as big as a calf, sniffing under the wheels of a goods wagon. He shifted the telescope a fraction to his left and there was a policeman dressed in a greatcoat that came down below his knees. Two policemen, in fact, and a second dog, on a leash.

He watched the little group for several minutes as they searched the empty train. Then the two teams split up, one passing further up the tracks and the other moving out of sight towards the little railway cottages opposite. He snapped the telescope shut.

Four men and two dogs for the railway yard. Say, a couple more teams to cover the station platforms. How many in the town? Twenty? And in the surrounding countryside?

'Got a photo of her? Something recent?'

He tapped the telescope against his cheek.

They must be watching every port and railway station in the country.

What would they do if they caught her?

Hang her?

258

Come on, Jericho. He could practically hear his housemaster's voice at his elbow. *Brace up, boy.*

Get through it somehow.

Wash. Shave. Dress. Make a little bundle of dirty laundry and leave it on the bed for Mrs Armstrong, more in hope than expectation. Go downstairs. Endure attempts to make polite conversation. Listen to one of Bonnyman's interminable, off-colour stories. Be introduced to two of the other guests: Miss Quince, rather pretty, a teleprincess in the naval hut, and Noakes, once an expert on Middle High German court epics, now a cryptanalyst in the weather section, vaguely known since 1940: a surly creature, then and now. Avoid all further conversation. Chew toast as stale as cardboard. Drink tea as grey and watery as a February sky. Half-listen to the wireless news: 'Moscow Radio reports the Russian Third Army under General Vatutin is making a strong defence of Kharkov in the face of the renewed German offensive . . .'

At ten to eight Mrs Armstrong came in with the morning post. Nothing for Mr Bonnyman ('thank God for that,' said Bonnyman), two letters for Miss Jobey, a postcard for Miss Quince, a bill from Heffers bookshop for Mr Noakes and nothing at all for Mr Jericho – oh, except this, which she'd found when she came down and which must have been put through the door some time in the night.

He held it carefully. The envelope was poor-quality, official-issue stuff, his name printed on it in blue ink, with 'By hand, Strictly Personal' added underneath and double-underlined. The 'e' in Jericho and in

'Personal' was in the Greek form. His nocturnal correspondent was a classicist, perhaps?

He took it into the hall to open, Mrs Armstrong at his heels.

Hut 6
4.45 A.M.

Dear Mr Jericho,

As you expressed such a strong interest in medieval alabaster figurework when we met yesterday, I wondered if you might care to join me at the same place at 8 this morning to view the altar tomb of Lord Grey de Wilton (15th cent. and really *very fine*)?

Sincerely,

H.A.W.

'Bad news, Mr Jericho?' She couldn't quite suppress the note of hope in her voice.

But Jericho was already dragging on his overcoat and was halfway out of the door.

Even after taking the hill at a fast trot he was still five minutes late by the time he passed the granite war memorial. There was no sign of her or anyone else in the graveyard so he tried the door to the church. At first he thought it was locked. It took both hands to turn the rusty iron ring. He put his shoulder to the weathered oak and it shuddered inwards.

The church inside was cave-like, cold and dark, the shadows pierced by shafts of dusty, slate-blue light, so solid they seemed to have been propped like slabs against the windows. He hadn't been in a church for years and the chilly stink of candle wax and damp and incense brought memories of childhood crawling back. He thought he could make out the shape of a head in one of the pews nearest the altar and began to walk towards it.

'Miss Wallace?' His voice was hollow and seemed to travel a great distance. But when he came closer he saw it wasn't a head, just a priest's vestment, draped neatly over the back of the pew. He passed on up the nave to the wood-panelled altar. To the left was a stone coffin with an inscription; next to it, the smooth, white effigy of Richard, Lord Grey de Wilton, dead these past five hundred years, reclining in full armour, his head resting on his helmet, his feet on the back of a lion.

'The armour is especially interesting. But then warfare in the fifteenth century was the highest occupation for a gentleman.'

He wasn't sure where she'd come from. She was simply there when he turned round, about ten feet behind him.

'And the face, I think, is also good, if unexceptional. You weren't followed, I trust?'

'No. I don't think so, no.'

She took a few steps towards him. With her dead complexion and tapering white fingers she might have been an alabaster effigy herself, climbed down from Lord Grey's tomb.

'Perhaps you noticed the royal arms above the north door?'

'How long have you been here?'

'The arms of Queen Anne, but, intriguingly, still of the Stuart pattern. The arms of Scotland were only added as late as 1707. Now that *is* rare. About ten minutes. The police were just leaving as I arrived.' She held out her hand. 'May I have my note back, please?'

When he hesitated she presented her palm to him again, more emphatically this time.

'The *note*, please, if you'd be so good. I'd prefer to leave no trace. Thank you.' She took it and stowed it away at the bottom of her voluminous carpet bag. Her hands were shaking so much she had trouble fastening the clasp. 'There's no need to whisper, by the way. We're quite alone. Apart from God. And He's supposed to be on our side.'

He knew it would be wise for him to wait, to let her come to it in her own time, but he couldn't help himself.

'You've checked it?' he said. 'The call sign?'

She finally snapped the bag shut. 'Yes. I've checked it.'

'And is it Army or Luftwaffe?'

She held up a finger. 'Patience, Mr Jericho. Patience. First there's some information I'd like from you, if you don't mind. We might begin with what made you choose those three letters.'

'You don't want to know, Miss Wallace. Believe me.'

She raised her eyes to heaven. 'God preserve me: another one.'

'I'm sorry?'

'I seem to move in an endless round, Mr Jericho, from one patronising male to another, for ever being told what I am and am not allowed to know. Well, that ends here.' She pointed to the flagstone floor.

'Miss Wallace,' said Jericho, catching the same tone of cool formality, 'I came in answer to your note. I have no interest in alabaster figurework – medieval, Victorian or ancient Chinese, come to that. If you've nothing else to tell me, good morning to you.'

'Then good morning.'

'Good morning.'

If he'd had a hat he would have raised it.

He turned and began his progress down the aisle towards the door. You fool, said a voice at his inner ear, you bloody conceited fool. By the time he'd gone half way his pace had slowed and by the time he reached the font he stopped. His shoulders sagged.

'Checkmate, I believe, Mr Jericho,' she called cheerfully from beside the altar.

'ADU was the call sign on a series of four intercepts our . . . mutual friend . . . stole from Hut 3.' His voice was weary.

'How do you know she stole them?'

'They were hidden in her bedroom. Under the floorboards. As far as I know, we're not encouraged to take our work home.'

'Where are they now?'

'I burned them.'

They were sitting in the second row of pews, side by side, facing straight ahead. Anyone coming into the church would have thought it was a confession – she playing the priest and he the sinner.

'Do you think she's a spy?'

'I don't know. Her behaviour is suspicious, to put it charitably. Others seem to think she is.'

'Who?'

'A man from the Foreign Office called Wigram, for one.'

'Why?'

'Obviously because she's disappeared.'

'Oh, come. There must be more to it than that. All this fuss for one missed shift?'

He ran his hand nervously through his hair.

'There are . . . indications – and don't, for God's sake, ask me to tell you what they are – just indications, all right, that the Germans may suspect Enigma is being broken.'

A long pause.

'But why would our mutual friend wish to help the *Germans*?'

'If I knew that, Miss Wallace, I wouldn't be sitting here with you, passing the time of day breaking the Official Secrets Act. Now, really, please, have you heard enough?'

Another pause. A reluctant nod of the head.

'Enough.'

She told it like story, in a low voice, without looking at him. She used her hands a lot, he noticed. She couldn't keep them still. They fluttered like tiny white birds – now pecking at the hem of her coat, pulling it demurely across her knees, now perching on the back of the pew in front, now describing, in rapid, circling motions, how she had gone about her crime.

She waits until the other girls have gone off on their meal break.

She leaves the door to the Index Room open a fraction, so as not to look suspicious and to ensure a good warning of anyone's approach.

She reaches up to the dusty metal shelf and drags down the first volume.

AAA, AAB, AAC . . .

She flicks through to the tenth page.

And there it is. The thirteenth entry.

ADU.

She runs her finger along the line to the row and column entries and notes their numbers on a scrap of paper.

She puts the index volume back. The row ledger is on a higher shelf and she has to fetch a stool to get it.

She stops off on her way to bob her head around the door and check the corridor.

Deserted.

Now she is nervous. Why? she asks herself. What is she doing that's so terribly wrong? She smooths her hands down over her grey skirt to dry her palms, then opens the book. She turns the pages. She finds the number. Again, she follows the line across.

She checks it once, and then a second time. There's no mistake.

ADU is the call sign of *Nachrichten-Regimenter* 537 – a motorised German Army signals unit. Its transmissions are on wavelengths monitored by the

Beaumanor intercept station in Leicestershire. Direction-finding has established that, since October, Unit number 537 has been based in the Smolensk military district of the Ukraine, presently occupied by Wehrmacht Army Group Centre under the command of Field Marshal Gunther von Kluge.

Jericho had been leaning forwards in anticipation. Now he drew back in surprise. 'A signals unit?'

He felt obscurely disappointed. What exactly had he been expecting? He wasn't sure. Just something a little more . . . *exotic*, he supposed.

'537,' he said, 'is that a front-line unit?'

'The line in that sector is shifting every day. But according to the situation map in Hut 6, Smolensk is still about a hundred kilometres inside German territory.'

'Ah.'

'Yes. That was my reaction – at first, anyway. I mean, this is a standard, rear-echelon, low-priority target. This is workaday in the extreme. But there are several . . . complications.' She fished in her bag for a handkerchief and blew her nose. Again, Jericho observed the slight trembling of her fingers.

After replacing the row volume it is the work of less than a minute to pull down the appropriate column book and make a note of the intercept serial numbers.

When she comes out of the Index Room, Miles ('that's Miles Mermagen,' she adds in parenthesis, 'Control Room duty officer: a bear of *very* little brain')

Miles is on the telephone, his back to the door, oiling up to someone in authority – 'No, no, that's absolutely fine, Donald, a pleasure to be of service . . .' – which suits Hester beautifully for it means he never even notices her collect her coat and leave. She clicks on her blackout torch and steps out into the night.

A gust of wind swirls down the alley between the huts and buffets her face. At the far end of Hut 8 the path forks: right will take her to the main gate and the warm bustle of the canteen, left leads into the blackness along the edge of the lake.

She turns left.

The moon is wrapped in a tissue of cloud but the pale light is just luminous enough to show her the way. Beyond the eastern perimeter fence lies a small wood which she can't see, but the sound of the wind moving through the invisible trees seems to pull her on. Past A- and B-Blocks, two hundred and fifty yards, and there it is, straight ahead, faintly outlined: the big, squat, bunkerlike building, only just completed, that now houses Bletchley's central Registry. As she comes closer her torch flashes on steel-shuttered windows, then finds the heavy door.

Thou shalt not steal, she tells herself, reaching for the handle.

No, no. Of course not.

Thou shalt not steal, thou wilt merely take a quick look, and then depart.

And, in any case, don't 'the secret things belong unto the Lord our God' (Deuteronomy 29.xxix)?

The rawness of the white neon is a shock after the

gloom of the hut, and so is the calm, ruffled only by the distant clatter of the Hollerith punch-card machines. The workmen still haven't finished. Brushes and tools are stacked to one side of a reception area that is thick with the smell of building work – fresh concrete, wet paint, wood-shavings. The duty clerk, a corporal in the Women's Auxiliary Air Force, leans across the counter in a friendly way as if she is serving in a shop.

'Cold night?'

'Rather.' Hester manages to smile and nod. 'I've got some serials to check.'

'Reference or loan?'

'Reference.'

'Section?'

'Hut 6 Control.'

'Pass?'

The woman takes the list of numbers and disappears into a back room. Through the open door Hester can see stacks of metal shelving, infinite rows of cardboard files. A man strolls past the doorway and takes down one of the boxes. He stares at her. She looks away. On the whitewashed wall is a poster, a Bateman cartoon showing a woman sneezing, accompanied by some typical, fatuous Whitehall busybodying:

THE MINISTRY OF HEALTH says:-
Coughs and sneezes spread diseases
Trap the germs by using your handkerchief
Help to keep the Nation Fighting Fit

There is nowhere to sit. Behind the counter is a large

clock with 'RAF' stamped on its face – so large, in fact, that Hester can actually see the big hand moving. Four minutes pass. Five minutes. The Registry is unpleasantly hot. She can feel herself starting to sweat. The stench of paint is nauseating. Seven minutes. Eight minutes. She would like to flee, but the corporal has taken her identity card. Dear God, how could she have been so utterly stupid? What if the clerk is now on the phone to Hut 6, checking up on her? At any instant, Miles will come crashing into the Registry: 'What the hell d'you think you're doing, woman?' Nine minutes. Ten minutes. Try to focus on something else. Coughs and sneezes spread diseases . . .

She's in such a state, she actually fails to hear the clerk come up behind her.

'I'm sorry to have been so long, but I've never come across anything like this . . .'

The girl, poor thing, is rather shaken.

'Why?' asked Jericho.

'The file,' said Hester. 'The file I'd asked her for? It was empty.'

There was a loud metallic crack behind them and then a series of short scrapes as the church door was pushed open. Hester closed her eyes and dropped to her knees on one of the cassocks, tugging Jericho down beside her. She clasped her hands and lowered her head and he did the same. Footsteps came halfway up the aisle behind them, stopped, and then resumed slowly on tiptoe. Jericho glanced surreptitiously to his left in time to see the elderly priest bending to retrieve his vestment.

'Sorry to interrupt your prayers,' whispered the vicar. He gave Hester a little wave and a nod. 'Hello there. So sorry. I'll leave you to God.'

They listened to his fussy tread fading towards the back of the church. The door was tugged shut. The latch fell with a crash. Jericho sat back on the pew and laid his hand over his heart and swore he could feel it beating through four layers of clothing. He looked at Hester – 'I'll leave you to *God*?' he repeated – and she smiled. The change it wrought in her was remarkable. Her eyes shone, the hardness in her face softened – and for the first time he briefly glimpsed the reason why she and Claire might have been friends.

Jericho contemplated the stained-glass window above the altar and made a steeple of his fingers. 'So what exactly are we to make of this? That Claire must have stolen the entire contents of the file? No –' he contradicted himself immediately ' – no, that can't be right, can it, because what she had in her room were the original cryptograms, not the decodes . . .?'

'Precisely,' said Hester. 'There was a typewritten slip in the Registry file which the clerk showed me – words to the effect that the enclosed serial numbers had been reclassified and withdrawn, and that all enquires should be addressed to the office of the Director-General.'

'The *Director-General*? Are you sure?'

'I *can* read, Mr Jericho.'

'What was the date on the slip?'

'March the 4th.'

Jericho massaged his forehead. It was the oddest thing he'd ever heard. 'What happened after the Registry?'

'I went back to the hut and wrote my note to you. Delivering that took the rest of my meal break. Then it was a matter of getting back into the Index Room whenever I could. We deep a daily log of all intercepts, made up from the blists. One file for each day.' Once again she rummaged in her bag and withdrew a small index-card with a list of dates and numbers. 'I wasn't sure where to start so I simply went right back to the beginning of the year and worked my way through. Nothing recorded till February the 6th. Only eleven interceptions altogether, four of which came on the final day.'

'Which was what?'

'March the 4th. The same day the file was removed from the Registry. What do you make of that?'

'Nothing. Everything. I'm still trying to imagine what a rear-echelon German signals unit could possibly say that would warrant the removal of its entire file.'

'The Director-General is who, as a matter of interest?'

'The chief of the Secret Intelligence Service. "C". I don't know his real name.' He remembered the man who had presented him with the cheque just before Christmas. A florid face and hairy country tweeds. He had looked more like a farmer than a spy master. 'Your notes,' he said, holding out his hand. 'May I?'

Reluctantly she handed him the list of interceptions. He held it towards the pale light. It certainly made a bizarre pattern. Following the initial interception, just after noon on 6 February, there had been two days of silence. Then there had been another signal at 1427 hours on the 9th. Then a gap of ten days. Then a broadcast at 1807 on the 20th, and another long gap, followed by a flurry of activity: two signals on 2 March (1639 and 1901), two on the 3rd (1118 and 1727), and finally four signals, in rapid succession, on the night of the 4th. These were the cryptograms he had taken from Claire's room. The broadcasts had begun just two days before his final conversation with Claire at the flooded clay pit. And they had ended a month later, while he was still at Cambridge, less than a week before the Shark blackout.

There was no shape to it at all.

He said: 'What Enigma key were they transmitted in? They *were* enciphered in Enigma, I take it?'

'In the Index they were catalogued as Vulture.'

'Vulture?'

'The standard Wehrmacht Enigma key for the Russian front.'

'Broken regularly?'

'Every day. As far as I know.'

'And the signals – how were they sent? They were, what, just carried on the usual military net?'

'I don't know, but I'd say almost certainly not.'

'Why?'

'There's not enough traffic, for a start. It's too irregular. And the frequency's not one I recognise. It feels to me like something rather more special – a private line, as it were. Just the two stations: a mother and a lone star. But we'd need to see the log sheets to be certain.'

'And where are they?'

'They should have been in the Registry. But when we checked we found they'd all been removed as well.'

'My, my,' murmured Jericho, 'they really have been thorough.'

'Short of tearing the sheets out of the Control Room Index, they couldn't have done much more. And *you* think *she's* behaving suspiciously? I'll have that back now, if I may.'

She took the record of the interceptions and bent forwards to hide it in her bag.

Jericho rested his head on the back of the pew and stared up at the vaulted ceiling. Special? he though. I'll say it was special, more than special for the Director-General himself to palm the entire bloody file, plus all the log sheets. There was no sense to it. He wished he weren't so damned tired. He needed to shut his study door for a day or two, sport his oak, find a good, fresh pile of clean notepaper and a set of sharpened pencils . . .

He slowly let his gaze descend to take in the rest of the church – the saints in their windows, the marble angels, the stone memorials to the respectable dead of Bletchley parish, the ropes from the belfry looped together like a hanging spider beneath the gloomy organ loft. He closed his eyes.

Claire, Claire, what have you done? Did you see something you weren't supposed to in that 'deadly dull' job of yours? Did you rescue a few scraps from the confidential waste when nobody was looking and spirit them home? And if you did that, why? And do they know you did it? Is that why Wigram's after you? Have you learned too much?

He saw her on her knees in the darkness at the foot of his bed, heard his own voice slurred with sleep – '*What on earth are you doing?*' – and her ingenuous reply: '*I'm just going through your things . . .*'

You were always looking for something, weren't you? And when I couldn't provide it, you just went on to someone else. ('*There's always someone else,*' you said: almost the last words you ever spoke to me, remember?) What is it, then, this thing you want so badly?

So many questions. He realised he was beginning to freeze. He huddled down into his coat, burying his chin in his scarf, thrusting his hands deep into his pockets. He tried to recall the images of the four cryptograms – LCNNR KDEMS LWAZA – but the letters were blurred. He had found this before. It was impossible mentally to photograph pages of gibberish: there had to be some meaning to them, some structure, to fix them in his mind.

'*A mother and a lone star . . .*'

The thick walls held a silence that seemed as old as the church itself – an oppressive silence, interrupted only occasionally by the rustling of a bird nesting in the rafters. For several minutes neither of them spoke.

Sitting on the hard bench, Jericho felt as though his bones had turned to ice, and this numbness, combined with the silence and the reliquaries everywhere and the sickly smell of incense, made him morbid. His father's funeral came to him for the second time in two days – the gaunt face in the coffin, his mother forcing him to kiss it goodbye, the cold skin beneath his lips giving off a sour reek of chemicals, like the school lab, and then the even worse stench at the crematorium.

'I need some air,' he said.

She gathered her bag and followed him down the aisle. Outside they pretended to study the tombs. To the north of the churchyard, screened by trees, was Bletchley Park. A motorcycle passed noisily down the lane towards the town. Jericho waited until the crack of its engine had dwindled to a drone in the distance and then said, almost to himself: 'The question I keep asking myself is why did she steal *cryptograms*? I mean, given what else she could have taken. If one was a spy –' Hester opened her mouth to protest and he held up his hand. 'All right, I'm not saying that she is, but if one was, surely one would want to steal proof that Enigma was being broken? What earthly use is an intercept?' He lowered himself to his haunches and ran his fingers over an inscription that had almost crumbled away. 'If only we knew more about them . . . To whom they were sent, for instance.'

'We've been over this. They've removed every trace.'

'But someone must know something,' he mused. 'For a start, someone must have broken the traffic. And someone else must have translated it.'

'Why don't you ask one of your cryptanalyst friends? You're all terrifically good chaps together, aren't you?'

'Not especially. In any case I'm afraid we're encouraged to lead quite separate lives. There *is* a man in Hut 3 who might have seen them . . .' But then he remembered Weitzman's frightened face ('*please don't ask me, I don't want to know . . .*') and he shook his head. 'No. He wouldn't help.'

'Then what a pity it is,' she said, with some asperity, 'that you burned our only clues.'

'Keeping them was too much of a risk.' He was still rubbing slowly at the stone. 'For all I knew, you might have told Wigram I'd asked you about the call sign.' He looked up at her uneasily. 'You didn't, I take it?'

'Credit me with some sense, Mr Jericho. Would I be here talking to you now?' She stamped off down the row of graves and began furiously studying an epitaph.

She regretted her sharpness almost at once. ('He that is slow to anger is better than the mighty; and he that ruleth his spirit than he that taketh a city.' Proverbs 16.xxxii.) But then, as Jericho pointed out later, when relations between them had improved sufficiently for him to risk the observation, if she hadn't lost her temper, she might never have thought of the solution.

'Sometimes,' he said, 'we need a little tension to sharpen our wits.'

She was jealous, that was the truth of it. She had thought she knew Claire as well as anyone but it was fast becoming apparent that she knew her hardly at all, scarcely better even than he did.

She shivered. There was no warmth in this March

sun. It fell on the stone tower of St Mary's as cold as light from a looking glass.

Jericho was back on his feet now, moving between the graves. She wondered whether she might have been like him if she'd been allowed to go to university. But her father wouldn't stand for it and her brother George had gone instead, as if it were God's law: men go to university, men break codes; women stay at home, women do the filing.

'Hester, Hester, just in time. Will you talk to Chicksands, there's a good girl, and see what they can do? And while you're on, the Machine Room reckon they've got a corrupt text on the last batch of Kestrel – the operator needs to check her notes and re-send. Then the eleven o'clocks from Beaumanor . . .'

She had been standing slack with defeat, gazing at a tombstone, but now she felt her body slowly coming to attention.

'The operator needs to check her notes . . .'

'Mr Jericho!'

He turned at the sound of his name to see her stumbling through the graves towards him.

It was almost ten o'clock and Miles Mermagen was combing his hair in his office, preparatory to returning to his digs, when Hester Wallace appeared at his office door.

'No,' he said, with his back to her.

'Miles, listen, I've been thinking, you were right, I've been an utter fool.'

He squinted suspiciously at her in the mirror.

'My application for a transfer – I want you to withdraw it.'

'Fine. I never submitted it.'

He returned his attention to himself. The comb slid through the thick black hair like a rake through oil.

She forced a smile. 'I was thinking about what you said, about needing to know where one fits into the chain . . .' He finished his grooming and turned his profile to the mirror, trying to look at his reflection sideways on. 'If you remember, we talked about my possibly going to an intercept station.'

'No problem.'

'I thought, well, I'm not due on shift till tomorrow afternoon – I thought I might go today.'

'Today?' He looked at his watch. 'Actually, I'm tied up, rather.'

'I *could* go on my own, Miles. And report my finding –' behind her back she dug her nails into her palm '– one evening.'

He gave her another narrowed look and she thought, No, no, really this is too obvious, even for him, but then he shrugged. 'Why not? Better call them first.' He waved his hand grandly. 'Invoke my name.'

'Thank you, Miles.'

'Lot's wife, what?' He winked. 'Pillar of salt by day, ball of fire by night . . .?'

On the way out he patted her bottom.

Thirty yards away, in Hut 8, Jericho was knocking on the door marked US NAVY LIAISON. A loud voice told him to 'come on in'.

Kramer didn't have a desk – the room wasn't big enough – just a card table with a telephone on it and wire baskets filled with papers stacked on the floor. There wasn't even a window. On one of the wooden partitions separating him from the rest of the hut he'd taped a recent photograph, torn out of *Life* magazine, showing Roosevelt and Churchill at the Casablanca conference, sitting side by side in a sunny garden. He noticed Jericho staring at it.

'When you fellers get me really down I look at it and think – well, hell, if they can do it, so can I.' He grinned. 'Got something to show you.' He opened his attaché case and pulled out a wad of papers marked MOST SECRET: ULTRA. 'Skynner finally got the order to give them me this morning. I'm supposed to get them off to Washington tonight.'

Jericho flicked through them. A mass of calculations that were half familiar, and some complex technical drawings of what looked like electronic circuitry.

Kramer said: 'The plans for the prototype four-wheel bombes.'

Jericho looked up in surprise. 'They're using valves?'

'Sure are. Gas-filled triode valves. GTIC thyatrons.'

'Good God.'

'They're calling it Cobra. The first three wheel-settings will be solved in the usual way on the existing bombes – that is, electro-mechanically. But the fourth – the *fourth* – will be solved purely electronically, using a relay rack and valves, linked to the bombe by this fat cable form, that looks like a –' Kramer cupped his hands into a circle '– well, that looks like a cobra, I guess. Using valves in sequence – that's a revolution. Never been done before. Your people say it should make the calculations a hundred times, maybe a thousand times, as fast.'

Jericho said, almost to himself: 'A Turing machine.'

'A what?'

'An electronic computer.'

'Well, whatever you want to call it. It works in theory, that's the good news. And from what they're saying, this may be just the start. It seems they're planning some kind of super-bombe, all electronic, called Colossus.'

Jericho had a sudden vision of Alan Turing, one winter afternoon, sitting cross-legged in his Cambridge study while the lamps came on outside, describing his dream of a universal calculating machine. How long ago had that been? Less than five years?

'And when will this happen?'

'That's the bad news. Even Cobra won't be operational till June.'

'But that's appalling.'

'Same old goddamn story. No components, no workshops, not enough technicians. Guess how many men are working on this thing right now, as we speak.'

'Not enough, I expect.'

Kramer held up one hand and spread his fingers close to Jericho's face. 'Five. *Five!*' He stuffed the papers back into his case and snapped the lock. 'Something's got to be done about this.' He was muttering and shaking his head. 'Got to get something moving.'

'You're going to London?'

'Right now. Embassy first. Then on across Grosvenor Square to see the admiral.'

Jericho winced with disappointment. 'I suppose you're taking your car?'

'Are you kidding. With this?' He patted the case. 'Skynner's making me go with an escort. Why?'

'I was just wondering – I know this is an awful cheek, but you said if I had a favour to ask – I was wondering if I might possibly borrow it?'

'Sure.' Kramer pulled on his overcoat. 'I'll probably be gone a couple of days. I'll show you where she's parked.' He collected his cap from the back of the door and they went out into the corridor.

By the entrance to the hut they ran into Wigram. Jericho was surprised at how unkempt he looked. He had obviously been up all night. A dusting of reddish-blond stubble glinted in the sunlight.

'Ah, the gallant lieutenant and the great cryptanalyst. I heard you two were friends.' He bowed with mock formality and said to Jericho: 'I'll need to talk to you again later, old chap.'

'Now there's a guy who gives me the creeps,' said Kramer, as they walked up the path towards the mansion. 'Had him in my room for about twenty minutes this morning, asking me questions about some girl I know.'

Jericho almost trod on his own feet.

'You know Claire Romilly?'

'There she is,' said Kramer, and for an instant Jericho thought he meant Claire but actually he was pointing to his car. 'She's still warm. The tank's full and there's a can in the back.' He fished in his pocket for the key and threw it to Jericho. 'Sure I know Claire. Doesn't everybody? Hell of a girl.' He patted Jericho on the arm. 'Have a nice trip.'

3

It was another half-hour before Jericho was able to get away.

He climbed the concrete steps to the Operations Room where he found Cave sitting alone at the end of the long table, telephones on either side of him, staring up at the Atlantic Plot. Eleven Shark signals had been intercepted since midnight, he said, none of them from the anticipated battle zone, which was bad news. Convoy HX-229 was within 150 miles of the suspected U-boat lines, steaming directly due east, full tilt towards them, at a speed of 10.5 knots. SC-122 was slightly ahead of her, to the north east. HX-229A was well back, heading north up the coast of Newfoundland. 'Nearly light,' he said, 'but the weather's getting worse, poor sods.'

Jericho left him to it and went in search, first, of Logie, who dismissed him with a wave of his pipe ('Fine, old love, you rest up, curtain rises twenty hundred'), and then of Atwood, who eventually agreed to lend him his pre-war AA touring atlas of the British Isles. ('"Roll up that map,"' he quoted wistfully, as he produced it from beneath his desk, "'it will not be wanted these ten years.'")

After that he was ready.

He sat in the front seat of Kramer's car and ran his hands over the unfamiliar controls and it occurred to him that he'd never quite got round to learning how to drive. He knew the basic principles, of course, but it must have been six or seven years since his last attempt, and that had been in his stepfather's huge and tanklike Humber – a vastly different proposition to this little Austin. Still, at least he wasn't doing anything illegal: in a country where one nowadays practically needed a permit to visit the lavatory, it was for some reason no longer necessary to have a driving licence.

He took several minutes trying to sort out clutch pedal from accelerator, handbrake from gear lever, then pulled out the choke and switched on the ignition. The car rocked and stalled. He put the gears into neutral and tried again and this time, miraculously, as his left foot lifted off the clutch, the car crawled forwards.

At the main gate he was waved down and managed to bring the car gliding to a halt. One of the sentries opened his door and he had to climb out while another got in to search the interior.

Half a minute later the barrier was rising and he was through.

He drove at a cyclist's pace along the narrow lanes towards Shenley Brook End, and it was this low speed that saved him. The plan he had agreed with Hester Wallace – assuming he could get Kramer's car – was that he would pick her up from the cottage, and he was just rounding the bend a quarter of a mile before the turning when something flashed dark in the field up ahead on the right. Immediately, he swerved up on to the verge and braked. He left the engine running then cautiously opened the door and clambered out on the running board to get a better view.

Policemen again. One moving stealthily around the edge of the field. Another half hidden in the hedge, apparently watching the road outside the cottage.

Jericho dropped back into the driver's seat and tapped his fingers on the steering wheel. He wasn't sure whether he had been seen but the sooner he got out of their range of vision the better. The gear change was stiff and it took both hands to jam the lever into reverse. The engine clanked and whined. First he nearly backed into the ditch, then he overcorrected and the car went weaving drunkenly across the road, mounted the opposite bank and stalled. It was not an elegant piece of parking but at least he was sufficiently far back around the curve for the policemen to be out of sight.

They had to have heard him, surely? At any moment one of them would come strolling down the lane to investigate, and he tried to think up some excuse for his lunatic behaviour, but the minutes passed and nobody appeared. He switched off the ignition and the only sound was birdsong.

No wonder Wigram looked so tired, he thought. He appeared to have taken over command of half the police force of the county – probably of the country, for all Jericho knew.

Suddenly, the scale of the odds stacked against them struck him as so overwhelming, he was seriously tempted to jack in the whole damn fool project. (*We must go to the intercept station, Mr Jericho — go to Beaumanor and get hold of the operator's handwritten notes. They keep them for at least a month and they'll never have dreamed of removing those — I'll take a wager on it. Only we poor drones have anything to do with them.*) Indeed, he might well have turned the car round that very minute and driven back to Bletchley if there hadn't been a loud tapping noise at the window to his left. He must have jumped a full inch in his seat.

It was Hester Wallace, although at first he didn't recognise her. She had exchanged her skirt and blouse for a heavy tweed jacket and a thick sweater. A pair of brown corduroy trousers were tucked into the tops of grey woollen socks, and her stout boots were so clogged with mud they seemed the size of a carthorse's hooves. She hefted her bulging carpetbag into the back of the Austin and sank down low in the passenger seat. She gave a long sigh of relief.

'Thank God. I thought I'd missed you.'

He leaned over and closed the door very quietly.

'How many are there?'

'Six. Two in the fields opposite. Two going from house to house in the village. Two in the cottage — one upstairs, dusting Claire's bedroom for fingerprints, and a policewoman downstairs. I told her I was going out. She tried to stop me but I said it was my one day off this week and I'd do as I pleased. I left by the back door and worked my way round to the road.'

'Did anybody see you?'

'I don't think so.' She blew warmth on her hands and rubbed them. 'I suggest we drive, Mr Jericho. And don't go back into Bletchley, whatever you do. I overheard them talking. They're stopping all cars on the main road out of town.'

She slid further down the seat so that she was invisible from outside the car unless someone came right up to the window. Jericho turned on the engine and the Austin rolled forwards. If they couldn't go back to Bletchley, he thought, then really he had no choice except to drive straight ahead.

They came round the curve and the road was clear. The turning to the cottage was on the left, deserted, but as they came level with it a policeman suddenly stepped out from the hedge opposite and held up his hand. Jericho hesitated and then pressed his foot down on the accelerator. The policeman stepped smartly out of the way and Jericho had a momentary impression of an outraged brick-red face. Then they were dropping down into the hollow and rising again and passing through the village. Another policeman was talking to a woman on the doorstep of her thatched cottage and he turned to stare at them. Jericho trod on the accelerator again and soon the village was behind them and the road was corkscrewing down into another leafy hollow. They rose into Shenley Church End, passed the White Hart Inn, where Jericho used to live, and then a church, and almost at once they had to stop at the junction of the A5.

Jericho glanced in his mirror to check there was no

one behind them. It seemed safe enough. He said to Hester: 'You can get up now.' He was in a daze. He couldn't believe what he was doing. He waited to let a couple of lorries go by, indicated, and then swung left on to the old Roman road. It ran straight and true ahead of them, northwest, for as far as they could see. Jericho changed up a gear, the Austin gathered speed, and they were clear.

Wartime England opened up before them – still the same but somehow subtly different: a little bit smudged, a little bit knocked about, like a prosperous estate going fast to ruin, or a genteel elderly lady fallen on hard times.

They didn't encounter any bomb damage until they reached the outskirts of Rugby, where what looked from a distance to be a ruined abbey turned out to be the roofless shell of a factory, but the depredations of war were everywhere. Fences beside the road, after three years without repairs, were sagging or collapsed. The gates and railings had gone from the fine country parks to be melted down for munitions. The houses were shabby. Nothing had been painted since 1940. Broken windows were boarded over, ironwork was rusted or coated in tar. Even the inn signs were blistered and faded. The country was degraded.

And we, too, thought Jericho, as they overtook yet another stooped figure trudging beside the road, don't we look slightly worse each year? In 1940 there had at least been the galvanising energy unleashed by the threat of invasion. And in 1941 there had been some hope when Russia and then America had entered the war. But 1942 had dragged into 1943, the U-boats had wrought murder on the convoys, the shortages had worsened and, despite the victories in Africa and on the eastern front, the war had begun to look endless – an unbroken, unheroic vista of rationing and exhaustion. The villages seemed almost lifeless – the men away, the women drafted into factories – while in Stony Stratford and in Towcester the few people who were about had mostly formed into queues outside shops with empty windows.

Beside him, Hester Wallace was silent, monitoring their progress with obsessive interest on Atwood's atlas. Good, he thought. With all the signposts and place names taken down, they would have no idea where they were if they once got lost. He didn't dare drive too quickly. The Austin was unfamiliar and (he was discovering) idiosyncratic. From time to time the cheap wartime petrol caused it to emit a loud bang. It tended to drift towards the centre of the road, and the brakes weren't too hot, either. Besides, a private car was such a rarity, he feared some officious policeman would pull them over if they went too fast and demand to see their papers.

He drove on steadily for more than an hour until, just before a market town she declared was Hinckley, she told him to turn off right on to a narrower road.

They had left Bletchley under a clear sky but the further north they had gone, the darker it had become. Grey clouds heavy with snow or rain had rolled across the sun. The tarmac pushed across a bleak, flat landscape, with not a vehicle to be seen, and for a second time Jericho experienced the curious sense that history was going backwards, that not for a quarter of a century could the roads have been this empty.

Fifteen miles further on she made him turn right again and suddenly they were climbing into much more hilly country, thickly wooded, with startling outcrops of bare rock striped white by snow.

'What place is this?'

'Charnwood Forest. We're almost there. You'd better pull over in a minute. Here, look,' she said, pointing to a deserted picnic area set just off the road. 'Here will do. I shan't be long.'

She hauled her bag from the back seat and set off towards the trees. He watched her go. She looked like a farm boy in her jacket and trousers. What was it Claire had said? *'She's got a bit of a crush on me'*? More than a bit, he thought, much more than a bit, to risk so much. It struck him that she was almost the exact physical opposite of Claire, that where Claire was tall and blonde and voluptuous, Hester was short and dark and skinny. Rather like him, in fact. She was changing her clothes behind a tree which wasn't quite wide enough and he got a sudden glimpse of her thin white shoulder. He looked away. When he looked back she was emerging from the dark woodland in an olive-green dress. The first drop of rain plopped on to the windscreen just as she got back into the car.

'Drive on then, Mr Jericho.' She found their position on the atlas again and rested her finger on it.

His hand paused on the ignition key. 'Do you think,

Miss Wallace,' he said, hesitantly, 'in view of the circumstances, we might now risk first-name terms?'

She gave him a faint smile. 'Hester.'

'Tom.'

They shook hands.

They followed the road through the forest for about five miles and then the trees thinned and they were into high, open country. The rain and melted snow had turned the narrow lane into a mud track and for five minutes they were forced to crawl in second gear behind a pony and trap. At last the driver raised his whip in apology and turned off to the right, towards a tiny village with curls of smoke rising from half a dozen chimneys, and very soon afterwards Hester shouted: 'There!'

If they hadn't been travelling so slowly, they might have missed it: a pair of lodge gates, a private road with a red-and-white pole slung across it, a sentry box, a cryptic sign: WOYG, BEAUMANOR.

War Office 'Y' Group, Beaumanor, 'Y' being the code name for the wireless interception service.

'Here we go.'

Jericho had to admire her nerve. While he was still fumbling sweatily for his pass, she had leaned across him to proffer hers to the guard and had announced briskly that they were expected. The Army private checked her name off on a clipboard, went round to the back of the car to make a note of their registration number, returned to the window, gave Jericho's card a cursory glance, and nodded them in.

Beaumanor Hall was another of those huge, secluded country houses that had been commandeered by the military from their grateful, almost bankrupt owners, and that would never, Jericho guessed, return to private use. It was early Victorian, with an avenue of dripping elms to one side and a stable yard to the other, into which they were directed. They drove under a fine arch. Half a dozen giggling ATS girls, their coats held over their heads like tents to ward off the rain, ran out in front of them and disappeared into one of the buildings. The courtyard held a couple of small Morris commercial trucks and a row of BSA motorcycles. As Jericho parked, a uniformed man hurried over to them carrying a vast and battered umbrella.

'Heaviside,' he said, 'Major Heaviside, as in the eponymous layer. And you must be Miss Wallace and you must be . . .?'

'Tom Jericho.'

'Mr Jericho. Excellent. Splendid.' He shook their hands vigorously. 'This is a treat for us, I must say. A visit from head office to the country cousins. Commander sends a thousand sorrows and says d'you mind if I do the honours? He'll try and catch us later. 'Fraid you've missed lunch, but tea? Cup of tea? *Filthy* weather . . .'

Jericho had been braced for some suspicious questions, and had used the journey to rehearse some careful answers, but the major merely ushered them under his leaking umbrella and guided them into the house. He was young, tall and balding, with spectacles so smeared with debris it was a wonder he could see through them. He had sloping shoulders, like a bottle, and the collar of his tunic was blanched white with dandruff. He took them into a cold and musty drawing room and ordered tea.

By now he'd finished his potted history of the house ('designed by the same bloke who built Nelson's Column, so they tell me') and was well embarked on a detailed history of the wireless interception service ('started out in Chatham till the bombing got too bad . . .'). Hester was nodding politely. A woman Army private brought them tea as thick and brown as shoe polish and Jericho sipped it and glanced impatiently around the empty walls. There were holes in the plaster where the picture hooks had been pulled out, and grimy shadows traced the outlines of large frames, now removed. An ancestral seat without ancestors, a house without a soul. The windows looking out on to the garden were crossed with strips of sticky tape.

He pointedly took out his watch and opened it. Almost three o'clock. They would need to be moving soon.

Hester noticed he was fidgeting. 'Perhaps,' she said, leaping into a brief lull in the major's monologue, 'we might take a look around?'

Heaviside looked startled and clattered his teacup into his saucer. 'Oh, crumbs, sorry. Right. If you're fit, then, we'll make a start.'

The rain was mixed with snow now, and the wind was blowing it hard, in waves, from the north. It lashed their faces as they came around the side of the big house and as they picked their way through the mud of a flattened rose garden they had to raise their arms against it, like boxers warding off blows. There was an odd keening, howling noise, like nothing Jericho had ever heard before, coming from beyond a wall.

'What the devil's that?'

'The aerial farm,' said Heaviside.

Jericho had only visited an intercept station once before, and that had been years ago, when the science was still in its infancy: a shack full of shivering Wrens perched on top of the cliffs near Scarborough. This was of a different order. They went through a gate in the wall and there it was – dozens of radio masts laid out in odd patterns, like the stone circles of the Druids, across several acres of fields. The metal pylons were bound together by thousands of yards of cable. Some of the taut steel hummed in the wind, some screamed.

'Rhombic and Beveridge configurations,' shouted the major above the racket. 'Dipoles and quadrahedrons . . . Look!' He tried to point and his umbrella was abruptly snapped inside out. He smiled hopelessly and waved it in the direction of the masts. 'We're about three hundred feet up here, hence this bloody wind. The farm's got two main harvests, can you see? One's pointing due south. That picks up France, the Med, Libya. The other's targeted east to Germany and the Russian front. The signals go by coaxial cables to the intercept huts.' He spread his arms wide and bellowed, 'Beautiful, isn't it? We can pick up everything for the best part of a thousand miles.' He laughed and waved his hands as if he were conducting an imaginary choir. 'Sing to me, you buggers.'

The wind slashed sleet in their faces and Jericho cupped his hands to his ears. It felt as though they were interfering with nature, tapping into some rushing elemental force they had no business dabbling in, like Frankenstein summoning down lightning into his laboratory. Another gust of wind knocked them backwards and Hester clutched at his arm for support.

'Let's get out of here,' yelled Heaviside. He gestured for them to follow him. Once they were on the other side of the wall they had some shelter from the wind. An asphalt road girdled what looked, at a distance, to be an estate village nestling in the grounds of the big house: cottages, farm sheds, a greenhouse, even a cricket pavilion with a clock tower. All dummy front-ages, explained Heaviside, cheerfully, designed to fool German air reconnaissance. This was where the work of interception was done. Was there anything they were especially interested in?

'How about the eastern front?' said Hester.

'Eastern front?' said Heaviside. 'Fine.'

He bounded ahead of them through the puddles, still trying to shake out his broken umbrella. The rain worsened and their fast walk turned into a run as they sprinted for the hut. The door banged shut behind them.

'We rely on the feminine element, as you can see,' said Heaviside, taking off his spectacles and drying them on the corner of his tunic. 'Army girls and civilian women.' He replaced his glasses and blinked around the hut. 'Good afternoon,' he said to a stout woman with sergeant's stripes. 'The supervisor,' he explained, then added in a whisper: 'Bit of a dragon.'

Jericho counted twenty-four wireless receivers, arranged in pairs, on either side of a long aisle, each with a woman hunched over it wearing headphones. The room was quiet apart from the hum of the machines and the occasional rustle of intercept forms.

'We've three types of sets,' Heaviside went on quietly. 'HROs, Hallicrafter 28 Skyriders and American AR-88s. Each girl has her own frequencies to patrol, though we'll double back if things get busy.'

'How many people d'you have working here?' asked Hester.

'Couple of thousand.'

'And you intercept everything?'

'Absolutely. Unless you tell us not to.'

'Which we never do.'

'Right, right.' Heaviside's bald head was glistening with rainwater. He bent forwards and shook himself vigorously, like a dog. 'Except that time the other week, of course.'

Afterwards, what Jericho would remember most was how coolly she handled it. She didn't even blink. Instead she actually changed the subject and asked Heaviside how fast the girls had to be ('we insist on a speed of ninety Morse characters a minute, that's the absolute minimum') and then the three of them began to stroll down the central aisle.

'These are sets tuned to the eastern front,' said Heaviside, when they were about halfway down. He stopped and pointed to the elaborate pictures of vultures stuck on the side of several of the receivers.

'Vulture's not the only German Army key in Russia, of course. There's Kite and Kestrel, Smelt for the Ukraine –'

'Are the nets particularly active at the moment?' Jericho felt it was time he should say something.

'Very much so, since Stalingrad. Retreats and counterattacks all along the front. Alarms and excursions. You've got to hand it to these Reds, you know – they can't half fight.'

Hester said casually: 'It would have been a Vulture station you were told not to intercept?'

'That's right.'

'And this would have been around the 4th of March?'

'Bang on. About midnight. I remember because we'd just sent four long signals and were feeling fairly well chuffed when your chap Mermagen comes on the blower in a frightful panic and says: "No more of *that*, thanks very much, not now, not tomorrow, not for ever more."'

'Any reason?'

'No reason. Just stop. Thought he was going to have a heart attack. Oddest damned thing I ever heard.'

'Perhaps,' suggested Jericho, 'knowing you were busy, they wanted to knock out low-priority traffic?'

'Balls,' said Heaviside, 'pardon me, but really!' His professional pride was wounded. 'You can tell your Mr Mermagen from me that it was nothing we couldn't handle, was it, Kay?' He patted the shoulder of a strikingly pretty ATS operator, who took off her headphones and pushed back her chair. 'No, no, don't get up, didn't mean to interrupt. We were just discussing our mystery station.' He rolled his eyes. 'The one we're not supposed to hear.'

'Hear?' Jericho looked at Hester sharply. 'You mean it's still broadcasting?'

'Kay?'

'Yes, sir.' She had a rather melodious Welsh accent. 'Not so often now, sir, but he was awful busy last week.' She hesitated. 'I don't, like, try to listen, on purpose, sir, but he does have the most beautiful fist. Real old school. Not like some of the *kids* –' she spat out the word '– they're using nowadays. Nearly as bad as the Italians, they are.'

'A man's style of Morse,' said Heaviside pompously, 'is as distinctive as his signature.'

'And what is his style?'

'Very fast but very clear,' said Kay. 'Rippling, I'd say. Fist like a concert pianist, he has.'

'Think she rather fancies this chap, don't you, Mr Jericho?' Heaviside laughed and gave her shoulder another pat. 'All right, Kay. Good work. Back to it.'

They moved on. 'One of my best,' he confided. 'Can be pretty ghastly, you know, eight hours listening at a stretch, just taking down gibberish. Specially at night, in the winter. Bloody freezing out here. We have to issue 'em with blankets. Ah, now, here, look: here's one coming in.'

They stood at a discreet distance behind an operator who was frantically copying down a message. With her left hand she kept fractionally adjusting the dial on the wireless set, with her right she was fumbling together message forms and carbon paper. The speed with which she then started to take down the message was astonishing. 'GLPES,' read Jericho over her shoulder, 'KEMPG NXWPD . . .'

'Two forms,' said Heaviside. 'Log sheet, on which she records the whispers: that's tuning messages, Q-code and so forth. And then the red form which is the actual signal.'

'What happens next?' whispered Hester.

'There are two copies of each form. Top copy goes to the Teleprinter Hut for immediate transmission to your people. That's the hut we passed that looks like the cricket pavilion. The other copies we keep here, in case there's a garble or something goes missing.'

'How long do you keep them?'

'Couple of months.'

'Can we see?'

Heaviside scratched his head. 'If you want. Not much to it, though.'

He led them to the far end of the hut, opened a door, turned on the light and stood back to show them the interior. A walk-in cupboard. A bank of about a dozen dark green filing cabinets. No window. Light switch on the left.

'How are they arranged?' asked Jericho.

'Chronologically.' He closed the door.

Not locked, noted Jericho, continuing his inventory. And the entrance not really visible, except to the four operators nearest to it. He could feel his heart beginning to thump.

'Major Heaviside, sir!'

They turned to find Kay standing, beckoning to them, one of her headphones pressed to her ear.

'My mystery piano player, sir. He's just started doing his scales again, sir, if you're interested.'

Heaviside took the headset first. He listened with a judicious expression, his eyes focused on the middle distance, like an eminent doctor with a stethoscope being asked to give a second opinion. He shook his head and shrugged and passed the headphones to Hester.

'Ours not to reason why, old chap,' he said to Jericho.

When it was Jericho's turn, he removed his scarf and placed it carefully on the floor next to the cable form that connected the wireless set to the aerials and the power supply. Putting on the headphones was rather like putting his head under water. There was a strange rush of sounds. A howl that reminded him of the wind in the aerial farm. A gunfire crackle of static. Two or three different and very faint Morse transmissions braided together. And suddenly, and most bizarrely, a German diva singing an operatic aria he vaguely recognised as being from the second act of *Tannhäuser*.

'I can't hear anything.'

'Must have drifted off frequency,' said Heaviside.

Kay turned the dial minutely anticlockwise, the sound wowed up and down an octave, the diva evaporated, more gunfire, and then, like stepping into an open space, a rapid, staccato *dah-dah-dah-dah-dah* of Morse, pulsing clearly and urgently, more than a thousand miles distant, somewhere in German-occupied Ukraine.

*

They were halfway to the Teleprinter Hut when Jericho raised his hand to his throat and said, 'My scarf.'

They stopped in the rain.

'I'll get one of the girls to bring it over.'

'No, no, I'll fetch it, I'll catch you up.'

Hester took her cue. 'And how many machines did you say you have?' She began to walk on.

Heaviside hesitated between the two of them, then hurried after Hester. Jericho could have kissed her. He never heard the major's answer. It was whipped away by the wind.

You are calm, he told himself, you are confident, you are doing nothing wrong.

He went back into the hut. The woman sergeant had her fat back to him, leaning over one of the interceptors. She never saw him. He walked swiftly down the central aisle, looking straight ahead, and let himself into the storeroom. He closed the door behind him and turned on the light.

How long did he have? Not long.

He tugged at the first drawer of the first filing cabinet. Locked. Damn it. He tried it again. Wait. No, it *wasn't* locked. The cabinet was fitted with one of these irritating anti-tilt mechanisms, which prevented two drawers being opened at once. He looked down and saw that the bottom drawer was protruding slightly. He closed it gently with his foot and to his relief the top drawer slid open.

Brown cardboard folders. Bundles of smudged carbons, held together by metal paperclips. Log sheets and W/T red forms. Day, Month and Year in the top right-hand corner. Meaningless jumbles of handwritten letters. This folder for 15 January 1943.

He stepped back and counted quickly. Fifteen four-drawer cabinets. Sixty drawers. Two months. Roughly a drawer a day. Could that be right?

He strode over to the sixth cabinet and opened the third drawer down.

February the 6th.

Bingo.

He held the image of Hester Wallace's neat notation steady in his mind. 6.2./1215. 9.2/1427. 20.2/ 1807. 2.3./1639, 1901 . . .

It would have helped if his fingers hadn't swollen to the size of sausages, if they weren't shaking and slippery with sweat, if he could somehow catch his breath.

Someone must come in. Someone must hear him, surely, opening and closing the metal drawers like organ stops, pulling out two, three, four cryptograms and the log sheets, too (Hester had said they'd be useful), stuffing them into his inside coat pocket, five, six – dropped it, damn – seven cryptograms. He almost gave up at that – 'Quit while you're ahead, old love' – but he needed the final four, the four Claire had hidden in her room.

He opened the top drawer of the thirteenth filing cabinet, and there they were, towards the back, virtually in sequence, thank you, God.

A footstep outside the storeroom. He grabbed the logs and red forms and had just about got them into his pocket and the drawer shut when the door opened to silhouette the trim figure of Kay the intercept girl.

'I thought I saw you come in,' she said, 'only you left your scarf, see?' She held it up and closed the door behind her, then slowly advanced down the narrow room towards him. Jericho stood paralysed with an idiot grin on his face.

'I don't mean to bother you, sir, but it is important, isn't it?' Her dark eyes were wide. He dimly registered again that she was very pretty, even in her Army uniform. The tunic was belted tight at her waist. Something about her reminded him of Claire.

'I'm sorry?'

'I know I shouldn't ask, sir – we're never meant to ask, are we? – but, well, *is it*? Only no one ever tells us, see? Rubbish, that's all it is to us, just rubbish, rubbish, all day long. And all night, too. You try to go to sleep and you can still hear it – beep-beep-bloody-beep. Drives you barmy after a bit. I joined up, see, volunteered, but it's not what I expected, this place. Can't even tell my mum and dad.' She had come up very close to him. 'You *are* making sense of it? It *is* important? I won't tell,' she added, solemnly, 'honest.'

'Yes,' said Jericho. 'We are making sense of it, and it is important. I promise you.'

She nodded to herself, smiled, looped his scarf around his neck and tied it, then walked slowly out of the storeroom, leaving the door open. He gave it twenty seconds, then followed her. Nobody stopped him as he went out through the hut and into the rain.

4

Heaviside didn't want them to leave. Jericho tried feebly to protest – the light was bad, he said, they had a long journey ahead, they had to beat the blackout – but Heaviside was horrified. He insisted, *insisted* they at least take a look at the direction finders and the high-speed Morse receivers. He was so enthusiastic, he looked as though he might burst into tears if they said no. And so they trailed meekly after him across the slick wet concrete, first to a row of wooden huts dressed up to look like a stable block and then to another fake cottage.

The chorus of the aerial farm sang weirdly in the background, Heaviside became increasingly excited describing abstruse technicalities of wavelength and frequency, Hester pretended heroically to be interested and carefully avoided meeting Jericho's eye, and all the time Jericho walked around unhearing, in a cocoon of anxiety, nerved for the distant sounds of discovery and alarm. Never had he been more desperate to get away from anywhere. From time to time his hand stole into his inside coat pocket, and once he left it there, reassured to feel the roughness of the intercepts safely between his fingers, until he realised he was doing a passable impersonation of Napoleon, whereupon he promptly snatched it out again.

As for Heaviside, such was his pride in Beaumanor's work, he clearly would have kept them there for another week if he could. But when, an interminable half-hour later, he suggested a visit to the motor pool and the auxiliary generators, it was Hester, so cool until then, who finally snapped and said, rather too firmly in retrospect, that no, thank you, but really they did have to get going.

'Honestly? It's a heck of a long way to have come for just a couple of hours.' Heaviside looked mystified. 'The commander will be disappointed to miss you.'

'Alas,' said Jericho. 'Some other time.'

'Up to you, old boy,' said Heaviside huffily. 'Don't want to press ourselves on you.' And Jericho cursed himself for hurting his feelings.

He walked them round to their car, halting on the way to point out an antique ship's figurehead of an admiral, perched on top of an ornamental horse trough. Some wit had draped a pair of Army knickers over the admiral's sword and they hung limply in the raw damp. 'Cornwallis,' said Heaviside. 'Found him in the grounds. Our lucky charm.'

When they said goodbye he shook hands with them each in turn, Hester first, then Jericho, and saluted as they got into the Austin. He turned as if to go, then froze, and suddenly ducked down to the window.

'What was it you said you did again, Mr Jericho?'

'Actually, I didn't.' Jericho smiled and turned the engine on. 'Cryptanalytic work.'

'Which section?'

'Can't say, I'm afraid.'

He jammed the gear stick into reverse and executed a clumsy three-point turn. As they pulled away he could see Heaviside in the rear-view mirror, standing in the rain, his hand protecting his eyes, watching them. The curve of the drive took them off to the left and the image vanished.

'Pound to a penny,' muttered Jericho, 'he's on his way to the nearest telephone.'

'You got them?'

He nodded. 'Let's wait till we get clear of here.'

Out through the gates, along the lane, past the village, towards the forest. The rain was blowing across the dark slope of woodland in ghostly white columns, like the banners of a phantom army. A large and lonely bird was flying through the cloudburst, very high and far away. The windscreen wipers scudded back and forth. The trees closed in around them.

'You were very good,' said Jericho.

'Until the end. By the end it was unendurable, not knowing if you'd managed it.'

He started to tell her about the storeroom, but then he noticed a track coming up, leading off from the side of the road into the privacy of the wood.

The perfect spot.

They bounced along the rough trail for about a hundred yards, plunging into puddles that turned out to be potholes a foot deep. Water fountained out on either side of them, tearing against the underside of the chassis. It spouted through a hole at Hester's feet and drenched her shoes. When at last the headlights showed a patch of bog too wide to negotiate, Jericho turned off the engine.

There was no sound except for the pattering of the rain on the thin metal roof. Overhanging branches blotted out the sky. It was almost too dark to read. He turned on the interior light.

'VVVADU QSA?K,' said Jericho, reading off the whispers on the first log sheet. 'Which, if I remember my days in traffic analysis, roughly translates as: This is station call sign ADU requesting reading of my signal strength, over.' He ran his finger down the carbon copy. Q-code was an international language, the Esperanto of wireless operators; he knew it off by heart. 'And then we get VVVCPQ BT QSA4 QSA?K. This is station call-sign CPQ, break, your signal strength is fine, what is my signal strength? Over.'

'CPQ,' said Hester, nodding. 'I recognise that call sign. That has something to do with Army High Command in Berlin.'

'Good. One mystery solved, then.' He returned his attention to the log sheet. 'VVVADU QSA3 QTC1 K: Smolensk to Berlin, your signal strength is reasonable, I have one message for you, over. QRV, says Berlin: I am ready. QXH K: broadcast your traffic, over. Smolensk then says QXA109: my message consists of 109 cipher groups.'

Hester fluttered the first cryptogram triumphantly. 'Here it is. One hundred and nine exactly.'

'OK. Fine. So that goes through – straight away, presumably, because Berlin replies: VVVCPQ R QRU HHVA. Message received and understood, I have nothing for you, Heil Hitler and good night. All very smooth and methodical. Right out of the manual.'

'That girl in the Intercept Hut said he was precise.'

'What we don't have, unfortunately, is Berlin's replies.' He riffled through the log sheets. 'Easy contact on the 9th as well, and again on the 20th. Ah,' he said, 'now on the 2nd of March it looks to have been more tricky.' The form was indeed a mass of terse dialogue. He held it up to the light. Smolensk to Berlin: QZE, QRJ, QRO. (Your frequency is too high, your signals are too weak, increase your power.) And Berlin snapping back: QWP, QRX10 (observe regulations, wait ten minutes) and finally an exasperated QRX (shut up). 'Now this is interesting. No wonder they suddenly start to sound like strangers.' Jericho squinted at the carbon copy. 'The call sign in Berlin has changed.'

'Changed? Absurd. Changed to what?'

'TGD.'

'*What*? Let me see that.' She snatched the form out of his hand. 'That's not possible. No, no. TGD simply isn't a Wehrmacht call sign.'

'How can you be sure?'

'Because I know it. There's a whole Enigma key named after TGD. It's never been broken. It's famous.' She had started to wind a lock of hair nervously around her right index finger. 'Notorious might be a better word.'

'What is it?'

'It's the call sign of Gestapo headquarters in Berlin.'

'Gestapo?' Jericho fumbled through the remaining log sheets. 'But all the messages from March the 2nd onwards,' he said, 'that's eight out of the eleven, all the long ones, including the four in Claire's room – they're all addressed to that sign.' He gave the forms to her so she could check for herself and sat back in his seat.

A gust of wind stirred the branches above them, sending a shower of rainwater rattling like a volley across the windscreen.

'Let's try and construct a thesis,' said Jericho after a minute or two, as much to hear a human voice as anything. The random pattering of the downpour and the crepuscular gloom of the forest were beginning to affect his nerves. Hester had pulled her feet up from the sodden floor and was huddled up very small on the front seat, staring out at the forest, hugging her legs, occasionally massaging her toes through her damp stockings.

'March the 4th is the key day,' he went on. (*Where was I on 4 March? In another world: reading Sherlock Holmes in front of a Cambridge gas fire, avoiding Mr Kite and learning to walk again.*) 'Up to that day, everything is proceeding normally. A signals unit hibernating in the Ukraine, dormant all winter, has come to life in the warmer weather. First, a few signals to Army HQ in Berlin, and then a burst of longer traffic to the Gestapo –'

'That's not normal,' said Hester scathingly. 'An Army unit transmitting reports in a Russian-front Enigma key to the headquarters of the secret police? Normal? I'd call that unprecedented.'

'Quite.' He didn't mind being interrupted. He was glad of a sign she was listening. 'In fact, it's so unprecedented, someone at Bletchley wakes up to what's happening and starts to panic. All previous signals are removed from the Registry. And just before midnight on that same day your Mr Mermagen telephones Beaumanor and tells them to stop interception. Ever happen before?'

'Never.' She paused, then moved her shoulder slightly in concession. 'Well, all right, *maybe*, when traffic's very heavy, a low-priority target *might* be neglected for a day or so. But you saw the size of Beaumanor. And that's not as big as the RAF's station at Chicksands. And there must be a dozen smaller places, maybe more. We're always being told by people like you that the whole point of the exercise is to monitor *everything*.'

He nodded. This was true. It had been their philosophy from the beginning: be inclusive, miss nothing. It isn't the big boys who give you the cribs – they're too good. It's the little fellows – the long-forgotten incompetents stuck in out-of-the-way places, who always begin their messages 'situation normal, nothing to report' and then use the same nulls in the same places, or who habitually encipher their own call-signs, or who set the rotors every morning with their girlfriend's initials . . .

Jericho said: 'So he wouldn't have told them to stop on his own authority?'

'Miles? God, no.'

'Who gives him his orders?'

'That depends. Hut 6 Machine Room, usually. Sometimes the Hut 3 Watch. They decide priorities.'

'Could he have made a mistake?'

'In what sense?'

'Well, Heaviside said Miles called Beaumanor just

before midnight on the 4th in a panic. I was wondering: what if Miles had been told earlier in the day that this unit was no longer to be intercepted, but forgot to pass on the message.'

'Eminently possible. Likely, in fact, knowing Miles. Yes, yes *of course*.' Hester turned round to face him. 'I see what you're driving at. In the time between Miles being told to pull the plug and the order reaching Beaumanor, four more messages had been intercepted.'

'Exactly. Which came into Hut 6 late on the night of the 4th. But by then the order had already been issued that they weren't to be decoded.'

'So they just got caught up in the bureaucracy and were passed along the line.'

'Until they ended up in the German Book Room.'

'In front of Claire.'

'Undecrypted.'

Jericho nodded slowly. Undecrypted. That was the crucial point. That explained why the signals in Claire's bedroom had showed no signs of damage. There had never been any strips of Type-X decode gummed to their backs. They had never been broken.

He peered into the wood but he didn't see trees, he saw the German Book Room on the morning after the night of 4 March, when the cryptograms would have arrived to be filed and indexed.

Would Miss Monk herself have rung the Hut 6 duty officer, or would she have delegated the task to one of her girls? 'We've got four orphan intercepts here, without the solutions. What, pray, are we supposed to do with them?' And the reply would have been – what?

Oh, Christ! File them? Forget them? Dump them in the bin marked CONFIDENTIAL WASTE?

Only none of those things had happened.

Claire had stolen them instead.

'*In theory?*' Weitzman had said. '*On an average day? A girl like Claire would probably see more operational detail about the German armed forces than Adolf Hitler. Absurd, isn't it?*'

Ah, but they weren't supposed to *read* it, Walter, that was the point. Well-bred young ladies wouldn't dream of reading someone else's mail, unless they were told to do so for King and country. They certainly wouldn't read it for themselves. That was the reason why Bletchley employed them.

But what was it Miss Monk had said of Claire? '*She'd really become much more attentive of late . . .*' Naturally she had. *She* had begun to read what was passing through her hands. And at the end of February or the beginning of March she had seen something that had changed her life. Something to do with a German rear-echelon signals unit whose wireless operator played Morse code to the Gestapo as if it were a Mozart sonata. Something so utterly 'un-boring, darling', that when Bletchley had decided they couldn't bear to read the traffic any more, she had felt compelled to steal the last four intercepts herself.

And why had she stolen them?

He didn't even need to pose the question. Hester had reached the answer ahead of him, although her voice was faint and disbelieving and almost drowned out by the rain.

'She stole them to read them.'

She stole them to read them. The answer slid beneath the random pattern of events and fitted it like a crib.

She stole the cryptograms to read them.

'But is it really feasible?' asked Hester. She seemed bewildered by the destination to which her logic had led her. 'I mean, could she really have done it?'

'Yes. It's possible. Hard to imagine. Possible.'

Oh, the nerve of it, thought Jericho. Oh, the sheer breathtaking bloody *nerve* of it, the cool deliberation with which she must have plotted it. Claire, my darling, you really are a wonder.

'But she couldn't have managed it on her own,' he said, 'not locked away at the back of Hut 3. She'd have needed help.'

'Who?'

He raised his hands from the steering wheel in a hopeless gesture. It was hard to know where to begin. 'Someone with access to Hut 6 for a start. Someone who could look up the Enigma settings for German Army key Vulture on March the 4th.'

'Settings?'

He glanced at her in surprise, then realised that the actual workings of an Enigma was not the sort of information she would have needed to know. And in Bletchley, what you didn't need to know you were never told.

'*Walzenlage*,' he said. '*Ringstellung. Steckerverbindungen.* Wheel order, ring setting and crossplugging. If Vulture was being read every day, they'd already have had those in Hut 6.'

'Then what would you have had to do?'

'Get access to a Type-X machine. Set it up in exactly the right way. Type in the cryptograms and tear off the plaintext.'

'Could Claire have done that?'

'Almost certainly not. She'd never have been allowed anywhere near the decoding room. And anyway she wasn't trained.'

'So her accomplice would have needed some skill?'

'Skill, yes. And nerve. And time, come to that. Four messages. A thousand cipher groups. Five thousand individual characters. Even an expert operator would need the best part of half an hour to decode that much. It *could* have been done. But she would have needed a superman.'

'Or woman.'

'No.' He was remembering the events of Saturday night: the sound downstairs in the cottage, the big male footprints in the frost, the cycle tracks and the red rear light of the bicycle shooting away from him into the darkness. 'No. It's a man.'

If only I'd been thirty seconds quicker, he thought. I'd have seen his face.

And then he thought: Yes, and maybe got a bullet in my own for my trouble: a bullet from a stolen Smith and Wesson .38, manufactured in Springfield, Massachusetts.

He felt a sudden prickle of ice-cold moisture on the back of his wrist and glanced up. He followed its trajectory to a spot in the roof, just before the windscreen. As he watched, another dark bubble of rainwater slowly swelled, ripened to a rich rust colour, and dropped.

Shark.

He realised guiltily he had nearly forgotten it.

'What's the time?'

'Almost five.'

'We should be getting back.'

He rubbed at his hand and reached for the ignition.

The car wouldn't start. Jericho twisted the key back and forth and pumped away frantically at the accelerator but all he managed to coax from the engine was a dull turning noise.

'Oh, hell!'

He turned up his collar, got out and went round to the boot. As he opened the lid a brace of pigeons took off behind him, wings snapping like firecrackers. There was a starting handle under the spare can of petrol and he inserted that into the hole in the front bumper. '*You do this the wrong way, lad,*' his stepfather had told him, '*and you can break your wrist.*' But which was the right way? Clockwise or anticlockwise? He gave the handle a hopeful tug. It was horribly stiff.

'Pull out the choke,' he shouted to Hester, 'and press your foot down on the third pedal if she starts to fire.'

The little car rocked as she slid across into the driver's seat.

He bent to his task again. The forest floor was only a couple of feet from his face, a pungent brown carpet of decaying leaves and fir cones. He heaved a couple more times until his shoulder ached. He was beginning to sweat now, perspiration mingling with the rainwater, dripping off the end of his nose, trickling down his neck. The insanity of their whole undertaking seemed encapsulated in this moment. The greatest convoy battle of the war was about to start, and where was he? In some primeval bloody forest in the middle of bloody nowhere poring over stolen Gestapo cryptograms with a woman he barely knew. What in the name of reason did they think they were doing? They must be – he tightened his grip – *crazy* . . . He jerked viciously on the starting handle and suddenly the engine caught, spluttered, nearly died, then Hester revved it loudly. The sweetest sound he'd ever heard, it split the forest. He slung the handle into the boot and slammed the lid.

The gearbox whined as he reversed along the track towards the road.

The overhanging branches made a tunnel of the soaking lane. Their headlights glinted on a film of running water. Jericho drove slowly around and around the same course, trying to find some landmark in the gloom, trying not to panic. He must have taken a wrong turning coming out of the clearing. The steering wheel beneath his hands felt as wet and slippery as the road. Eventually they came to a crossroads beside a vast and decaying oak. Hester bent her head again to the map. A lock of long black hair fell across her eyes. She used both hands to pile it up. She clenched a pin between her teeth and muttered through it: 'Left or right?'

'You're the navigator.'

'And you're the one who decided to drive us off the main road.' She skewered her hair savagely back in place. 'Go left.'

He would have chosen the other way but thank God he didn't because she was right. Soon the road ahead began to brighten. They could see patches of weeping sky. He pressed his foot down and the speedometer touched forty as they passed out of the forest and into the open. When, after a mile or so, they came to a village, she told him to pull up outside the tiny post office.

'Why?'

'I need to find out where we are.'

'You'd better be quick.'

'I've really no intention of sight-seeing.'

She slammed the door behind her and ran through the rain, sidestepping the puddles with a gym mistress's agility. A bell tinkled inside the shop as she opened the door.

Jericho glanced ahead, then checked in his mirror. The village appeared to consist of nothing more than this one street. No parked vehicles that he could see. No one about. He guessed that a private car, especially one driven by a stranger, would be a rarity, a talking-point. In the little red-brick cottages and the half-timbered houses he could already imagine the curtains being twitched back. He turned off the windscreen wipers and sank lower in his seat. For the twentieth time his hand went to the bulge of cryptograms in his inside pocket.

Two Englands, he thought. One England – this one – familiar, safe, obvious. But now another, secret England, secluded in the grounds of stately houses – Beaumanor, Gayhurst, Woburn, Adstock, Bletchley – an England of aerial farms and direction finders, clattering bombes and, soon, the glowing green and orange valves of Turing machines ('*it should make the calculations a hundred times, maybe a thousand times as fast*'). A new age beginning to be born in the parklands of the old. What was it that Hardy had written in his *Apology*? 'Real mathematics has no effect on war. No one has yet discovered any warlike purpose to be served by the theory of numbers.' The old boy couldn't guess the half of it.

The bell tinkled again and Hester emerged from the post office holding a newspaper over her head like an umbrella. She opened the car door, shook the paper and threw it, not very gently, into his lap.

'What's this for?' It was the *Leicester Mercury*, the local rag: that afternoon's edition.

'They print appeals for help, don't they? From the police? When someone is missing?'

It was a good idea. He had to concede it. But although they checked the paper carefully – twice, in fact – they could find no photograph of Claire and no mention of the hunt for her.

Dropping southwards, heading for home. A different route for the return journey, more easterly – this was Hester's plan. To keep their spirits up, she occasionally recited the names of the villages and checked them in the gazetteer as they rattled down their empty high streets. Oadby, she said, ('note the early English to Perpendicular church'), Kibworth Harcourt, Little Bowden, and on across the border out of Leicestershire and into Northamptonshire. The sky over the distant pale hills brightened from black to grey and finally to a kind of glossy, neutral white. The rain slowed, then stopped. Oxendon, Kelmarsh, Maidwell . . . Square Norman towers with arrow-slits, thatched pubs, tiny Victorian railway stations nesting in a bosky countryside of high hedges and dense copses. It was enough to make you want to burst into a chorus of 'There'll Always Be an England' except that neither of them felt like singing.

Why had she run? That was what Hester said she couldn't understand. Everything else seemed logical enough: how she would have got hold of the cryptograms in the first place, why she might have wanted to read them, why she would have needed an accomplice. But why then commit the one act guaranteed to draw attention to yourself? Why fail to turn up for your morning shift?

'You,' she said to Jericho, after she had thought it over for a few more miles. There was a hint of accusation in her voice. 'I think it must be you.'

Like a prosecuting counsel she took him back over the events of Saturday night. He had gone to the cottage, yes? He had discovered the intercepts, yes? A man had arrived downstairs, yes?

'Yes.'

'Did he see you?'

'No.'

'Did you *say* anything?'

'I may have shouted "Who's there?" or something of the sort.'

'So he could have recognised your voice?'

'It's possible.'

But that would mean I knew him, he thought. Or at least that he knew me.

'What time did you leave?'

'I don't know exactly. About half past one.'

'There you are,' she said. 'It *is* you. Claire returns to the cottage after you've gone. She discovers the intercepts are missing. She realises that you must have them because this mysterious man has told her you were there. She believes you'll take them straight to the authorities. She panics. She runs . . .'

'But that's madness.' He took his eyes off the road to stare at her. 'I'd never have betrayed her.'

'So *you* say. But did *she* know that?'

Did she know that? No, he realised, returning his attention to the wheel, no, she did not know that. Indeed, on the basis of his behaviour on the night she found the cheque, she had good reason to assume he was a fanatic about security – a pretty ironic conclusion, given he now had eleven stolen cryptograms stuffed inside his overcoat pocket.

A twenty-year-old bus with an outside staircase to its upper deck, like something out of a transport museum, pulled over to the grass verge to let them overtake. The schoolchildren on board waved frantically as they passed.

'Who were her boyfriends? Who was she seeing apart from me?'

'You don't want to know. *Believe me.*' There was relish in the way she threw back at him the words he had used to her in church. He couldn't blame her for it.

'Come on, Hester.' He gripped the steering wheel grimly and glanced into the mirror. The bus was receding from view. A car was emerging from behind it. 'Don't spare my blushes. Let's keep it simple. Just confine it to men from the Park.'

Well, they were impressions, she said, rather than names. Claire had never mentioned names.

Give me the impressions, then.

And she did.

The first one she'd encountered had been young, with reddish hair, clean-shaven. She'd met him on the stairs with his shoes in his hand one morning in early November.

Reddish hair, clean-shaven, repeated Jericho. It didn't sound familiar.

A week later she'd cycled past a colonel parked in the lane in an Army staff car with the headlights dowsed. And then there was an Air Force man called Ivo Something, with a weird vocabulary of 'prangs' and 'crates' and 'shows' that Claire used to mimic fondly. Was he Hut 6 or 3? She was fairly sure Hut 3. There was an Honourable Evelyn double-barrelled someone-or-other – 'thoroughly *dis*honourable, darling' – whom Claire had met in London during the Blitz and who now worked in the mansion. There was an older man who Hester thought had something to do with the

Navy. And there was an American: he was definitely Navy.

'That would be Kramer,' said Jericho.

'You know him?'

'He's the man who lent me the car. How recent was that?'

'About a month ago. But I got the impression he was just a friend. A source of Camels and nylons, nothing special.'

'And before Kramer there was me.'

'She never talked about you.'

'I'm flattered.'

'Given the way she used to talk about the others, you should be.'

'Anyone else?'

She hesitated. 'There may have been someone new in the last month. She was certainly away a good deal. And once, about two weeks ago, I had a migraine and came home early off shift and I *thought* there was a man's voice coming from her room. But if there was they stopped talking when they heard me on the stairs.'

'That's eight then, by my count. Including me. And leaving out any others you've forgotten or don't know about.'

'I'm sorry, Tom.'

'It's quite all right.' He managed to arrange his face into a parody of a smile. 'If anything it's rather fewer than I'd thought.' He was lying, of course, and he guessed she knew it. 'Why is it, I wonder, that I don't hate her for it?'

'Because that's the way she is,' said Hester, with

unexpected ferocity. 'Well, she never made much secret of it, did she? And if one hates her for what she is – then, really, one can't have loved her very much in the first place, can one?' Her neck had blushed a deep pink. 'If all one wants is a reflection of oneself – well, honestly, there's always the mirror.'

She sat back, apparently as surprised by this speech as he was.

He checked the road behind them. Still empty apart from the same, solitary car. How long since he'd first noticed it? About ten minutes? But now he came to think of it, it had probably been there a good while longer, certainly since before they overtook the school bus. It was lying about a hundred yards back, low and wide and dark, its belly close to the ground, like a cockroach. He squeezed his foot harder on the accelerator and was relieved to see the gap between them widen until at last the road dipped and turned and the big car disappeared.

A minute later it was back again, maintaining exactly the same distance.

The narrow lane ran between high, dark hedges flecked with buds. Through them, as through a magic lantern, Jericho caught odd glimpses of tiny fields, a ruined barn, a bare, black elm, petrified by lightning. They came to a longish stretch of flat road.

There was no sun. He calculated there must be about half an hour of daylight left.

'How far is it to Bletchley?'

'Stony Stratford coming up, then about six miles. Why?'

He looked again in the mirror and had just begun to say, 'I fear —' when a bell started to clamour behind them. The big car had finally tired of following and was flashing its headlights, ordering them to pull over.

Until this moment, Jericho's encounters with the police had been rare, brief and invariably marked by those exaggerated displays of mutual respect customary between the guardians of the law and the lawful middle classes. But this one would be different, he saw that at once. An unauthorised journey between secret locations, without proof of ownership of the car, without petrol coupons, at a time when the country was being scoured for a missing woman: what would that earn them? A trip to the local police station, for sure. A lot of questions. A telephone call to Bletchley. A body search.

It didn't bear contemplating.

And so, to his astonishment, he found himself measuring the road ahead, like a long-jumper at the start of his run. The red roofs and the grey church spire of Stony Stratford had begun to poke above the distant line of trees.

Hester grabbed the edges of her seat. He jammed his foot down hard to the floor.

The Austin gathered speed slowly, as in a nightmare, and the police car, responding to the challenge, began to gain on them. The speedometer climbed past forty, to fifty, to fifty-five, to nearly sixty. The countryside seemed to be racing directly at them, only swerving at the last second to flash by narrowly on either side. A main road appeared ahead. They had to stop. And if Jericho had been an experienced driver that is what he would have done, police or no police. But he hesitated until there was nothing he could do but brake as hard as he dared, change down into second gear and yank the steering wheel hard left. The engine screamed. They spun and cornered on two tyres, he and Hester pitched sideways by the force. The clanging bell was drowned by the roar of an engine and suddenly the radiator grille of a tank transporter was rushing to fill the rear-view mirror. Its bumper touched them. An outraged blast from its hooter, as loud as a foghorn, seemed to blow them forwards. They shot across the bridge over the Grand Union Canal and a swan turned lazily to watch them and then they were doglegging through the market town – right, left, right, shuddering over cobbled alleys, the wheel shaking in Jericho's hands – anything to get off this wretched Roman road. Abruptly the houses receded and they were out in open country again, running alongside the canal. A narrowboat was being towed by a weary carthorse. The bargeman, lying stretched out beside the tiller, raised his hat to them.

'Left here,' said Hester, and they swung away from the canal into a lane that was not much better than the forest track: just two strips of potholed, tarmaced road, extending ahead like tyre tracks, separated by a mound of grass that scraped the bottom of the car. Hester turned and knelt on her seat, staring out of the back window for any sign of the police, but the countryside had closed behind them like a jungle. Jericho drove on slowly for two miles. They passed through a tiny hamlet. A mile the other side of it a space had been dug out to allow cars – or, more likely, carts – to pass one another. He drove up into it and switched off the engine.

They did not have much time.

Jericho kept watch on the lane while she changed in the back seat of the Austin. According to the map, they were only about a mile due west of Shenley Brook End and she was insistent she could make it back to the cottage on foot across open country before dark. He marvelled at her nerve. To him, after the encounter with the police, everything had taken on a sinister aspect: the trees gesticulating at one another in the wind, the patches of dense shadow now gathering at the edges of the fields, the rooks that had erupted, cawing, from their nests and were now circling high above them.

'Can't we read them?' Hester had asked, after they had parked. He had taken the cryptograms from his pocket so that they could decide what to do with them. 'Come on, Tom. We can't just burn them. If she thought she could read them, why can't we?'

Oh, a dozen reasons, Hester. A hundred. But here were three to be going on with. First, they would need the Vulture settings that were in use on the days the signals were sent.

'I can try to get those,' she had said. 'They must be in Hut 6 somewhere.'

Very well, maybe she could. But even if she managed it, they would still need several *hours* to themselves on a Type-X machine – and not one of the Type-Xs in Hut 8, either, because naval Enigmas were wired differently from Army ones.

She had made no answer to that.

And, third, they would need to find a place to hide the cryptograms, because otherwise, if they were caught with them, they'd both be on trial *in camera* at the Old Bailey.

No answer to that, either.

There was a movement in the hedge about thirty yards ahead of him. A fox came nosing out of the undergrowth and stepped into the lane. Halfway across it stopped and stared directly at him. It held itself perfectly still and sniffed the air, then slouched off into the opposite hedgerow. Jericho let out his breath.

And yet, and yet . . . Even as he had ticked off all the obvious objections, he had known that she was right. They couldn't simply destroy the cryptograms now, not after all they had gone through to get them. And once that was conceded then the only logical reason for keeping them was to try to break them. Hester would have to steal the settings somehow while he looked for a way of gaining access to a Type-X machine. But it was dangerous – he prayed that she could see that. Claire was the last person to steal the cryptograms and there was no telling what had happened to her. And somewhere – maybe looking for them now, for all they knew – was a man who left large footprints in the frost; a man apparently armed with a stolen pistol; a man who knew that Jericho had been in Claire's room and had taken away the signals.

I am no hero, he thought. He was scared half to death.

The car door opened and Hester emerged, dressed again in trousers, sweater, jacket and boots. He took her bag and stowed it in the Austin's boot.

'Are you sure you don't want me to drive you?'

'We've been over this. It's safer if we split up.'

'For God's sake then be careful.'

'You should worry about yourself.' The air was milky with the approaching dusk – damp and cold. Her face was beginning to blur. She said: 'I'll see you tomorrow.'

She swung herself easily over the gate and set off directly across the field. He thought she might turn and wave but she never looked back. He watched her for about two minutes, until she had safely reached the far side. She searched briefly for a gap in the hedge, then vanished like the fox.

5

The lane led him up over the Chase, past the big wireless masts of the Bletchley Park out-station at Whaddon Hall, and down to the Buckingham Road. He peered along it, cautiously.

According to the map, only five roads, including this one, connected Bletchley with the outside world, and if the police were still watching the traffic they would stop him, he was certain. Short of flying a swastika the

Austin could hardly have looked more suspicious. Mud was spattered over the bodywork to the height of the windows. Grass was wrapped tightly around the axles. The back bumper was buckled where the tank transporter had struck it. And the engine, after Stony Stratford, had acquired a kind of urgent death rattle. He wondered what on earth he would say to Kramer.

The road was quiet in both directions. He passed a couple of farmhouses and within five minutes he was entering the outskirts of the town. He drove on past the suburban villas with their white pebble-dashed frontages and their fake Tudor beams, then left up the hill towards Bletchley Park. He turned into Wilton Avenue and immediately braked. Parked at the end of the street beside the guard post was a police car. An officer in a greatcoat and cap was talking earnestly to the sentry.

Once again, Jericho had to use both hands to jam the gear lever into reverse, then he backed out very slowly into Church Green Road.

He had moved beyond panic now and was in some calm place at the centre of the storm. 'Act as normally as possible', that had been his advice to Hester when they had decided to keep the cryptograms. 'You're not on duty until four tomorrow afternoon? Fine, then don't go in before that time.' The injunction must apply to him as well. Normality. Routine. He was expected in Hut 8 for the night's attack on Shark? He would be there.

He drove on up the hill and parked the car in a street of private houses about three hundred yards from St

Mary's Church. Where to hide the cryptograms? The Austin? Too risky. Albion Street? Too likely to be searched. A process of elimination brought him to the answer. Where better to hide a tree than in a forest? Where better to conceal a cryptogram than in a code-breaking centre? He would take them into the Park.

He transferred the wad of paper from the inside pocket of his overcoat to the hiding place he had made in the lining and locked the car. Then he remembered Atwood's atlas and unlocked it again. Bending to retrieve the book he casually checked the road. A woman in the house opposite was standing on her doorstep, in an oblong of yellow light, calling her children in from play. A young couple strolled past, arm in arm. A dog loped miserably along the gutter and stopped to cock its leg against the Austin's front tyre. An ordinary, English provincial street at twilight. *The world for which we fight.* He closed the door quietly. Head down, hands in pockets, he set off at a brisk walk for the Park.

It was a matter of pride with Hester Wallace that, when it came to walking, she had the stamina of any man. But what had looked on the map to be a straight and easy mile had turned into a crooked ramble three times as long, across tiny fields enclosed by tangled hedges and by ditches swollen wide as moats with brown meltwater, so that it was almost dark by the time she reached the lane.

She thought she might be lost but after a minute or two the narrow road began to seem familiar to her – a pair of elms grown too close together, as if from the same root; a mossy and broken stile – and soon she could smell the fires in the village. They were burning green wood and the smoke was white and acrid.

She kept a look out for policemen, but saw none – not in the field opposite the cottage, nor in the cottage itself, which had been left unlocked. She bolted the front door behind her, stood at the bottom of the stairs and called out a greeting.

Silence.

Slowly she climbed the stairs.

Claire's room was in chaos. *Desecrated* was the word that came to mind. The personality it had once reflected was disarranged, destroyed. Her clothes had all been strewn about, the sheets stripped off her bed, her jewellery scattered, her cosmetics opened up and spilled by clumsy male hands. At first she thought the surfaces were coated in talcum, but the fine white dust had no smell, and she realised it must be fingerprint powder.

She made a start at clearing it up, but soon abandoned it and sat on the edge of the naked mattress with her head in her hands until a great wave of self-disgust made her leap to her feet. She blew her nose angrily and went downstairs.

She lit a fire in the sitting room and set a kettle full of water on the hearth. In the kitchen she riddled the stove and managed to coax a glow from the pale ash, piled on some coal and set a saucepan to boil. She carried in the tin bath from the outhouse, bolting and locking the back door behind her.

She would stifle her terrors with routine. She would bathe. She would eat the remains of last night's carrot flan. She would retire early and hope for sleep.

Because tomorrow – *tomorrow* – would be a frightening day.

Inside Hut 8 there was a crowded, nervous atmosphere, like the green room of a theatre on opening night.

Jericho found his usual place next to the window. To his left: Atwood, leafing through Dilly Knox's edition of the mimes of Herodas. Pinker opposite, dressed as if for Covent Garden, his black velvet jacket slightly too long in the sleeve, so that his stubby fingers protruded like mole's paws. Kingcome and Proudfoot were playing with a pocket chess-set. Baxter was rolling a series of spindly cigarettes with a little tin contraption that didn't work properly. Puck had his feet up on the desk. The Type-Xs clacked sporadically in the background. Jericho nodded a general good evening, gave Atwood back his atlas – 'Thank you, dear boy. Good trip?' – and draped his overcoat over the back of his slatted chair. He was just in time.

'Gentlemen!' Logie appeared in the doorway and clapped twice to draw their attention, then stepped aside to allow Skynner to precede him into the room.

There was a general clatter and scraping of chair legs as they all clambered to their feet. Someone stuck their head round the door of the Decoding Room and the racket of the Type-Xs ceased.

'Easy, everybody,' said Skynner and waved them

back into their seats. Jericho found that by tucking his feet under his chair he could rest his ankle against the stolen cryptograms. 'Just stopped by to wish you luck.' Skynner's heavy body was swathed like a Chicago gangster's in half an acre of pre-war, double-breasted pinstripe. 'I'm sure you're all aware of what's at stake here as well as I am.'

'Shut up, then,' whispered Atwood.

But Skynner didn't hear him. This was what he loved. He stood with his feet planted firmly apart, his hands clasped behind his back. He was Nelson before Trafalgar. He was Churchill in the Blitz. 'I don't think I'm exaggerating when I say this could be one of the most decisive nights of the war.' His gaze sought out each of them in turn, coming last of all to Jericho and sliding away with a flicker of distaste. 'A mighty battle – probably the greatest convoy battle of the war – is about to start. Lieutenant Cave?'

'According to the Admiralty,' said Cave, 'at nineteen hundred hours this evening, convoys HX-229 and SC-122 were both warned they had entered the presumed operational area of the U-boats.'

'There we are, then. "Out of this nettle, danger, may we pluck this flower, safety."' Skynner nodded abruptly. 'Go to it.'

'Haven't I heard that before somewhere?' said Baxter.

'*Henry IV* Part One.' Atwood yawned. 'Chamberlain quoted it before he went off to meet Herr Hitler.'

After Skynner had gone, Logie went round the room handing out copies of the convoy contact section of the

Short Signal Code Book. To Jericho, as a mark of recognition, he gave the precious original.

'We're after convoy contact reports, gentlemen: as many of them as possible in the twenty-four hours between midnight tonight and midnight tomorrow – in other words, the maximum amount of crib covering one day's Enigma settings.'

The instant an E-bar signal was heard, the duty officer of the receiving station would telephone to alert them. When the contact report arrived by teleprinter a minute later, ten copies would be made and distributed. No fewer than twelve bombes – Logie had the personal guarantee of the Hut 6 bombe controller – would be placed at their disposal the moment they had a worthwhile menu to run.

As he finished his speech, the blackout shutters began to be fixed to the windows and the hut battened down for the night.

'So, Tom,' said Puck pleasantly. 'How many contact reports do you think we will need for this scheme of yours to succeed?'

Jericho was leafing through the Short Signal Code Book. He glanced up. 'I tried to work it out yesterday. I'd say about thirty.'

'Thirty?' repeated Pinker, his voice rising in horror. 'But that would m-m-mean a mmm-mmm-mmm –'

'Massacre?'

'Massacre. Yes.'

'How many U-boats would be needed to produce thirty signals?' asked Puck.

Jericho said: 'I don't know. That would depend on the time between the initial sighting and the start of the attack. Eight. Perhaps nine.'

'Nine,' muttered Kingcome. 'Christ! Your move, Jack.'

'Will someone tell me, then, please,' said Puck, 'for what I am supposed to be hoping? Am I hoping that the U-boats find these convoys or not?'

'Not,' said Pinker, looking round the table for support. 'Obviously. We w-w-want the convoys to escape the U-boats. That's what this is all about.'

Kingcome and Proudfoot nodded but Baxter shook his head violently. His cigarette disintegrated, sprinkling shreds of tobacco down the front of his cardigan. 'Damn it,' he said.

'You'd really s-s-sacrifice a c-c-convoy?' asked Pinker.

'Of course.' Baxter carefully brushed the loose tobacco into his palm. 'For the greater good. How many men has Stalin had to sacrifice so far? Five million? Ten million? The only reason we're still in the war is the butcher's bill on the eastern front. What's a convoy in comparison, if it gets us back into Shark?'

'What do you say, Tom?'

'I don't have an answer. I'm a mathematician, not a moral philosopher.'

'Bloody typical,' said Baxter.

'No, no, in terms of moral logic, Tom's is actually the only rational reply,' said Atwood. He had laid aside his Greek. This was the sort of discussion he liked. 'Consider. A madman seizes both your children at knife-point and says to you: "One must die, make your choice." Towards whom do you direct your reproaches? Towards yourself, for having to make a decision? No. Towards the madman, surely?'

Jericho said, staring at Puck: 'But that analogy doesn't answer Puck's point about what one should *hope* for.'

'Oh, but I would argue that that is *precisely* what it does answer, in that it rejects the premise of his question: the presumption that the onus is on us to make a moral choice. *Quod erat demonstrandum.*'

'Nobody can split a hair f-finer than F-Frank,' said Pinker, admiringly.

'"The *presumption* that the onus is on us to make a moral choice,"' repeated Puck. He smiled across the table at Jericho. 'How very Cambridge. Excuse me. I think I must visit the lavatory.'

He made his way towards the back of the hut. Kingcome and Proudfoot returned to their chess game. Atwood picked up Herodas. Baxter fiddled with his cigarette-rolling machine. Pinker closed his eyes. Jericho leafed through the Short Signal Code Book and thought of Claire.

Midnight came and went without a sound from the North Atlantic and the tension which had been building all evening began to slacken.

The 2 a.m. offering from the cooks of the Bletchley Park canteen was enough to make even Mrs Armstrong blanch – boiled potatoes in cheese sauce with barracuda, followed by a pudding made from two slices of bread stuck together with jam and then deep-fried in batter – and by four, the digestive effects of this, combined with the dim light in Hut 8 and the fumes from the paraffin heater, were casting a soporific pall over the naval cryptanalysts.

Atwood was the first to succumb. His mouth dropped open and the top plate of his dentures came loose so that he made a curious clicking sound as he breathed. Pinker wrinkled his nose in disgust and went off to make a nest for himself in the corner, and soon afterwards Puck, too, fell asleep, his body bent forwards, his left cheek resting on his forearms on the table. Even Jericho, despite his determination to stand guard over the cryptograms, found himself slipping over the edge of unconsciousness. He pulled himself back a couple of times, aware of Baxter watching him, but finally he couldn't fight it any longer and he slid into a turbulent dream of drowning men whose cries sounded in his ears like the wind in the aerial farm.

SIX

STRIP

STRIP: to remove one layer of encipherment from a cryptogram which has been subjected to the process of super-encipherment (US, qv), i.e., a message which has been enciphered once, and then re-enciphered to provide double security.

A Lexicon of Cryptography
('Most Secret', Bletchley Park, 1943)

1

LATER, IT WOULD transpire that Bletchley Park knew almost everything there was to know about *U-653*.

They knew she was a Type VIIc – 220 feet long, 20 feet wide, with a submerged displacement of 871 tons and a surface range of 6,500 miles – and that she had been manufactured by the Howaldts Werke of Hamburg, with engines by Blohm und Voss. They knew she was eighteen months old, because they had broken the signals describing her sea-trials in the autumn of 1941. They knew she was under the command of Kapitänleutnant Gerhard Feiler. And they knew that on the night of 28 January 1943 – the final night, as it happened, that Tom Jericho had spent with Claire Romilly – *U-653* had slipped her moorings at the French naval port of Saint-Nazaire and had moved out under a dark and moonless sky into the Bay of Biscay to begin her sixth operational tour.

After she had been at sea for a week, the cryptanalysts in Hut 8 broke a signal from U-boat headquarters – then still in their grand apartment building off the Bois de Boulogne in Paris – ordering *U-653* to proceed on the surface to naval grid square KD 63 'AT MAXIMUM MAINTAINABLE SPEED WITHOUT REGARD TO THE THREAT FROM THE AIR'.

On 11 February she joined ten other U-boats in a new mid-Atlantic patrol line code-named Ritter.

Weather conditions in the North Atlantic were particularly foul in the winter of 1942-3. There were a hundred days when the U-boats reported winds topping force 7 on the Beaufort scale. Sometimes the gales reached over 100 miles per hour, whipping up waves more than 50 feet high. Snow, sleet, hail and frozen spray lashed submarines and convoys alike. One Allied ship rolled over and sank in minutes simply from the weight of ice on her superstructure.

On 13th February, Feiler broke radio silence to report that his watch officer, one Leutnant Laudon, had been washed overboard — a blatant disregard of operational procedure on Feiler's part which brought no condolences but a terse rebuke from his controllers, broadcast to the entire submarine fleet:

FEILER'S MESSAGE ABOUT LOSS OF WATCH OFFICER SHOULD NOT HAVE BEEN SENT UNTIL W/T SILENCE WAS BROKEN BY GENERAL CONTACT WITH ENEMY.

It was only on the 23rd, after nearly four weeks at sea, that Feiler redeemed himself by at last making contact with a convoy. At 6 p.m. he dived to avoid an escorting destroyer, and then, when night came, rose to attack. He had at his disposal twelve torpedoes, each 23 feet long with its own electric motor, capable of running through a convoy, turning in a half circle and running back, turning again and so on, and on, until either its power ran out or a ship was sunk. The sensing mechanism was crude; it was not unknown for a U-boat to find itself being pursued by its own armaments. They were called FATs: *Flachenabsuchendertorpedos*, or 'shallow searching torpedoes'. Feiler fired four of them.

```
FROM: FEILER
IN NAVAL GRID SQUARE BC 6956 AT 0116. FOUR-FAN
AT A CONVOY PROCEEDING ON A SOUTHERLY COURSE AT
7 KNOTS. ONE STEAMSHIP OF 6,000 GROSS REGISTERED
TONS: LARGE EXPLOSION AND A CLOUD OF SMOKE, THEN
NOTHING MORE SEEN. ONE STEAMSHIP OF 5,500 GRT
LEFT BURNING. 2 FURTHER HITS HEARD, NO
OBSERVATIONS.
```

On the 25th, Feiler radioed his position.
On the 26th, his luck turned bad again.

```
FROM: U-653
AM IN NAVAL GRID SQUARE BC 8747. HIGH PRESSURE
GROUP 2 AND STARBOARD NEGATIVE BUOYANCY TANK
UNSERVICEABLE. BALLAST TANK 5 NOT TIGHT. IS
MAKING ODD NOISES. DIESEL PRODUCING DENSE WHITE
SMOKE.
```

Headquarters took all night to consult its engineers and replied at ten the following morning.

```
TO: FEILER
THE CONDITION OF BALLAST TANK NO 5 IS THE ONLY
THING WHICH MAY ENFORCE RETURN PASSAGE. DECIDE
FOR YOURSELF AND REPORT.
```

By midnight, Feiler had made his decision.

```
FROM: U-653
AM NOT RETURNING.
```

On 3 March, in mountainous seas, *U-653* came alongside a U-boat tanker and took on board 65 cubic metres of fuel and provisions sufficient for another fourteen days at sea.

On the 6th, Feiler was ordered into station in a new patrol line, code-named *Raubgraf* (Robber Baron).

And that was all.

On 9 March the U-boats abruptly changed their Weather Code Book, Shark was blacked out, and *U-653*, along with one hundred and thirteen other German submarines then known to be operating in the Atlantic, vanished from Bletchley's view.

At 5 a.m. GMT on Tuesday 16 March, some nine hours after Jericho had parked the Austin and walked into Hut 8, *U-653* was heading due east on the surface, returning to France. In the North Atlantic it was 3 a.m.

After ten days on station in the *Raubgraf* line, with no sign of any convoy, Feiler had finally decided to head for home. He had lost, along with Leutnant Laudon, four other ratings washed overboard. One of his petty officers was ill. The starboard diesel was still giving trouble. His one remaining torpedo was defective. The boat, which had no heating, was cold and damp, and everything – lockers, food, uniforms – was covered in a greenish-white mould. Feiler lay on his wet bunk, curled up against the cold, wincing at the irregular beat of the engine, and tried to sleep.

Up on the bridge, four men made up the night watch: one for each point of the compass. Cowled like monks in dripping black oilskins, lashed to the rail by metal belts, each had a pair of goggles and a pair of Zeiss binoculars clamped firmly to his eyes and was staring blindly into his own sector of darkness.

The cloud cover was ten-tenths. The wind was a steel attack. The hull of the U-boat thrashed beneath their feet with a violence that sent them skidding over the wet deck plates and knocking into one another.

Facing directly ahead, towards the invisible prow, was a young Obersteurmann, Heinz Theen. He was peering into such an infinity of blackness that it was possible to imagine they might have fallen off the edge of the world, when suddenly he saw a light. It flared out of nowhere, several hundred yards in front of him, winked for two seconds, then disappeared. If he hadn't had his binoculars trained precisely upon it, he would never have seen it.

Astonishing though it seemed, he realised he had just witnessed someone lighting a cigarette.

An Allied seaman lighting a cigarette in the middle of the North Atlantic.

He called down the conning tower for the captain.

By the time Feiler had scrambled up the slippery metal ladder to the bridge thirty seconds later the cloud had shifted slightly in the high wind and shapes were moving all around them. Feiler swivelled through 360 degrees and counted the outlines of nearly twenty ships, the nearest no more than 500 yards away on the port side.

A whispered cry, as much of panic as command: 'Alarrrmm!'

The *U-653* came out of her emergency dive and hung motionless in the calmer water beneath the waves.

Thirty-nine men crouched silently in the semidarkness listening to the sounds of the convoy passing overhead: the fast revs of the modern diesels, the ponderous churning of the steamers, the curious singing noises of the turbines in the warship escorts.

Feiler let them all go by. He waited two hours, then surfaced.

The convoy was already so far ahead as to be barely visible in the faint dawn light – just the masts of the ships and a few smudges of smoke on the horizon, and then, occasionally, when a high wave lifted the U-boat, the ironwork of bridges and funnels.

Feiler's task under standing orders was not to attack – impossible in any case, given his lack of torpedoes – but to keep his quarry in sight while drawing in every other U-boat within a radius of 100 miles.

'Convoy steering 070 degrees,' said Feiler. 'Naval grid square BD 1491.'

The first officer made a scrawled note in pencil then dropped down the conning tower to collect the Short Signal Code Book. In his cubbyhole next to the captain's berth the radioman pressed his switches. The Enigma came on with a hum.

2

At 7 a.m., Logie had sent Pinker, Proudfoot and Kingcome back to their digs to get some decent rest. 'Sod's law will now proceed to operate,' he predicted, as he watched them go, and sod's law duly did. Twenty-five minutes later, he was back in the Big Room with the queasy expression of guilty excitement which would characterise the whole of that day.

'It looks like it may have started.'

St Erith, Scarborough and Flowerdown had all reported an E-bar signal followed by eight Morse letters, and within a minute one of the Wrens from the Registration Room was bringing in the first copies. Jericho placed his carefully in the centre of his trestle table.

RGHC DMIG. His heart began to accelerate.

'Hubertus net,' said Logie. '4601 kilocycles.'

Cave was listening to someone on the telephone. He put his hand over the mouthpiece. 'Direction finders have a fix.' He clicked his fingers. 'Pencil. Quick.' Baxter threw him one. '49.4 degrees north,' he repeated. '38.8 degrees west. Got it. Well done.' He hung up.

Cave had spent all night plotting the convoys' courses on two large charts of the North Atlantic – one issued by the Admiralty, the other a captured German naval grid, on which the ocean was divided into thousands of tiny squares. The cryptanalysts gathered round him. Cave's finger came down on a spot almost exactly midway between Newfoundland and the British Isles. 'There she is. She's shadowing HX-229.' He made a cross on the map and wrote 0725 beside it.

Jericho said: 'What grid square is that?'

'BD 1491.'

'And the convoy course?'

'070.'

Jericho went back to his desk and in less than two minutes, using the Short Signal Code Book and the current Kriegsmarine address book for encoding naval grid squares ('Alfred Krause, Blucherplatz 15': Hut 8 had broken that just before the blackout) he had a five-letter crib to slide under the contact report.

```
R G H C D M I G
D D F G R X ? ?
```

The first four letters announced that a convoy had been located steering 070 degrees, the next two gave the grid square, the final two represented the code name of the U-boat, which he didn't have. He circled R-D and D-R. A four-letter loop on the first signal.

'I get D-R/R-D,' said Puck a few seconds later.

'So do I.'

'Me too,' said Baxter.

Jericho nodded and doodled his initials on the pad. 'A good omen.'

After that, the pace of events began to quicken.

At 8.25, two long signals were intercepted emanating from Magdeburg, which Cave at once surmised would be U-boat headquarters ordering every submarine in the North Atlantic into the attack zone. At 9.20, he put down the telephone to announce that the Admiralty had just signalled the convoy commander with a warning that he was probably being shadowed. Seven minutes later, the telephone rang again. Flowerdown intercept station. A second E-bar flash from almost the same location as the first. The Wrens hurried in with it: KLYS QNLP.

'The same hearse,' said Cave. 'Following standard operating procedure. Reporting every two hours, or near as damn it.'

'Grid square?'

'The same.'

'Convoy course?'

'Also the same. For now.'

Jericho went back to his desk and manipulated the original crib under the new cryptogram.

```
K L Y S Q N L P
D D F G R X ? ?
```

Again, there were no letter clashes. The golden rule of Enigma, its single, fatal weakness: *nothing is ever itself – A can never be A, B can never be B* . . . It was working. His feet performed a little tap dance of delight beneath the table. He glanced up to find Baxter staring at him and he realised, to his horror, that he was smiling.

'Pleased?'

'Of course not.'

But such was his shame that when, an hour later, Logie came through to say that a second U-boat had just sent a contact signal, he felt himself personally responsible.

SOUY YTRQ.

At 11.40, a third U-boat began to shadow the convoy, at 12.20, a fourth, and suddenly Jericho had seven signals on his desk. He was conscious of people coming up and looking over his shoulder – Logie with his burning hayrick of a pipe and the meaty smell and heavy breathing of Skynner. He didn't look round. He didn't talk. The outside world had melted for him. Even Claire was just a phantom now. There were only the loops of letters, forming and stretching out towards him from the grey Atlantic, multiplying on his sheets of paper, turning into thin chains of possibility in his mind.

They didn't stop for breakfast, nor for lunch. Minute by minute, throughout the afternoon, the cryptanalysts followed, at third hand, the progress of the chase two thousand miles away. The commander of the convoy was signalling to the Admiralty, the Admiralty had an open line to Cave, and Cave would shout each time a fresh development looked like affecting the hunt for cribs.

Two signals came at 13.40 – one a short contact report, the other longer, almost certainly originating from the U-boat that had started the hunt. Both were for the first time close enough to be fixed by direction finders on board the convoy's own escorts. Cave

listened gravely for a minute, then announced that
HMS *Mansfield*, a destroyer, was being dispatched
from the main body of merchantmen to attack the U-
boats.

'The convoy's just made an emergency turn to the
southeast. She's going to try to shake off the hearses
while *Mansfield* forces them under.'

Jericho looked up. 'What course is she steering?'

'What course is she steering?' repeated Cave into the
telephone. 'I *said*,' he yelled, 'what fucking *course* is she
steering?' He winced at Jericho. The receiver was
jammed tight to his scarred ear. 'All right. Yes. Thank
you. Convoy steering 118 degrees.' Jericho reached for
the Short Signal Code Book.

'Will they manage to get away?' asked Baxter.

Cave bent over his chart with a rule and protractor.
'Maybe. It's what I'd do in their place.'

A quarter of an hour passed and nothing happened.

'Perhaps they have done it,' said Puck. 'Then what
do we do?'

Cave said: 'How much more material do you need?'

Jericho counted through the signals. 'We've got
nine. We need another twenty. Another twenty-five
would be better.'

'Jesus!' Cave regarded them with disgust. 'It's like
sitting with a flock of carrion.'

Somewhere behind them a telephone managed half
a ring before it was snatched out of its cradle. Logie
came in a moment later, still writing.

'That was St Erith reporting an E-bar signal at 49.4
degrees north, 38.1 degrees west.'

'New location,' said Cave, studying his charts. He made a cross, then threw his pencil down and leaned back in his chair, rubbing his face. 'All she's managed to do is run straight from one hearse into another. Which is what? The fifth? Christ, the sea must be teeming with them.'

'She isn't going to get away,' said Puck, 'is she?'

'Not a chance. Not if they're coming in from all around her.'

A Wren moved among the cryptanalysts, doling out the latest cryptogram: BKEL UUXS.

Ten signals. Five U-boats in contact.

'Grid square?' said Jericho.

Hester Wallace was not a poker player, which was a mistake on her part as she had been blessed with a poker face that could have made her a fortune. Nobody watching her wheel her bicycle into the shed beside the canteen that afternoon, or seeing her flick her pass at the sentry, or squeezing up against the corridor wall in Hut 6 to let her march by, or sitting opposite her in Intercept Control – nobody would have guessed the turmoil in her mind.

Her complexion was, as ever, pale, her forehead slightly creased by a frown that discouraged conversation. She wore her long, dark hair like a headache, savagely twisted up and speared. Her costume was the usual uniform of the West Country schoolmistress: flat shoes, grey woollen stockings, plain grey skirt, white shirt and an elderly but well-cut tweed jacket which she would shortly take off and hang over the back of the chair, for the afternoon was warm. Her fingers moved across the blist in a short, staccato pecking motion. She had hardly slept all night.

Name of intercept station, time of interception, frequency, call sign, letter groups . . .

Where was the record of settings kept? That was the first matter to determine. Not in Control, obviously. Not in the Index Room. Not in the Registry. And not next door in the Registration Room, either: she had already made a quick inspection there. The Decoding Room was a possibility, but the Type-X girls were always complaining they were cramped for space, and sixty separate Enigma keys, their settings changed daily – in the case of the Luftwaffe, sometimes twice a day – well, that was a minimum of five hundred pieces of information every week, 25,000 in a year, and this was the war's fourth year. That would suggest a sizeable catalogue; a small library, in fact.

The only conclusion was that they had to be kept where the cryptanalysts worked, in the Machine Room, or else close by.

She finished blisting Chicksands, noon till three, and moved towards the door.

Her first pass through the Machine Room was spoiled by nerves: straight through it to the other end of the hut without even glancing from side to side. She stood outside the Decoding Room, cursing her fears, pretending to study the noticeboard. With a shaking hand she made a note about a performance of *Die Fledermaus* by the Bletchley Park Music Society which she had no intention of ever attending.

ROBERT HARRIS

The second run was better.

There was no machinery in the Machine Room – the origin of its name was lost in the glorious mists of 1940 – just desks, cryptanalysts, wire baskets filled with signals and, on the wall to the right, shelf after shelf of files. She stopped and looked around distractedly, as if searching for a familiar face. The problem was, she knew nobody. But then her gaze fell upon a bald head with a few long, ginger hairs combed pathetically across a freckled crown, and she realised that wasn't entirely true.

She knew Cordingley.

Dear old, dull old Donald Cordingley, the winner – in a crowded field – of the Dullest Man in Bletchley contest. Ineligible for military service due to a funnel chest. By profession: actuary. Ten years' service with the Scottish Widows Assurance Society in the City of London, until a lucky third place in the *Daily Telegraph* crossword competition won him a seat in the Hut 6 Machine Room.

Her seat.

She watched him for a few more seconds, then moved away.

When she got back to Control Miles Mermagen was standing by her desk.

'How was Beaumanor?'

'Engrossing.'

She had left her jacket over her chair and he ran his hand over the collar, feeling the material between his thumb and forefinger, as if checking it for quality.

'How'd you get there?'

'A friend gave me a lift.'

'A male friend, I gather.' Mermagen's smile was wide and unfriendly.

'How do you know that?'

'I have my spies,' he said.

The ocean was alive with signals. They were landing on Jericho's desk at the rate of one every twenty minutes.

At 16.00 a sixth U-boat fastened on to the convoy and soon afterwards Cave announced that HX-229 was making another turn, to 028 degrees, in her latest and (in his opinion) hopeless attempt to escape her pursuers.

By 18.00 Jericho had a pile of nineteen contact signals, out of which he had conjured three four-letter loops and a mass of half-sketched bombe menus that looked like the plans for some complex game of hopscotch. His neck and shoulders were so knotted with tension he could barely straighten up.

The room by now was crowded. Pinker, Kingcome and Proudfoot had come back on shift. The other British naval lieutenant, Villiers, was standing next to Cave, who was explaining something on one of his charts. A Wren with a tray offered Jericho a curling Spam sandwich and an enamel mug of tea and he took them gratefully.

Logie came up behind him and tousled his hair.

'How are you feeling, old love?'

'Wrecked, frankly.'

'Want to knock off?'

'Very funny.'

'Come into my office and I'll give you something. Bring your tea.'

The 'something' turned out to be a large, yellow Benzedrine tablet, of which Logie had half a dozen in an hexagonal pillbox.

Jericho hesitated. 'I'm not sure I should. These helped send me funny last time.'

'They'll get you through the night, though, won't they? Come on, old thing. The commandos swear by them.' He rattled the box under Jericho's nose. 'So you'll crash out at breakfast? So what? By then we'll either have this bugger beaten. Or not. In which case it won't matter, will it?' He took one of the pills and pressed it into Jericho's palm. 'Go on. I won't tell Nurse.' He closed Jericho's fingers around it and said quietly: 'Because I can't let you go, you know, old love. Not tonight. Not you. Some of the others, maybe, but not you.'

'Oh, Christ. Well, since you put it so nicely.'

Jericho swallowed the pill with a mouthful of tea. It left a foul taste and he drained his mug to try and swill it away. Logie regarded him fondly.

'That's my boy.' He put the box back in his desk drawer and locked it. 'I've been protecting your bloody back again, incidentally. I had to tell him you were much too important to be disturbed.'

'Tell who? Skynner?'

'No. Not Skynner. Wigram.'

'What does he want?'

'You, old cock. I'd say he wants you. Skinned, stuffed and mounted on a pole somewhere. Really, I don't know, for such a quiet bloke, you don't half make some enemies. I told him to come back at midnight. All right by you?'

Before Jericho could reply the telephone rang and Logie grabbed it.

'Yes? Speaking.' He grunted and stretched across his desk for a pencil. 'Time of origin 19.02, 52.1 degrees north, 37.2 degrees west. Thanks, Bill. Keep the faith.'

He replaced the receiver.

'And then there were seven . . .'

It was dark again and the lights were on in the Big Room. The sentries outside were banging the blackout shutters into place, like prison warders locking up their charges for the night.

Jericho hadn't set foot out of the hut for twenty-four hours, hadn't even looked out of the window. As he slipped back into his seat and checked his coat to make sure the cryptograms were still there, he wondered vaguely what kind of day it had been and what Hester was doing.

Don't think about that now.

Already, he could feel the Benzedrine beginning to take effect. The muscles of his heart seemed feathery, his body charged. When he glanced across his notes, what had seemed inert and impenetrable a half-hour ago was suddenly fluid and full of possibility.

The new cryptogram was already on his desk: YALB DKYF.

'Naval grid square BD 2742,' called Cave. 'Course 055 degrees. Convoy speed nine and a half knots.'

Logie said: 'A message from Mr Skynner. A bottle of Scotch for the first man with a menu for the bombes.'

Twenty-three signals received. Seven U-boats in contact. Two hours to go till nightfall in the North Atlantic.

20.00: nine U-boats in contact.
20.46: ten.

The Control Room girls took a table near the serving hatch for their evening meal. Celia Davenport showed them all some pictures of her fiancé, who was fighting in the desert, while Anthea Leigh-Delamere brayed endlessly about a meet of the Bicester Hunt. Hester passed on the photographs without looking at them. Her eyes were fixed on Donald Cordingley, queuing to collect his lump of coelacanth, or whatever other obscure example of God's aquatic creatures they were now required to eat.

She was cleverer than he, and he knew it.

She intimidated him.

Hello, Donald, she thought. *Hello, Donald . . . Oh, nothing much, just this new back-break section, coming along with bucket and shovel after the Lord Mayor's parade . . . Now, listen, Donald, there's this funny little wireless net, Konotop-Prihiki-Poltava, in the southern Ukraine. Nothing vital, but we've never quite broken it and Archie — you must know Archie? — Archie has a theory it may be a variant on Vulture . . . Traffic runs through February and the first few days in March . . . That's right . . .*

She watched him as he sat alone and picked at his

lonely supper. She watched him, indeed, as if she *were* a vulture. And when, after fifteen minutes, he rose and scraped the leftovers from his plate into the swill bins, she rose as well, and followed him.

She was vaguely aware of the other girls staring after her in astonishment. She ignored them.

She tracked him all the way back to Hut 6, gave him five minutes to settle down, then went in after him.

The Machine Room was shaded and somnolent, like a library at dusk. She tapped him lightly on the shoulder.

'Hello, Donald.'

He turned round and blinked up at her in surprise. 'Oh, hello.' The effort of memory was heroic. 'Hello, Hester.'

'It's almost dark out there,' said Cave, looking at his watch. 'Not long now. How many have you had?'

'Twenty-nine,' said Baxter.

'I believe you said that would be enough, Mr Jericho?'

'Weather,' said Jericho, without looking up. 'We need a weather report from the convoy. Barometric pressure, cloud cover, cloud type, wind speed, temperature. Before it gets too dark.'

'They've got ten U-boats on their backs and you want them to tell you the *weather*?'

'Yes, please. Fast as they can.'

The weather report arrived at 21.31.

There were no more contact signals after 21.40.

*

Thus convoy KX-229 at 22.00.

Thirty-seven merchant vessels, ranging in size from the 12,000-ton British tanker *Southern Princess* to the 3,500-ton American freighter *Margaret Lykes*, making slow progress through heavy seas, steering a course of 055 degrees, direct to England, lit up like a regatta by a full moon to a range of ten miles visibility – the first such night in the North Atlantic for weeks. Escort vessels: five, including two slow corvettes and two clapped out, elderly ex-American destroyers donated to Britain in 1940 in exchange for bases, one of which – HMS *Mansfield* – had lost touch with the convoy after charging down the U-boats because the convoy commander (on his first operational command) had forgotten to signal her with his second change of course. No rescue ship available. No air cover. No reinforcements within a thousand miles.

'All in all,' said Cave, lighting a cigarette and contemplating his charts, 'what you might fairly call a bit of a cock-up.'

The first torpedo hit at 22.01.

At 22.32, Tom Jericho was heard to say, very quietly, 'Yes.'

3

It was chucking-out time at the Eight Bells Inn on the Buckingham Road and Miss Jobey and Mr Bonnyman had virtually exhausted the main topic of their evening's conversation: what Bonnyman dramatically termed the 'police raid' on Mr Jericho's room.

They had heard the details at supper from Mrs Armstrong, her face still flushed with outrage at the memory of this violation of her territory. A uniformed officer had stood guard all afternoon on the doorstep ('in full view of the entire street, mind you'), while two plain-clothes men carrying a box of tools and waving a warrant had spent the best part of three hours searching the upstairs back bedroom, before leaving at teatime with a pile of books. They had dismantled the bed and the wardrobe, taken up the carpet and the floorboards, and brought down a heap of soot from the chimney. 'That young man is out,' declared Mrs Armstrong, folding her hamlike arms, 'and all rent forfeit.'

"*All rent forfeit*," repeated Bonnyman into his beer, for the sixth or seventh time. 'I love it.'

'And such a quiet man,' said Miss Jobey.

A handbell rang behind the bar and the lights flickered.

'Time, gentlemen! Time, please!'

Bonnyman finished his watery bitter, Miss Jobey her port and lemon, and he escorted her unsteadily, past the dartboard and the hunting prints, towards the door.

The day that Jericho had missed had given the town its first real taste of spring. Out on the pavement the night air was still mild. Darkness touched the dreary street with romance. As the departing drinkers stumbled away into the blackout, Bonnyman playfully pulled Miss Jobey towards him. They fell back slightly into a doorway. Her mouth opened on his, she pressed herself up against him, and Bonnyman squeezed her waist in return. Whatever she might have lacked in beauty – and in the blackout, who could tell? – she more than made up for in ardour. Her strong and agile tongue, sweet with port, squirmed against his teeth.

Bonnyman, by profession a Post Office engineer, had been drafted to Bletchley, as Jericho had guessed, to service the bombes. Miss Jobey worked in the upstairs back bedroom of the mansion, filing Abwehr hand-ciphers. Neither, in accordance with regulations, had told the other what they did, a discretion which Bonnyman had extended somewhat to cover in addition the existence of a wife and two children at home in Dorking.

His hands slipped down her narrow thighs and began to hoist her skirt.

'Not here,' she said into his mouth, and brushed his fingers away.

Well (as Bonnyman would afterwards confide with a wink to the unsmiling police inspector who took his statement), the things a grown man has to do in wartime, and all for a simple you-know-what.

First, a cycle ride, which took them along a track and under a railway bridge. Then, by the thin beam of a torch, over a padlocked gate and through mud and brambles towards the hulk of a broken building. A great expanse of water somewhere close by. You couldn't see it, but you could hear the lapping in the breeze and the occasional cry of a waterfowl, and you could sense a deeper darkness, like a great black pit.

Complaints from Miss Jobey as she snagged her precious stockings and wrenched her ankle: loud and bitter imprecations against Mr Bonnyman and all his works which did not augur well for the purpose he had in mind. She started whining: 'Come on, Bonny, I'm frightened, let's go back.'

But Bonnyman had no intention of turning back. Even on a normal evening, Mrs Armstrong monitored every peep and squeak in the ether of the Commercial Guesthouse like a one-woman intercept station; tonight, she'd be on even higher alert than usual. Besides, he always found this place exciting. The light flashed on bare brick and on evidence of earlier liaisons – *AE + GS*, *Tony = Kath*. The spot held an odd erotic charge. So much had clearly happened here, so many whispered fumblings . . . They were a part of a great flux of yearning that went back long before them and would go on long after them – illicit, irrepressible, eternal. This was *life*. Such, at any rate, were Bonnyman's thoughts, although naturally he didn't express them at the time, nor afterwards to the police.

'And what happened next, sir? Precisely.'

He won't admit to this either, thank you very much, precisely or imprecisely.

But what did happen next was that Bonnyman wedged the torch in a gap in the brickwork where something had been torn from the wall, and threw his arms around Miss Jobey. He encountered a little light resistance at first – some token twisting and turning and 'stop it', 'not here' – which quickly became less convincing, until suddenly her tongue was up to its tricks again and they were back where they'd left off outside the Eight Bells Inn. Once again his hands began to ride up her skirt and once again she pushed him away, but this time for a different reason. Frowning slightly, she ducked and pulled down her knickers. One step, two steps, and they had vanished into her pocket. Bonnyman watched, enraptured.

'What happened next, inspector, *precisely*, is that Miss Jobey and myself noticed some hessian sacking in the corner.'

She with her skirt up above her knees, he with his trousers down around his ankles, shuffling forwards like a man in leg-irons, dropping heavily to his knees, a cloud of dust from the sacks rising and blossoming in the torch-beam, then much squirming and complaining on her part that something was digging into her back.

They stood and pulled away the sacks to make a better bed.

'And that was when you found it?'

'That was when we found it.'

The police inspector suddenly brought his fist down hard on the rough wooden table and shouted for his sergeant.

'Any sign of Mr Wigram yet?'

'We're still looking, sir.'

'Well, bloody well find him, man. Find him.'

4

The bombe was heavy – Jericho guessed it must weigh more than half a ton – and even though it was mounted on castors it still took all his strength, combined with the engineer's, to drag it away from the wall. Jericho pulled while the engineer went behind it and put his shoulder to the frame to heave. It came away at last with a screech and the Wrens moved in to strip it.

The decryptor was a monster, like something out of an H. G. Wells fantasy of the future: a black metal cabinet, eight feet wide and six feet tall, with scores of five-inch-diameter drum wheels set into the front. The back was hinged and opened up to show a bulging mass of coloured cables and the dull gleam of metal drums. In the place where it had stood on the concrete floor there was a large puddle of oil.

Jericho wiped his hands on a rag and retreated to watch from a corner. Elsewhere in the hut a score of other bombes were churning away on other Enigma keys and the noise and the heat were how he imagined a ship's engine room might be. One Wren went round to the back of the cabinet and began disconnecting and replugging the cables. The other moved along the front, pulling out each drum in turn and checking it. Whenever she found a fault in the wiring she would hand the drum to the engineer who would stroke the tiny brush wires back into place with a pair of tweezers. The contact brushes were always fraying, just as the belt which connected the mechanism to the big electric motor had a tendency to stretch and slip whenever there was a heavy load. And the engineers had never quite got the earthing right, so that the cabinets had a tendency to give off powerful electric shocks.

Jericho thought it was the worst job of all. A pig of a job. Eight hours a day, six days a week, cooped up in this windowless, deafening cell. He turned away to look at his watch. He didn't want them to see his impatience. It was nearly half past eleven.

His menu was at that moment being rushed into bombe bays all across the Bletchley area. Eight miles north of the Park, in a hut in a clearing in the forested estate of Gayhurst Manor, a clutch of tired Wrens near the end of their shift were being ordered to halt the three bombes running on Nuthatch (Berlin-Vienna-Belgrade Army administration), strip them and prepare them for Shark. In the stable block of Adstock Manor, ten miles to the west, the girls were actually sprawled with their feet up beside their silent machines, drinking Ovaltine and listening to Tommy Dorsey on the BBC Light Programme, when the supervisor came storming through with a sheaf of menus and told them to stir themselves, fast. And at Wavendon Manor, three miles northeast, a similar story: four bombes in a dank and windowless bunker were abruptly pulled off Osprey (the low-priority Enigma key of the Organisation Todt) and their operators told to stand by for a rush job.

Those, plus the two machines in Bletchley's Hut 11, made up the promised dozen bombes.

The mechanical check completed, the Wren went back to the first row of drums and began adjusting them to the combination listed on the menus. She called out the letters to the other girl, who checked them.

'Freddy, Butter, Quagga . . .'

'Yes.'

'Apple, X-ray, Edward . . .'

'Yes.'

The drums slipped on to their spindles and were fixed into place with a loud metallic click. Each was wired to mimic the action of a single Enigma rotor: 108 in all, equivalent to thirty-six Enigma machines running in parallel. When all the drums had been set, the bombe was trundled back into place and the motor started.

The drums began to turn, all except one in the top row which had jammed. The engineer gave it a whack with his spanner and it, too, began to revolve. The bombe would now run continuously on this menu – certainly for one day; possibly, according to Jericho's calculations, for two or three – stopping occasionally when the drums were so aligned they completed a circuit. Then the readings on the drums would be checked and tested, the machine restarted, and so it would go on until the precise combination of settings had been found, at which point the cryptanalysts would be able to read that day's Shark traffic. Such, at any rate, was the theory.

The engineer began dragging out the other bombe and Jericho moved forward to help, but was stopped by a tugging on his arm.

'Come on, old love,' shouted Logie above the din.

'There's nothing more we can do here.' He pulled at his sleeve again.

Reluctantly, Jericho turned and followed him out of the hut.

He felt no sense of elation. Maybe tomorrow evening or maybe on Thursday, the bombes would give them the Enigma settings for the day now ending. Then the real work would begin – the laborious business of trying to reconstruct the new Short Weather Code Book – taking the meteorological data from the convoy, matching it to the weather signals already received from the surrounding U-boats, making some guesses, testing them, constructing a fresh set of cribs . . . It never ended, this battle against Enigma. It was a chess tournament of a thousand rounds against a player of prodigious defensive strength, and each day the pieces went back to their original positions and the game began afresh.

Logie, too, seemed rather flat as they walked along the asphalt path towards Hut 8.

'I've sent the others home to their digs for some kip,' he was saying, 'which is where I'm going. And where you ought to go, too, if you're not too high to sleep.'

'I'll just clear up here for a bit, if that's all right. Take the code book back to the safe.'

'Do that. Thanks.'

'And then I suppose I'd better face Wigram.'

'Ah, yes. Wigram.'

They went into the hut. In his office, Logie tossed Jericho the keys to the Black Museum. 'And your prize,' he said, holding up a half-bottle of scotch. 'Don't let's forget that.'

Jericho smiled. 'I thought you said Skynner was offering a full bottle.'

'Ah, well, yes, I did, but you know Skynner.'

'Give it to the others.'

'Oh, don't be so bloody pious.' From the same drawer Logie produced a couple of enamel mugs. He blew away some dust and wiped their insides with his forefinger. 'What shall we drink to? You don't mind if I join you?'

'The end of Shark? The future?'

Logie splashed a large measure of whisky into each mug. 'How about,' he said, shrewdly, offering one to Jericho, 'how about *your* future?'

They clinked mugs.

'*My* future.'

They sat in their overcoats, in silence, drinking.

'I'm defeated,' said Logie at last, using the desk to pull himself to his feet. 'I couldn't tell you the year, old love, never mind the day.' He had three pipes in a rack and he blew noisily through each of them, making a harsh, cracking sound, then slipped them into his pocket. 'Now don't forget your scotch.'

'I don't want the bloody scotch.'

'Take it. Please. For my sake.'

In the corridor, he shook Jericho's hand, and Jericho feared Logie was going to say something embarrassing. But whatever it was he had in mind, he thought better of it. Instead, he merely gave a rueful salute and lurched along the passage, banging the door behind him.

*

The Big Room, in anticipation of the midnight shift, was almost empty. A little desultory work was being done on Dolphin and Porpoise at the far end. Two young women in overalls were on their knees around Jericho's desk, gathering every scrap of waste paper into a couple of sacks, ready for incineration. Only Cave was still there, bent over his charts. He looked up as Jericho came in.

'Well? How's it going for you?'

'Too early to tell,' said Jericho. He found the code book and slipped it into his pocket. 'And you?'

'Three hit so far. A Norwegian freighter and a Dutch cargo ship. They just went straight to the bottom. The third's on fire and going round and round in circles. Half the crew lost, the other half trying to save her.'

'What is she?'

'American Liberty ship. The *James Oglethorpe*. Seven thousand tons, carrying steel and cotton.'

'American,' repeated Jericho. He thought of Kramer. *'My brother died, one of the first . . .'*

'It's a slaughter,' said Cave, 'an absolute bloody slaughter. And shall I tell you the worst of it? It's not going to finish tonight. It's going to go on and on like this for days. They're going to be chased and harried and torpedoed right the way across the bloody North Atlantic. Can you imagine what that feels like? Watching the ship next to you blow up? Not being allowed to stop and search for survivors? Waiting for your turn?' He touched his scar, then seemed to realise what he was doing and let his hand fall. There was a terrible resignation in the gesture. 'And now, apparently, they're picking up U-boat signals swarming all around SC-122.'

His telephone began to ring and he swung away to answer it. While his back was turned, Jericho quietly placed the half-empty half-bottle of scotch on his desk, then made his way out into the night.

His mind, on a fuel of Benzedrine and scotch, seemed to be wheeling away on a course of its own, churning like the bombes in Hut 11, making bizarre and random connections – Claire and Hester and Skynner, and Wigram with his shoulder holster, and the tyre tracks in the frost outside the cottage, and the blazing Liberty ship going round and round over the bodies of half her crew.

He stopped by the lake to breathe some fresh air and thought of all the other occasions when he had stood here in the darkness, gazing at the faint silhouette of the mansion against the stars. He half-closed his eyes and saw it as it might have been before the war. A midsummer evening. The sounds of an orchestra and a bubble of voices drifting across the lawn. A line of Chinese lanterns, pink and mauve and lemon, stirring in the arboretum. Chandeliers in the ballroom. White crystal fracturing on the smooth surface of the lake.

The vision was so strong that he found he was sweating in his overcoat against the imagined heat, and as he climbed the slope towards the big house he fancied he saw a line of silver Rolls-Royces, their chauffeurs leaning against the long bonnets. But as he drew closer he saw that the cars were merely buses, come to drop off the next shift, pick up the last, and that the music in the mansion was only the percussion of telephone bells and the tapping of hurrying footsteps on the stone floor.

In the labyrinth of the house he nodded cautiously to the few people he passed – an elderly man in a dark grey suit, an Army captain, a WAAF. They appeared seedy in the dingy light and he guessed, by their expressions, he must look pretty odd himself. Benzedrine could do funny things to the pupils of your eyes, he seemed to remember, and he hadn't shaved or changed his clothes for more than forty hours. But nobody in Bletchley was ever thrown out for simply looking strange, or the place would have been empty from the start. There was old Dilly Knox, who used to come to work in his dressing gown, and Turing who cycled in wearing a gas mask to try to cure his hay fever, and the cryptanalyst from the Japanese section who had bathed naked in the lake one lunchtime. By comparison, Jericho was as conventional as an accountant.

He opened the door to the cellar passage. The bulb must have blown since his last visit and he found himself peering into a darkness as chill and black as a catacomb. Something gleamed very faintly at the foot of the stairs and he groped his way down the steps towards it. It was the keyhole to the Black Museum, traced in luminous paint: a trick they had learned in the Blitz.

Inside the room the light switch worked. He unlocked the safe and replaced the code book and for a moment he was seized by the crazy notion of hiding the stolen cryptograms inside it as well. Folded into an envelope they might pass unnoticed for months. But when, after tonight, was he likely to pass this way again? And one day they would be discovered. And then all it would take would be a telephone call to Beaumanor and everything would be unravelled – his involvement, Hester's . . .

No, no.

He closed the steel door.

But still he couldn't quite bring himself to leave. So much of his life was here. He touched the safe and then the rough, dry walls. He drew his finger through the dust on the table. He contemplated the row of Enigmas on the metal shelf. They were all encased in light wood, mostly in their original German boxes, and even in repose they seemed to exude a compelling, almost menacing power. These were far more than mere machines, he thought. These were the synapses of the enemy's brain – mysterious, complex, *animate*.

He stared at them for a couple of minutes, then began to turn away.

He stopped himself.

'Tom Jericho,' he whispered. 'You bloody fool.'

The first two Enigmas he lifted down and inspected turned out to be badly damaged and unusable. The third had a luggage label attached to its handle by a bit of string: 'Sidi Bou Zid 14/2/43'. An Afrika Korps Enigma, captured by the Eighth Army during their attack on Rommel last month. He laid it carefully on the table and unfastened the metal clasps. The lid opened easily.

This one was in perfect condition: a beauty. The letters on the keys were unworn, the black metal casing unscratched, the glass bulbs clear and gleaming. The three rotors – stopped, he saw, at ZDE – glinted silver beneath the naked light. He stroked it tenderly. It must only just have left its makers. 'Chiffreirmaschine Gesellschaft,' read their label. 'Heimsoeth und Rinke, Berlin-Wilmersdorf, Uhlandstrasse 138.'

He pushed a key. It was stiffer than on a normal typewriter. When he had depressed it far enough, the machine emitted a clunk and the right-hand rotor moved on a notch. At the same time, one of the bulbs lit up.

Hallelujah!

The battery was charged. The Enigma was live.

He checked the mechanism. He stooped and typed C. The letter J lit up. He typed L and got a U. A, I, R and E yielded, successively, X, P, Q and Q again.

He lifted the Enigma's inner lid and detached the spindle, set the rotors back at ZDE and locked them into place. He typed the cryptogram JUXPQQ and C-L-A-I-R-E was spelled out letter by letter on the bulbs in little bursts of light.

He fumbled through his pockets for his watch. Two minutes to twelve.

He folded the lid back into place and hoisted the Enigma up on its shelf. He made sure to lock the door behind him.

To the people whom he ran past in the mansion's corridors, who was he? Nothing. Nobody. Just another peculiar cryptanalyst in a flap.

Hester Wallace, as agreed, was in the telephone box at midnight, the receiver in her hand, feeling more foolish than afraid as she pretended to make a call. Beyond the glass, two currents of pale sparks were flowing quietly in the dark, as one shift streamed in from the main gate and the other ebbed towards it. In her pocket was a sheet of Bletchley's wood-flecked, brownish notepaper on which were jotted six entries.

Cordingley had swallowed her story whole – indeed, he had been, if anything, a little *too* eager to help. Unable at first to locate the relevant file, he had called in aid a pimply, jug-eared youth with wispy yellow hair. Could this child, she had wondered, this foetus-face, really be a cryptanalyst? But Donald had whispered yes, he was one of the best: now the professions and the universities had all been picked over, they were turning to boys straight out of school. Unformed. Unquestioning. The new elite.

The file had been procured, a space cleared in a corner, and never had Miss Wallace made a pencil move more quickly. The worst part had been at the end: keeping her nerve and not fleeing when she'd finished, but checking the figures, returning the file to the Foetus, and observing the normal social code with Donald –

'*We really must have a drink one of these evenings.*'
'*Yes really we must.*'

'*I'll be in touch, then.*'

'*Absolutely. So shall I.*'

– neither, of course, having the slightest intention of ever doing so.

Come on, Tom Jericho.

Midnight passed. The first of the buses lumbered by – invisible, almost, except for its exhaust fumes, which made a puff of pink cloud in its red rear lights.

And then, just as she was beginning to give up hope, a blur of white. A hand tapped softly on the glass. She dropped the telephone and shone her torch on to the face of a lunatic pressed close to the pane. Dark wild eyes and a convict mask of shadowed beard. 'There's really no need to scare me half to death,' she muttered, but that was in the privacy of the phone booth. As she came out, all she said was: 'I've left your numbers on the telephone.'

She held the door open for him. His hand rested on hers. A brief moment of pressure signalled his thanks – too brief for her to tell whose fingers were the coldest.

'Meet me here at five.'

Exhilaration gave a fresh energy to her tired legs as she pedalled up the hill away from Bletchley.

He needed to see her at five. How else could one interpret that, except as meaning he had found a way? A victory! A victory against the Mermagens and the Cordingleys!

The gradient steepened. She rose to tread the pedals. The bicycle waved from side to side like a metronome. The light danced on the road.

Afterwards, she was to reproach herself severely for this premature jubilation, but the truth was she would probably never have seen them anyway. They had positioned themselves quite carefully, drawn up parallel with the track and hidden by the hawthorn hedge – a professional job – so that when she came round the corner and began to bounce over the potholes towards the cottage she passed them in the shadows without a glance.

She was six feet from the door when the headlights came on – slitted blackout headlights, but dazzling enough to splash her shadow against the whitewashed wall. She heard the engine cough and turned, shielding her eyes, to see the big car coming at her – calm, unhurried, implacable, nodding over the bumpy ground.

5

Jericho told himself to take his time. There's no hurry. You've given yourself five hours. Use them.

He locked himself into the cellar room, leaving the key half turned in the keyhole, so that anyone trying to insert *their* key from the other side would find it blocked. He knew he'd have to open up eventually – otherwise, what was he? Just a rat in a trap. But at least he would now have thirty seconds' warning, and to give himself a cover story, he reopened the Naval Section safe and spread the handful of maps and code books across the narrow table. To these he added the stolen cryptograms and key settings, and his watch, which he placed before him with its lid open. Like preparing for an examination, he thought. *'Candidates must write on one side of the paper only; this margin to be left blank for the use of the examiner.'*

Then he lifted down the Enigma and removed the cover.

He listened. Nothing. A dripping pipe somewhere, that was all. The walls bulged with the pressure of the cold earth; he could smell the soil, taste the spores of damp lime plaster. He breathed on his fingers and flexed them.

He would work backwards, he decided, deciphering the last cryptogram first, on the theory that whatever had caused Claire's disappearance was contained somewhere in those final messages.

He ran his fingers down the columns of notation to find the Vulture settings for 4 March – panic day in the Bletchley Registry.

III V IV GAH CX AZ DV KT HU LW GP EY MR FQ

The Roman numerals told him which three out of the machine's five rotors were to be used that day, and what order they were to be placed in. GAH gave him the rotor starting positions. The next ten letter pairs represented the cross-pluggings he needed to make on the plugboard at the back of the Enigma. Six letters were left unconnected which, by some mysterious and glorious fold in the laws of statistics, actually increased the number of potential different cross-pluggings from almost 8 million million (25 x 23 x 21 x 19 x 17 x 15 x 13 x 11 x 9 x 7 x 5 x 3) to more than 150 million million.

He did the plugging first. Short lengths of corded, chocolate-coloured flex, tipped at either end by brass plugs sheathed in bakelite that sank with satisfying precision into the lettered sockets: C to X, A to Z . . .

Next he lifted the Enigma's inner lid, unlocked the spindle, and slid off the three rotors that were already loaded. From a separate compartment he withdrew the two spares.

Each rotor was the size and thickness of an ice-hockey puck, but heavier: a code wheel with twenty-six terminals – pin-shaped and spring-loaded on one side, flat and circular on the other – with the letters of the alphabet engraved around the edge. As the rotors turned against one another, so the shape of the electrical circuit they completed varied. The right-hand rotor always moved on a letter each time a key was struck. Once every twenty-six letters, a notch in its alphabet ring caused the middle rotor also to move on a place. And when, eventually, the middle rotor reached its turnover position, the third rotor would move. Two rotors moving together was known at Bletchley as a crab; three was a lobster.

He sorted the rotors into the order of the day – III, V and IV – and slipped them on to the spindle. He twirled III and set it at the letter G, V at A and IV at H, and closed the lid.

The machine was now primed just as its twin had been in Smolensk on the evening of 4 March.

He touched the keys.

He was ready.

The Enigma worked on a simple principle. If, when the machine was set in a particular way, pressing key A completed a circuit that illuminated bulb X, then it followed – because electric current is reciprocal – that, in the same position, pressing key X would illuminate bulb A. Decoding was designed to be as easy as encoding.

Jericho realised quite quickly that something was going wrong. He would type a letter of the cryptogram with his left index finger and with his right hand make a note of the character illuminated on the display panel. T gave him H, R gave him Y, X gave him C . . . This was no German he recognised. Still, he went on in the increasingly desperate hope it would start to come right. Only after forty-seven letters did he give up.

HYCYKWPIOROKDZENAJEWICZJPTAKJHRUTBPYSJMOTYLPCIE

He ran his hands through his hair.

Sometimes an Enigma operator would insert meaningless padding around proper words to disguise the sense of his message, but never this much, surely? There *were* no proper words that he could discern hidden anywhere in this gibberish.

He groaned, leaned back in his chair and stared at the flaking plaster ceiling.

Two possibilities, each equally unpleasant.

One: the message had been super-enciphered, its

plaintext scrambled once, and then again to make its meaning doubly obscure. A time-consuming technique, usually reserved for only the most secret communications.

Two: Hester had made a mistake in transcription – had got, perhaps, just one letter wrong – in which case he could sit here, literally for the rest of his life, and still he would never make the cryptogram disgorge its secrets.

Of the two explanations, the latter was the more likely.

He paced around his cell for a while, trying to get some circulation back into his legs and arms. Then he set the rotors back at GAH and made an attempt to decipher the second message from 4 March. The same result:

```
SZULCJK UKAH _
```

He didn't even bother with the third and fourth but instead played around with the rotor settings – GEH, GAN, CAH – in the hope she might simply have got one letter wrong, but all the Enigma winked at him was more gobbledygook.

Four in the car. Hester in the back seat next to Wigram. Two men in the front. The doors all locked, the heater on, a stench of cigarette smoke and sweat so strong that Wigram had his paisley scarf pressed delicately to his nose. He kept his face half-turned from her all journey and didn't say a word until they reached the main road. Then they pulled across the white lines to overtake another car and their driver switched on a police bell.

'Oh, for Christ's sake, Leveret, cut it out.'

The noise stopped. The car swerved left, then right. They jolted down a rutted track and Hester's fingers sank deeper into the leather upholstery as she strained to avoid toppling into Wigram. She hadn't spoken, either – it was her single, token gesture of defiance, this silence. She was damned if she was going to show her nerves by babbling like a girl.

After a couple of minutes they stopped somewhere and Wigram sat motionless, a statesman, while his men in the front seats scrambled out. One of them opened his door. Torches flashed in the darkness. Shadows appeared. A welcoming committee.

'Got those lights up yet, inspector?' asked Wigram.

'Yes, sir.' A deep male voice; a Midlands accent. 'A lot of complaints from the air raid people, though.'

'Well, they can frig off for a start. Jerry wants to bomb this place, he's welcome. Got the plans?'

'Yes, sir.'

'Good-oh.' Wigram grabbed the roof and hoisted himself out on the running board. He waited a second or two and when Hester didn't move he ducked back inside and flexed his fingers irritably. 'Come on, come on. D'you expect me to carry you?'

She slid across the seat.

Two other cars – no, *three* other cars with their headlights on, showing the cut-out patterns of men moving, plus a small Army truck and an ambulance. It was the ambulance that shook her. Its doors were open and, as Wigram guided her past it, his hand lightly on her elbow, she caught the smell of disinfectant, saw the dun-coloured oxygen cylinders, the stretchers with their coarse brown blankets, their leather straps, their innocent white sheets. Two men sat on the rear bumper, legs outstretched, smoking. They stared at her without interest.

'Been here before?' said Wigram.

'Where are we?'

'Lovers' lane. Not your scene, I fancy.'

He was holding a flashlight and as he stood aside to usher her through a gate she saw a sign: DANGER: FLOODED CLAY PIT — VERY DEEP WATER. She could hear a guttural engine somewhere ahead, and the cry of sea-birds. She started to shake.

'The hand of the Lord was upon me, and carried me out in the spirit of the Lord, and set me down in the midst of the valley which was full of bones.'

'D'you say something?' asked Wigram.

'I don't believe so.'

Oh, Claire, Claire, Claire . . .

The engine noise was louder now, and seemed to be coming from inside a brick building to her left. A faint white light shone up through the gaps in its roof to reveal a tall, square chimney, its lower part engulfed by ivy. She was vaguely aware that they were at the head of a procession. Behind them came the driver, Leveret, and then the second man from the car wearing a belted gaberdine, and then the police inspector.

'Mind yourself here,' warned Wigram, and he tried

to take her arm again but she shook him off. She picked her own way between the clumps of brick and the towering weeds, heard voices, turned a corner, and was confronted by a dazzling line of arc lights illuminating a broad path. Six policemen were working their way along it, in parallel, on their hands and knees among a glitter of broken glass and rubble. Behind them, one soldier tended a shuddering generator; another unreeled a drum of cable; a third was rigging more lights.

Wigram grinned and winked at her, as if to say: See what I can command. He was pulling on a pair of light brown, calfskin gloves. 'Got something to show you.'

In a corner of the building, a police sergeant stood beside a rumpled heap of sacks. Hester had to will her legs to move forwards. *Please, Lord, don't let it be her.*

'Get your notebook out,' said Wigram to the sergeant. He hoisted the tails of his overcoat and squatted on his haunches. 'I am showing the witness, first, one lady's coat, ankle-length by the look of it, colour grey, trimmed with black velvet.' He drew it completely out of the sack and turned it over. 'Grey satin lining. Quite badly stained. Probably blood. Need to check it. Collar label: "Hunters, Burlington Arcade". And the witness responded?' He held it up, without looking round.

Remember, I said, 'That's too beautiful to put on every day,' and you said, 'Silly old Hester, that's the only reason there is to wear it'?

'And the witness *responded?*'

'It's hers.'

' "It's hers." Got that? Good. OK. Next. One lady's

shoe. Left foot. Black. High heel. Heel snapped off. Hers, d'you think?'

'How can I tell? One shoe –'

'Largish. Say, size seven. Eight. What size did she take?' A pause, then Hester, quietly: 'Seven.'

'We've found the other one outside, sir,' said the inspector. 'Near the water's edge.'

'And a pair of knickers. White. Silk. Badly blood-stained.' He held them out at arm's length between finger and thumb. 'Recognise these, Miss Wallace?' He let them drop and rummaged in the bottom of the sack. 'Final item. One brick.' He shone his flashlight onto it; something glinted. 'Also bloodstained. Blonde hairs attached.'

'Eleven main buildings,' said the inspector. 'Eight of them with kilns, four with chimneys still standing. Rail spur here with sidings, linking into the main line, and a branch going off here, right through the site.'

They were outside now, at the spot where the second shoe had been found, and the map was spread over a rusting water rank. Hester stood away from them, Leveret watching her, his hands hanging loosely by his sides. There were more men moving down by the water's edge, torches stabbing the night.

'Local fishing club use a shed here, near the jetty. Three rowing boats usually stored.'

'Usually?'

'Door's been kicked in, sir. Season's over. That's why nobody discovered it. A boat's missing.'

'Since?'

'Well, there was some fishing on Sunday. Deep ledgering for carp. That was the last day of the season. Everything was all right then. So any time from Sunday night onwards.'

'Sunday. And we're now into Wednesday.' Wigram sighed and shook his head.

The inspector spread his hands. 'With respect, sir, I have three men stationed in Bletchley. Bedford lent us six, Buckingham nine. We're two miles from the centre of town. There is a limit. Sir.'

Wigram didn't seem to hear him. 'And how big's the lake?'

'About a quarter of a mile across.'

'Deep?'

'Yes, sir.'

'What – twenty, thirty feet?'

'At the edges. Shelving to sixty. Could be seventy. It's an old working. They built the town with what they dug out here.'

'Did they really?' Wigram flashed his light across the lake. 'Makes sense, I suppose. Making one hole out of another.' Mist was rising, swirling in the breeze like steam above a cauldron. He swung the beam round and pointed it back at the building. 'So what happened here?' he said softly. 'Our man lures her out for a shag on Sunday night. Kills her, probably with that brick. Drags her down here . . .' The beam traced the path from the kilns to the water. 'Strong man – must have been, she was a big girl. Then what? Gets a boat. Stuffs the body in a sack maybe. Weights it with bricks. That's obvious. Rows it out. Dumps it. A muffled splash at midnight, just like in the pictures . . . He probably meant to come back for the clothes as well, but something put him off. Perhaps the next pair of lovebirds had already arrived.' He played the light over the mist again. 'Seventy feet deep. Frigging hell! We'll need to put a submarine down there to find her.'

'May I go now?' said Hester. She had kept herself very quiet and composed so far, but now the tears had started and she was drawing in great gulps of air.

Wigram aimed the beam at her wet face. 'No,' he said sadly. 'I'm rather afraid you can't.'

Jericho was replugging the cipher machine as quickly as his numb fingers would permit him.

Enigma settings for German Army key Vulture, 6 February 1943:

```
I V III DMR EY JL AK NV FZ CT HP MX BQ GS
```

The final four cryptograms were hopeless, a disaster, mere chaos out of chaos. He had wasted too much time on them already. He would begin again, this time with the first signal. E to Y, J to L. And if this didn't work? Don't even think it. A to K, N to V . . . He lifted the lid, unfastened the spindle, slid off the rotors. Above his head, the great house was silent. He was too deeply entombed to hear a footstep. He wondered what they were doing up there. Looking for him? Probably. And if they woke up Logie it wouldn't take them long to find him. He slid the rotors into place – first, fifth, third – and clicked them round to DMR.

Almost at once he began to sense success. First C and X, which were nulls, and then A, N, O, K, H.

An OKH . . .

To OKH. *Oberkommando des Heeres.* The High Command of the Army.

A miracle.

His finger hammered away at the key. The lights flashed.

An OKH/BEFEHL. To the office of the Commander-in-Chief.

Dringend.

Urgent.

Melde Auffindung zahlreicher menschlicher Überreste zwölf Km westlich Smolensk . . .

Discovered yesterday twelve kilometres west Smolensk human remains . . .

Hester was locked in the car with Wigram, Leveret standing guard outside.

Jericho. He was asking her about Jericho. Where was he? What was he doing? When did she last see him?

'He's left the hut. He's not at his digs. He's not at the cottage. I ask you: Where the hell else is there to go in this frigging town?'

She said nothing.

He tried shouting at her, pounding his fist on the seat in front, and then, when that didn't work, he gave her his handkerchief and tried sympathy, but the scent of cologne on the silk and the memory of the blonde hair gilding the brick made her want to be sick and he had to wind his window down and get

Leveret to come round and open her door.

'They've found the boat, sir,' said Leveret. 'Blood in the bottom.'

Just before three o'clock, Jericho had the first message deciphered.

```
TO THE OFFICE OF THE COMMANDER IN CHIEF. URGENT.
DISCOVERED TWELVE KILOMETRES WEST SMOLENSK
EVIDENCE HUMAN REMAINS. BELIEVED EXTENSIVE,
POSSIBLY THOUSANDS. HOW AM I TO PROCEED?
LACHMAN, OBERST, FIELD POLICE.
```

Jericho sat back and contemplated this marvel. Well, yes, Herr Oberst, how are you to proceed? I die to know.

Once again he began the tedious procedure of replugging and re-rotoring the Enigma. The next signal had been sent from Smolensk three days later, on 9 February. A, N, O, K, H, B, E, F, E, H, L . . . The exquisite formality of the German armed forces unfolded before him. And then a null, and then G, E, S, T, E, R, N, U, N, D, H, E, U, T, E.

Gestern und heute. Yesterday and today.

And so on, letter by letter, inescapably, remorselessly – press, *clunk*, light, note – stopping occasionally to massage his fingers and straighten his back, the whole ghastly story made worse by the slowness with which he had to read it, his eyeballs pressed to the crime. Some of the words gave him difficulty. What was *mumifiziert*? Could it be 'mummified'? And *Sagemehl geknebelt*? 'Gagged with sawdust'?

```
PRELIMINARY EXCAVATION UNDERTAKEN IN FOREST
NORTH DNIEPER CASTLE YESTERDAY AND TODAY. SITE
APPROXIMATELY TWO HUNDRED SQUARE METRES. TOPSOIL
COVERING TO DEPTH OF ONE POINT FIVE METRES
PLANTED PINE SAPLINGS. FIVE LAYERS CORPSES.
UPPER MUMMIFIED LOWER LIQUID. TWENTY BODIES
RECOVERED. DEATH CAUSED BY SINGLE SHOT HEAD.
HANDS BOUND WIRE. MOUTHS GAGGED CLOTH AND
SAWDUST. MILITARY UNIFORMS, HIGH BOOTS AND
MEDALS INDICATE VICTIMS POLISH OFFICERS. SEVERE
FROST AND HEAVY SNOWFALL OBLIGE US SUSPEND
OPERATIONS PENDING THAW. I SHALL CONTINUE MY
INVESTIGATIONS. LACHMAN, OBERST, FIELD POLICE.
```

Jericho took a tour around his little cell, flapping his arms and stamping his feet. It seemed to him to be peopled with ghosts, grinning at him with toothless mouths blasted into the backs of their heads. He was walking in the forest himself. The cold sliced his flesh. And when he stopped and listened he could hear the sound of trees being uprooted, of spades and pickaxes ringing on frozen earth.

Polish officers?

Puck?

The third signal, after a gap of eleven days, had been sent on 20th February. *Nach Eintreten Tauwetter Exhumierungen im Wald bei Katyn fortgesetzt . . .*

FOLLOWING THAW KATYN FOREST EXCAVATIONS RESUMED
EIGHT HUNDRED YESTERDAY. FIFTY-TWO CORPSES
EXAMINED. QUANTITIES OF PERSONAL LETTERS,
MEDALS, POLISH CURRENCY RECOVERED. ALSO SPENT
PISTOL CARTRIDGE CASES SEVEN POINT SIX FIVE
MILLIMETRE STAMPED QUOTE GECO D UNQUOTE.
INTERROGATION LOCAL POPULATION ESTABLISHES ONE
EXECUTIONS CONDUCTED NKVD DURING SOVIET
OCCUPATION MARCH AND APRIL NINETEEN HUNDRED AND
FORTY. TWO VICTIMS BELIEVED BROUGHT FROM
KOZIELSK DETENTION CAMP BY RAIL TO GNIEZDOVO
STATION TAKEN INTO FOREST AT NIGHT IN GROUPS ONE
HUNDRED SHOTS HEARD. THREE TOTAL NUMBER VICTIMS
ESTIMATED TEN THOUSAND REPEAT TEN THOUSAND.
ASSISTANCE URGENTLY REQUIRED IF FURTHER
EXCAVATION DESIRED.

Jericho sat motionless for fifteen minutes, gazing at the
Enigma, trying to comprehend the scale of the
implications. This was a secret it was dangerous to
know, he thought. This was a secret big enough to
swallow a person whole. Ten thousand Poles – our
gallant Allies, survivors of an army that had charged the
Wehrmacht's Panzers on horseback, waving swords –
ten thousand of them trussed, gagged and shot by our
other, more recent, gallant Allies, the heroic Soviet
Union? No wonder the Registry had been cleared.

An idea occurred to him and he went back to the
first cryptogram. For if one looked at it thus:

HYCYKWPIOROKDZENAJEWICZJPTAKJHRUTBPYSJMOTYLPCIE

it was meaningless, but if one rearranged it thus:

```
HYCYK, W . , PIORO, K . , DZENAJEWICZ, J . ,
PTAK, J . , HRUT, B . , PYS, J . , MOTYL, P . , _
```

then out of the chaos was conjured order. Names.

He had enough now. He could have stopped. But he went on anyway, for he was never a man to leave a mystery partially solved, a mathematical proof only half worked-out. One had to sketch in the route to the answer, even if one had guessed at the destination long before the journey's end.

Enigma settings for German Army key Vulture, 2 March 1943:

```
III IV II LUK JP DY QS HL AE NW CU IK FX BR
```

An Ostubaf Dorfmann. Ostubaf for *Obersturmbann-führer.* A Gestapo rank.

```
TO OBERSTURMBANNFUHRER DORFMANN RHSA
ON ORDERS OFFICE COMMANDER IN CHIEF NAMES OF
POLISH OFFICERS IDENTIFIED TO DATE IN KATYN
FOREST AS FOLLOWS
```

He didn't bother to write them down. He knew what he was looking for and he found it after an hour, buried in a babble of other names. It wasn't sent to the Gestapo on the 2nd, but on the 3rd:

```
PUKOWSKI, T.
```

6

A few minutes after 5 a.m., Tom Jericho surfaced, molelike, from his subterranean hole, and stood in the passage of the mansion, listening. The Enigma had been returned to its shelf, the safe locked, the door to the Black Museum locked as well. The cryptograms and the settings were in his pocket. He had left no trace. He could hear footsteps and male voices coming towards him and he drew back against the wall, but whoever they were they didn't come his way. The wooden staircase creaked as they passed on, out of sight, up to the offices in the bedrooms.

He moved cautiously, keeping close to the wall. If Wigram had gone looking for him in the hut at midnight and failed to find him, what would he have done? He would have gone to Albion Street. And seeing Jericho hadn't turned up there, he might by now have roused a considerable search party. And Jericho didn't want to be found, not yet. There were too many questions he had to ask, and only one man had the answers.

He passed the foot of the staircase and opened the double doors that led to the lobby.

You became her lover, didn't you, Puck? The next after me in the great revolving door of Claire Romilly's men. And somehow – how? – you knew that something terrible was going on in that ghastly forest. Wasn't that why you sought her out? Because she had access to information you couldn't get to? And she must have agreed to help, must have started copying out anything that looked of interest. ('*She'd really been much more attentive of late . . .*') And then there came the nightmare day when you realised – who? your father? your brother? – was buried in that hideous place. And then, the next day, all she could bring you was cryptograms, because the British – the British: your trusty Allies, your loyal protectors, to whom the Poles had entrusted the secret of Enigma – the British had decided that in the higher interest they simply didn't want to know any more.

Puck, Puck, what have you done?

What have you done with her?

There was a sentry in the Gothic entry hall, a couple of cryptanalysts talking quietly on a bench, a WAAF with a stack of box files struggling to find the doorhandle with her elbow. Jericho opened it for her and she smiled her thanks and made a rolling motion with her eyes, as if to say: *What a place to find ourselves at five o'clock on a spring morning*, and Jericho smiled and nodded back, a fellow sufferer: *Yes, indeed, what a place . . .*

The WAAF went one way and he went the other, towards the morning star and the main gate. The sky was black, the telephone box almost invisible in the shadows of the arboretum. It was empty. He walked straight past it and pushed his way into the vegetation. Sir Herbert Leon, the last Victorian master of the Park, had been a dedicated arborist, planting his realm with three hundred different species of tree. Forty years of re-seeding, followed by four years without pruning, had turned the arboretum into a labyrinth of secret chambers, and here Jericho squatted on the dry earth and waited for Hester Wallace.

By five fifteen it was clear to him she wasn't coming, which suggested she had been detained. In which case, they were almost certainly looking for him.

He had to get out of the Park, and he couldn't risk the main gate.

At five twenty, when his eyes were thoroughly used to the dark, he began to move northwards through the arboretum, back towards the house, his bundle of secrets heavy in his pocket. He could still feel the effects of the Benzedrine – a lightness in his muscles, an acuteness in his mind, especially to danger – and he offered a prayer of thanks to Logie for making him take it, because otherwise by now he'd be half-dead.

Puck, Puck, what have you done?

What have you done with her?

He came out cautiously from between two sycamores and stepped on to the lawn at the side of the mansion. Ahead of him was the long, low outline of the old Hut 4, with the mass of the big house behind it. He skirted it and went around the back, past some rubbish bins and into the courtyard. Here were the stables where he'd started work in 1939, and beyond those the cottage where Dilly Knox had first pried into the mysteries of the Enigma. Drawn up in a semicircle on the cobbles he could just make out the gleaming cylinders and exhausts of half a dozen motorcycles. A door opened and in the brief glow he saw a dispatch rider, padded, helmeted and gauntleted, like a medieval knight. Jericho pressed himself against the brickwork and waited while the motorcyclist adjusted his pillion, then kicked the machine into life and revved it. Its red light dwindled and disappeared through the rear gate.

He considered, briefly, trying to get out using the same exit, but reason told him that if the main entrance was probably being watched, then so was this. He stumbled on past the cottage, past the back of the tennis courts, and finally past the bombe hut, throbbing like an engine shed in the darkness.

By now a faint blue stain had begun to seep up from the rim of the sky. Night – his friend and ally, his only cover – was preparing to desert him. Ahead, he could begin to make out the contours of a building site. Pyramids of earth and sand. Squat rectangles of bricks and sweet-smelling timber.

Jericho had never before paid much notice to Bletchley's perimeter fence, which turned out, on inspection, to be a formidable stockade of seven-foot-high iron stakes, tapering at their tips into triple spears, bent outwards to deter incursion. It was as he was running his hands over the galvanised metal that he heard a swish of movement in the undergrowth just beyond it, to his left. He took a few steps backwards and retreated behind a stack of steel girders. A moment later, a sentry ambled past, in no great state of alertness, to judge by his slouched silhouette and the shuffle of his step.

Jericho crouched lower, listening as the sounds faded. The perimeter was perhaps a mile long. Say, fifteen minutes for a sentry to complete a circuit. Say, two sentries patrolling. Possibly three.

If there were three, he had five minutes.

He looked around to see what he could see.

A two-hundred-gallon drum proved too heavy for him to shift, but there were planks, and some thick sections of concrete drainage pipe, both of which he found he was able to drag over to the fence. He started to sweat again. Whatever they were building here, it was going to be vast – vast and bombproof. In the gloom the excavations were fathomless. 'FIVE LAYERS CORPSES. UPPER MUMMIFIED LOWER LIQUID . . .'

He upended the pipes and stood them about five feet apart. He laid a plank on top. Then he hefted a second set of pipes on to the first, picked up another length of timber and staggered over with it balanced on his shoulder. He set it down carefully, making a platform with two steps – about the first practical thing he had made since boyhood. He climbed on to the rickety structure and seized the iron spears. His feet scrabbled for a purchase on the rails. But the fence was designed to keep people out, not in. Fuelled by chemicals and desperation, Jericho was just able to pull himself astride it, twist, and lower himself down the other side. He dropped the last three feet and stayed there, squatting in the long grass, recovering his breath, listening.

His final act was to put his foot through the railings and kick away the planks.

He didn't wait to see if the noise had attracted attention. He set off across the field, walking at first, then trotting and finally running, sliding and skidding over the dewy grass. There was a big military camp to his right, concealed by a line of trees only just now materialising. Behind him, he could sense the dawn on his shoulders, brightening by the minute. He looked back only when he reached the road, and that was his last impression of Bletchley Park: a thin line of low, black buildings – mere dots and dashes along the horizon – and above them in the eastern sky an immense arc of cold blue light.

He had been to Puck's digs once before, on a Sunday afternoon a year ago, for a game of chess. He had a vague memory of an elderly landlady who doted on Puck pouring them tea in a cramped front room, while her invalid husband wheezed and coughed and retched upstairs. He could remember the game quite clearly, it had a curious shape to it – Jericho very strong in the opening, Puck in the middle, and Jericho again at the end. A draw agreed.

Alma Terrace. That was it. Alma Terrace. Number nine.

He was moving quickly – long strides and an occasional, loping run – keeping to the side of the pavement, down the hill and into the sleeping town. Outside the pub lingered a soapy smell of last night's beer. The Methodist chapel a few doors down was dark and bolted, its blistered sign unchanged since the outbreak of war: 'Repent ye: for the Kingdom of Heaven is at hand.' He went under the railway bridge. On the opposite side of the road was Albion Street, and a little further along the Bletchley Working Men's Club ('The Co-Operative Society Presents a Talk by Councillor A. E. Braithwaite: The Soviet Economy, Its Lessons for Us'). After another twenty yards he turned left into Alma Terrace.

It was a street like so many others: a double row of tiny red-brick houses running parallel with the railway. Number nine was a clone of all the rest: two little windows upstairs and one downstairs, all three swathed in blackout curtains as though in mourning, a spade's length of front yard with a dustbin in it, and a wooden gate to the road. The gate was broken, the timber splintered grey and smooth like driftwood, and Jericho had to hoist it open. He tried the door – locked – and hammered on it with his fist.

A loud coughing – as loud and immediate as a woken guard dog. He stepped back a pace and after a couple of seconds one of the upstairs curtains flickered open. He shouted: 'Puck, I need to talk to you.'

A steady clop-clop of hooves. He glanced up the road to see a coal dray turning into the street. It passed by slowly and the driver took a good, long look at him, then flicked the reins and the big horse responded, the tempo of its hooves increasing. Behind him Jericho heard a bolt being worked and drawn back. The door opened a crack. An old woman peered out.

'I'm so sorry,' said Jericho, 'but it's an emergency, I need to speak to Mr Pukowski.'

She hesitated, then let him in. She was less than five feet tall, a wraith, with a pale blue, quilted housecoat clutched across her nightdress. She spoke with her hand held in front of her mouth and he realised she was embarrassed because she didn't have her teeth in.

'He's in his room.'

'Could you show me?'

She shuffled down the passage and he followed. The coughing from upstairs had intensified. It seemed to shake the ceiling, to swing the grimy lampshade.

'Mr Puck?' She tapped on the door. 'Mr Puck?' She said to Jericho: 'He must be still asleep. I heard him come in late.'

'Let me. May I?'

The little room was empty. Jericho was across it in three strides, pulling back the curtains. Grey light lit the kingdom of the exile: a single bed, a washstand, a wardrobe, a wooden chair, a small mirror of thick, pink, crystalled glass with birds carved into it, suspended above the mantelpiece by a metal chain. The bed had been lain on rather than slept in, and a saucer by the bedhead was filled with cigarette stubs.

He turned back to the window. The inevitable vegetable patch and hooped bomb shelter. A wall.

'What's over there?'

'But the door was bolted –'

'On the other side of the wall? What's over there?'

With her hand in front of her mouth she looked aghast. 'The station.'

He tried the window. It was jammed shut.

'Is there a back door?'

She led him through a kitchen that couldn't have altered much since Victorian days. A mangle. A hand pump for raising water to the sink . . .

The back door was unlocked.

'He's all right, isn't he?' She'd stopped worrying about her teeth. Her mouth was trembling, the skin around it furrowed, sunken, brown.

'I'm sure. You go back to your husband.'

He was following Puck's trail now. Footprints – large footprints – led across the vegetable patch. A tea chest stood against the wall. It bowed and splintered as Jericho mounted it, but he was just able to fold himself over the top of the sooty brickwork. For a moment he almost tumbled head first on to the concrete path, but then he managed to brace himself and brought his legs up.

In the distance: the whistle of a train.

He hadn't run like this for fifteen years, not since he was a schoolboy being screamed at on a five-mile steeplechase. But here they were again, as grim as ever, the familiar instruments of torture – the knife in his side, the acid in his lungs, the taste of rust in his mouth.

He tore through the back entrance into Bletchley Station and flailed around the corner on to the platform, through a cloud of leaden-coloured pigeons that flapped and rose heavily and settled again. His feet rang on the ironwork of the footbridge. He took the stairs two at a time and ran across the gantry. A fountain of white smoke spurted up to his left, his right, and filtered through the floorboards, as the locomotive passed slowly underneath.

The hour was early, the waiting crowd was small, and Jericho was halfway down the steps to the northbound platform when he spotted Puck about fifty yards away, standing close to the tracks, holding a small suitcase, his head turning to follow the slow parade of compartments. Jericho stopped and clutched the hand rail, bent forwards, struggling for air. The Benzedrine, he realised, was wearing off. When the train at last jolted to a stop, Puck looked around, walked casually towards the front, opened a door and disappeared.

Using the rail to support himself, Jericho picked his way down the last few steps and almost toppled into an empty compartment.

He must have blacked out, and for several minutes, because he never heard the door slam behind him or the whistle blow. The next thing he was conscious of was a rocking motion. The banquette was warm and dusty to his cheek and through it he could feel the soothing rhythm of the wheels – *dah-dah-dee-dee, dee-dee-dah-dah, dah-dah-dee-dee* . . . He opened his eyes. Smudges of bluish cloud edged in pink slipped slowly across a square of white sky. It was all very beautiful, like a nursery, and he could have fallen asleep again, but for a vague recollection that there was something dark and threatening he was supposed to be afraid of, and then he remembered.

Levering himself up, he ministered to his aching head – shook it, rotated it in a figure of eight, then pushed down the window and thrust it into the cold draught of rushing air. No sign of any town. Just flat, hedged countryside, interspersed with barns and ponds that glinted in the morning light. The track was curving slightly and ahead he could see the locomotive flying its long pennant of smoke above a black wall of carriages. They were heading north on the main west-coast line, which meant – he tried to recall – Northampton next, then Coventry, Birmingham, Manchester (probably), Liverpool . . .

Liverpool?

Liverpool. And the ferry across the Irish Sea.

Jesus.

He was stunned by the unreality of it all, yet at the same time by its simplicity, its obviousness. There was a communication cord above the opposite row of seats ('Penalty for improper use: £20') and his immediate reaction was to pull it. But then what? *Think.* He would be left, unshaven, ticketless, drug-eyed, trying to convince some sceptical guard there was a traitor on board, while Puck – what would Puck do? He would climb down from the train and disappear. Jericho suddenly saw the full absurdity of his own situation. He didn't even have enough money to buy a ticket. All he had was a pocketful of cryptograms.

Get rid of them.

He pulled them from his pocket and tore them into fragments, then hung his head back out of the window and released them into the slipstream. They were whipped away, borne up and over the top of the carriage and out of sight. Craning his head the other way, he tried to guess how far up the train Puck was. The force of the wind stifled him. Three carriages? Four? He pulled back in and closed the window, then crossed the swaying compartment and slid open the door to the corridor.

He peered out, carefully.

The rolling stock was standard, pre-war, dark and filthy. The corridor, lit for the blackout by faint blue bulbs, was the colour of a poison bottle. Four compartments off to one side. A connecting door at the front and rear led into the adjacent carriages.

Jericho lurched towards the head of the train. He glanced into each compartment as he passed. Here were a pair of sailors playing cards, there a young couple asleep in one another's arms, there again a family – mother, father, boy and girl – sharing sandwiches and a flask of tea. The mother had a baby at her breast and turned away, embarrassed, when she saw him looking.

He opened the door leading to the next carriage and stepped into no man's land. The floor shifted and pitched beneath his feet like a catwalk at a funfair. He stumbled and banged his knee. Through a three-inch gap he could see the couplings clanking and, beneath them, the rushing ground. He let himself into the other carriage in time to see the big, unsmiling face of the guard emerging from a compartment. Jericho slipped smartly into the lavatory and locked himself in. For a moment he thought he was sharing it with some tramp or derelict but then he realised that this was *him* – the yellowish face, the dwindled and feverish eyes, the windblown hair, the two days' growth of blue-black beard – this was *his* reflection. The toilet was blocked and stinking. A trail of sodden, soiled paper curled from its bowl and wrapped around his feet like an unravelled bandage.

'Ticket please.' The guard rapped loudly. 'Slide your ticket under the door, please.'

'It's in my compartment.'

'Oh, is it then?' The handle rattled. 'You'd better come and show me.'

'I'm not feeling awfully well.' (Which was true.) 'I've left it out for you.' He pressed his burning forehead to the cool mirror. 'Just give me five minutes.'

The guard grunted. 'I'll be back.' Jericho heard the rush of wheels as the connecting door opened, then the slam of it closing. He waited a few seconds then flipped open the lock.

There was no sign of Puck in this carriage, or in the next, and by the time he'd leaped the gyrating iron plates into the third he could sense the train beginning to slow. He moved on down the corridor.

Two compartments filled with soldiers, six in each, sullen-looking, their rifles stacked at their feet.

Then one empty compartment.

Then Puck.

He was sitting with his back to the engine, leaning forwards – the same old Puck, handsome, intense, his elbows on his knees, engrossed in conversation with someone just out of Jericho's line of sight.

It was Claire, thought Jericho. It had to be Claire. It would be Claire. He was taking her with him.

He turned his back on the compartment and moved discreetly crabwise, pretending to look out of the dirty window. His eyes registered an approaching town – scrubland, goods wagons, warehouses – and then an anonymous platform with a clock frozen at ten to twelve, and faded posters with jolly, buxom girls advertising long-dead holidays in Bournemouth and Clacton-on-Sea.

The train crawled along for a few more yards, then stopped abruptly opposite the station buffet.

'Northampton!' shouted a man's voice. 'Northampton Station!'

And if it was Claire, what would he do?

But it wasn't her. He looked and saw a *man*, a young man – neat, dark, tanned, aquiline: in every essence, *foreign* – saw him only briefly because the man was already up on his feet and releasing Puck's hand from a double clasp. The young man smiled (he had very white teeth) and nodded – some transaction had been completed – and then he was stepping out of the compartment and was moving quickly across the platform, sharp shoulders slicing through the crowd. Puck watched him for a moment, then pulled the door shut and sank back into his seat, out of sight.

Whatever his escape plans, they did not appear to include Claire Romilly.

Jericho jerked his gaze away.

Suddenly he saw what must have happened. Puck cycling over to the cottage on Saturday night to retrieve the cryptograms – and instead finding Jericho. Puck returning later to discover the cryptograms were missing. And Puck assuming, naturally, that Jericho had them and was about to do what any loyal servant of the state would do: run straight to the authorities and turn Claire in.

He glanced back at the compartment. Puck must have lit a cigarette. Films of smoke were settling into wide, steel-blue strata.

But you couldn't allow that, could you, because she was the only link between you and the stolen papers? And you needed time to plan this escape with your foreign friend.

So what have you done with her?

A whistle. A frantic working-up of steam. The platform shuddered and began to slide away. Jericho barely noticed, unconscious of everything except the inescapable sum of his calculations.

What happened next happened very quickly and if there was never to be a single, coherent explanation of events, that was due to a combination of factors: the amnesia induced by violence, the deaths of two of the participants, the bureaucratic fog-machine of the Official Secrets Act.

But it went something like this.

About two miles north of Northampton Station, close to the village of Kingsthorpe, a set of points connected the west-coast main line with the branch line to Rugby. With five minutes' notice, the train was diverted off its scheduled course, westwards down the branch line, and very shortly afterwards a red signal warned the driver of an obstruction on the tracks ahead.

The train was therefore already slowing, although he didn't recognise it, when Jericho slid open the door to Puck's compartment. It moved very easily, at a finger's pressure. The layers of smoke rippled and erupted.

Puck was just extinguishing the cigarette (his ashtray was subsequently found to contain five stubs) and he was pushing down the window – presumably because he had noticed the loss of speed, and maybe the diversion, and was suspicious and wanted to see what was happening. He heard the door behind him and turned, and his face, in that instant, became a skull. His flesh was shrunken, tautened, masklike. He was already a dead man, and he knew it. Only his eyes were still alive, glittering beneath his high forehead. They flickered from Jericho to the corridor to the window and back to Jericho. A frantic effort was going on behind them, you could see, a mad and hopeless attempt to compute odds, angles, trajectories.

Jericho said: 'What have you done with her?'

Puck had the stolen Smith and Wesson in his hand, safety catch off. He brought it up. His eyes went through the same routine: Jericho, corridor, window, then Jericho again and finally the window. He tilted his head back, keeping the gun held out at arm's length, and tried to see up the track.

'Why are we stopping?'

'What have you done with her?'

Puck waved him back with the gun, but Jericho didn't care what happened now. He took a step closer.

Puck began to say something like 'Please don't make me' and then – farce, as the door slid open and the guard came in for Jericho's ticket.

For a long moment they stood there, this curious trio – the guard with his large, bland face, creasing with surprise; the traitor with his wavering pistol; the cryptanalyst between them – and then several things happened more or less at once. The guard said 'Give me that' and made a lunge at Puck. The gun went off. The noise of it was like a physical blow. The guard said 'Ooof?' in a puzzled way, and looked down at his stomach as if he had a bad twinge of indigestion. The wheels of the train locked and screamed and suddenly they were all on the floor together.

It may have been that Jericho was the first to crawl free. Certainly he had a memory of actually helping Puck to his feet, of pulling him out from beneath the guard, who was making a ghastly keening sound and leaking blood everywhere – from his mouth and his nose, from the front of his tunic, even from the bottom of his trouser legs.

Jericho knelt over him and said, rather fatuously, because he'd never seen anyone injured before: 'He needs a doctor.' There was a commotion in the corridor. He turned to find that Puck had the outside door open and the Smith and Wesson pointed at him. He was clasping the wrist of his gun hand and wincing as if he'd sprained it. Jericho closed his eyes for the bullet and Puck said – and this Jericho was sure of, because he spoke the words very deliberately, in his precise English: 'I killed her, Thomas. I am so terribly sorry.'

Then he vanished.

The time by now was just after a quarter past seven – 7.17, according to the official report – and the day was coming up nicely. Jericho stood on the threshold of the carriage and he could hear blackbirds singing in the nearby copse, and a skylark above the field. All along the train, doors were banging open in the sunshine and people were jumping out. The locomotive was leaking steam and beyond it a group of soldiers were scrambling down the slight embankment, led – Jericho was surprised to see – by Wigram. More soldiers were deploying from the train itself, to Jericho's right. Puck was only about twenty yards away. Jericho jumped down to the grey stones of the track and set off after him.

Someone shouted, very loudly, almost directly behind him: 'Get out of the fucking way, you fucking idiot!' – wise advice, which Jericho ignored.

It couldn't end here, he thought, not with so much still to know.

He was all in. His legs were heavy. But Puck wasn't making much progress either. He was hobbling across a meadow, trailing a left ankle which autopsy analysis would later show had a hairline fracture – whether from his fall in the compartment or his leap from the train, no one would ever know, but every step must have been agony for him. A small herd of Jersey cattle watched him, chewing, like spectators at a running track.

The grass smelled sweet, the hedges were in bud, and Jericho was very close to him when Puck turned and fired his pistol. He couldn't have been aiming at Jericho – the shot went wide of anything. It was just a parting gesture. His eyes were dead now. Sightless, blank. There was an answering crackle from the train. Bees buzzed past them in the spring morning.

Five bullets hit Puck and two hit Jericho. Again, the order is obscure. Jericho felt as though he had been struck from behind by a car – not painfully, but terrifically hard. It winded him and pitched him forward. He somehow kept on going, his legs cartwheeling, and saw tufts flying out of Puck's back, one, two, three, and then Puck's head exploded in a red blur, just as a second blow – irresistible this time – spun Jericho from his right shoulder round in a graceful arc. The sky was wet with spray and his final thought was what a pity it was, what a *pity* it was, *what a pity it was* that rain should spoil so fine a morning.

SEVEN

PLAINTEXT

PLAINTEXT: The original, intelligible text, as it was before encipherment, revealed after successful decoding or cryptanalysis.

A Lexicon of Cryptography
('Most Secret', Bletchley Park, 1943)

THE APPLE TREES wept blossom in the wind. It drifted across the graveyard and piled like snow against the slate and marble tombs.

Hester Wallace leaned her bicycle beside the low brick wall and surveyed the scene. Well, this was life, she thought, and no mistake about it; this was nature going on regardless. From inside the church rolled the booming notes of the organ. 'O God, Our Help in Ages Past . . .' She hummed to herself as she tugged on her gloves, tucked a few stray hairs under the band of her hat, straightened her shoulders and strode on up the flagstone path towards the porch.

The truth was, if it hadn't been for her, there would never have been a memorial service. It was she who persuaded the vicar to open the doors of St Mary's, Bletchley, even though she had to concede that 'the deceased', as the vicar primly put it, was not a believer. It was she who booked the organist and told him what to play (Bach's Prelude and Fugue in E flat major to see them all in, the Sanctus from Fauré's *Requiem* to get them all out). It was she who chose the hymns and the readings and had the service cards printed, she who decorated the nave with spring flowers, she who wrote out the notices and posted them around the Park ('a short service of remembrance will be held on Friday 16

April at 10 o'clock . . .'), she who lay awake the night before, worrying in case nobody bothered to come.

But they came all right.

Lieutenant Kramer came in his American naval uniform, and old Dr Weitzman came from the Hut 3 Watch, and Miss Monk and the girls from the German Book Room, and the heads of the Air Index and the Army Index, and various rather sheepish-looking young men in black ties, and many others whose names Hester never knew but whose lives had clearly been touched by the six-month presence at Bletchley Park of Claire Alexandra Romilly, born 21.12.22 and died (according to the police's best estimate) 14.3.43: Rest in Peace.

Hester sat in the front pew with her Bible marked at the passage she intended to read (I Corinthians 15.li-lv: 'Behold, I show you a mystery . . .') and every time someone new came in she turned to see if it was *him*, only to glance away in disappointment.

'We really ought to begin,' said the vicar, fussing with his watch. 'I've a christening due at half past.'

'Another minute, vicar, if you'd be so good. Patience is a Christian virtue.'

The scent of the Easter lilies rose above the nave – virgin-white lilies with green, fleshy stems, white tulips, blue anemones . . .

It was a long time since she had seen Tom Jericho. He might be dead for all she knew. She had only Wigram's word that he was still alive, and Wigram wouldn't even tell her which hospital he was in, let alone allow her to visit. He had, though, agreed to pass on an invitation to the service, and the following day he announced that the answer was yes, Jericho would love to come. 'But the poor chap's still quite sick, so don't count on it is my advice.' Soon Jericho would be going away, said Wigram, going away for a good long rest. Hester hadn't cared for the way he had said this, as if Jericho had somehow become the property of the state.

By five past ten the organist had run out of music to play and there was an awkward hiatus of shuffling and coughing. One of the German Book Room girls began to giggle until Miss Monk told her loudly to hush.

'Hymn number 477,' said the vicar, with a glare at Hester. '"The Day Thou gavest, Lord, is ended."'

The congregation stood. The organist hit a shaky D. They started to sing. From somewhere near the back she could hear Weitzman's rather beautiful tenor. It was only as they reached the fifth verse ('So be it, Lord; thy throne shall never,/Like earth's proud empires, pass away') that Hester heard the door scrape open behind them. She turned, and so did half the others, and there, beneath the grey stone arch – thin and frail and supported by the arm of Wigram, but alive, thank God: indisputably alive – was Jericho.

Standing at the back of the church, in his overcoat with its bullet holes freshly darned, Jericho wished several things at once. He wished, for a start, that Wigram would take his bloody hands off him, because the man made his flesh crawl. He wished they weren't playing this particular hymn because it always reminded him of the last day of term at school. And he wished it hadn't been necessary to come. But it was. He couldn't have avoided it.

He detached himself politely from Wigram's arm and walked, unaided, to the nearest pew. He nodded to Weitzman and to Kramer. The hymn was ending. His shoulder ached from the journey. 'Thy Kingdom stands and grows for ever,' sang the congregation, 'Till all Thy creatures own Thy sway.' Jericho closed his eyes and inhaled the rich aroma of the lilies.

The first bullet, the one that had hit him like a blow from a car, had struck him in the lower left-hand quadrant of his back, had passed through four layers of muscle, nicked his eleventh rib and had exited through his side. The second, the one that had spun him round, had buried itself deep in his right shoulder, shredding part of the deltoid muscle, and that was the bullet they had to cut out surgically. He lost a lot of blood. There was an infection.

He lay in isolation, under guard, in some kind of military hospital just outside Northampton – isolated, presumably, in case, in his delirium, he babbled about Enigma; guarded in case he tried to get away: a ludicrous notion, as he didn't even know where he was.

His dream – it seemed to him to go on for days, but perhaps that was just a part of the dream: he could never tell – his dream was of lying at the bottom of a sea, on soft white sand, in a warm and rocking current. Occasionally he would float up and it would be light, in a high-ceilinged room, with a glimpse of trees through tall, barred windows. At other times, he would rise to find it dark, with a round and yellow moon, and someone bending overhead.

The first morning he woke up he asked to see a doctor. He wanted to know what had happened.

The doctor came and told him he had been involved in a shooting accident. Apparently, he had wandered too close to an Army firing range ('you bloody silly fool') and he was lucky he hadn't been killed.

No, no, protested Jericho. It wasn't like that at all. He tried to struggle up but the pain in his back made him cry out loud.

They gave him an injection and he went back to the bottom of the sea.

Gradually, as he started to recover, the equilibrium of his pain began to shift. In the beginning, it was nine-tenths physical to one-tenth mental; then eight-tenths to two-tenths; then seven to three, and so on, until the original proportions were reversed and he almost looked forward to the daily agony of the changing of his dressings, as an opportunity to burn away the memory of what had happened.

He had part of the picture, not all of it. But any attempt to ask questions, any demand to see someone in authority – any behaviour, in short, that might be construed as 'difficult' – and out would come the needle with its little cargo of oblivion.

He learned to play along.

He passed the time by reading mystery stories, Agatha Christie mostly, which they brought him from the hospital library – little red-bound volumes, warped with use, with mysterious stains on their pages which he preferred not to study too closely. *Lord Edgeware Dies, Parker Pyne Investigates, The Seven Dials Mystery, Murder at the Vicarage*. He got through two, sometimes three a day. They also had some Sherlock Holmes and one afternoon he lost himself for a blissful couple of hours by trying to solve the Abe Slaney cipher in *The Adventure of the Dancing Men* (a simplified Playfair grid system, he concluded, using inverted and mirror images) but he couldn't check his findings as they wouldn't let him have pencil and paper.

By the end of the first week, he was strong enough to take a few steps down the corridor and visit the lavatory unaided.

In all this time, he had only two visitors: Logie and Wigram.

Logie must have come to see him some time at the beginning of April. It was early evening, but still quite light, with shadows dividing the little room – the bed of tubular metal, painted white and scratched; the trolley with its jug of water and metal basin; the chair. Jericho was dressed in blue-striped pyjamas, very faded; his wrists on the counterpane were frail. After the nurse had gone, Logie perched uneasily on the edge of the bed and told him that everyone sent their best.

'Even Baxter?'

'Even Baxter.'

'Even Skynner?'

'Well, no, maybe not Skynner. But then I haven't seen much of Skynner to be honest. He's got other things on his mind.'

Logie talked for a bit about what everyone was

doing, then started telling him about the convoy battle, which had gone on for most of the week, just as Cave had predicted. Twenty-two merchantmen sunk by the time the convoys reached air-cover and the U-boats could be driven off. 150,000 tons of Allied shipping destroyed and 160,000 tons of cargo lost – including the two weeks' supply of powdered milk that Skynner had made that disastrous joke about, remember? Apparently, when the ship went down, the sea had turned white. '*Die grösste Geleitzugschlacht aller Zeiten,*' German radio had called it, and for once the buggers weren't lying. The greatest convoy battle of all time.

'How many dead?'

'About four hundred. Mostly Americans.'

Jericho grunted. 'Any U-boats sunk?'

'Only one. We think.'

'And Shark?'

'Hanging in there, old love.' He patted Jericho's knee through the bedclothes. 'You see, it *was* worth it in the end, thanks to you.'

It had taken the bombes forty hours to solve the settings, from midnight on Tuesday until late on the Thursday afternoon. But by the weekend the Crib Room had made a partial recovery of the Weather Code Book – or enough of it to give them a toehold – and now they were breaking Shark six days out of seven, although sometimes the breaks came in quite late. But it would do. It would do until they got the first of the Cobra bombes in June.

A plane passed low overhead – a Spitfire, to judge by the crack of its engine.

After a while, Logie said quietly: 'Skynner's had to hand over the plans for the four-wheel bombes to the Americans.'

'Ah.'

'Well, *of course*,' said Logie, folding his arms, 'it's all *dressed up* as cooperation. But nobody's fooled. Leastways, *I'm not*. From now on, we're to teleprinter a copy of all Atlantic U-boat traffic to Washington the moment we receive it, then it's two teams working in friendly consultation. Blah, blah, blah. What bloody have you. But it'll come down to brute force in the end. It always does. And when they've got ten times the bombes we have — which won't take very long, I reckon, six months at the outside — what chance do we stand? We'll just do the interception and they'll do all the breaking.'

'We can hardly complain.'

'No, no. I know we can't. It's just . . . Well, we've seen the best days, you and I.' He sighed and stretched out his legs, contemplating his vast feet. 'Still, there is one bright side, I suppose.'

'What's that?' Jericho looked at him, then saw what he meant, and they both said 'Skynner!' simultaneously, and laughed.

'He is *bloody* upset,' said Logie contentedly. 'Sorry about your girl, by the way.'

'Well . . .' Jericho made a feeble gesture with his hand and winced.

There was a difficult silence, mercifully ended by the nurse coming in and telling Logie his time was up. He got to his feet with relief and shook Jericho's hand.

420

'Now you get well, old love, d'you hear what I'm saying, and I'll come and see you again soon.'

'Do that, Guy. Thank you.'

But that was the last time he saw him.

Miss Monk approached the pulpit to give the first reading: 'Say Not the Struggle Naught Availeth' by Arthur Hugh Clough, a poem she declaimed with great determination, glaring at the congregation from time to time, as if defying them to contradict her. It was a good choice, thought Jericho. Defiantly optimistic. Claire would have enjoyed it:

> 'And not by eastern windows only,
>   When daylight comes, comes in the light,
> In front the sun climbs slow, how slowly,
>   But westward, look, the land is bright.'

'Let us pray,' said the vicar.

Jericho lowered himself carefully to his knees. He covered his eyes and moved his lips like all the others, but he had no faith in any of it. Faith in mathematics, yes; faith in logic, of course; faith in the trajectory of the stars, yes, perhaps. But faith in a God, Christian or otherwise?

Beside him, Wigram uttered a loud 'Amen'.

Wigram's visits had been frequent and solicitous. He would shake Jericho's hand with the same peculiar and tenuous grip. He would plump his pillows, pour his water, fuss with his sheets. 'They treating you well? You want for nothing?' And Jericho would say yes, thank you, he was being well looked after, and Wigram would always smile and say *super*, how *super* everything was – how *super* he was looking, what a *super* help he had been, even, once, how *super* the view was from the sickroom window, as if Jericho had somehow created it. Oh yes, Wigram was charming. Wigram dispensed charm like soup to the poor.

In the beginning it was Jericho who did most of the talking, answering Wigram's questions. Why hadn't he reported the cryptograms in Claire's room to the authorities? Why had he gone to Beaumanor? What had he taken? How? How had he broken the inter-cepts? What had Puck said to him as he leaped from the train?

Wigram would then go away, and the next day, or the day after, come back and ask him some more. Jericho tried to mix in some questions of his own, but Wigram always brushed them away. Later, he would say. Later. All in good time.

And then one afternoon he came in beaming even more broadly than usual to announce that he had completed his enquiries. A little web of wrinkles appeared at the edges of his blue eyes as he smiled down at Jericho. His lashes were thick and sandy, like a cow's.

'So, my dear chap, if you're not too exhausted, I suppose I should tell you the story.'

Once upon a time, said Wigram, settling himself at the bottom of the bed, there was a man called Adam Pukowski, whose mother was English and whose father was Polish, who lived in London until he was ten, and who, when his parents divorced, went away with his father to live in Cracow. The father was a professor of mathematics, the son showed a similar aptitude, and in due course found his way into the Polish Cipher Bureau at Pyry, south of Warsaw. War came. The father was called up with the rank of major to rejoin the Polish Army. Defeat came. Half the country was occupied by the Germans, the other half by the Soviet Union. The father disappeared. The son escaped to France to become one of the fifteen Polish cryptanalysts employed at the French cipher centre at Gretz-Armainvillers. Defeat came again. The son escaped via Vichy France to neutral Portugal, where he made the acquaintance of one Rogerio Raposo, a junior member of the Portuguese diplomatic service and an extremely dodgy character.

'The man on the train,' murmured Jericho.

'Indeed.' Wigram sounded irritated at being interrupted: this was his moment of glory, after all. 'The man on the train.'

From Portugal, Pukowski made his way to England.

Nineteen-forty passed with no news of Pukowski's father or, indeed, of any of the other ten thousand missing Polish officers. In 1941, after Germany invaded Russia, Stalin unexpectedly became our ally. Representations were duly made about the vanished Poles. Assurances were duly given: there were no such prisoners in Soviet hands; any there might have been had been released long ago.

'Anyway,' said Wigram, 'to cut a long story a whole

lot shorter, it appears that at the end of last year, rumours began to circulate among the Poles in exile in London that these officers had been shot and then buried in a forest near Smolensk. I say, is it hot in here or is it me?' He got up and tried to open the window, failed, and returned to his perch on the bed. He smiled. 'Tell me, was it you who introduced Pukowski to Claire?'

Jericho shook his head.

'Ah, well,' sighed Wigram, 'I don't suppose it matters. A lot of the story is lost to us. Inevitably. We don't know how they met, or when, or why she agreed to help him. Or even what she showed him exactly. But I think we can guess what must have happened. She'd make a copy of these signals from Smolensk, and sneak them out in her knickers or whatever. Hide them under her floorboards. Lover-boy would collect them. This may have gone on for a week or two. Until the day came when Pukowski saw that one of the dead men was his own father. And then the next day Claire had nothing to bring him but the undecoded intercepts, because *someone* –' Wigram shook his head in wonder '– someone very, very senior *indeed*, I have since discovered, had decided they just didn't want to know.'

He suddenly reached over and picked up one of Jericho's discarded mystery stories, flicked through it, smiled, replaced it.

'You know, Tom,' he said thoughtfully, 'there's never been anything like Bletchley Park in the history of the world. There's never been a time when one side knew so much about its enemy. In fact, sometimes, I think, it's possible to know too much. When Coventry was bombed, remember? Our beloved Prime Minister discovered from Enigma what was going to happen about four hours in advance. Know what he did?'

Again Jericho shook his head.

'Told his staff that London was about to be attacked and that they should go down to the shelters, but that he was going upstairs to watch. Then he went out on to the Air Ministry roof and spent an hour waiting in the freezing cold for a raid he *knew* was going to happen somewhere else. Doing his bit, d'you see? To protect the Enigma secret. Or, another example: take the U-boat tankers. Thanks to Shark, we know where they're going to be, and when, and if we knocked them out we might save hundreds of Allied lives – in the short term. But we'd jeopardise Enigma, because if we did that, Dönitz would know we must be reading his codes. You see what I'm driving at? So Stalin has killed ten thousand Poles? I mean, *please*, Uncle Joe's a national hero. He's winning the frigging war for us. Third most popular man in the country, after Churchill and the King. What's that Hebrew proverb? "My enemy's enemy is my friend"? Well, Stalin's the biggest enemy Hitler's got, so as far as we're concerned, for present purposes, he's a bloody good friend of ours. Katyn massacre? Katyn frigging *massacre?* Thanks awfully, but, really, do shut up.'

'I don't suppose Puck would have seen it quite like that.'

'No, old chap, I don't suppose he would. Shall I tell you something? I think he rather hated us. After all, if it hadn't been for the Poles, we might not even have broken Enigma in the first place. But the people he really hated were the Russians. And he was prepared to do anything to get revenge. Even if it meant helping the Germans.'

'"My enemy's enemy is my friend,"' murmured Jericho, but Wigram wasn't listening.

'And how could he help the Germans? By warning them Enigma wasn't safe. And how could he do *that*?' Wigram smiled and spread his hands. 'Why, with the assistance of his old friend from 1940, Rogerio Raposo, recently transferred from Lisbon and now employed as a courier at the Portuguese legation in London. How about some tea?

> For the dear ones parted from us
> We would raise our hymns of prayer;
> By the tender love which watcheth
> Round thy children everywhere . . .

Senhor Raposo, said Wigram, sipping his tea after the nurse had gone, Senhor Raposo, presently a resident of His Majesty's Prison, Wandsworth, had confessed to everything.

On 6 March, Pukowski had gone to see Raposo in London, handed him a thin, sealed envelope and told him he could make a great deal of money if he delivered it to the right people.

The following day, Raposo flew on the scheduled British Imperial Airways flight to Lisbon carrying said envelope, which he passed to a contact of his on the staff of the German naval attaché.

Two days after that, the U-boat service changed its Short Weather Code Book, and a general review of cipher security began – Luftwaffe, Afrika Korps . . . Oh, the Germans were interested, of course they were. But they weren't about to abandon what their experts still insisted was the most secure enciphering system ever devised. Not on the basis of one letter. They suspected a trick. They wanted proof. They wanted this mysterious informant in Berlin, in person.

'That's our best guess, anyway.'

On 14 March, two days before the start of the convoy battle, Raposo made his next weekly trip to Lisbon and returned with specific instructions for Pukowski. A U-boat would be waiting to pick him up off the coast of northwest Ireland on the night of the 18th.

'And that was what they were discussing on the train,' said Jericho.

'And that was what they were discussing on the train. Quite right. Our man Puck was collecting his ticket, so to speak. And shall I tell you the really frightening thing?' Wigram took another sip of tea, his little finger delicately crooked, and looked at Jericho over the rim of his cup. 'If it hadn't been for you, he might just have got away with it.'

'But Claire would never have gone along with this,' protested Jericho. 'Passed on a few intercepts – yes. For a lark. For love, even. But she wasn't a *traitor.*'

'Lord, no.' Wigram sounded shocked. 'No, I'm sure Pukowski never even told her for *one minute* what he was planning to do. Consider it from his point of view.

She was the weak link. She could have given him away at any moment. So imagine how he must have felt when he saw *you* walk back through the door from Cambridge on that Friday night.'

Jericho remembered the look of horror on Puck's face, that desperate attempt to force a smile. He had already seen what must have happened: Puck leaving a message at the cottage that he needed to talk to her, Claire hurrying back into the Park at four in the morning – *click click click* on her high heels in the darkness. He said quietly, almost to himself: 'I was her death warrant.'

'I suppose you were. He must've known you'd try and get in touch with her. And then, the next night, when he went round to the cottage to get rid of the evidence, the stolen cryptograms, and found you there . . . Well . . .'

Jericho lay back and stared at the ceiling as Wigram rattled through the rest of the story. How, on the night the convoy battle had started, just before midnight, he'd been called by the police and told that a sack full of women's clothing had been found. How he'd tried to find Jericho, but Jericho had disappeared, so he'd grabbed Hester Wallace instead and taken her down to the lakeside. How it had been obvious at once what had happened, that Claire had been bludgeoned, or maybe bludgeoned and strangled, and her body rowed out into the lake and dumped.

'Mind if I smoke?' He lit up without waiting for a reply, using his saucer as an ashtray. He examined the tip of his cigarette for a moment. 'Where was I exactly?'

Jericho didn't look at him. 'The night of the convoy battle.'

Ah, yes. Well, Hester had refused to talk at first, but there's nothing like shock to loosen the tongue and eventually she'd told him everything, at which point Wigram had realised that Jericho wasn't a traitor; realised, in fact, that if Jericho had broken the cryptograms he was probably closer to discovering the traitor than *he* was.

So he had deployed his men. And watched.

This would have been about five in the morning.

First, Jericho was seen hurrying down Church Green Road into the town. Then he was observed going into the house in Alma Terrace. Then he was identified boarding the train.

Wigram had men on the train.

'After that, the three of you were just flies in a jam jar, frankly.'

All passengers disembarking at Northampton were stopped and questioned, and that took care of Raposo. By then, Wigram had arranged for the train to be diverted into a branch line where he was waiting to search it at leisure.

His men had orders not to shoot unless they were shot at first. But no chances were going to be taken. Not with so much at stake.

And Pukowski had used his pistol. And fire had been returned.

'You got in the way. I'm sorry about that.' Still, as he was sure Jericho would agree, preserving the Enigma secret had been the most important objective. And that had been accomplished. The U-boat that had been sent to pick up Puck had been intercepted and sunk off the coast of Donegal, which was a double bonus, as the Germans probably now thought that the whole business had been a set-up all along, designed to trap one of their submarines. At any rate, they hadn't abandoned Enigma.

'And Claire?' Jericho was still staring at the ceiling. 'Have you found her yet?'

'Give us time, my dear fellow. She lies under at least sixty feet of water, somewhere in the middle of a lake a quarter of a mile across. That may take us a while.'

'And Raposo?'

'The Foreign Secretary spoke to the Portuguese ambassador that morning. Under the circumstances, he agreed to waive diplomatic immunity. By noon we'd taken Raposo's flat apart. Dreary place at the wrong end of Gloucester Road. Poor little sod. He really was only in it for the money. We found two thousand dollars the Germans had given him, stuffed in a shoe box on top of his wardrobe. Two grand! Pathetic.

'What will happen to him?'

'He'll hang,' said Wigram pleasantly. 'But never mind about him. He's history. The question is, what are we going to do with *you?*'

After Wigram had gone, Jericho lay awake for a long time, trying to decide which parts of his story had been true.

'Behold, I show you a mystery,' said Hester.

'We shall not all sleep, but we shall all be changed,

'In a moment, in the twinkling of an eye, at the last trump: for the trumpet shall sound, and the dead shall be raised incorruptible, and we shall be changed.

'For this corruptible must put on incorruption, and this mortal must put on immortality.

'So when this corruptible shall have put on incorruption, and this mortal shall have put on immortality, then shall be brought to pass the saying that is written, Death is swallowed up in victory.

'O death, where is thy sting? O grave, where is thy victory?'

She closed her Bible slowly and regarded the congregation with a dry and level eye. In the end pew she could just make out Jericho, white-faced, staring straight ahead.

'Thanks be to God.'

She found him waiting for her outside the church, the white blossom raining down on him like confetti. The other mourners had gone. He had his face raised to the sun and she guessed from the way he seemed to be drinking in the warmth that he hadn't seen it for a long while. As he heard her approach, he turned and smiled and she hoped her own smile hid her shock. His cheeks were concave, his skin as waxy as one of the candles in church. The collar of his shirt hung loosely from his gaunt neck.

'Hello, Hester.'

'Hello, Tom.' She hesitated, then held out her gloved hand.

'Super service,' said Wigram. 'Absolutely super. Everybody's said so, haven't they, Tom?'

'Everybody. Yes.' Jericho closed his eyes for a second and she understood immediately what he was signalling: that he was sorry Wigram was there, but that he couldn't do anything about it. He released her hand. 'I didn't want to leave,' he said, 'without seeing how you were.'

'Oh, well,' she said, with a jollity she didn't feel, 'bearing up, you know.'

'Back at work?'

'Yes, yes. Still blisting away.'

'And still in the cottage?'

'For now. But I think I'll move out, as soon as I can find myself another billet.'

'Too many ghosts?'

'Something like that.'

She suddenly found herself loathing the banality of the conversation but she couldn't think of anything better to say.

'Leveret's waiting,' said Wigram. 'With the car. To run us to the station.' Through the gate Hester could see the long black bonnet. The driver was leaning against it, watching them, smoking a cigarette.

'You're catching a train, Mr Wigram?' asked Hester.

'*I'm* not,' he said, as if the notion was offensive. 'Tom is. Aren't you, Tom?'

'I'm going back to Cambridge,' explained Jericho. 'For a few months' rest.'

'In fact we really ought to push off,' continued Wigram, looking at his watch. 'You never know – there's always a *chance* it may be on time.'

Jericho said, irritably: 'Will you excuse us for just one minute, Mr Wigram?' Without waiting for a reply, he guided Hester away from Wigram, back towards the church. 'This bloody man won't leave me alone for a second,' he whispered. 'Listen, if you can bear it, will you give me a kiss?'

'What?' She wasn't sure she could have heard him correctly.

'A kiss. Quickly. Please.'

'Very well. It's no great hardship.'

She took off her hat, reached over and brushed his thin cheek with her lips. He held her shoulders and said softly in her ear: 'Did you invite Claire's father to the service?'

'Yes.' He had gone mad, she thought. The shock had affected his mind. 'Of course I did.'

'What happened?'

'He didn't reply.'

'I knew it,' he whispered. She felt his grip tighten.

'Knew what?'

'*She isn't dead . . .*'

'How touching,' said Wigram loudly, coming up behind them, 'and I hate to break things up, but you're going to miss your train, Tom Jericho.'

Jericho released her and took a step back. 'Look after yourself,' he said.

For a moment she couldn't speak. 'And you.'

'I'll write.'

'Yes. Please. Be sure you do.'

Wigram tugged at his arm. Jericho gave her a final smile and a shrug, then allowed himself to be led away.

She watched him walk painfully up the path and through the gate. Leveret opened the car door and as he did so, Jericho turned and waved. She raised her hand in return, saw him manoeuvre himself stiffly into the back seat, then the door slammed shut. She let her hand drop.

She stayed there for several minutes, long after the big car had pulled away, then she replaced her hat and went back into the church.

2

'I almost forgot,' said Wigram, as the car turned down the hill. 'I bought you a paper. For the journey.'

He unlocked his briefcase and took out a copy of *The Times*, opened it to the third page and handed it to Jericho. The story consisted of just five paragraphs, flanked by an illustration of a London bus and an appeal for the Poor Clergy Relief Corporation:

MISSING POLISH
OFFICERS

GERMAN ALLEGATIONS

The Polish Minister of National Defence, Lieutenant-General Marjan Kukiel, has issued a statement concerning some 8,000 missing Polish officers who were released from Soviet prison camps in the spring of 1940. In view of German allegations that the bodies of many thousands of Polish officers had been found near Smolensk and that they had been murdered by the Russians, the Polish Government has decided to ask the International Red Cross to investigate the matter . . .

'I particularly like that line,' said Wigram, 'don't you: "released from Soviet prison camps"?'

'That's one way of putting it, I suppose.' Jericho tried to give him back the paper, but Wigram waved it away.

'Keep it. A souvenir.'

'Thanks.' Jericho folded the paper and slipped it into his pocket, then stared firmly out of the window to forestall any further conversation. He'd had enough of Wigram and his lies. As they passed under the blackened railway bridge for the final time he surreptitiously touched his cheek and he suddenly wished he could have brought Hester with him for this last act.

At the station, Wigram insisted on seeing him on to the train, even though Jericho's luggage had been sent on ahead at the beginning of the week and there was nothing for him to carry. And Jericho consented in return to have Wigram's hand for support as they crossed the footbridge and strolled along the length of the Cambridge train in search of an empty seat. Jericho was careful to make sure that he, rather than Wigram, chose the compartment.

'Well, then, my dear Tom,' said Wigram, with

mock sadness, 'I'll bid you goodbye.' That peculiar handshake again, the little finger somehow tucked up into the palm. Final things: did Jericho have his travel warrant? Yes. And he knew that Kite would be meeting him at Cambridge to escort him by taxi to King's? Yes. And he'd remembered that a nurse would be coming in from Addenbrooke's Hospital every morning to change the dressing on his shoulder? Yes, yes, yes.

'Goodbye, Mr Wigram.'

He settled his aching back into a seat facing away from the engine. Wigram closed the door. There were three other passengers in the compartment: a fat man in a dirty fawn raincoat, an elderly woman in a silver fox, and a dreamy-looking girl reading a copy of *Horizon*. They all looked innocent enough, but how could one tell? Wigram tapped on the window and Jericho struggled to his feet to lower it. But the time he had it open, the whistle had blown and the train was beginning to pull away. Wigram trotted alongside.

'We'll be in touch when you're fit again, all right? You know where to get hold of me if anything comes up.'

'I certainly do,' said Jericho, and slid the window up with a bang. But still Wigram kept pace with the compartment – smiling, waving, running. It had become a challenge for him, a terrific joke. He didn't stop until he reached the end of the platform, and that was Jericho's final impression of Bletchley: of Wigram leaning forwards, his hands on his knees, shaking his head and laughing.

*

Thirty-five minutes after boarding the train at Bletchley, Jericho disembarked at Bedford, bought a one-way ticket to London, then waited in the sunshine at the end of the platform, filling in *The Times* crossword. It was hot, the tracks shimmered; there was a strong smell of baking coal dust and warm steel. When he'd finished the final clue he stuffed the newspaper, unread, into a rubbish bin and walked slowly up and down the platform, getting used to the feel of his legs. A crowd of passengers was beginning to build up around him and he scanned each face automatically, even though logic told him it was unlikely he was being followed: if Wigram had feared he might abscond, he surely would have arranged for Leveret to drive him all the way to Cambridge.

The tracks began to whine. The passengers surged forwards. A military train passed slowly southwards, with armed soldiers on the engine footplate. From the carriages peered a line of gaunt, exhausted faces, and a murmur went through the crowd. German prisoners! German prisoners under guard! Jericho briefly met the eyes of one of the captives – owlish, bespectacled, unmilitary: more clerk than warrior – and something passed between them, some flash of recognition across the gulf of war. A second later the white face blurred and disappeared, and soon afterwards the London express pulled in, packed and filthy. 'Worse than the bloody Jerries' train,' complained a man.

Jericho couldn't find a seat, so he stood, leaning against the door to the corridor, until his chalk complexion and the sheen of perspiration on his forehead prompted a young Army officer to give up his place. Jericho sat down gratefully, dozed, and dreamed of the German prisoner with his sad owl's face, and then of Claire on that first journey, just before Christmas, their bodies touching.

By 2.30 he was in London, at St Pancras Station, moving awkwardly through the mass of people towards the entrance to the Underground. The lift was out of action so he had to take the stairs, stopping on every landing to recover his strength. His back was throbbing and something wet was trickling down his spine, but whether it was sweat or blood he couldn't tell.

On the eastbound Circle Line platform, a rat scurried through the rubbish beneath the rails towards the tunnel mouth.

When Jericho failed to emerge from the Bletchley train, Kite was irritated but unconcerned. The next train was due in within a couple of hours, there was a good pub just around the corner from the station, and that was where the college porter chose to do his waiting, in the amiable company of two halves of Guinness and a pork pie.

But when the second train terminated at Cambridge, and still there was no sign of Jericho, Kite went into a sulk that lasted him throughout the half hour it took him to trudge back to King's.

He informed the domestic bursar of Jericho's non-appearance, and the domestic bursar told the Provost, and the Provost dithered over whether or not to call the Foreign Office.

'No consideration,' complained Kite to Dorothy Saxmundham in the Porter's Lodge. 'Just no bloody consideration at all.'

With the solution in his pocket, Tom Jericho left Somerset House and made his slow way westwards, along the Embankment, towards the heart of the city. The south bank of the Thames was a garden of ruins. Above the London docks, silver-coloured barrage balloons turned and glinted and nodded in the late afternoon sun.

Just beyond Waterloo Bridge, outside the entrance to the Savoy, he managed at last to find a taxi for hire and directed the driver to Stanhope Gardens in South Kensington. The streets were empty. They reached it quickly.

The house was big enough to be an embassy, wide and stucco-fronted, with a pillared entrance. It must have been impressive once, but now the plasterwork was grey and flaking and in places great chunks of it had been blasted away by shrapnel. The windows of the top two storeys were curtained, blind. The house next door was bombed out, with weeds growing in the basement. Jericho climbed the steps and pressed the bell. It seemed to ring a long way off, deep within the bowels of the dead house, and left a heavy silence. He tried again, even though he knew it was useless, then retreated across the road to wait, sitting on the steps of the opposite house.

Fifteen minutes passed, and then, from the direction of Cromwell Place, a tall, bald man appeared, startlingly thin – a skeleton in a suit – and Jericho knew at once it must be him. Black jacket, grey-striped trousers, a grey silk tie: all that was needed to complete the cliché was a bowler hat and a rolled umbrella. Instead, incongruously, he carried, as well as his briefcase, a string bag full of groceries. He approached his vast front door wearily, unlocked it and vanished inside.

Jericho stood, brushed himself down and followed.

The door bell tolled again; again, nothing happened. He tried a second time, and a third, and then, with difficulty, got down on his knees and opened the letter flap.

Edward Romilly was standing at the end of a gloomy passage with his back to the door, perfectly still.

'Mr Romilly?' Jericho had to shout through the flap. 'I need to speak to you. Please.'

The tall man didn't move. 'Who are you?'

'Tom Jericho. We spoke once on the telephone. Bletchley Park.'

Romilly's shoulders sagged. 'For God's sake, will you people just *leave me alone!*'

'I've been to Somerset House, Mr Romilly,' said Jericho, 'to the Registry of Births, Marriages and Deaths. I have her death certificate here.' He pulled it out of his pocket. 'Claire Alexandra Romilly. Your daughter. Died on 14 June 1929. At St Mary's Hospital, Paddington. Of spinal meningitis. At the age of six.' He propelled it through the letter flap and watched it slither across the black and white tiles towards Romilly's feet. 'I'm going to have to stay here, sir, I'm afraid, for as long as it takes.'

He let the flap snap shut. Weary with self-disgust, he turned away and leaned his good shoulder against one of the pillars. He looked across the street to the little communal gardens. From beyond the houses opposite came the pleasant hum of the early-evening traffic on Cromwell Road. He grimaced. The pain had begun to move out from his back now, establishing lines of communication into his legs, his arms, his neck; everywhere.

He wasn't sure how long he knelt there, looking at the budding trees, listening to the cars, until at last behind him Romilly unlocked the door.

He was fifty or thereabouts, with an ascetic, almost monkish face, and as Jericho followed him up the wide staircase, he found himself thinking, as he often did on meeting men of that generation, that this would be roughly the age of his father now, if he had lived. Romilly led Jericho through a doorway into darkness and tugged open a pair of heavy curtains. Light spilled into a drawing room full of furniture draped in white sheets. Only a sofa was uncovered, and a table, pushed up close to a marble fireplace. On the table was some dirty crockery; on the mantelpiece, a large pair of matching silver photograph frames.

'One lives alone,' said Romilly apologetically, fanning away the dust. 'One never entertains.' He hesitated, then walked over to the fireplace and picked up one of the photographs. 'This is Claire,' he said, quietly. 'Taken a week before she died.'

A tall, thin girl with dark ringlets smiled up at Jericho.

'And this is my wife. She died two months after Claire.'

The mother had the same colouring and bone-structure as the daughter. Neither looked remotely like the woman Jericho knew as Claire.

'She was driving alone in a motorcar,' went on Romilly, 'when it ran off an empty road and struck a tree. The coroner was kind enough to record it as an accident.' His Adam's apple bobbed as he swallowed. 'Does anyone know you're here?'

'No, sir.'

'Wigram?'

'No.'

'I see.' Romilly took the pictures from him and replaced them on the mantelpiece, realigning them precisely as they had been. He stared from mother to daughter and back again.

'This will sound absurd to you,' he said eventually, without looking at Jericho, 'it sounds absurd to *me*, now – but it seemed to be a way of *bringing her back*. Can you understand that? I mean, the idea that another girl of exactly her age would be going around, using her name, doing what she might have done . . . Living her life . . . I thought it might make sense of what had happened, d'you see? Give her death a purpose, after all these years. Foolish, but . . .' He raised a hand to his eyes. It was a minute before he could speak. 'What exactly do you want from me, Mr Jericho?'

Romilly lifted a dustsheet and found a bottle of whisky

and a pair of tumblers. They sat on the sofa together staring at the empty fire.

'What exactly do you want from me?'

The truth, at last, perhaps? Confirmation? Peace of mind? An ending . . .

And Romilly seemed to want to give it, as if he recognised in Jericho a fellow sufferer.

It had been Wigram's bright idea, he said, to put an agent into Bletchley Park. A woman. Someone who could keep an eye on this peculiar collection of characters, so essential to the defeat of Germany, yet so alien to the tradition of intelligence; who had, indeed, destroyed that tradition, turning what had been an art – a game, if you like, for gentlemen – into a science of mass production.

'Who *were* you all? *What* were you? Could *all* of you be trusted?'

No one at Bletchley was to know she was an agent, that was important, not even the commander. And she had to come from the right kind of background, that was absolutely vital, otherwise she might have been dumped at some wretched out-station somewhere, and Wigram needed her *there*, at the heart of the place.

Romilly poured himself another drink and offered to top up Jericho's, but Jericho covered his glass.

Well, he said, sighing, putting the bottle at his feet, it was harder than one might think to manufacture such a person: to conjure her into life complete with identity card and ration books and all the other paraphernalia of wartime life, to give her the right background ('the right *legend*,' as Wigram had termed it), without at the very least dragging in the Home Office and half a dozen government agencies who knew nothing of the Enigma secret.

But then Wigram had remembered Edward Romilly.

Poor old Edward Romilly. The widower. Barely known outside the Office, abroad these past ten years, with all the right connections, initiated into Enigma – and, more importantly, with the birth certificate of a girl of exactly the right age. All that was required of him, apart from the use of his daughter's name, was a letter of introduction to Bletchley Park. In fact, not even that, since Wigram would write her letter: a signature would suffice. And then Romilly could continue with his solitary existence, content to know he had done his patriotic duty. And given his daughter a kind of life.

Jericho said: 'You never met her, I suppose? The girl who took your daughter's name?'

'Good God, no. In fact, Wigram assured me I'd never hear another word about it. I made that a condition. And I didn't hear anything, for six months. Until you called one Sunday morning and told me my daughter had disappeared.'

'And you got straight on the telephone to Wigram to report what I'd said?'

'Of course. I was horrified.'

'And naturally you demanded to know what was happening. And he told you.'

Romilly drained his scotch and frowned at the empty tumbler. 'The memorial service was today, I think?'

Jericho nodded.

'May I ask how it went?'

'"For the trumpet shall sound,"' said Jericho, '"and the dead shall be raised incorruptible, and we shall be changed . . ."' He looked away from the photograph of the little girl above the fireplace. 'Except that Claire – my Claire – isn't dead, is she?'

The room darkened, the light was the colour of the whisky, and now Jericho was doing most of the talking.

Afterwards, he realised he never actually told Romilly how he had worked it all out: that host of tiny inconsistencies that had made a nonsense of the official version, even though he recognised that much of what Wigram had told him must have been the truth.

The oddity of her behaviour, for a start; and the failure of her supposed father to react to her disappearance, or to show up at her memorial service; the puzzle of why her clothes had been so conveniently discovered when her body had not; the suspicious speed with which Wigram had been able to halt the train . . . All these had clicked and turned and rearranged themselves into a pattern of perfect logic.

Once one accepted she was an informer, everything else followed. The material which Claire – he still called her Claire – had passed to Pukowski had been leaked with Wigram's approval, hadn't it?

'Because really – in the beginning, anyway – it was nothing, just chickenfeed, compared with what Puck already knew about naval Enigma. Where was the harm? And Wigram let her go on handing it over because he wanted to see what Puck would do with it. See if anyone else was involved. It was bait, if you like. Am I right?'

Romilly said nothing.

It was only later that Wigram had realised he'd made the most almighty miscalculation – that Katyn, and more especially the decision to stop monitoring it, had tipped Puck over the edge into treason, and that somehow he'd managed to tell the Germans about Enigma.

'I assume it wasn't Wigram's decision to stop the monitoring?'

Romilly gave a barely perceptible shake of his head. 'Higher.'

How high?

He wouldn't say.

Jericho shrugged. 'It doesn't matter. From that point on, Puck must have been under twenty-four-hour watch, to find out who his contact was and to catch them both red-handed

'Now, a man under round-the-clock surveillance is not in a position to murder anyone, least of all an agent of the people doing the watching. Not unless they are spectacularly incompetent. No. When Puck discovered I had the cryptograms he knew Claire would have to disappear, otherwise she'd be questioned. She had to vanish for at least a week, so he could get away. And preferably for longer. So between them they *staged* her murder – stolen boat, bloodstained clothes beside the lake. He guessed that would be enough to make the police call off their hunt. And he was right: they have stopped looking for her. He never suspected she was betraying *him* all the time.'

Jericho took a sip of whisky. 'Do you know, I really think he may have loved her – that's the joke of it. So much so that his last words, literally, were a lie – "*I killed her, Thomas, I'm so very sorry*" – a deliberate lie, a gesture from the edge of the grave, to give her a chance to get away.

'And that, of course, was the cue for Wigram, because from his point of view, that confession neatly tied up everything. Puck was dead. Raposo would soon be dead. Why not leave "Claire" to rest at the bottom of the lake as well? All that he needed to do to round the story off was to pretend that it was *me* who led him to the traitor.

'So to say that she's still alive is not an act of faith, but merely logical. She *is* alive, isn't she?'

A long pause. Somewhere a trapped fly barged against a window pane.

Yes, said Romilly, hopelessly. Yes, he understood that to be the case.

What was it Hardy had written? That a mathematical proof, like a chess problem, to be aesthetically satisfying, must possess three qualities: inevitability, unexpectedness and economy; that it should 'resemble a simple and clear-cut constellation, not a scattered cluster in the Milky Way'.

Well, Claire, thought Jericho, here is my proof.

Here is my clear-cut constellation.

*

Poor Romilly, he didn't want Jericho to leave. He had bought some food, he said, on his way home from the office. They could have supper together. Jericho could stay the night – God knew, he had enough room . . .

But Jericho, looking around at the furniture dressed as ghosts, the dirty plates, the empty whisky bottle, the photographs, was suddenly desperate to get away.

'Thank you, but I'm late.' He managed to push himself to his feet. 'I was due back in Cambridge hours ago.'

Disappointment settled like a shadow across Romilly's long face. 'If you're sure I can't persuade you . . .' His words were slightly slurred. He was drunk. On the landing he bumped against a table and switched on a tasselled lamp, then conducted Jericho, unsteadily, down the stairs to the hall.

'Will you try and find her?'

'I don't know,' said Jericho. 'Perhaps.'

The death certificate was still lying on the letter-stand in the hall. 'Then you'll need this,' said Romilly, picking it up. 'You must show it to Wigram. If you like, you can tell him you've seen me. In case he tries to deny everything. I'm sure he'll have to let you see her then. If you insist.'

'Won't that get you into trouble?'

'Trouble?' Romilly gave a laugh. He gestured behind him, at his mausoleum of a house. 'D'you think I care about *trouble*? Come on, Mr Jericho. Take it.'

Jericho hesitated, and in that moment he had a vision of himself – a few years older, another Romilly, struggling vainly to breathe life into a ghost. 'No,' he said at last. 'You are very kind. But I think I ought to leave it here.'

He left the silent street with relief and walked towards the sound of traffic. On Cromwell Road he hailed a cab.

The spring evening had brought out the crowds. Along the wide pavements of Knightsbridge and in Hyde Park it was almost like a festival: a profusion of uniforms, American and British, Commonwealth and exile – dark blue, khaki, grey – with everywhere the splashes of colour from the summer dresses.

She was probably here, he thought, tonight, somewhere in the city. Or perhaps that would have been considered too risky, and she had been sent abroad by now, to lie low until the whole business had been forgotten. It occurred to him that a lot of what she had told him might actually be true, that she could well be a diplomat's daughter.

On Regent Street, a blonde-haired woman on the arm of an American major came out of the Café Royal.

He made a conscious effort to look away.

ALLIED SUCCESS IN NORTH ATLANTIC read a newspaper placard on the opposite side of the street. NAZI U-BOATS SUNK.

He pulled down the window and felt the warm night air on his face.

And here was something very odd. Staring out at the teeming streets he began to experience a definite sense of – well, he could not call it *happiness*, exactly. *Release*, perhaps, would be a better word.

449

He remembered their last night together. Lying beside her as she wept. What had that been? Remorse, was it? In which case, perhaps she *had* felt something for him.

'*She never talked about you,*' Hester had said.

'*I'm flattered.*'

'*Given the way she used to talk about the others, you should be . . .*'

And then there had been that birthday card: 'Dearest Tom . . . always see you as a friend . . . perhaps in the future . . . Sorry to hear about . . . in haste . . . Much love . . .'

It was a solution, of a sort. As good a solution, at any rate, as he was likely to get.

At King's Cross Station he bought a postcard and a book of stamps and sent a message to Hester asking her to visit him in Cambridge as soon as she could.

On the train he found an empty compartment and stared at his reflection in the glass, an image which gradually became clearer as the dusk gathered and the flat countryside disappeared, until he fell asleep.

The main gate to the college was closed. Only the little doorway cut into it was unlocked and it must have been ten o'clock when Kite, dozing beside the coke stove, was woken by the sound of it opening and closing. He lifted the corner of the blackout curtain in time to see Jericho walking into the great court.

Kite quietly let himself out of the Porter's Lodge to get a better view.

It was unexpectedly bright – there were a lot of stars

– and he thought for a moment that Jericho must have heard him, for the young man was standing at the edge of the lawn and seemed to be listening. But then he realised that Jericho was actually looking up at the sky. The way Kite told it afterwards, Jericho must have stood that way for at least five minutes, turning first towards the chapel, then the meadow, and then the hall, before moving off purposefully towards his staircase, passing out of sight.

Acknowledgements

I OWE A debt of gratitude to all those former employees of Bletchley Park who spoke to me about their wartime experiences. In particular, I would like to thank Sir Harry Hinsley (Naval Section, Hut 4), Margaret Macintyre and Jane Parkinson (Hut 6 Decoding Room), the late Sir Stuart Milner-Barry (former head of Hut 6), Joan Murray (Hut 8) and Alan Stripp (Japanese ciphers).

Roger Bristow, Tony Sale and their colleagues at the Bletchley Park Trust answered my questions with great patience and allowed me to wander about the site at will.

None of these kind people bears any responsibility for the contents of this book, which is a work of the imagination, not of reference.

For those readers who would like the facts on which this novel is based, I strongly recommend *Top Secret Ultra* by Peter Calvocoressi (London, 1980), *Codebreakers* edited by F. H. Hinsley and Alan Stripp (Oxford, 1993), *Seizing the Enigma* by David Kahn (Boston, USA, 1991), *The Enigma Symposium* by Hugh Skillen (Middlesex, two volumes, 1992 and 1994), *The Hut 6 Story* by Gordon Welchman (New York, 1982) and *GCHQ* by Nigel West (London, 1986).

Details of the action in the North Atlantic are drawn from the original, decoded signals of the U-boats, held at the Public Record Office in London, and also from *Convoy* by Martin Middlebrook (London, 1976) and *The Critical Convoy Battles of March 1943* by Jürgen Rohwer (English translation, London, 1977).

Finally, I would like to record my special thanks to Sue Freestone and David Rosenthal, neither of whom ever lost faith in *Enigma*, even on those occasions when it was a mystery to its author.

Robert Harris
June 1995

About the author

ROBERT HARRIS WAS born in 1957 and is the author of three international bestselling novels: *Fatherland* (1992), *Enigma* (1995) and *Archangel* (1998). His work has been translated into 30 languages. Before becoming a novelist he worked as a television reporter on *Panorama* and *Newsnight*, as political editor of the *Observer*, and as a columnist on the *Sunday Times*. His non-fiction books include *Selling Hitler* (1986), the story of the forging of the Hitler diaries.

He lives near Hungerford in Berkshire with his wife, Gill Hornby, and their four children.